- You can return this item to any Bournemouth library but not all libraries are open every day.

- Items must be returned on or before the due date. Please note that you will be charged for items returned late.

- Items may be renewed unless requested by another customer.

- Renewals can be made in any library, by telephone, email or online via the website. Your membership card number and PIN will be required.

- Please look after this item - you may be charged for any damage.

Bournemo

www.bournemouth.gov

D1352262

"Well-written and fascinating, this
Fresh Fiction

Also by Eve Berlin

The Edge Trilogy
Pleasure's Edge
Desire's Edge
Temptation's Edge

Writing as Eden Bradley
The Dark Garden
Forbidden Fruit

Temptation's Edge

Edge

Give in to temptation...

EVE BERLIN

BLACK
LACE

1 3 5 7 9 10 8 6 4 2

First published in the United States of America in 2012
by The Berkley Publishing Group, part of Penguin (USA) Inc.
Published in the UK in 2013 by Black Lace,
an imprint of Ebury Publishing
A Random House Group Company

The Random House Group Limited Reg. No. 954009

Addresses for companies within the Random House Group
can be found at www.randomhouse.co.uk

A CIP catalogue record for this book is
available from the British Library

The Random House Group Limited supports the Forest
Stewardship Council® (FSC®), the leading international
forest-certification organisation. Our books carrying the FSC
label are printed on FSC®-certified paper. FSC is the only
forest-certification scheme supported by the leading
environmental organisations, including Greenpeace.
Our paper procurement policy can be found at:
www.randomhouse.co.uk/environment

Printed and bound by CPI Group (UK) Ltd, Croydon, CR0 4YY

ISBN 9780352347282

To buy books by your favourite authors and register for offers visit
www.randomhouse.co.uk
www.blacklace.co.uk

one

Mischa Kennon was a perfectionist. In her work as a tattoo artist. As an author of the short erotic stories she'd had published. In the maintenance of her platinum blonde hair, which she wore in long, polished waves around her shoulders, and her red-lacquered nails, which she kept short to accommodate her work. Her San Francisco apartment was as immaculate as the tattoo shop she owned, Thirteen Roses. She worked hard, played harder. And she was never, ever late. Which made the delay in her flight to Seattle for her best friend's engagement party particularly frustrating.

Finally she was there. The cab pulled up in front of the restaurant—she'd already dropped her luggage at Dylan's apartment, where she would be staying—and she paid the driver and stepped onto the rainy sidewalk in front of Wild Ginger. She swung open the door and moved into the warm interior. She'd been there before when she'd visited Dylan and met her fiancé,

Alec. It was their favorite restaurant and the perfect place for the party to celebrate their upcoming wedding in only a few weeks. Mischa took in a breath as she nodded at the hostess and moved through the busy Thai fusion restaurant toward the back room, where they held private parties.

She was happy for her friend, although the whole marriage thing wasn't for her, personally. She was the independent type. Well, so was Dylan, but she and Alec had something special.

"Honey, you made it!" Dylan's smile was brilliant as she rose from the long table and came to wrap her arms around Mischa in a cloud of the spicy vanilla scent she always wore.

"I'm so sorry I'm late, honey," Mischa apologized. "The damn weather."

"I know. It's our fault for wanting to get married this fall, but we just couldn't wait, and we really want to be married by Thanksgiving."

"Look at you—you have that bridal glow," she told Dylan, holding her friend at arm's length. It was true. Her gray eyes shone as lustrous as her long, curly red hair. "Or maybe you and Alec had some alone time before the party?" she teased with a wink.

Dylan grinned as her fiancé came up behind them. Alec Walker was a wall of a man, well over six feet tall, with the breadth of a linebacker.

"Maybe we did," he said, laughing as he leaned in to kiss Mischa's cheek. "But a gentleman never kisses and tells. How are you?"

"Fine, thanks. Just glad to be here."

"Dylan mentioned you have a possible business proposal to investigate while you're here?" Alec helped her off with her rain-spattered coat.

Mischa nodded, patted her hair into place. "Thanks, Alec.

Yes, another tattoo artist I know may want to open a new shop in Seattle and is hoping I'll be interested in a partnership, so I thought I'd look into it while I'm here to help with the wedding plans."

Dylan squeezed her hand. "I can't believe I get to have you for two whole weeks. You're sure it's not an inconvenience? Your shop will be all right?"

"I wouldn't dream of letting you do this whole wedding alone. And Billy is the best shop manager I could ask for. Which is why I can even consider expanding here. I figure I can work half time in both places. Which means I'll get to see more of you. But we can talk about that later—tonight is all about you two."

"And we've left you standing here after your long trip. Come on and say hi to everyone."

Dylan grabbed her hand and they moved toward the table where Dylan's friend Kara, whom Mischa had met on previous visits, was just getting out of her chair. Kara reached to give her a quick hug.

"So nice to see you. Do you remember Dante?"

Kara's boyfriend shook her hand. Dante was as tall as Alec, but leaner, with dark hair and eyes that were a sparkling golden brown. He hovered over Kara as protectively as Alec did with Dylan.

Mischa wondered if that unusual protective thing was something that was a natural part of the fact that both men were dominants. She'd played with that a bit herself—the domination and submission dynamic. She'd even been to a few BDSM clubs. Not that she required kink. But it was fun when she was with a guy who was into it. She'd never been able to give herself over to it completely, though. Certainly not the way Dylan and Kara must have, to be in relationships with dominant men. Not that *she'd* be in a relationship, period. But it was lovely to see people who were so happy. The glow these two pairs were giving off was almost enough to make her think about it . . . for a moment or two, anyway.

"Mischa, you have to meet our fabulous baker."

She turned—and caught herself pulling in a long breath as her eyes met a stunning gaze that was a shimmering sea green shot through with amber. He was looking at her, staring at her from beneath dark brows. He had a rugged face. A generous mouth that looked stern until he smiled at her. Then it was all flawless white teeth and frank sensuality. It took her a moment to realize she had to tilt her head back to really see him—he stood taller than even Alec, had shoulders just as broad. She felt a small stirring in her veins, a fluttering in her stomach.

"You're their baker?"

He laughed, a rich, booming sound. "Lord, no. I'm Connor."

His deep tone was laced with a distinctly Irish accent.

God, she loved a man with an accent. It really made her swoon. Hell, she'd been swooning since the moment she'd laid eyes on him.

"Connor Galloway, Mischa Kennon. Connor is a friend of Alec's. He'll be in the wedding party. And I seriously doubt Connor can boil water, never mind bake. He burned the hot dogs the last time the guys went camping."

"Hey, I learned to microwave mac and cheese at my mother's knee," he protested, his brogue a low, rolling thunder that made her belly stir with need.

Down, girl.

Dylan laughed, putting Mischa's hand into that of a petite, smiling blonde woman. "*This* is our baker—and friend—Lucie."

"Hi, Mischa. I've heard so much about you."

"Mischa?" Dylan gave her a nudge with her elbow, making her realize she was still focused on Connor.

Get it together.

She turned and smiled. "It's great to meet you, Lucie. Do we know what kind of cake they want yet?"

The blonde's smile widened into a grin. "We're doing cupcakes. Wait until you see what I have in mind. We're having a tasting session on Wednesday."

"I'll look forward to it."

Sugar was one of her favorite things. She wasn't a dieting girl—she loved food too much—and she was comfortable with her curves. But even the idea of a cupcake tasting couldn't distract her from the towering presence of Connor Galloway as Dylan led her around the table, introducing her to their friends.

He wasn't exactly following them, yet she had the sense that he was watching her from under those dark brows. Whenever she'd glance up for a moment—which she did more often than she'd like to admit—she found his gaze on her. No matter where he was in the room, leaning over the table, talking to various people. That gaze was dark. Penetrating. She wasn't sure what it was he wanted, but it was clear he wanted *something*. It was more than desire—that she recognized easily enough. She was no wallflower. She welcomed desire, from the right man. Knew exactly how to deal with it. She felt his desire. But there was something else . . . some sort of deeper curiosity that *commanded* her attention.

Ah, that must be it. He must be another dominant. But where that air of command elicited a bantering response from her when it came to most of the toppy men she'd come into contact with, Connor's direct searching gaze made her feel . . . warm all over. A sort of odd, melting sensation. As though her knees were actually weak.

Don't be silly.

He was just a man. A dominant man. But many a dominant

man had met his match in her. She wasn't about to be taken down by the admittedly scorchingly sexy Connor Galloway.

Lord, he was sexy.

She sighed, tucked her blonde hair behind her ear as Alec held a chair for her. She thanked him as she seated herself at the long banquet table. And had to pull in a breath as Connor sat down next to her.

"We're to be dinner partners," he said.

A simple remark, yet it felt loaded. As if he meant more than that they would sit next to each other through the meal.

She was reading far too much into things with this man. She must be tired from the long trip up from San Francisco. Either that or it had been too long since she'd been laid.

Was two months too long?

"Shall I order you a drink?" he asked. "I see you don't have one yet."

"Oh . . . yes, a drink would be good." Maybe that was exactly what she needed to relax and pull herself together. "I'll have some cold sake. They have a good selection here."

He raised a brow. "Nothing stronger?"

"Why would you think I'd need something stronger?"

He leaned in and she caught a whiff of his scent, a blend of the rain outside and something dark and earthy. "You strike me as a strong woman. Who may require a stronger drink after your long journey." He grinned, a warm grin she found infectious.

She couldn't help but laugh. "You're right, I could use something stronger. How about a vodka on ice?"

"Grey Goose?"

"Why not?"

The man knew his vodka. She couldn't help but wonder what else he might know. What those large hands had experienced . . .

Okay, this really had to stop. She was sitting at her best friend's engagement party and her panties were going damper by the minute. Over a guy she'd just met. Of course, that was how it usually worked with her. She knew the moment she met a man if she wanted him. There was no dancing around it, the way it often seemed to go for other women. No doubts. She always knew she *wanted* someone. But rarely to this ridiculous degree.

Maybe never.

Even more ridiculous how utterly girly she found herself feeling when he ordered her drink for her, saying to the waiter, "A Grey Goose over ice for the lady. Add two olives, if you will."

That accent . . . the tone of authority in his voice, no matter how polite he'd been. It made her shiver. Distracted her. From the fact that this was Dylan and Alec's party, not some personal meat market for *her*. Although the shopping was quite nice.

Their drinks came and Connor took them from the waiter with an almost imperial nod of his head that was still somehow charming. She noted he drank whiskey straight up. She could smell the perfumy fragrance after he sipped and leaned in close to her.

"How's yours?" he asked.

She lifted her glass, sipped. "Perfect."

"Ah, I may not be able to bake, but I have other talents."

She laughed. "You say that as though you made the drinks yourself."

"That wasn't necessarily what I was referring to."

She lowered her voice, batted her lashes. "Are you flirting with me, Connor Galloway?"

"Why? Are you opposed to the idea?"

"On the contrary."

He grinned, those brilliant white teeth contrasting with his plush red lips. So damn kissable she could feel her own lips twitch.

He took her hand, pulled it to his mouth, and brushed a quick kiss over her knuckles that sent desire spiraling through her in sharp, fluttering arcs.

"You have long fingers," he said, keeping his tone low. "The hands of an artist."

"Do you think so?"

He was still grinning at her. Still making her feel like a teenager with a mad crush. "Well, I admit Alec and Dylan may have mentioned that you are indeed an artist, but yes, you have beautiful hands."

Why was his little compliment making her blush? That and his heavy Irish brogue. She felt a surge of disappointment when he released her hand.

"Thank you."

"You have your own tattoo shop down in San Francisco, they tell me. That's a hard road, running your own business."

"Hard, but wonderful. After years of apprenticing in other people's shops, then renting chair space, I love being my own boss."

"I'll bet you do." His green eyes were twinkling. He was teasing her, and she liked it.

"I do, as a matter of fact. I like being in charge of my life. Doing my art my way."

He nodded. "That I understand. I'm an artist myself, though of a different sort."

She took another sip of her vodka, leaned toward him, intrigued. "What do you do?"

"I'm a concept artist. I design for video games, some for film and television. Spaceships, robots, that sort of thing."

She laughed. "That's like every kid's dream come true."

"It is. Except that it gives me little time to do my own work."

"And what is your own work?"

"I like to sketch in charcoal."

"But not spaceships and robots?"

He shrugged, his massive shoulders rippling with muscle beneath his dark button-down shirt. "I've been more interested in the human form the last couple of years. I've started to do some erotic pieces."

She smiled at him. "Every young *boy's* dream come true."

He nodded. "When I have the time. Which I'm just now beginning to have. I'm at a point where I can start to pick and choose which contracts I want to accept. You're lucky to be your own boss, in charge of your schedule, although I imagine running the show is a lot of work."

"It is, but I have a great team, which helps. And I love it."

Being able to open her own shop was one of her biggest achievements, bigger, even, than getting her art degree. Her business was everything, the one thing in her life she *knew* she'd done right.

"What does your family think of you doing tattoos for a living?" Connor asked.

"My younger sister, Raine, is . . . different from me. She's an English professor, married to a professor of mathematics. She's been supportive, in her way, even though I think she finds it hard to relate. Evie is more of a free spirit, an artist herself, so she loves the idea."

"Evie? Another sister?" he asked.

"My mother."

"You call your mother by her first name?" He wasn't the first to ask about it.

She laughed, but there was a raw edge to it that stuck in her throat. "If you knew Evie . . . she's never really been anyone's mother."

Why had she said that? She was certain he didn't want to hear her sob story about her flaky mother. He was quiet for a moment, watching her again. She shook her head, a little appalled at herself.

"Change of subject?" he suggested kindly.

"Yes. Sure. What about you? Do you have family here?"

"Just me. Family is back in Dublin. It's just my mum and my sisters, Molly and Clara. I try to get back every year to visit."

"What brought you to the States? Did you come here for work?"

It was his turn to stall. He shrugged again, but the gesture wasn't quite as casual as it had been before. "I married an American. I've been divorced for a long time."

"Ah." He was obviously uncomfortable talking about it, so she switched tracks. "But you stayed here."

"I like it here. I'd made a life here, got my degree in graphic arts, started a career."

Why did she suspect there was something else to it that he wasn't saying? Maybe because for the first time since they'd been talking he was looking away, his gaze resting on the rain-spattered window for several moments before he turned back to her.

"Change of subject?" she suggested this time.

"Yes. Definitely."

He smiled, and she watched his tight features loosen. Noticed the merest hint of creases at the edges of his eyes. She'd always loved that on a man, for some reason.

"What shall we talk about?" she asked.

"We can talk more about you." He leaned in toward her.

"There isn't really that much more to say."

"Ah, I disagree. I find you fascinating."

"Are you flirting with me again?"

"I am."

She smiled at him. "I like it."

He lifted her hand once more and his voice was a quiet murmur against it before he laid a soft kiss there. His sea-green eyes burned into her. He had long lashes, dark and full. She could see a small scar, about an inch long, below his right eye. Which only made him more masculine. Sexier. "We have much to discuss later, then."

"Discuss?"

God, she could barely speak, her entire body feeling like she'd been engulfed by flames. He'd only kissed her hand!

He moved in even closer. "You may have guessed who—and what—I am, knowing Alec and Dylan, yes?"

"Yes."

"Then you may know that I never take a woman without negotiating first."

She straightened, pulled her hand from his. "You think you'll 'take' me?"

"I do. And I think you'll like it. I can see it in the sparkle in your lovely blue eyes. Eyes like the sky off the coast of Dun Laoghaire in the summertime."

"Dun Laoghaire?"

"Just outside of Dublin. Have you ever been to Ireland?"

"No, never. I'd love to see it someday."

How had he managed to change the subject so smoothly? Oh, he was smooth. Still, she'd never met a man who could maneuver around her. This man would be no different, despite her response to him. He could play the role of boss in the bedroom—and she knew already they'd end up there—but if he thought to pull that anywhere else, he'd be dead wrong.

She took a long swallow of her vodka, set the glass down on the table beside the square red porcelain plate. "So, back to these negotiations you mentioned."

"Ah, lass, don't you agree that should wait until after this party is done?"

He was right, of course. What was wrong with her? A totally inappropriate conversation while they were supposed to be celebrating with Dylan and Alec. But he'd talked her in circles . . . hadn't he?

She gave a small nod of her chin, sipped her drink once more. And was relieved when Dylan stopped by to chat with her for a few minutes, shifting the mood. Allowing her some time to think, to get her head back on straight.

"I'm so glad you're here, Mischa. There are a thousand things to do."

"Don't worry, sweetie, we'll get it all done. I'm completely at your disposal."

"You're sure you don't mind staying at my place without me being there? I just . . . I don't want to be away from him." Dylan ducked her head, but Mischa could see her blush.

"Oh, you've got it bad, hon," she laughed. "But honestly, I'm used to living alone. And we'll be together all the time to work on the wedding plans. You'll be plenty sick of me by the end of the trip."

"I will not," Dylan insisted. "I'm grateful you're here. I need a right hand. I've never done this girly bridal stuff."

"Me neither. But we'll figure it out."

"Thanks, Misch."

"No problem, chica."

Dinner arrived, a gorgeous array of sushi, spicy curries, noodles and rice, and Dylan went back to her seat, where she cuddled up with her groom-to-be. Mischa wondered for one brief moment if any guy would ever want to stick with her the way Alec did with Dylan—their mutual devotion was an almost palpable thing. But why was she even considering it? She'd always been fine on her own. Just like her admittedly eccentric mother had finally learned, she didn't need a man to make a happy, full life. Her life was already full with running her business, her friends, her art, her writing. Men were a pleasant pastime, and one she didn't want to do without. But anything more? No, that wasn't for her. She'd learned that lesson early on through the absence of her own father. It had only been confirmed when Raine's father had left when Evie was pregnant with her. He'd been around for Raine through the years, but Evie had been left alone again. And again and again, until she'd had an epiphany about the value of independence a few years ago. No, she was just fine on her own. More than fine. Hadn't her success as a businesswoman proved that?

"Gathering wool?" Connor asked, the deep timber of his voice breaking into her wandering thoughts.

"Hmm, yes, I guess I was."

"What about?"

She turned to look at him more fully. His face was serious. Too damn handsome. "Oh, I doubt you really want to know."

He shrugged again, reminding her of the breadth of his shoulders. He paused to eat a piece of sushi, chewing thoughtfully for several moments. "Maybe I do."

Good Lord, he did. Connor realized he wanted to know exactly what was going through that gorgeous head of hers. He wanted to know everything about her. And it had nothing to do with his usual thorough investigation of a woman he was going to play. He simply wanted to *know*.

What the hell was wrong with him? He was as taken as a teenager with his first warm tit in his hand. And he didn't even have his hands on her tits, although Lord knew he wanted to. Wanted to have her *under* his hands. Under his command. But Mischa was no quiet, passive, submissive girl. She was full of fire, this one. Which made the idea that much more tempting.

He didn't mind a little power struggle. Not as long as he came out on top. He always did, no question about it. But he had the sense that it'd be one hell of a struggle with this girl.

The idea intrigued him. Fascinated him. Hell, he hadn't been able to think of anything else since he'd first set eyes on her. With those lush curves, that fall of pale blonde hair, the way it kept falling over one eye like some old Hollywood siren. Full lips painted a wicked scarlet that was meant to imply sex. A woman as confident as she was, as cocky as any man, wouldn't go down easily. But despite what she thought—and it was obvious she thought *she* was in control, through and through—he'd seen it in her. That unconscious response that signaled a spark of submissive desire. It may only be a small spark, but he was just the man to bring it out in her. It wasn't simple ego talking. He was good at what he did in the BDSM arena. Or maybe it *was* some ego. Or just the power of his desire for this girl, which was frankly throwing him a bit. He wanted to sleep with her. Spank her. Feel her naked flesh under his hands. See what her body looked like beneath the tight-fitting black dress she wore. She looked like some 1950s pinup girl with that platinum blonde hair waving around her shoulders. Gorgeous.

He was almost getting hard just thinking about it. He had to will his cock down, to remember they were at a friend's dinner table, and not the Pleasure Dome, which is where he'd much prefer they be.

The BDSM club was where he and Alec had met, where Alec had later introduced him to Dante. Their tastes all ran in the same vein, and it was a pleasure to have friends he could be completely open with. But this was not the time and place. Not to do more than flirt with the girl, at least until after the party was over. To tease her. To gauge her reaction.

She was definitely reacting. And he was sure as hell reacting to her. Enough that he almost wanted to order another finger of scotch to help him calm down. But that was something he never did. One drink was his limit. He was as tough on himself as he ever was on any subbie girl he played with. Rules were rules. They were always there for a reason, and Lord knew he had his reasons. So why was he allowing this girl to challenge that rule, even for a moment? He'd best get things back under control.

He forced himself to talk with the others seated near their section of the table through dinner. Even though Mischa was the only one he wanted to talk to. But if he was going to be an idiot over this girl—and it seemed maybe he was—then he thought he'd at least put it off until he had her alone somewhere.

Ah, yes. Alone. Naked. Just strip that tight black dress off her and see the rise of her breasts, fill his hands with them. His mouth . . .

He groaned quietly, took the last swallow of his scotch, savored the burn as it slid down his throat.

"Was it good?"

"What?"

He whipped his head around to find Mischa's pale brow arched.

"The chicken *satay*," she said. "I haven't tried it yet."

He just sat and stared at her for several moments before he managed to collect himself. He forced his gaze from her plush red lips to her brilliant blue eyes.

"The food here is always excellent. You should try the *satay*. Here, have some of mine."

He picked up a tender piece of grilled chicken, dipped it in the small bowl of peanut sauce and held it to her lips. She flashed him a quick grin full of sensual promise before she parted those gorgeous lips and took the food into her mouth.

The woman knew exactly the power she held over men. He

wasn't immune to it—that was damn certain. But just as certain was the fact that he *would* gain control over her. He just had to wait until he could get her alone. Judging from her flirtatious behavior, that shouldn't be an issue. The only question was when?

"Mmm, that was delicious."

She licked her lips. His groin tightened.

"So are you, if you don't mind my saying so."

"I don't mind at all."

She smiled, and once more he felt that same jolt of desire he'd felt every time she'd smiled, every time she'd spoken to him. Need ran hot in his veins.

He leaned in a little closer, keeping his voice low. "Then perhaps you won't mind an invitation."

"An invitation?"

"To have that discussion I mentioned."

"The negotiations, you mean?"

Ah, she was still flirting with him. This was a fine game they were playing, but they both had some idea of how it would end.

"Yes. And after that . . ."

"After that, what?" she asked.

The look on her beautiful face was pure sex. They both knew the answer. And they both understood the small thrill in having this conversation in front of all these people, their low voices making an intimate bubble around them.

Yes, pure sex, this girl.

"After that will depend on how the negotiations go. On how you answer my questions."

"And if I have questions for you?"

"That's part of it, isn't it?" He let his pinky brush the back of her hand, watched her cheeks warm, the plump rise of her breasts flush pink. Which was exactly why he'd done it—to see that response. "Power play is all about the give and take, regardless of what those less well versed in these things may think. It's a power *exchange*. It works both ways. Except that I will be the one in command."

She blinked, her cheeks going a darker, lovely shade of pink.

"Ah, you're thinking to argue that, are you? I don't think so, my girl. Are you still in?"

She paused for one long beat, then said, a little breathlessly, "Yes."

Damn it. He couldn't get her out of there soon enough.

"Mischa, you're sure you don't mind riding with Connor? I didn't realize our car would be full of gifts."

"Don't worry about me, Dylan. It's fine."

It was more than fine. Alone in a car with Connor. Then alone at Dylan's apartment. They'd flirted all through dinner. He was every bit as interested as she was—he'd made that very clear. And she was *very* interested.

"You're sure?" Dylan asked again.

"Of course. You and Alec go relax, open your gifts. I'll see you in the morning anyway, won't I?"

"Yes, dress shopping after a late breakfast, if that's okay with you."

"I *love* late." Mischa grinned at her.

Dylan laughed. "Okay. But you have my cell if you need anything."

"Knowing you, I'm certain your apartment is lacking nothing I might need."

"There's nothing to eat . . . I haven't been home much."

It was Mischa's turn to laugh. "Like you've ever done anything other than live off takeout. Stop worrying. I know where the menus are. Go home and curl up with your man."

Dylan gave her a quick kiss on the cheek, then Alec led her out the door of the restaurant just as Connor came with her coat.

"I took a cab tonight," he said, slipping her coat over her shoulders. "Parking is hell here. I didn't mention it to Alec and Dylan. Hope you don't mind."

"A cab is fine." She was trying to ignore the way her pulse was running hot and thready again. He really was an amazing-looking man, all hard muscle and sculpted features, and eyes that seemed to look through her. "San Francisco doesn't have any decent parking, either, which is one reason why I rent an apartment within walking distance of my shop. I cab it almost everywhere else."

She was trying to have a normal conversation with him when all she wanted was for him to slam her up against a wall and kiss her senseless. Instead, she was babbling. Totally unlike her. She took in a breath of the cold air as he led her outside. It was only now that they were both standing that she realized the full extent of his towering height, how massive his frame was beneath his black wool peacoat. The acute awareness of his hulking form beside her made her shiver as much as the damp night air.

Calm down.

He was just another man. This would be just another night of friendly, strings-free sex, which was the way she preferred things. Why did he have her so shaken up?

"You haven't told me the name of your tattoo shop there," he said as they stepped to the curb.

"It's called Thirteen Roses. I've had it for almost four years."

"Business is good?"

"Really good. Better than I'd expect in this economy. Actually, part of this trip will be to discuss opening a new location here with another artist I met in the first shop I apprenticed in."

"There's a good customer base for tattoos in this town, I'd think."

"Do you have any yourself?" she asked, hoping he did. Even before she'd started tattooing herself, body art had been a bit of a fetish for her. She thought it was beautiful—when done well, of course—but she really had a thing for tattoos. For hot men with tattoos, specifically.

God, to see ink on his skin . . .

"I have two," he answered. "I'm looking for a third, once I find the right artist. Mine has moved to New York. If you're a good girl, maybe I'll show them to you later."

She laughed. But inside, she was trembling all over.

Good girl.

No one had ever said such a thing to her before. No one had dared, frankly. Not even those few men she'd let tie her up, spank her, at the BDSM clubs in San Francisco. The submission thing had never been that serious for her, and just as often she'd been the one on top. But coming from him, it was sexy as hell.

He was staring at her again. Watching her closely.

She shook her head. "What is it?"

"I'm just wondering . . ."

"What?"

"If you'll be coming home with me tonight. To have that discussion, you know." His tone lowered until she had to strain over the noise of passing traffic on the wet streets to hear him. "I'm hoping you will. Because, to be honest, I can't wait to get my hands on you, Mischa. I can't wait to feel your lovely, smooth flesh beneath my palms. To have you over my knee. To hear your breath catch when I spank you." He paused. "Exactly as you're doing now. Which tells me what your answer will be. But I have to hear it from you. Will you come with me? Or do I drop you at Dylan's place so you can think it over some more?"

Had any man ever talked to her this way? So utterly sure of himself. Despite that he was basically asking her permission . . . to what? To do things to her she'd only ever played at. But never, she was certain, as seriously as this man could play. With him, it would be a whole new world of experience. One she found herself eager for.

"What will it be, Mischa?" he urged.

He was close enough that she could smell the faint, sweet tinge of good scotch on his breath. His hand was at her waist. Somehow, even through the heavy wool of her coat, she swore she could feel the heat of his touch. She shivered.

"I'll come with you, Connor. Let's go."

two

Connor smiled, gave a small nod with his square chin before stepping into the street. He hailed a taxi with a loud whistle and a brief wave of his hand, commanding the cab as easily as he did everything else. Including, it seemed, her. She was surprised by it. Enticed by it.

"Come on, then," he said.

He handed her into the cab, an old-world gesture she loved immediately, then he climbed in beside her and gave the driver an address in Belltown, the same section of Seattle where Dylan lived. It was made up of older structures and much of the old architecture had been preserved in the apartment buildings, warehouses that had been turned into lofts, the charming, funky retail stores and cafes. It reminded her a bit of home.

As soon as the cab pulled onto the street Connor wrapped an arm around her waist and pulled her closer, sliding her across the seat effortlessly, as if she were nothing more than a doll. His cheek was next to hers.

"I've been waiting all night for this. To get you alone. To kiss you."

She turned to look up at him, at his glittering gaze reflecting the amber streetlights. Desire was stark on his rugged face, mirroring her own.

She licked her lips. "What are you waiting for?" she asked.

He flashed a grin, but it faded quickly, his face going serious as he moved in to press his mouth to hers.

Oh, his lips were soft. So damn soft as he brushed them over hers. Too lightly; she wanted more. She reached up to lay her hand on his cheek, but he took it, held it firmly in his. Pressed her palm to his chest as he opened her lips with his, his warm tongue slipping inside.

He tasted like the tiniest bit of the whiskey he'd had with dinner. Mostly he tasted like pure man. Pure desire.

She sighed, opened to him, and he pulled her closer. His arm around her held her firmly, so hard he was nearly bruising her. But she needed it, somehow. Craved that rough touch. That hard kind of passion. And he kept kissing her, kissing her, until she could barely breathe. Kisses full of wanting. Full of demand. It was making her go hot and soft all over. Wet between her thighs. When he slipped a hand down to caress her knee, then higher, she let him do it. Parted her thighs for him. Waited for him to reach higher.

He pulled back long enough to murmur, "Good girl, that's it," before bending to kiss her once more.

His tongue drove into her mouth and she sucked it in. He still held her hand to his chest, where she could feel his heart hammering as hard as her own. As hard as the pulse beat of desire in her breasts, her sex. And as his hand moved up her thigh, leaving a trail of heat as it went, she pulled in a gasping breath. Pulled in the heady scent of him: rain and the earth and the night.

She trembled when she felt that first brush of his fingers at the edge of her lace panties. At the idea that he'd feel right away how wet she was, the lace soaked. He groaned into her mouth, and she felt a strange sort of satisfaction at his realization, at his reaction to it.

He spread her thighs wider with a firm hand, and she let him do it. Held perfectly still as he brushed his fingertips over the wet fabric, against her aching cleft, over the hard nub of her clitoris.

Need him. Need more.

As if reading her mind, he slid his fingers under the fabric, moving right away in between the swollen folds of her sex.

"Mmm . . . ," she moaned against his mouth.

He didn't pause, didn't stop kissing her. Instead he began a steady, lovely rhythm, his fingers rubbing over her slit, his tongue pushing into her mouth. Desire rose, burned into her like a flame. She arched, coming up off the seat of the cab, but immediately he used his other hand to press down on her hip, to hold her still.

Some part of her rebelled against his control. Another part of her loved it even more. She was too far gone to question it.

She breathed him in, kissed him harder—it was the only thing she could do. She was helpless against him, against the tide of pleasure washing over her. When he pushed his fingers inside her she gasped again. Was sure she felt him smiling against her mouth. Then he was fucking her with his fingers with a steady pressure. In, then out, his thumb circling her clit until she was sure she would come at any moment.

He pulled back.

"We're here."

Oh yes, almost there . . .

She blinked. Her breath was a rasping pant. He was watching

her. His fingers were still working inside her. She could barely stand to see him watching her face.

"Are you ready, my girl?"

"Yes." She bit her lip.

He smiled, a wicked grin on his gorgeous face as his fingers stilled.

Bastard.

He slipped his fingers from her, and she wanted to cry out. She was so close to climax she was shaking all over.

"Shh, Mischa. Let me help you out."

She was dizzy with it all—his lovely manners, her body burning with almost-met need. Who the hell was this man?

Her legs were shaky, but he helped her from the cab, one strong arm around her. They were standing on the sidewalk in front of an older brick building. He pulled her right up against him, and she felt the hard-packed muscle of his big body.

"I'm going to get you upstairs. And I'm going to make you come. We can talk after you've come for me. After you've come down from it. Still with me, girl?"

Was he crazy? Where else could she possibly be at this moment?

She nodded. "Yes, damn it."

He laughed, a low, rumbling chuckle of delight.

"Oh, we're going to have ourselves a night. I can hardly wait."

Neither could she. In fact, if he didn't hurry and take her up to his apartment, if he didn't carry through with his promise, bring her to orgasm soon, she was going to explode right there on the sidewalk. It was all she could think about.

Connor.

Need.

Out of control.

Totally out of control.

Why didn't it matter as much as it should?

He led her up two flights of stairs, keeping her hand in his. It was large, warm. She remembered how it had felt between her thighs, which were rubbing together as they climbed the wide staircase, teasing her heated flesh. She was breathless when they got to the third floor. Not from the climb. It was everything he'd done to her in the cab. What he would do once they got inside. The possessiveness of his touch.

He opened a door painted bright blue, took her into his apartment. There was light coming from a floor lamp, illuminating the space. In a brief glance she took in the sleek, modern furnishings, the long wall of exposed brick. There were sketches all over the walls, framed in simple black or pewter frames. Robots, spaceships. One really excellent nude of a woman reclining in a chair. But she didn't have time to think about it. He was slipping her coat from her shoulders, leading her to the big L-shaped sofa done in a heavy dark blue canvas.

"Have a seat."

It wasn't a question. Why did that make her entire body vibrate with need? She sat, and he settled next to her. She noticed once more the way his dark shirt pulled against his broad chest, making her want to reach out and stroke the fabric. To feel the bulging muscle she knew lay beneath. She flexed her fingers.

"Are you nervous, Mischa?"

"What? No, of course not."

"What, then?"

"I . . . I don't know," she admitted. "Maybe just that I know something different will happen tonight. Something more than what I've experienced before. I've done a few things . . . been to a couple of fetish clubs. But you're more . . . serious about it, I think."

"Does it make you afraid?"

"No." She shook her head, not wanting to admit it. "No."

He smiled. "We'll see if that turns out to be true."

"You seem to take some pleasure in the idea," she said.

He grinned, his green-and-gold eyes glittering. "I *am* a sadist, Mischa."

That made her laugh. "Fair enough."

He took her hand then, brought it to his mouth. Brushed his lips over the back of her fingers, making her shiver. With his gaze still on hers, he unfolded her fingers, one at a time, kissed each one. She'd never had such attention paid to her hands before. Had never imagined what it might do to her. With each press of his warm lips against her skin, her body was going hot, melting all over.

He paused to ask, "Do I have your consent, Mischa?"

"Mmm . . . what?"

"To have my way with you." He grinned gorgeously.

She grinned back. "Definitely."

"What about a little pain with our pleasure? And I'm asking now in this abbreviated way because, to be honest, I can hardly wait."

She loved to hear him admit that he wanted her, loved the husky tone in his voice. "Yes. Definitely."

"We still need to have that talk before anything more serious happens. But right now I just need to touch you." He slipped one hand around the back of her neck, exerted the smallest pressure there, and she was surprised—shocked, really—at her response to it. It made her feel commanded by him. And also taken care of in some weird indefinable way she couldn't explain to herself.

"Yes, later," she murmured in agreement.

"Come on, now," he said, his tone low. "Lie back for me, my girl."

He used the hand on her neck to guide her, until she was reclining on the sofa. He got up so that he had one knee on the cushions, leaning over her.

"You really are beautiful," he murmured, almost as if he were talking to himself.

He let the hand slide from around her neck to her collarbone, then down between her breasts, stroking her cleavage, the tops of her breasts. The heat of his hand scorched her, her nipples going hard.

"I love these stiletto heels. That you wear these thigh-high fishnets beneath your dress. Come now, let me see you." He kept his gaze on her body as he swept the soft knit fabric of her dress up her thighs, revealing her black lace panties. "Very nice," he murmured. "But let's have off with them, shall we?"

He slipped them off, smiling as her bare flesh came into view. His gaze flicked up to hers for one moment before he looked back at her shaved sex. He touched her, just his fingertips, a light, feathering touch over her aching cleft, and pleasure shimmered over her like heat lightning, making her squirm.

"Ah, I have to taste you," he said.

She had one brief moment to think *Yes, please*. Then he was bent over her, his tongue stroking her swollen folds, pushing between them.

"Ah, Connor . . ."

Her hands went into his short crop of dark hair, and she watched his fingers biting into her thigh. Loved that hard pressure on her skin. Loved even more the lapping motion of his tongue as he moved up her damp slit to the hard nub of her clit.

"God . . ."

He kept licking her pussy in a slow, steady rhythm. She wanted to come, but it was just the tiniest bit too slow to allow her to reach climax.

"Please, Connor. Faster."

He paused, and when he began again he moved even more slowly, licking her almost lazily.

"Oh, you're torturing me."

There was no response from him, simply another pause in which she understood that the more she complained or begged, the slower he would go.

Wicked man.

She loved it.

She sighed, settled into the soft cushions, let her thighs fall farther apart. And as soon as she did he really went to work, his tongue pushing inside her, then moving back to her needy clit and licking, licking, then sucking hard.

"Oh!"

She felt her climax bearing down on her, let the pleasure shiver through her body as the spasms began. And as she began to come, he thrust his fingers inside her.

She exploded, calling out, hips arching hard against his mouth, his surging fingers. Pleasure was a hammering jolt, echoing through her over and over.

"Connor . . . ah, God . . ."

The waves subsided, but he didn't stop. He was fucking her with his fingers, as he had in the cab, but this time with hard, almost punishing strokes. And he was sucking on her clit, making it hurt a little. But she loved it, *needed* it, somehow. In moments, it seemed, she was coming again. Unbelievably. Her body trembled with pleasure, her hips bucking so hard he had to hold her down with his hand. Or maybe he simply wanted to. She loved it all—his hard hands, his lovely, hot mouth. His command of her.

After, she lay shivering, small frissons of pleasure still shimmering through her. Connor raised his head, wiped his mouth with the back of his hand, smiled at her.

"That was beautiful, my girl. To feel you come like that, in my mouth. Shall we do it again?"

She laughed shakily. "I may need a few minutes to recover."

"I'll use that time, then, to get you undressed and into my bed."

Before she had time to answer he'd lifted her in his arms and was carrying her down a short hallway. She couldn't remember the last time a man had held her this way—in his *arms*. It made her feel small. Utterly feminine.

Out of the corner of her eye she caught sight of more framed sketches on the walls of the hallway, then he was moving into the bedroom, flicking on the light switch with his elbow. The room was thoroughly masculine, with large pieces of sleek black furniture, an enormous bed in the same black wood, framed by four posts. The downy comforter was varying shades of gray, from dark to pale, done in bold horizontal stripes. But all she could really think about was that he was going to fuck her there.

He set her down on the edge of the bed.

"Stay right there, Mischa," he said, his voice low, quiet. But there was still unquestioning authority in his tone, and it was making her hot all over. Making her heart pound.

She watched as he kicked his way out of his shoes, then unbuttoned his shirt, slipped it off. She took in a breath as his muscular shoulders and chest, the tight six-pack of his abs, came into view. His skin was a pale gold, as if he'd seen a little sun over the summer. Around his right biceps he had a tattoo in black and red—a Celtic warrior armband, complicated knotwork with thorny tribal spikes. As purely male as the rest of him. There was heavy black text in Gaelic in a line down the inside of his left forearm, but she had trouble focusing on his tattoos as he stepped out of his black slacks, revealing strong thighs, and the even stronger bulge of his erect cock under his black boxer briefs.

A shudder of need went through her.

Have to touch him, to feel his cock in my hand . . .

She licked her lips.

"Now you," he said, moving toward her, a glint in his eyes.

He bent over her, helped her unzip her dress and slip it over her head.

"Ah, you're fucking beautiful," he said, real awe in his voice. "But let's get this off."

He reached around her, unsnapped her black lace bra, and she felt the weight of her breasts, the heat of them, her nipples hardening in the cool air.

"Yes, gorgeous girl. Lord. Even better than I'd imagined."

He knelt on the bed, towering over her as he pressed her down onto the mattress. The cotton quilt was soft against her back. His breath was hot on her cheek as he whispered, "I need to see your tattoos. To see how you've marked your skin before I do that myself: mark you. To see just how beautiful you are."

He gathered her breasts in his hands as he spoke, and all she could do was sigh at the warmth of his palms, his skin pressed against her stiff nipples. He kissed her cheek, her neck, playing with her breasts, gently at first, then he gave her nipples a small pinch.

"Oh!"

"Does it hurt?"

"A . . . a little. But it's good, too."

"Very good. Do you know about safe words?"

"Yes."

"Tell me your safe words."

"*Yellow* for too much. It means slow down. *Red* means stop."

"Yes. Excellent. Trust that I will respect them absolutely. Yes?"

"Yes."

He pinched her again, hard enough this time to make her pull in a gasping breath.

"Is it still good?"

"Oh yes . . ."

Her pussy was aching, soaking wet. She needed to come again.

"Touch me, girl," he commanded.

She reached for him, stroked her hand over the cotton of his boxer briefs, reveled in his sharp intake of breath. He was big. Hard as iron. She looked down as she reached into the gap and pulled his cock free.

Oh, it was beautiful. So damn hard, the tip dark and swollen. The flesh was like velvet, the same golden brown as the rest of his body. So thick her fingers couldn't quite wrap around it. She licked her lips again.

"Stroke me," he told her.

She started a slow slide of her fisted hand, up the heavy shaft, down again.

"Ah, that's good," he said.

He was caressing her breasts, his palms soft, pausing to pinch her nipples again and again. She was on fire, burning for him. Loving every moment of this delicate torture. Loving the contrast of his soft touch, the sharp pinches. Loving it enough that she felt no desire to question his absolute authority over her at this moment.

He moved in until one of his thighs was between hers, used it to press the tiniest bit against her aching cleft.

"I love how wet you get for me, Mischa. For *me*. How slippery you feel. Like fucking heaven, if you want to know the truth. I love how you stroke my cock. That delicate female hand around me. Ah . . ."

She squeezed his cock, felt him jump a little in response, smiled to herself.

His hips arched into her hand. His voice was a little breath-less now. "As much as I love this, I'm going to love fucking you even more, especially with you wearing these fishnet stockings, the tall heels. It's too good. But now I want you to stop."

He released her breasts, took her hand from his rigid cock, his fingers closing over hers tightly.

"Your tattoos are beautiful. All these flowers spilling over your shoulder. I love that they're all black and gray. It makes for an almost chiaroscuro effect. Like my charcoal drawings."

"Yes. That was the intention," she told him, barely able to think straight.

"I'm going to turn you over now, to see what else is there."

Desire was like some living thing, coiling through her body. She wanted him to admire her tattoos, to admire her body. "Yes. Do it, Connor."

Connor took a long breath, forcing his body to calm enough to handle her the way he wanted to. He put his hands on her waist, slid them down until they were under her bare, silky buttocks. Amaz-ing skin on this woman; the texture of it. He gave her gorgeous breasts one last glance—they were some of the finest he'd ever seen, beautifully plump, with dark red nipples, making him think of her red mouth. They were hard as stones, a contrast against her pale, pale skin.

He turned her, and she let him do it. He felt her yielding, knew her orgasms had something to do with it. That had he tried to take her over in this way before making her come, she'd have fought him more.

He loved that it was working.

Her back was just as beautiful as her breasts, her face: the soft lines and curves of her form, the sway of her lower back. The plump buttocks, just rounded enough, and shaped like a heart. And her skin covered in a sinuous line of flowers, all done in classic Japanese style: chrysanthemums, lilies, cherry and plum blossoms, a few tiny orchids. Amazing detail. They were scattered over her fair flesh, from her right shoulder to her left hip, then curling just over the side of her hip and onto the top of her thigh. He'd caught sight of it when he'd gone down on her, but he'd been too distracted by her scent—all warm woman and perfume and need—to really focus on the design.

He could barely focus now, even though he wanted to. He wanted to take her all in, to know every inch of her plush, flawless body. Exactly the kind of body he preferred, all beautifully rounded curves. Flesh he could hang on to. All the better for a good, hard spanking.

He bent over her, leaned down to place a kiss between her shoulder blades. She was laying perfectly still, her arms over her head, which excited him in some strange way. He always loved compliance in a woman. But knowing how feisty this one was made it more thrilling.

She trembled beneath his lips, just the tiniest bit. He kissed her again, softly, felt her answering shiver. He did it again and again, moving his mouth lower, until he reached that luscious valley at the small of her back. He let his tongue dart out. She squirmed in response. He moved lower, kissed the rise at the top of her firm buttocks, bit a little into the flesh.

"Ah, Connor . . ."

"Shh."

He laid another kiss there, bit again. Felt her quiet intake of breath. She remained quiet. Obeying him. He kissed his way back up her spine, slowly, enjoying the taste of her, her soft skin beneath his lips. He pushed her hair aside, saw the kanji symbols tattooed in a line down the back of her neck, the small black and amber Japanese fan done in exquisite detail where her neck met her hairline, above the kanji.

"Spread your lovely thighs. Yes, that's it."

He reached between them, pushed his fingers right into that wet heat, felt her pussy clench, hot and tight around his fingers.

"Ah!"

He pumped a few times, his cock growing impossibly hard.

He had to have her soon. But first . . .

He rose up and gave her ass a hard smack. She jumped a little, then he felt her body melt all over, inside and out.

Oh, she was lovely, this girl. Her response was really something.

He smacked her again. She jumped less this time, her body absorbing the impact. Her ass was growing pink already; her skin was that pale. He loved it.

He paused to massage the flesh of her buttocks, lightly at first, then harder, working the pain in. He flexed his fingers in her pussy, pushed deeper, slipped them almost out. Then he smacked her ass, plunged his fingers deep inside her all at once, and she cried out.

"Connor!"

He stilled.

"What is it?"

"I just . . . God, do it again."

He smiled to himself. His cock pulsed with need. He said very quietly, "Just so you know, my girl, it doesn't work that way. I had some idea you'd gotten the message earlier. But I'll tell you plainly now, if you're to play with me, then you'll have to know that the more you ask for something, the less likely you are to get it. I am a sadist, as I believe I mentioned. I take enormous pleasure in seeing you squirm with unmet need. I'll take even greater pleasure in seeing you come. But only when I determine it's time. But before the end of the night you will also come to trust me, that I will do these things in such a way that the end result is the building of your desire. That I will take you to dizzying heights that can never be reached when you're given what you want the moment you want it."

"Yes," she said, her voice a mere whisper.

"Yes, what, Mischa? Yes, this makes sense to you? Yes, you want it this way?"

She paused for one long moment. Then, "Yes to everything."

"Oh, that is the right answer. Exactly what I wanted to hear from you."

Mischa trembled, her sex clenching. Why did it turn her on like this to know she had pleased him? It was so much against her nature. And yet . . . everything with this man was different. She had no control over her response to him. It disturbed her on some deep level she could barely connect with. She was too far gone. In pleasure. The pain. His command. Her head lost in that ethereal place she'd heard of, but had never reached in her BDSM experiments before. Subspace. Oh yes, she was there now. Finally.

He bent over her. She could feel the heat of his body against her back. The heat of his breath as he spoke into her ear. "I am going to fuck you now, Mischa. Just like this. Hold still."

She waited, felt the small draft as he moved away from her, heard him open a drawer in the night table next to the bed, the small tearing sound of a foil packet. Then he was on her again, this time really lowering his big body onto hers. She felt absolutely taken over simply by the size of him. Dwarfed by him in a way that once more made her feel absolutely feminine. He was resting on his elbows, his muscled forearms on either side of her head.

"Spread wide," he told her. "There's a girl."

She felt his thighs on either side of hers. Then he moved his hips in between them, and she felt the first luscious touch of the head of his sheathed cock at the entrance to her sex.

If she hadn't been soaking wet before, she was now. She took in a breath, waited.

Connor said quietly, his voice a rasping pant, "I really want to fuck your ass, Mischa. Not now, but later. Would you like that?"

She shuddered with desire. "Yes. Yes."

"Ah, you are too good, aren't you? Let me see how good your pussy is."

He wrapped one arm around her hips, pulled them up so that her ass was raised off the bed. He was holding her as if she weighed nothing, but so tightly she could feel his firm ab muscles against her buttocks. He arched and slipped just the tip of his big cock inside her.

"Oh . . ."

She had to take a breath, relax around the sheer girth of him. At the notion of what his heavy shaft would feel like buried deep inside her.

"So damn hot inside. So wet," he murmured. "I'll take it slow, until I know if you can take me."

He surged an inch and she was stretching already, he was so enormous.

He kissed the back of her neck. "Okay, my girl?"

"Oh yes."

He angled his hips, sank deeper, pushing pleasure into her body, her pussy, her womb. He slid out a bit, surged back in, really filling her this time.

"Take a breath," he commanded her, and she did. He pushed hard, making her gasp.

"Ah, God . . ."

"I know, darlin'. But you can take it. You're tight, but wet as the sea. I can feel it. Your beautiful cunt around me. Holding my cock in your body. Come on now. Breathe. Relax. You can do it."

She did as he said, taking long breaths. Letting her body relax around his thick shaft. He moved, pulling out a little at a time, pushing back inside her, his cock buried to the hilt. She could feel the softer flesh of his balls pressed up against her. And over her, the hard planes of his body were firm against her back.

He began to pump, a slow, hard thrust. Driving pleasure deep. Making her arch her back to raise her ass to meet his thrusts. He was kissing the back of her neck, biting the flesh, kissing her again as he moved faster. Her body was loosening, her pussy adapting to his size as desire spiraled, dazzling her. His scent was all around her, the dark earth, the rainy night. She breathed him in, breathed in the pleasure and the pain of this enormous man fucking her.

She spread her thighs wider, needing more. There was a low chuckle from him.

"You are perfect, my girl," he muttered as his strong hips thrust harder. "Come on. Really take it, now."

He began a hard, pummeling rhythm, his cock driving deep. Pleasure was sharp, growing by the moment with each punishing plunge of his hips.

"Gonna come again," she gasped.

"Yes, come, darlin'. Do it now."

Pleasure crested, carrying her higher, higher, and burst inside her with the brilliance of a thousand stars. Lights flashed behind her eyes as she heard him call out, felt him slam into her.

"Mischa . . . fuck!"

His hand curled around hers, his fingers holding tight, as tight as his arm around her waist, and something inside her opened up.

They were both still coming, and he held on to her as he shuddered against her, his cock pulsing inside her. He collapsed onto her for one moment, then he rolled, taking her with him. His breath was a ragged pant. So was hers. Her body was lit up with sensation, in a small state of overload. Something about his big body . . . God, she loved the size of him. His muscles. His beautiful cock.

Something about the way he'd held on to her as he came . . .

When he pulled her closer to him, right against his side, one strong arm around her body, she didn't want to acknowledge what it did to her. That he *wanted* to hold her. That she wanted—needed—him to in a way that made her heartbeat race.

What was this?

Great sex. Absolutely amazing, mind-blowing sex. A foray into the real dominance thing—not yet in terms of outward kink, but absolutely in the way she'd given herself over to him, in the way he'd commanded her to. This amazing sex with one of the hottest men she'd ever seen. But that was it.

Why did she even have to question how she was feeling?

Maybe because she was feeling things she'd never felt before. An absolute driving *need* to do it again. Tonight. Tomorrow.

Could any sex be that good? Or was there something more?

Her mind automatically rejected the idea. It was sex, a hot man. Nothing more, damn it.

Damn it.

Because she knew there was a small lie in there somewhere. One she didn't want to explore too closely. She'd learned her lessons early from her mother. Every man Mischa had slept with—and she'd shamelessly sampled plenty—had only confirmed what she knew: that men were playthings, companions. Nothing more. Nothing she needed, certainly. She had a good life. She was busy, successful. Happy.

Wasn't she?

Why then was she suddenly feeling that she'd be a lot happier with Connor around?

He's not that kind of man. And you're not that kind of girl.

No. She knew herself. When this fling was over—and that's exactly what this was—even if it was going to last a few days longer than she'd intended, it was still that: a fling. She'd never required anything more. She didn't intend to start now. Even if Connor made her pulse hammer in her veins, her body surge with melting desire. Even now, after coming three times in the last hour.

Even if the way he held her made her *heart* melt, for the first time in her life.

She was being ridiculous. They'd just met. And she was not that kind of girl. She'd just have to keep telling herself that until this terrible, strange yearning went away.

three

Moonlight shone through the pale rice paper of the window shades, just enough that he could see her still form outlined beneath the down quilt. It had slipped from her shoulders in her sleep, revealing the curve of one luscious breast pressed beneath her arm. He glanced at the clock; it was after two. Which meant they hadn't been asleep for long. He felt as though he'd been sleeping for hours, he was so groggy. Or maybe it was the softness that was *her* that made him feel a little dizzy. Out of his head.

He *was* a little out of his head. He'd dreamed of her. They'd just met, and he was dreaming of her, for fuck's sake! Even now he couldn't stop staring at her. Wondering . . . what? If she would stay in his bed for as long as possible in the morning, certainly. Maybe take a long, hot shower with him. Soap her up, feel her lush body slippery with soap. Maybe fuck her again in the shower. Even better, maybe bend her over his big glass dining room table and give her a good spanking. The one he couldn't give her until they'd worked through their negotiations. He'd been too caught up in her earlier to talk. He'd had to have her as soon as he could. He'd barely been able to hold off long enough to make her come a few times, even though he'd wanted her to. Watching a woman come always really killed him. Watching Mischa come . . .

He moaned, remembering the sounds she made, her hot, panting breath, her clenching pussy.

When was the last time any woman had challenged his sense of absolute control the way she did? The control that was too necessary to his role as a dominant—to the way he lived his life—to even question.

He scrubbed a hand over his stubbled jaw. This woman was different. He'd come to understand that right away. The way she made his blood run hot, just looking at her. Talking with her. Unbelievable.

And now, seeing her in his bed, her skin washed silver in the moonlight . . . Hell, he was turning into some kind of romantic, suddenly. But romance wasn't what had his pulse hammering, his cock coming up hard. It was the scent of sex that hung in the cool night air. The scent of woman next to him. The heat of her body under the covers.

He reached out, pulled the covers down a bit to see her better. She sighed in her sleep, rolled onto her back. Lord, she had the most perfect breasts he'd ever seen in his life. They were full, her nipples large. They were hardening, from the cold air, probably. Tempting as hell. His cock pulsed.

Need to touch her . . .

He leaned in, whispered in her ear, "Come on, Mischa. Wake up."

"Hmm?"

"Wake up, darlin'. I need to fuck you again."

"Ah, Connor."

She reached for him, still half asleep, her eyes not even open. There was a small smile on her mouth as she wrapped a soft hand behind his neck and pulled him in.

He didn't need to be told twice. He slid on top of her, her plush breasts crushed beneath his chest. She was spreading her thighs already. And he was hard as stone for her. It was all he could do to reach for a condom, to raise himself up long enough to sheath himself before he slid into her.

Ah, but she was hot and silky—he could feel it through the latex. And so damn tight. She wrapped her legs around his back, her arms around his neck, her hands in his hair. He began to move, trying not to hurt her, but really needing to just fuck her, to push into her until he was as deep as he could go. Her hips were arching into his, harder and harder, taking him in, and she was making small rasping, panting noises that were driving him crazy.

"Connor, please . . ."

"What do you need?"

"I just . . . God, I need more."

He slipped his hands under her, held on tight to her fine ass, raising her hips so he could change angles, move even deeper inside her.

She was really moving, fucking him as much as he was her, her nails digging into his shoulders. Pleasure was like a coiled snake in his belly, tighter and tighter, making him shiver. It spread, into his balls, his *brain*.

"That's it, darlin' . . . yes. Come on, fuck me. That's it."

He reached in between them, pressed his fingers onto her hard little clit.

"Oh, that's good," she murmured.

They moved faster, moved together. He rubbed at her clit as he thrust into her, and soon she was crying out.

"Ah, Connor! Yes!"

He felt her pussy clamp hard around his cock as she came, a hot, clasping fist. She was trembling all over, her nails digging deeper into his flesh. Pleasure crested, the small bit of pain from her nails driving him on—the sharp spasms, the scent of her climax, driving him even harder.

He came, his body shaking with it. His head reeling. One shock of pleasure after another, reverberating through his system, his balls pulling tight.

He was groaning—he could hear himself as if from a distance. Heard her soft sighs. It was several moments before he became aware that he was still fucking her, even after his climax, and hers, were over. He couldn't get enough of her—her soft body, her sweet, silky pussy.

Her.

Ridiculous.

She was just all hot woman. Fucking beautiful. Responsive as hell. What man wouldn't be taken with her?

He pulled out of her, meant to pull away. But he caught a glimpse of her face, so damn lovely in the light of the moon, with her recent pleasure making her features soft and loose. Her eyes were gleaming from beneath half-closed lids, her red lips were parted. And he couldn't help himself, he had to kiss her, his mouth coming down on hers.

She was soft and hot inside her mouth as she opened to him. Her lips were sweet, her tongue even sweeter. And soon they were making out like two teenagers. Just kissing like crazy, eating each other up. He couldn't get hard again; not so soon. But there was some strange driving *need* there he didn't understand. They were just kissing, hands in each other's hair, and hers was like satin, tangling in his fingers.

She was panting into his mouth. He loved the feel of it. Of her rising excitement. He wanted to touch her, make her come again. He wasn't about to stop kissing her—it was too good. He moved to the side just enough that he could reach down between her thighs, slip over the smooth skin of her shaved cleft. Found her soaking wet again. It made his belly, his worn cock, clench. He'd fuck her again right now if he could. But while he waited to recover, he'd just slide in her juices, let his hand fuck her.

She moaned as he stroked her wet slit, angled his hand so he could press two fingers inside her and circle her hard clitoris with his thumb. Immediately her hips were pumping. Her hot pussy taking his fingers in, clenching hard. He thrust into her, pressed hard onto her clit. Merciless. Desperate. He needed her to come into his hand. Needed to feel that pleasure in her body. Needed to keep on kissing her like this: mouths open, tongues twining. Everything wet and hot and *her*.

In moments she was coming again, moaning into his mouth. Her pussy flooded, soaking his hand. And unbelievably, his cock went hard once more.

He muttered something—he didn't know what—as he reached, half blind, for another condom. Then he was on her, pushing into that silken flesh.

"Connor, please, just fuck me . . . I need you to . . . just . . . ah . . ."

He wanted to fuck her hard, fuck her through the wall, his need was so urgent. But once he was inside her she melted all over, her whole body softening under his. He was still kissing her, but more slowly now, letting her set the pace. And somehow the desperation turned into something else, some wild need for this slow, almost sleepy motion. Their hips pumped together. Her tongue surged softly into his mouth. And his cock pushed into her. But it was as if the whole world had slowed down so that he could really *feel* it all.

Softness.

Woman.

Mischa.

Her hands went to his hips, smoothed over his buttocks, pulled him in tighter. Her fingers flexed, dug a little into his flesh. But even that was softer, somehow.

When he came this time, it was like heat and water, the sensation liquid, undulating through him. And when it was over he was still kissing her, and she was kissing him back, making quiet little sighing sounds, just breathing into him.

His cock softened, he slipped out, and still they were kissing. Until they both grew sleepy, the kissing slowing until it was just their lips resting together. He fell asleep.

Mischa blinked in the dim light of dawn. She felt the heat of Connor's big body beside her, heard the gentle rhythm of his breathing. And remembered that quiet space they'd shared in the middle of the night.

She ran her hands through her hair, staring up at the ceiling, exhaling slowly. Had it really happened? That slow, sleepy sex. The intensity of it, even though it had all flowed without effort, without thought, even. As if they were in a dream.

No man had ever kissed her that way. As if he'd die without it. They'd never stopped kissing for a moment. And it had been . . . wonderful.

But now, she had to question what it had really been about. Was the intensity simply what happened with a guy who was so deeply into the power play thing? She'd heard those heavy BDSM relationships were very impassioned, the connections strong— not that this was a relationship, by any means. Or was it just some momentary romantic fantasy? Not that she was the kind of woman who had those sorts of fantasies. And Connor hadn't struck her as being that kind of man. The idea that he'd want anything more than a night or two of hot sex was frankly silly.

But three or four wouldn't be bad . . . and maybe more. She did plan to stay in Seattle for two weeks, until Dylan's wedding arrangements were settled and she'd made a decision about going into business with Greyson. Two weeks with Connor . . .

She sat up, holding the down comforter over her bare breasts. Bad idea. Very bad. If she was feeling this confused, this vulnerable, after one night with him, before they'd even had a chance to get to the real kink, how much more might that open her to him? She knew very well where that could lead—down a bumpy road she had no intention of following, one with inevitable damage at the end. The kind of damage her mother had suffered at the hands of the men she had loved.

She saw it in her mind's eye like a movie playing, the haunting memories from her childhood she couldn't seem to shake blending together into one raw, aching image. Her mother lying in a darkened room for days, her face swollen with tears. The inevitable ashtray overrun with ashes, the acrid scent of pot smoke in the air. The bed or couch or futon may have been different from year to year as Evie moved them around from apartment to commune to funky cottage, but her mother was always the same. Falling hard for some man, immersing herself in romantic fantasies that were crushed when the guy left. And the guy *always* left. Her mother's inability to get a grasp on reality had too often left Mischa to care for her younger sister, to care for her *mother*, from too young an age. She remembered shaking Evie awake, trying to get her to eat. To get up and take a shower, take her and Raine to school. No kid should have to do that. No kid should have to witness the way Evie had allowed herself to be ravaged by love. No woman should allow that to happen.

Mischa shook herself. She was *not* falling in love. That wasn't what this was about. She didn't know what it was, exactly. But every alarm bell in her head was going off, shrieking at her, and she wasn't going to stick around to find out.

She got out of the bed as quietly as she could, found her clothes, slipped into them, trying very hard not to look at Connor. But it was impossible. He was too large, too imposing, even as he slept.

The light filtering through the shades was a pale, misty gray. But she could see him, the sheer size of him, the muscles in his shoulder as he lay on his side. His face was as beautiful as any man she'd ever seen, despite the rugged bone structure, the purely masculine lines, that scar beneath his right eye. Somehow, even as he slept his expression, his *presence*, held authority.

She shivered and told herself she was just cold as she turned away, tiptoeing down the hall, her shoes in her hand. She glanced up and found a row of erotic drawings on the long hallway wall, women in various states of undress, various states of bondage. She paused in front of one sketch—the woman looked very much like her, with long, wavy pale hair, a lot of tattoos. Some other woman he'd had sex with, probably. Had he slept with them all? Not that it was any of her business. None of her concern. Connor Galloway could do whatever he liked. Except fuck with her head. Which was why she was leaving.

She found her coat on the big sofa, had a brief flash of him pushing her down on the cushions, going down on her, doing things with his mouth she'd only ever *thought* she'd experienced before.

She shook her head against the next shiver that tried to tremble through her, put on her coat and opened the front door. She couldn't resist one final glance over her shoulder before pulling it shut behind her.

Good-bye, Connor.

*   *   *

The cafe downtown where Dylan had asked to meet her for breakfast was a bustling place on a Saturday morning, the warm air carrying the lovely scents of strong coffee and baking pastries. Like so many Seattle buildings this one was older, with high ceilings, a wide front window and old wood floors that had been refinished to a glossy sheen. Dylan waved to her from a small table in the back and Mischa made her way through the crowd.

"Morning, Misch."

"Hi. Have you been waiting long?" She took off her coat and hung it over the back of the wooden chair.

"Only long enough to get seated. I just ordered some coffee for you."

"Bless you."

The waitress arrived with their coffee, set a mug down in front of each of them, telling them she'd leave them to look over the menu.

"Mischa? Are you all right?"

"What?" She looked up from her coffee. "Sure, fine."

"Okay . . . then why did you just put four packets of sugar in your coffee?"

"Did I?" Mischa looked into her cup, as if there might be some explanation there. "Doesn't matter. I'll drink it, anyway. I need it this morning."

"But you're fine?" Dylan raised one dark auburn eyebrow.

Mischa felt her gaze on her. She shrugged. "Don't worry about me, Dylan. I'm a big girl. I'll figure this out for myself."

"Is it the new shop? Have you spoken with Greyson already?"

"No, we're not due to meet until Wednesday."

"Hangover?"

"Nope. I hardly drank last night."

"Are you worried about opening the new shop with Greyson?"

"Maybe a little. But I've decided I definitely want to do it, if we can work out all the details, so I'm feeling good about it."

"You look tired," Dylan remarked, her gaze sharp on her now.

"I am a little tired."

"And you didn't get much sleep because . . . ?"

There was a small smile quirking the corner of Dylan's mouth, and Mischa realized she wasn't going to let it go.

"You can be a real bulldog sometimes, you know?"

"So Alec tells me." She was really grinning now.

Mischa blew out a long breath, wrapping her hands around the coffee mug. "Okay. But it's really . . . nothing. I went home with Connor last night. No big deal. I'm just short on sleep. But I promise it won't hinder my shopping capabilities today at all."

"I'm not worried about the shopping. I'm worried about you."

"A little lack of sleep never killed anyone." She sipped her coffee, winced at how sweet it was.

"If he was an asshole to you, Misch, I will have Alec kick his ass, close friends or not."

Mischa laughed. "That won't be necessary, but thanks for the offer. He was an absolute gentleman." She realized then it was true; he had been. He'd taken great care with her. In a way that made her feel absolutely *cared for*.

Maybe that was the most dangerous part.

She shook her head.

"See, I knew there was something more."

"Dylan, I just . . . Look, you're right, there is something else going on. But it's just all in my head. He was perfectly nice to me, we had crazy hot sex, and now I'm just . . . being stupid. I'll sort it out."

"Wow. I don't know that I've ever heard *you* getting stupid over a man."

"Yeah, me neither," she muttered, hating that she was admitting out loud that anything was wrong.

Dylan was watching her, her gray eyes narrowing.

"Come on, Dylan," Mischa protested. "It's nothing. I mean, it's *something*, but I'll deal with it. I always do."

"True."

"So why don't you show me the pictures of the dresses you have in mind while we get some food?"

Dylan pursed her lips for a moment, but she said, "Okay."

They were just finishing their breakfast and getting back into their coats to go shopping when Mischa's cell phone buzzed in her purse. She pulled it out and looked at the number. It was unfamiliar, but had a Seattle area code. She knew somehow that it was him.

Connor.

"Aren't you going to answer that?" Dylan asked.

"Nope. Today I'm all yours. Anything else can wait."

Especially a direct reminder of the man she was doing her best to forget about.

Like that's ever going to happen.

She huffed and pulled the belt to her coat tight. "Come on, let's go."

Mischa unlocked the door to Dylan's apartment and pushed her way inside. Her feet were killing her, even though she'd worn her favorite pair of flat, knee-high boots with her warm sweater tights and her standard dress—she rarely wore pants. Still, she was dying to get into a hot tub and soak. This wedding dress shopping thing wasn't for wimps, and she was worn out.

She dropped her coat on the gorgeous peridot suede couch

she'd always admired, sat down long enough to unlace her boots and pull them off.

"Ah."

She flexed her toes for a moment, then carried the boots across the big loft apartment, the sleek, white-washed wood floors smooth under her bare feet, and into the bedroom with its pristine white bed linens set against soft green walls. It was a comfortable room, all the furnishings in the clean, contemporary lines that were everywhere in the apartment, but the wall color and the fluffy white comforter softened the look. She set her boots on the floor and her purse on the big white bed, pulling out her cell phone. There were three missed calls, all from the same number she'd seen that morning. She pulled in a long breath as a surge of need rippled through her.

Why did she want to talk to him so damn badly?

Defiantly, she tossed the phone on the bed, marched into the bathroom and started the hot water for her bath. She pinned up her hair, catching sight of her face in the mirror. The flush on her cheeks, her dilated pupils, had nothing to do with being tired. She'd been in an odd state all day. Half of her was struggling with the firm resolve to stop thinking about Connor. The other half was losing badly. She was doing no better now.

Just sex. It was just sex.

The hottest freaking sex of my entire sordid life.

Her nipples went hard at that thought. She couldn't help but remember the way he'd touched her. How she'd come over and over.

She sighed, shut off the faucet and got into the tub, and sat back.

Connor.

He had the broadest shoulders she'd ever seen up close. And

the way his heavily muscled body had felt under her hands . . . the way it had felt held over her. Unbelievably powerful. She'd felt . . . completely overtaken by him. Even by the thick Irish brogue, the low, gravelly tone of his voice.

She moaned, a quiet sound in the still air.

Maybe it wouldn't be such a bad thing, just this once . . .

She closed her eyes, let herself remember his hands on her body. His mouth—God, his mouth—as he kissed her so damn hard. As he went down on her, sucking on her clit until she came.

"Oh . . ."

She lowered her hands, let one cup her breast, her fingers caressing her nipple. The other went between her parted thighs, pressing onto her hard clitoris.

She remembered the hot silk of his tongue against hers. The way he held her so firmly. As if he owned her. How she'd loved it.

She began to circle her clitoris, pressing, pressing, pausing only to dip down, to push one finger inside herself, then two.

"Oh yes," she murmured.

She tilted her hips, beginning a pumping rhythm, fucking herself with her fingers. Letting the pleasure drift over her in lovely waves.

She remembered the strange pale green shot with gold of his eyes, the dark brows that looked almost menacing when he was holding himself over her, fucking her. So much intensity there, a thrilling darkness. It was as though pleasure *changed* him, opened up something, turned him into something more primal. She loved it.

She pressed her fingers deeper, angled them to hit her G-spot. Remembered his big, beautiful cock. She spread her thighs wider, added a third finger, trying to duplicate that sensation of being utterly filled.

Pleasure surged, deep in her belly, her clit, her breasts, pulsing with need. She gave her nipple a sharp pinch, let the pain and the pleasure wash over her. Knew that he did it better. It was still good. But less so, without the interplay, the power exchange.

Connor.

She remembered her response to his command, the way it made her shiver. Remembered how her body had felt, crushed beneath his. The thrill that he had taken her from behind their first time together, how it felt a little dirty. She loved that, too.

Connor.

She moved her hand faster, fucking herself hard, her hips pumping. She twisted her nipple between her fingers. Pleasure shafted through her with a keen, lovely edge, and she felt herself nearing her peak.

"Come on," she whispered. "Come on, Connor. Fuck me."

She plunged her fingers into her aching sex, let her nipple go to pinch her clit, hard. Pleasure roared through her, along with the small bit of pain that took her over the edge.

"Ah, Connor!"

She shivered with it, wave after wave, her body jerking, the water splashing around her.

Finally it was over, and she let herself drift in the heat of the water, her muscles loose.

Somehow, it wasn't enough.

She washed herself, the soapy sponge seeming to light her sensitized skin on fire. Needing more. Needing him.

She rinsed off, got out of the bath, wrapped a thick moss-green towel around herself, not wanting to see her reflection in the mirror. To have to look at her own post-climax gratification. At the hunger she knew would be clear in her eyes, a hunger that was still somehow unsated.

She marched back into the bedroom. She'd get into her yoga

pants, order some dinner from one of the many take-out menus Dylan kept in the kitchen and distract herself with a movie. Or maybe she'd draw until it was time for bed.

Her gaze flicked to the bed, to her small silver train case sitting on the floor next to it that held her vibrators. Oh yes, she knew what she'd be doing at bedtime. But not yet. She'd just had a ripping orgasm in the bathtub; she didn't need to come again so soon.

Except that she did.

She huffed out a breath. Where the hell had she put her yoga pants?

Her cell phone buzzed. She'd left it on vibrate all day. Now she could barely listen to that sound without her body lighting up, craving the vibration. She'd do better to put the ringer back on.

She picked up the phone, checking to see who it was, saw Dylan's cell number on the screen.

"Hey, what's up?"

"Sorry, Misch, but I just realized our appointment tomorrow at the florist is at ten, not eleven."

"No problem. I'll be ready."

"What are you up to? Have you eaten?"

"I was just about to order something. I just got out of the bath."

And just had one of the best solo orgasms of her life, which she didn't need to mention. Or that she planned to do it again in a few hours—if she could manage to wait that long.

"Okay, Misch. See you in the morning."

"Night, hon."

She was about to toss the phone back onto the bed when it rang again. She pressed the talk button. "What did you forget, Dylan?"

"Mischa."

Oh, this was *so* not Dylan.

"Connor? How did you get my number?"

"I asked Alec for it."

God, her heart was going a million miles an hour. Excitement warred with annoyance that he hadn't gotten the message to leave her alone. If she'd wanted to talk to him, she would have returned one of his calls—she was certain it had been him trying to reach her all day.

"What's up?" she asked.

"We need to talk."

"What about?"

"You running out this morning."

"Come on. You can't tell me that bothered you."

"I'd rather we talk in person, Mischa."

"I've had a long day. I'm not up to going anywhere."

"That won't be necessary. I'm at your front door."

"What?"

She stomped through the apartment, the wood floors hard under her bare feet, and flung open the door.

"What are you doing here, Connor?"

He grinned, his lush mouth quirking at the corners.

"Lovely outfit."

She glanced down at her green towel, huffed and pulled it tighter. "You didn't answer my question."

"You did warn me you'd have questions."

Why was he still grinning at her? And filling up the doorway like some sort of giant. But she wasn't about to be intimidated.

"So?" she said, her jaw clenching.

Why did he have to look so damn gorgeous? And why did he have to be so even-tempered? The man was going to drive her crazy. Not to mention the way her nipples were hardening beneath the towel, the slight *zing* of desire between her thighs.

Stop it.

"So," he started. "This would be easier if you'd invite me in."

"I don't know that I want to."

Oh, that was a lie. She simply didn't *want* to want to.

He stepped closer, not quite inside the door. But close enough that when she inhaled she caught a little of his dark scent.

"Obviously things didn't end as well as I assumed they did. I thought we had a pretty splendid evening together." He lowered his tone. "I thought you enjoyed yourself as much as I did—all three orgasms . . . or was it four?"

"Five," she muttered.

"Well, then." He paused, reached out and stroked her cheek with one big fingertip, let it rest just under her chin. "I'd thought to do it again; spend an evening together. I'd thought you might be amenable. But I can see now how five orgasms might sour your mind on me."

He grinned at her, gave a wink, a gesture that would have been far too camp on almost any other man. On him, it was charming.

Damn it.

She sighed. "Look, Connor, I just don't need any . . . complications, you know?"

That was certainly true enough. She had a lot to accomplish while she was in town. Not only was Dylan's wedding important, but opening a new shop with Greyson could be an enormous step in securing her future. She needed to maintain her focus if she was going to make it happen.

"I would never think to complicate your life, Mischa. You and I, we're the uncomplicated types, aren't we? Birds of a feather."

It was true—on the surface, anyway. Underneath, she knew she had some heavy stuff to work out. Maybe he did, too. But as far as sex went . . . why not? Maybe it could be that simple.

"Invite me in, Mischa."

She blinked up at him, her head already spinning with the thought.

"Do it," he said softly, but there was as much command in his low tone as there ever was with him.

She stepped back, held the door wide, and he moved in, closing it behind him.

He took her in his arms, leaned in to kiss her, and they had a few breathless moments in which his tongue surged into her mouth, hot and sweet, his lips soft on hers, yet demanding at the same time. Then he pulled back, held her at arm's length.

"Oh no you don't," he said. "We'll talk first this time."

"Me?"

He laughed. "All right, maybe it was my fault. But kissing you is too damn good. But yeah, we have to talk a few things through."

"Okay. Let me go change."

"I don't mind the towel."

She smiled at him. "I'm sure you don't, but you can't ask me to sit next to you and think straight enough to have these negotiations after the way you just kissed me when I'm half naked."

"Mmm, point taken." He grinned at her, then settled on the sofa as easily as if he owned it. But then, that was how Connor did everything.

She hurried back to the bedroom, found her red satin kimono robe and slipped into it. She took a few moments in the bathroom to take her hair down and brush it into place in front of the big pewter-framed mirror. She tried to ignore the gleam in her blue eyes, the pink blush on her cheeks.

She'd have to accept that this was what he did to her. With one kiss. Hell, just by being there. She could pretend to be annoyed with him, but what she was really annoyed with was her lack of control over her own response to him.

She had been, anyway.

Seeing him again made it all come back to her—the way he made her feel. Which was too damn good not to have another taste of it.

She was strong enough, independent enough, to simply let it go when her trip was over, or when one of them decided it was time to part ways. She always had been before. There was no reason for her to think she wouldn't be now.

She could have sex with Connor Galloway again. And oh, how she was melting already, knowing it was about to happen. She could explore his brand of kink. It didn't have to mean anything more than that. It didn't have to make her head spin. And even if it did, she would handle it. Just as she'd told Dylan, she always did.

There was another small lie in there somewhere. But she was too distracted by the knowledge that he was in the next room, waiting for her, to pay it any attention.

"You are in big trouble, girl," she told her reflection in the mirror. But that reflection only smiled back at her with a lustful gleam in her eyes.

four

"Come sit by me," he said.

She did, next to him but not too close. If they had serious issues to discuss, she'd have to maintain a certain distance in order
to keep a clear head. Semi-clear, anyway. The man was still in the
room. And she suspected up close he'd smell too good to resist.

"Do you want something to drink?" she asked him. "A glass
of wine?"

"No alcohol when we play. No alcohol when we negotiate.
Clear heads."

"Okay. How do these negotiations go?"

"I have a list of questions. You answer. Simple in essence, except that you need to think your answers through, be honest with
yourself about what you want, where your boundaries and fears
are. And it's just as crucial that you're honest with me. This will
determine what we might do, and perhaps more important, what
we won't do. You'll be telling me yes, no or maybe for each ques-

tion. 'Maybe' means it's something I can push you on in the moment, or bring up again later, if I determine you're in the right space to approach it."

"If *you* determine?" She crossed her arms over her chest. That didn't sit well with her at all.

Connor leaned forward, his elbows braced on his knees. "Mischa, being a dominant is a great pleasure, but with it comes great responsibility. I know we've just met, but can you trust in what you've seen of me so far? Can you trust that I am Alec's friend? We play in the same circles, by the same code of ethics. Are you familiar with the Safe, Sane and Consensual credo?"

"Yes. I've heard it at the clubs I've been to. And I've read about it."

"Then you have some idea of what that code means to me. I take it very seriously. All right?"

She nodded. Her heart was beginning to pound. This was serious stuff. The few men she'd "played" with at the clubs had been just that—play—but Connor was the real thing. It aroused her, excited her, so much more than she'd expected. But with Connor every time she thought she knew what to expect, he surprised her. Including, right now, how quickly her irritation at his bossiness dissolved under the powerful force of his natural command. It was real—he wasn't some wannabe, which, she now realized, was probably what those other men she'd experimented with were. And somehow, that changed everything.

"I should also tell you," he went on, "that when we're done, if you still have any questions for me, you let me know, and I will answer as thoroughly as I can."

She nodded again. Licked her lips.

"Remember: yes, no or maybe. Do you want to be spanked?"

She smiled, a little surprised at how quickly the conversation had shifted, how he'd gotten right down to business. But this question was easy enough. "Yes. Sure."

"Pinched?"

Also easy. "Yes."

"Hit with a flogger, a slapper, a crop?"

A lovely chill ran through her. "Yes. I've had a flogger used on me, but it was one of those soft suede ones. And frankly, he was far too tentative with it."

"What about with a single-tail?"

"Is that like a short bullwhip?"

He nodded. "Yes."

"I don't know. I don't know the level of pain I can handle, what I might enjoy past a certain point."

"But you do enjoy the pain?"

"Yes. I always have. From rough sex to a good spanking."

"But you have never felt that you were a submissive." It was phrased as a statement, but she knew he was asking her.

"Not in the past. But . . . it's different with you. Not that I'll ever be truly submissive. The submission is part of the pain-pleasure thing. An offshoot of that."

"And you're not entirely happy about it?"

She smiled again, a little wryly. "Not entirely."

"But you are willing to explore these things with me?"

"Yes."

"What about anal sex?"

"Yes. I like it a lot."

A slow smile from him at that. "Ah, good girl."

There it was, those two simple words again that just made her melt into a pathetic little puddle.

Only for him.

She'd been telling him the truth. Although she'd been spanked, tied up, she'd never felt that sensation of going under, of letting go of control, handing that to another person. It had been more about seeking out extreme forms of sex. Having an adventure. The adventure with him would be something else altogether.

"How do you feel about being tied up? Handcuffed? Chained?"

"Being tied up has never really done much for me. I don't get the fascination with ropes, and definitely not with silk scarves. That seems . . . amateurish to me. I love the handcuffs. Really love the idea of chains, although I've never used them before."

"Ah, we are a perfect match, you and I. What about being blindfolded?"

"I . . . I don't like it. Enough that I've never allowed anyone to try it with me. I don't like that total disconnect from my environment."

"You always need a shred of control to hang on to, is that it?"

She raised her chin. "Yes."

"All right. We don't have to go there right now. What about hot wax?"

"I've played with it before, but I wasn't the one on the bottom that time."

He laughed. "And?"

"I like the idea of it. We'll have to see if I like the sensation."

"Tell me about the kanji tattoo on the back of your neck— what does it say?"

"My tattoo?"

"Yes."

She shrugged, trying not to squirm, although she wasn't sure why *now*, rather than during all the questions about the floggers and chains. "It says 'pain is love.'"

He raised one dark brow. "Do you really believe that?"

There was no hesitation before she answered this time. Loving anyone always meant that a certain amount of pain was inevitable. That's what her life had taught her. What witnessing her mother's life had taught her. Love equaled loss. Life with her mother had been one loss after another. Her father . . . there was nothing but a sense of loss there, other than the constant yearning to be loved by a man who didn't care that she existed. That's what her tattoo was about. "Yes. Don't you?"

He smiled a little, although at the same time he no longer looked quite so happy. "Yes. I guess I do."

He paused, still looking at her. She stared back, watching as he rearranged his features, let the shadow there, a flicker of emotion, fade away. She wasn't going to ask him about that. She knew the feeling well enough herself.

"Do you have any questions for me?" he asked her finally.

"Are the negotiations done?"

"For now."

"Then yes, I have a question."

"Ask."

"When are you going to take me to that club, the Pleasure Dome?"

He laughed again. "You like the public play, do you?"

"That's the biggest draw of those places for me, or it has been in the past. More than the equipment, my partners."

"You like to put on a show, do you? So do I. If you really want to go, then I'll certainly take you. Not tonight. Maybe next weekend. If you're still interested, that is. You might run from me again."

"I don't think so."

"What makes you so certain of that?"

"I just . . ." How could she explain to him, without saying more than she wanted to? Without admitting more than she was willing to look at herself? "I want to go. And I have a feeling this is going to work out. That we'll be good together."

"You're not a shy one, are you?"

It was her turn to laugh. "Hardly."

He stood, towering over her. He looked a bit intimidating, she could admit to that. The man was a *wall*. Big and dark, his eyes glittering with mischief. But she also loved it—his size, that shadowed side of him. His wickedness.

He held out a hand to her. "Shall we begin, then?"

She smiled, got to her feet. And was swept into his arms so fast it made her head spin. He turned her until she was facedown on the sofa, her robe gone as if by magic. He held both her wrists behind her back in one of his hands. She was panting instantly, shocked at how quickly he'd gotten her naked and into this submissive position. She also understood, in some distant way, that he'd used that element of surprise to break right through any walls she may have put up. It didn't scare her. Little did. She trusted him, for all the reasons he'd stated. And it was working beautifully. There was nothing but that small voice in the back of her head that was trying to tell her to slow down, to regain some balance in the power between them. But she was turned on enough to overcome it.

He leaned over and whispered into her ear, as if he could see right into her head, "Just relax now. Give it all over to me. You don't need to struggle. To argue with yourself about it. Just do it. It can be that easy."

"It's not easy," she gasped, realizing only then that part of her *was* holding back, hanging on to some small sense of control. God, this really was a mind fuck.

"It's as easy as you make it, Mischa."

She tried to shake her head, but he pressed down on the back of her neck with one hand. Gently, but it was enough to press her cheek right into the cushions of the sofa. And he was still using the other hand to hold both of her wrists at the small of her back. She began to tremble all over. It was half nerves, half desire, which was shivering through her in a series of tiny sparks, like small electric shocks. How had he known she would respond like this when she hadn't known herself?

He leaned over her until he was whispering into her hair. "I know what you're going through, Mischa. You're fighting it. The fight makes it harder on you. I admit I'll enjoy it a bit. But when you let go of the fight, that's when it can really begin. That's when you'll feel it all in some new, sublime way. That's my goal with you, sweetheart. To take you there."

"I . . . I don't know . . ." Her anxiety was mounting as she squirmed, and she realized she truly could not break from his hold on her.

"Ah, but I do. I can see it in you, the ability. The submissive response to even the most subtle tone of voice, the most subtle touch. It doesn't have to mean you'll ever be some kind of slave girl. There's a world of difference there. Don't you worry about that. Just be in the moment. Let it happen, as much as you can." His fingers flexed on the back of her neck, the fingers of his other hand flexing on her wrists, a small reminder. "Breathe for me, now. Deep breath in, let it out slow. Like meditation. It *is* a sort of meditation, as strange as it may sound. As odd as it may be to think of being able to relax while I hold you down like this. But that's exactly the point. You are in *my* hands."

As soon as he said that, she did get it. She did as he said, pulling in a long breath, letting it out a little at a time. Trying desperately to quiet the voice in her head that was telling her it was time to panic. But his soothing tone instructing her to breathe, over and over, was drowning it out.

Time passed. She didn't know how much. Finally he said, "Very good." And spanked her.

"Oh!"

"Can you take it, Mischa?"

She paused, let out a panting breath. "Yes."

"Are you being stubborn? Or do you really want it?"

"I want it," she said without hesitation this time. She didn't want to think. She only wanted to feel. And it was crucial that it was Connor doing these things to her.

He smacked her again, the sound ringing through the high-ceilinged loft. His hand came down once more, really stinging her flesh this time, and she gasped.

"Shh, you're okay," he told her, his voice a rough whisper.

He smoothed his hand over her tender skin. It felt lovely. His voice in her ears. His hand on her. The sting of the spanking. It all seemed to merge.

"Ready, my girl?"

"Yes."

There was a long enough pause that she had a moment to wonder what was going to happen. Then his hand came down again. And again. A sharp volley of slaps on her ass, one cheek, then the other, in a kind of slow, even rhythm. His hand came down harder with each smack. And with the sting came pleasure just as sharp. In minutes she was soaking wet, needy. She tilted her hips, pressing her cleft into the sofa.

"Ah, none of that," he said, the hand holding her wrists gripping tighter and pressing down a bit, into the small of her back, so that there was no question what he was talking about. "If you have a need, *I* will fill it. Do you understand?"

"Yes . . . I understand."

Inside she was pouting a little at being spoken to that way. But she was also as turned on as she'd ever been in her life. That it was *him* telling her these things, laying down these rules for her.

For her.

It felt like a small epiphany—the discovery, on some deep level, that this was truly for her as much as for him. But she couldn't think now. He was spanking her again, faster this time. Harder. The pain built and built. And just when she thought she couldn't bear it any longer, he let her wrists go and slipped his hand between her thighs and right into the soft folds of her pussy.

"Oh . . ."

"Ah, so wet. This is beautiful to me, darlin'. To feel your pleasure under my hands. To know it's more than sheer stubbornness that keeps you here. To know that your sweet pussy is as wet as my cock is hard."

Her sex clenched. She turned her face into the cushions, moaned as he pressed a finger inside her.

"So damn wet. So tight, no matter how wet you are. You held my cock so tightly inside you when I was fucking you last night."

She groaned.

"You like that, to hear me talk of fucking you, don't you? I can see that you do. I can feel it. Need coming off you in waves, like heat from the sun. I like it, too. To speak of fucking you. To say the words."

There was a long pause while he pumped his fingers into her until she was squirming; she couldn't help it, couldn't hold still. Pleasure was spiraling inside her, deeper and deeper.

"I want to fuck you, Mischa, my girl. I want to fuck you so hard. I want to fuck you until you can't stop coming. I want to fuck you until you scream. And I will, my girl. Take that as a promise."

Oh, she was shivering all over, her pussy squeezing his thrusting fingers, needing more. Needing his big cock inside her. Needing to be spanked some more.

"Connor . . ."

"Shh." His fingers stopped. "You will speak only when I ask you to. Is that clear?"

"Yes. Yes . . . oh . . ."

"Good girl." He began to pump into her again. "Hold as still as you can, now. Do it for me."

He gathered her wrists in his hand again, holding them tight, seeming to hold *on to* her, to help her control her body as he shifted his hand, withdrawing his fingers and replacing them with his broad thumb so he could press onto her tight clit with his fingers. She needed to move, to arch her hips into his hand, but she didn't do it. Because he didn't want her to.

Her head was absolutely empty of everything but the most exquisite, torturous pleasure. She was going to come.

He stopped, gave her wrists a hard squeeze, hard enough to really hurt, to bring her a bit away from where she hovered on the edge of climax.

She whimpered, hardly believing she was doing it.

He was close to her ear again. "I know, my darlin' girl. I know it's hard. But you'll be the better for it. Trust me. When I do let you come, you'll explode like a fucking rocket. You'll have the best orgasm of your life. Just put yourself into my hands. Completely. Let's do some breathing again."

She tried, but her breath was shaky. He kept talking to her, his voice soft, until she was able to fill up her lungs, despite the hard, driving need in her body. And eventually, under his instruction, she was able to get it back under control.

Under control.

Wasn't that exactly what she wanted? But she'd had to hand the control over to him first . . .

She couldn't make sense of it.

She didn't have time to; he flipped her over onto her back and bent to press his mouth to her aching slit.

"Oh . . . God . . ."

His lips were warm, his tongue like damp silk as it slid up her cleft, in between the swollen folds of her pussy lips, then inside her. He let it surge into her, all soft and moist. It felt amazing. Pleasure was rising once more. He took his time, just letting his wide tongue press softly against her sex, slipping inside her, out again. And all the while he had his hands beneath her buttocks, his fingers digging in just enough. Possessively.

She felt the silk of his dark hair against her inner thighs. Loved the contrasts: his soft mouth, his hard hands, the satin of his hair, the gentle scrape of his beard stubble. She was writhing a little, but he was letting her, not controlling her as much this time. She was so close . . . so close . . .

He pulled away.

"Mischa, look at me."

She opened her eyes, hadn't realized they'd been closed. And caught his gaze. His pupils were wide, the green of his eyes glowing, sparking with bits of gold. The eyes of a wildcat. His mouth was damp with her juices, loose with desire. A stab of need went through her, simply seeing the expression on his face.

"You're going to come now," he said quietly.

"Yes . . . please."

"You're going to come for me, my girl. Do you understand? For *me*."

"Yes. Yes."

He kept his gaze on her as he thrust his hand between her thighs. He pushed three fingers into her wet sex, used his thumb to rub her swollen clitoris. He brought the other hand to his mouth, sucked one finger, brought it out again and slipped it under her.

She knew what he was going to do with it. But still, it was like some exquisite surprise when he pushed the wet tip into her ass.

She moaned, panted.

"Good?" he asked.

"God, yes!"

"Then come for me. Come hard, my girl."

Pleasure invaded her system: clit, pussy, ass. It all came together, sensation overload, and her body went wild with a burst of heat. It consumed her, dazzled her. She was yelling, jerking. And he kept his gaze on hers, so that she had the sensation of coming *into* his sea-green eyes.

"Connor!"

"I'm here with you, sweetheart. I'm riding it out with you."

And he did; he stayed with her, his fingers plunging into her, working her ass, her clitoris. His gaze locked on hers, going darker by the second.

She wasn't sure she was quite done when he slipped his fingers from her, unzipped his jeans and slipped a condom onto his erect cock.

"Can't fucking wait a moment longer," he muttered.

Then he was on her, using his hands to wrap her legs around him. The fabric of his jeans was rough against her thighs. She didn't care. Her hands went into his hair and held on as he worked the tip of his cock into her.

He was as big as ever, but she was so incredibly wet, she took him all in one stroke.

"Mischa, fuck, girl . . ."

He thrust into her, his hands snaking around her body to pinch her buttocks, squeezing her flesh hard between his fingers. It hurt like hell. It felt amazing. The pleasure, the pain, melted together, became one sensation. That and the scent of him in her nostrils. The knowledge that it was Connor riding her.

She latched on to his neck, tasting him with her tongue, then biting down hard, feeling the silky flesh of his throat between her teeth. He cried out, an animal sound. But he never stopped fucking her in long, punishing strokes.

They were gasping together, moving together. And as he dug his fingers into her flesh, he came, shuddering, calling her name.

"Mischa . . . Mischa!"

She grabbed his head in her hands, forced him to look into her eyes as he was coming, and it was overwhelming, seeing him so lost in pleasure. Seeing the dark intensity there. The *connection*.

There was too much there. She couldn't comprehend it all, or if what she thought she was seeing was real. Chills ran up her spine for several moments. Then her body arced as another orgasm washed over her, his hips slamming into her still, his pelvic bone crashing against her clitoris.

Her head spun, everything went dark, and she lost herself in sensation. Lost herself in him.

Connor.

She wanted to call for him. To tell him what she was feeling, talk out her confusion. But she was too far gone to speak his name.

His weight grew heavy on her, but she was too weak, too out of it, to ask him to move. She didn't really want him to. The small part of her mind that was gradually clearing was a little afraid that if he got off her she'd bolt from the room. But instead of her panic calming as they both caught their breath, it grew. With each passing moment she became more and more certain that she had given him far too much of herself. That doing so was dangerous. That she was out of her depths with this man.

Finally she said, "Connor."

"Hmm? What is it, darlin'?"

"I have to . . . I have to get up. I have to move."

He raised his head to look into her eyes. He stayed there for several moments, searching her face as the tension mounted inside her, until she thought she would scream. She had to bite down on her lip to hold it inside.

"Are you bottoming out?"

"No. No. I just . . . Connor, let me up."

"Of course."

He rolled off her, stripping the condom from his softening cock. She sat upright, breathing as hard as she had been while he was fucking her.

"Okay. Okay." She pushed a hand through her tangled hair. "I just . . . have to go."

He put a hand on her arm. She tried to shake him off, but he wasn't having it. He said softly, "Where do you need to go, Mischa?"

"Out of here." She swallowed hard, hating the tears she felt prick the back of her eyelids.

"It's okay," he said.

She turned to him, her eyes feeling hot. Blazing, she was sure. "It is *not* okay!"

"What's not? Tell me."

She shook her head. She knew she was being childish. She couldn't help it.

He placed both hands on her shoulders. His eyes were gleaming, a little sleepy, still, but they held his usual authority. "Mischa, you're panicking."

"Damn right I am."

"Why?"

"Because this is not right! I am not some little subbie girl you can tell what to do. I am not some . . . weak woman who can't think for herself."

"I never said you were."

"No, but your actions imply it." She was trembling now, hard shudders running through her body.

"Mischa," he said again, as if he knew saying her name would catch her attention. It did. "This *is* bottoming out. The panic.

The shivering. I'm not saying you don't have some real concerns. But the panic is simply a chemical response to an overload of stimulation. Let me help you."

"Why would you? You don't care about me. And you don't have to—that's not what I'm saying."

What *was* she saying? She wasn't even sure any longer. All she knew was she had to get out of there—or get *him* out of there. She didn't care that she was getting a little hysterical.

"I don't have to, it's true," he said, his tone still low. "But I do."

"What are you saying?"

"Maybe I'm not exactly certain. But I do care, as I would for any human being. And more . . . because it's you. I don't understand it." He shrugged, his hands loosening on her shoulders, stroking the skin a little. "Maybe I'm not meant to. But there it is."

"You feel responsible for me," she said, knowing she sounded sulky.

"Yes. I'm supposed to, aren't I? But it's not all about that. And even if it were, that would be enough for me to *want* to soothe you. This is what I do. It's very real for me. More real with you, now . . ."

She saw a flash of uncertainty in his eyes. She didn't understand why that calmed her. Maybe because it made him more human?

She pushed her hair from her face. "Connor . . . I'm sorry I'm being such a bitch."

"You're not, darlin'. You're in a scary place. We've all been there, haven't we? Let me help you out of it. Yes?"

He'd bent closer, his head lowered to meet her gaze more easily.

She swallowed again. Nodded. "Yes. Okay."

He pulled her into his arms without another word, holding

her against his wide chest. She laid her head on his shoulder and he rocked her. She felt a bit foolish, but she let him do it. Let him pull a soft throw blanket from the arm of the sofa and drape it around her shoulders. Let her fingers rub over the ink on his biceps, feeling the slightly raised skin there.

They stayed that way for a long time, until her body grew stiff. She couldn't believe his patience with her. That he could sit with her this way, without demanding anything in return.

He was an unusual man, unlike any other she'd ever met. Which frightened her as much as it attracted her. But she was too tired to figure it out now. She wanted to simply stay where they were. Wanted him to hold her. Something she'd never really wanted—had never allowed herself to want—in her life.

He wouldn't stick around. She wasn't fooling herself into thinking he would. That wasn't what men did, other than a rare few. And she wasn't looking for that. Not long term. If only he'd stay with her tonight . . .

"Shall we go to bed?" he asked, finally.

"You're not leaving?"

"Why would I?"

She didn't have an answer for him. All the reasons were in her head. Her father. Raine's father. The many men she'd been with who had left because those were always the kind of men she chose. How she *had* to do it that way. But she didn't want to say any of that out loud, as if talking about why men always left would make it manifest, somehow. She didn't think she could take it right now.

"I think I am . . . bottoming out," she admitted finally.

"Yes."

"You'll stay with me?" she asked, hating how pitiful she sounded. But she couldn't help it.

"I'll stay with you. I'm right here."

For now. But *now* was all she needed.

That's what she told herself, anyway.

Connor blinked, letting his eyes adjust to the strange-colored glow of neon signs from the street below the apartment, which was diffused by the quiet rain coming down outside. He wasn't used to it, these vaulted windows, the light showing through the sheer curtains. He wasn't used to spending the night away from home.

He usually played a woman at the Pleasure Dome. And if it was followed by sex, it was most often in one of the small curtained rooms set aside for that very purpose at the club. It was rare he'd take a woman back to his place, and even then, once he was sure she was stable, he'd drive her home or put her in a cab. There was too much chance for false hopes to be built up if he let a woman stay the night at his place. Even more, in his mind, if he stayed the night at hers. And yet he'd done both with Mischa. There had been no question Friday night. No question tonight. Or had it been last night?

He glanced at a small clock glowing on the table next to the bed. Almost five in the morning. He *had* stayed the night. And once more he'd awakened in the half-dark with Mischa beside him. And he liked it.

He turned to see the soft curve of her body beneath the covers. As utterly feminine as any woman he'd seen in his life. Curved all over—hips, breasts. The slight roundness of her stomach and thighs and bottom that was so much more attractive to him than those starving model types. Everything round and soft on her. She was completely covered, just her head above the snowy white quilt. Her pale hair spilled like reams of silk all over the pillows. It was cast in the pink and amber light showing through the high windows. Yet he knew the color of it, how it was almost white with just the merest hint of gold. Like something precious . . .

He rubbed at his chin, the stubble biting into his fingertips.

Something precious about *her* . . . Something he didn't understand, didn't really want to. She was doing some number on his head, this woman. And it was more than the sex, which was nothing short of amazing, from her raw, wanton abandon to her gorgeous face when she came. How *hard* she came. The contrast of her competence and strength in her daily life—he had a feeling Mischa was the kind of woman who didn't let anyone fuck with her—to the raw vulnerability she'd shown him last night. Christ, it was something, to see that.

It was something to see her at any given moment.

Which might explain why he was sitting there, watching her sleep, for the second time in a row.

That *might* explain it.

He didn't know what the hell was going on with him. Something, that was certain. He couldn't remember behaving this way with anyone. Not any of the girls he played at the club, had sex with. Not even in the early days with his ex-wife, Ginny.

That had been one of his biggest mistakes. They'd been totally unsuited for each other. Hell, he wasn't suited for any woman long term. He knew that—had always known it. He was his father's son, after all, wasn't he? Had his father's temper, even if he'd managed to keep it under control for years. Genes were genes. He knew he'd keep it together within the strict bounds of BDSM play, understood how it was almost therapeutic for him. But in a real relationship?

He'd often been surly with Ginny. A real punk. She hadn't deserved it. Youth was no damn excuse. He'd been a man already, at twenty. Or he should have been. He should never have married the girl—he didn't know what he'd been thinking. He'd had no right.

He scrubbed harder at his stubble. Why was he thinking of this now? He wasn't considering marrying this girl. He was just . . . looking at her. Appreciating her. What man wouldn't? Even though all he could see was her hair, her pale cheek, her luscious red mouth that was nearly as red now as when she had her lipstick on. Her hand curled beside her face.

He reached out, touched her fingertips with his own, felt the faint heat of her skin. There was nothing sexual there. No, that wasn't true. The chemistry was there, burning, but banked for the moment. It was something else . . .

He shook his head.

A man could think some strange things in the rainy hour before dawn. That was all.

A part of him wanted to get up and leave. Run out of there. But he couldn't do it. Not after the way she'd bottomed out last night.

He was so full of shit.

That wasn't why he was staying. He was there because he *wanted* to be.

Indulgent of him. He wasn't going to lead her on. And he damn well wasn't going to stay forever. He didn't even know what that meant, did he? If Ginny hadn't left him, he would have left sooner or later. Hell, the marriage hadn't lasted two years. Totally his fault. Him and his temper.

At least he'd gotten a handle on that. Getting into the BDSM scene had cured him of those juvenile outbursts, but he could never forget what he was capable of. Control had become the key. And it would be no less key now in dealing with Mischa. In these foolish mental meanderings he was having.

Have to get her to the club.

Yes, he was in his element at the Pleasure Dome. It would be a useful reminder of what he was about—and what he wasn't. The control, the responsibility. He was a hell of a lot more responsible as a dominant than he'd been without that dynamic in his life. Those leanings had always been there, but now he knew how to channel that energy.

The Pleasure Dome.

She'd asked to go. And the timing was right. There was a Tuesday evening play party for VIP members, which he was. He was sure Alec and Dylan wouldn't be there, with all the wedding preparations. That might prove too awkward for Mischa and he needed her to be relaxed for what he planned to do to her.

He felt a wicked grin steal over his face. This was safer ground—thinking about what he wanted to do with this girl. Put her on the St. Andrew's cross and flog her right. Chain her down to one of the padded tables and pour hot wax over her. Make her come. Make her scream. Make her *his* in the only way that would work.

He laid his head back down on the pillow and watched the rain on the windows, the run of watercolors on the glass.

Yes, just get her to the club, where he was in charge, in command of himself, as well as her. All he had to do was get her there and everything would be all right. Everything would make sense again.

five

"Mischa?"

"Hmm . . . what?"

She looked up to find Dylan's gray eyes peering at her from behind the small bunch of white roses she was holding. "You going to tell me what went on last night?"

Mischa shrugged. "Connor came over . . ."

"And?"

"And it was . . . amazing."

Dylan put the roses back into the tall metal pot on the concrete floor of Rose and Thorn, the florist's shop where they had their appointment to discuss the flowers for the wedding. She placed her hands firmly on her hips. "Why so vague with me, suddenly? You've always shared your adventures before."

Mischa paused. "Yes, but they've never been with a friend of yours before."

Dylan dropped her arms to her sides. "I guess that makes

sense. Are you sure it's not something else? You seem a little dazed."

"Well . . ."

How much did she want to share with Dylan? She was her best friend, but whatever was happening in her head about Connor—and there were definitely some weird thoughts going on in there—it felt private. She hadn't had a chance to figure it out herself yet. It had almost been a relief that they'd woken up late, giving her just enough time to hop in the shower to get ready to meet Dylan. No time for sex or long good-byes. Just a brief talk with him letting him know she really was okay.

But was she?

"Misch?"

"My apologies for the interruption, ladies. Now, what about calla lilies?" Andre Rose, the small, wiry florist with a shaved head and dark-rimmed glasses asked them as he came back from the phone call that had disturbed their consultation with a single blossom in his hand. "I think the small variety would suit you. Simple and elegant."

"Mischa?" Dylan asked. "Tell me what you think. You're my floral expert."

"I like them." She reached out, stroked a finger over the smooth, creamy flower the florist held out for them. "Elegant, I agree. I love the smaller Green Goddess variety. Maybe mixed with the white, and with some of the tiny white dendrobium or-chids?"

Andre clapped his hands together. "Perfect with the bride's red hair. We can add some delicate greens, nothing too full and fluffy. I'm thinking we should keep all the arrangements very streamlined and on the smaller side. We don't want to detract from the setting at the Asian Art Museum. Now, what about the bouquets?"

"I don't want to carry one. That feels too traditional for me. What do you think, Misch?"

The truth was, she could barely think at all today. But at least flowers she knew. "I think . . . maybe just three or four of the white orchids in your hair." She bundled Dylan's red curls into her hands, held it up off her neck. "Just in the back. Subtle."

Dylan's smile was radiant. "I love it."

"And for your attendants?" Andre asked.

"That's just you and Kara," Dylan said.

"What if we each just had one orchid tucked behind our ear?"

"Beautiful!" Andre clapped again. "Dylan?"

"That's perfect. Let's go ahead and place the order."

Andre led them to a pair of white padded iron stools at the counter and moved behind it, pulling out his order book. They spent a little time giving him the number of tables, confirming the flower types and picking out the narrow glass vases for the arrangements. When they were done they bundled themselves back into their coats and stepped out onto the rainy street, opening their umbrellas.

"Are you ready for lunch?" Dylan asked. "I'm starving."

Mischa wasn't hungry—she hadn't had more than a tall coffee she'd picked up on her way to meet the florist. Her stomach was strangely upset. But she nodded her agreement. "Sure. Where do you want to go?"

"There's a nice cafe just up the street, if you don't mind walking in the rain."

"Let's go."

They walked the two blocks in comfortable silence. Fairly comfortable, anyway. She was sure Dylan would want to hash out what was going on with her and Connor as soon as they sat down. She was right.

They found the cafe, hung their coats on hooks by the door,

folded their umbrellas and left them in a wide trough made for the purpose. The scent of coffee and food was in the air and Mischa's stomach rumbled as they perused the menu. They ordered and the waitress quickly brought their drinks back—hot tea for them both.

"So?" Dylan had one eyebrow quirked.

Mischa sighed. "So . . ." She gave a small shake of her head. "I don't know what to say. Which is why I haven't said more. I'm sorry. I know I'm not making a lot of sense. But this doesn't make much sense to *me*."

"What doesn't make sense?"

"This thing with Connor. My reaction to it."

"Tell me what's different with him than other guys you've been with."

"Everything. And nothing. I mean, on the surface it's just a very kinky fling." She looked at Dylan, who just nodded. "I assume you'd know it was kinky, since it's him."

"Yes. But it's not like you've never gone there before. And it's not like I'd be shocked by it, of all people."

Mischa leaned her elbows on the table. "Dylan, is it normal to respond very strongly to this stuff?"

"Of course. Extreme sex would equal a strong response. And it often does."

"I've played around with this before. You and I have talked about it. But with Connor, we've taken it to some new levels. The whole power exchange thing . . . I'm experiencing it for the first time with him. The guys I've been with before just didn't have his skill, or maybe I simply didn't connect with them in the same way. I don't know . . ." She paused, bit her lip. "Before, it's been a sensation thing. That little edge of danger. The forbidden. But it was just for fun. With Connor it's a lot more real. I'm finally getting it."

Dylan nodded once more. "I understand. It's like a whole new level opens up when the power dynamic becomes apparent. It's pretty damn thrilling. But it can also be a little scary."

"It is. As much as I'm enjoying it there's always this small voice in my head telling me not to give up control. I know you understand what I mean because you've always had some control issues yourself. Well, not anymore, maybe."

"Oh no, they're still there. I've just learned to channel them differently. And . . . Look, I don't want to beat you over the head with the stuff you've confided in me about your mom and what happened when you were growing up, but maybe you have more reason to have control issues than I do."

"It's all right. I wouldn't have told you about it if I wasn't okay discussing it with you. And it was . . . pretty rough. I spent my entire childhood feeling like I had no control over anything—my life, Evie. Hell, the fact was, I didn't. One of the best things about hitting adulthood was that my life was in my hands for the first time. I don't like the idea of giving that up, even for a moment. But Connor makes me *like* it, which freaks me out."

Dylan nodded. "I understand. I really do."

"Honestly, it scares the crap out of me. But not while it's happening. Only in retrospect. Which makes it worse, somehow. That I'm letting this happen is pretty damn frightening."

"It can be even scarier if you get attached."

"Oh, I'm not getting attached." She waved the idea away with her hand.

"No?" Dylan was watching her, in much the same way Connor did. Searching her face. "Misch, you don't have to tell me. But you'd better think about it or you could really get hurt. I don't want to see that happen to you."

"Why do you think I'll get hurt? I already know Connor isn't into more than a fling while I'm in town, if even for that long. And I don't want any more than that myself. I'm here to focus on your wedding and looking into opening another shop with Greyson. My friends and my work are my whole life, you know that. My priorities."

"Yes. But I also know priorities can change."

Mischa blew out a breath. "You and Alec are an exception to the rule."

"Are we?" Dylan leaned in closer. "I didn't used to think so. You remember the talks we had on the phone when Alec and I were first seeing each other?"

"Of course."

"They sounded an awful lot like this one."

"They did not," Mischa protested.

Dylan shrugged. "Have it your way. Since I know you will." She grinned a little, easing her words.

"Yeah, well, not Tuesday night, I won't," she muttered, sipping her tea.

"What do you mean? What happens Tuesday night?"

Mischa put her cup down. "He's taking me to the Pleasure Dome." She couldn't help the small smile that quirked the corners of her mouth.

"Ah."

"What do you mean, 'ah'?"

"The club with Connor can be some serious stuff."

"I've been to BDSM clubs before."

"Not with Connor. He's the real thing, as you said."

"I know that. I'm ready for it."

But was she? The hard play—floggers and chains and whatever else he might have in mind for her, sure. But after what had happened last night the idea that she could bottom out again was a little daunting. Still, her desire to go there, to experience these things with him, was powerful enough to let her move past her fears. Even thinking about it made her pulse race hot in her veins—being at the club with him. The pain play. The power dynamics. The exhibitionism she loved.

She was ready for all of that. Ready enough to convince herself she would simply deal with the rest—any bottoming out, any emotional reaction—if and when it happened.

Connor was due to pick her up in less than an hour and she still hadn't decided what to wear to the club. Should she go with classic black lace, go more bold with red silk, or wear the sexy, yet innocent white mesh set?

Not that she imagined she'd be allowed to wear her lingerie for long once they were there, but presentation was everything.

She didn't want to admit how badly she wanted to please him.

Standing in front of the bathroom mirror, she saw how dark and hard her nipples were, the flush on her breasts, her cheeks. She stroked her fingers over her nipples, felt them stiffen even more, and sighed. He was going to touch her tonight. Do all sorts of wicked things to her. With other people watching . . .

Her sex gave a sharp squeeze, and she groaned. She shook her head as she gathered the pile of lingerie from the bathroom counter and went back into the bedroom. She pulled another pile of filmy lace and satin from the drawer Dylan had given her and tossed it all on the bed. It was a good thing she always traveled with such a good selection.

She held up a pair of turquoise silk bikini panties that had two wide strips of black lace on either side, found the matching bra. The color suited her blue eyes perfectly. The bra had a clasp in the front for easy access and just that small touch of padding that would give her already generous breasts a nice lift and killer cleavage.

She stepped into the two pieces and turned to the closet. The dress was an easier choice, a short sheath of black stretch lace. She decided to forgo stockings despite the cold weather—she could wear her long trench coat—and slipped into her highest pair of black stiletto-heeled peep-toe pumps. Per the instructions Connor had sent via text that morning, she wore her pale blonde hair up in a tight chignon at the back of her neck with one of her signature silk flowers in black pinned into it. She added a pair of tiny black enamel rosebud drop earrings, fixed her red lipstick and moved into the living room to wait for him.

She sat on the couch, picked up a magazine, flipped through it and put it down again a moment later. A glance at the clock told her she still had a good fifteen minutes before he was due to arrive. She got up and moved to the tall bank of windows overlooking the street below.

It was raining again, but that was Seattle for you. She felt at home there. San Francisco didn't rain as much, but like Seattle, it was often gray and foggy. Some people hated the weather, but being so heavily tattooed it was better not to spend too much time in the sun. And the gray weather soothed her, for some reason. It made the world look softer.

She watched the cars splashing through the puddle at the corner, the people walking down the sidewalks—or rather, the tops of their umbrellas. Dylan's apartment was in Belltown, a funky neighborhood close to the water, full of exactly the kinds of places where Mischa felt most at home: small cafes, a few galleries, tattoo shops, boutiques. She watched the colorful array of umbrellas moving down the street, a few people *sans* umbrellas running to get out of the rain. She was about to force herself to go sit down again when she saw a sleek black Hummer park in front of the building, and a large man get out.

Connor.

Her heart began to pound.

The enormous vehicle suited him. She hadn't thought about what he might drive, but she doubted he could fit comfortably into most cars.

Moments later the downstairs buzzer rang and she went to the intercom mounted on the wall by the front door and pressed the button. His voice came through, a little tinny, the sound of the rain in the background.

"Mischa, it's me."

"I'll come right down."

"Don't be daft, I'm coming up. Buzz me in."

She did, then rushed back into the bathroom to take one last look at her reflection, making sure her hair was in place, her hem straight.

A knock on the front door had her scurrying as fast as she could in her heels across the wood floor. She took a deep breath, patted her hair once more.

Don't be silly.

But she couldn't help herself. Not when it came to Connor. She may as well accept that before their big evening together. She just *would* be a girl around him.

She opened the door.

He was dressed all in black, which she knew most of the doms did for a play party or dungeon night. Dark jeans, tight black T-shirt beneath his black leather jacket. Heavy black boots, which she really loved. She had a thing for big black boots on a man. Something so masculine, so bad boy about them.

"Hi. Ah, don't you look gorgeous," he said, pulling her into him as he stepped through the door, nearly dragging her off her feet, making her stumble a little.

"Hi, yourself." She laughed, her heart thumping out a hard, even rhythm.

"Come here and kiss me, girl," he ordered.

As if she could do anything else. He held her so damn tight, his big hands wrapped possessively around her waist. He bent his head, crushed his lips to hers, the kiss soft and hard all at once. When he opened her lips with his, she melted, her body going loose and hot all over.

God, the man could kiss! Like the devil himself. Slow, hard, thoroughly wicked kisses.

When he let her go she was breathless.

"Ready for our night at the club?" he asked, his hands still at her waist.

"Yes. Absolutely."

"You look ready." He grinned. "Dressed for an evening of fun. Dressed for sex. You always do, though, don't you? But I love that about you. Sexiest woman I've ever met."

Did he have any idea what that did to her, hearing him say that to her? But he didn't look as if it was calculated. He looked as if he was simply saying what was on his mind. Not that she'd never had a man compliment her before; quite the contrary. But coming from him it meant more . . .

"Come on. Get your coat and we'll go."

She nodded, pulled her long black trench from the front closet by the door. He insisted on helping her into it, which she loved. All these small, gentlemanly gestures. Most of the guys she'd dated were devoid of any chivalry. It was something she'd noted in many of the dominant men at the BDSM clubs she'd been to. Most of them were as careful with the submissive girls they played with as they were rough, in some odd combination she'd always admired. He even took the key from her hand and locked the door behind them.

He kept one hand at the small of her back as they took the

elevator down and led her outside, popping open a black umbrella, helping her into his car.

"I'll turn the seat warmers on for you, just give them a minute," he said as the big engine purred to life. He pulled into the street.

The car felt strangely luxurious. It wasn't what she'd expected of a Hummer. She'd always thought of them as military vehicles. But the seat was plush and growing warmer by the second, just as he'd said, which was lovely in the cold evening air. The dashboard held an array of small dials and lights, giving off a soft amber glow.

"Do you have any questions about how things will happen at the club?" he asked her, glancing at her before returning his gaze to the road.

"I imagine it's very much the same as going to the clubs in San Francisco."

"Tonight is a VIP night. Which means the rules are a bit looser. The Safe, Sane and Consensual credo still stands, of course, but only the most serious players are allowed in—those with a special membership. There are no gawkers on a VIP night. There may be some very heavy scenes going on. Fire play. Piercing. The bullwhip. How do you feel about seeing these things? Do I need to hurry you through to a private play area? Or are you all right with that sort of stuff?"

"I can handle seeing just about anything."

"There may be sex on the open floor, as well."

She shrugged. "Sex is just sex. It doesn't bother me."

"And would you like to have sex there, in front of everyone?"

"I . . ." Her sex went damp so suddenly it took her by surprise. "I've never done that. I've been tied up, flogged in front of other people. I loved that. Being seen. Watched."

"But sex with an audience of admirers?"

They stopped at a signal and he turned to look at her.

"I . . . don't know."

He reached over, took her hand and brought it to his lips, laid a gentle kiss there. He said very softly, "I can hear you, you know. The catch in your breath. It's very much the sound of desire hitting you hard in the stomach, not of shock. Unless it's shock at how much the idea excites you. But we'll leave that decision for later. Except that I must hear you tell me now if that breath means a maybe, rather than a no. Because we will not do anything you tell me you're absolutely opposed to before I take you down into subspace."

"What about the things I tell you once I'm there?"

"Ah, at that point you may be willing to do something you might later regret. I won't let that happen. We don't negotiate once you're spaced. So?"

She nodded, her throat dry. "It's a maybe."

Her body was screaming "yes." Why couldn't she admit that to him? Why did it seem as if that would be handing too much of herself over to him? Especially when she knew, on some level, anyway, that handing herself over to him was what the club experience was going to be about—that it was his intention in taking her there. That it was what she had agreed to in going.

It's just sex. Just some kinky play.

But it was much more than that, and she knew it. Had known it all along. But now it was making her panic a little. She wasn't afraid of the whips and chains, of people watching her as these things happened, even the sex. She didn't think that would scare her. But how Connor made her feel? That was a different matter.

He brushed another quick kiss across her knuckles, dropped her hand onto his strong thigh as the light changed and the car moved through the wet streets. It was calming that he held on to her hand. Possessive, as he always was with her. And lovely, the heat of his big fingers wrapped around hers.

By the time they reached the Pleasure Dome her body was on fire, full of heat and need, thinking about the evening ahead. It was all doing a number on her head, and maybe that was part of his intention. She understood the mind-fuck dynamic of the dom/sub thing. Not that she was a real subbie girl in the true sense of the word. She was into the sensation, the extreme sex. That was all. Yet, it was working. His treatment of her. The sense of anticipation. The way he handled her like some rare doll as he helped her from the car.

The building was a bit imposing, one of the old converted warehouses so common around the downtown areas of Seattle. Four stories of dark gray brick with the big warehouse windows painted over.

A tall man let them through an enormous red door. The moment they stepped inside her head was spinning. She could barely take it all in. She wasn't really paying attention to what the small foyer looked like as she stood quietly at Connor's side while he checked in at the front desk, left their coats there. All she knew was the low throb of music, Connor's scent as he laid a heavy arm across her shoulders and took her into the club itself. And the large black leather bag she was just now noticing he had over his shoulder. She knew what must be in there—his tools of pain and delight. She was dying to see what he had in the bag, to know what he might do to her. The idea that she was about to have this experience with *Connor* was dizzying. Maybe because she knew that he would open her up in ways she'd never been open before.

The place was a blur of heavy play equipment: enormous bondage frames made of wood and studded with metal eyebolts, which rope could be threaded through to weave spiderweb-like patterns where people were bound. It looked like some sort of mad decoration. There were a number of spanking benches of various designs, and long padded tables with chains and padded cuffs attached to them, all done in red leather. The cleaning stations, which held spray bottles of bleach, paper towels, first-aid kits. And in between were plush red leather sofas and chairs around the edges of the low-lit room, where a few people lounged.

There were people kneeling on the floor, naked, or mostly so. All of them beautiful in their submissive poses, some with their hands raised palms up on their thighs, others with hands clasped behind their backs, or behind their collared necks. None of this was anything new. She'd seen such things at the San Francisco clubs. What was different tonight was *her*. Being there with Connor. How he made her feel.

She felt submissive, for the first time. Felt that melting sense of yielding, her mind emptying out. She realized in a small flash that maybe this was what she'd been looking for every time she'd gone to one of the clubs with a man. What she'd sought and never found. Until now.

Her throat went tight as he led her across the room, and she gripped his hand.

"You all right, darlin'?" he asked immediately.

She nodded, but he stopped where they were, peering closely at her face.

"Tell me what's going on with you," he demanded in a quiet voice.

She tried to shake her head but he was still watching her face, waiting for an answer. She knew by his serious expression he would stand for no argument or avoidance.

"I'm just . . . I feel different here. It's not the club. That part is familiar. The equipment. The people. It's *me* that's different.

I'm . . ." She stopped, shook her head. Not because she was being stubborn, but because she didn't know how to go on.

To her surprise, his features softened in a way that made her heart beat a little faster with something warm and lovely.

"I like that it's different for you. I can feel it. It's as though your body is going a little limp. It's you giving yourself over to it. And that's exactly what I want from you." He paused, his tone lowering. "I can see that it's good for you, knowing that you're pleasing me. I understand what that's about, even if you're not clear on it just yet. But this is perfect, you giving yourself in this way, Mischa. It's what has to happen in order for this evening to go as I'd planned. As I'd hoped. Because there was some doubt as to whether or not you'd be able to, wasn't there?"

She nodded, her throat thick with emotion she didn't understand.

"I can see how it's affecting you," he told her. "It's all right, you know, to have some sort of response to this. It's normal, in fact. I know you said you'd played before, but not at this level. And with the more extreme practices comes the more extreme response, if you've opened yourself to it. And you have. It's all right for you to be scared." He smiled then, a little wickedly. "The sadist in me loves it, in fact."

That made her smile. He really was wicked, in exactly the right way. She wasn't even sure she knew what she meant by that. But it was making her relax a bit, talking with him like this. Knowing he understood, even though he was doing most of the talking.

He reached out, stroked his fingertips over her cheek, touched her lower lip.

"There's going to be another shift when I bind you. You may feel some sense of losing yourself. Just know that I'm right here with you at all times. Know that I will do everything in my power to make it good for you. That it will be what I want, what will please me. But it will also be exactly what you need. Are you ready?"

Was she? She wasn't one hundred percent certain. But as ready as she was going to be, maybe.

"Yes."

"Come on, then, my girl."

He took her by the hand and led her to one of the tall, free-standing crosses that stood almost in the middle of the room. It was a good six feet in height, with a thick pole topped by a T-bar from which hung a suspension bar with a heavy leather cuff dangling at each end.

She glanced at Connor. He swung the leather bag down, setting it on the floor to one side of the cross. He hadn't let go of her hand.

He used his other hand at her waist to guide her to one of the red leather chairs that stood just behind the cross. He sat down, pulling her into his lap, and he started kissing her right away. His mouth on hers, hard, demanding, yet his lips, his tongue, like hot silk. He tasted a little of toothpaste. He tasted like Connor. His hand slipped under her buttocks, holding her closer, his tongue making a soft exploration of her mouth. And her body began that lovely, sensual buzz she felt whenever he kissed her, touched her.

His other hand started on her shoulder, slipped around the back of her neck, pressing there in that way he had of making her feel his command of her. It was a subtle signal, but effective. He moved down, over the side of her breast, then gathering it in his big hand.

She moaned into his mouth, arched her body, pressing into his hand. And he let her do it, cupping her breast, kneading her nipple through the fabric with his thumb, then slipping his hand into the neckline of her dress, beneath her bra, and finding her hard-ening nipple with his fingertips.

He pressed the rigid nub of flesh, rubbed it, took it between his fingers and tugged. Pleasure swarmed her, making her wet with need. She squirmed in his lap and he shifted until she could feel the solid ridge of his erection beneath her thigh. She squirmed again, pressing onto his hard cock. He kissed her harder, began to really pinch her nipple, making it hurt, sending stinging cur-rents through her body. But the pain was pure pleasure, simmer-ing in her system, sharp and lovely.

She was growing wetter and wetter. Needing to be touched, wanting her clothes off. As if he could hear her thoughts he slid his hands down to the hem of her dress and pulled it over her head, taking his mouth from hers to do it.

"Oh . . ."

She arched, needing to feel his body against hers. The air was wonderful on her almost bare skin.

"You are beautiful, Mischa. Fucking gorgeous. There are a number of eyes on you already, sweetheart. They envy me. I can see it in the way they stare. No, don't look. Look only at me. Sim-ply know they're there. I want you to focus."

She swallowed, nodded. Her pulse was racing.

He gathered her breasts in his hands, pushing them to-gether. "How did you know I'd love this on you? So damn sexy. But let's have it off, shall we?"

He unsnapped the catch in one deft motion, and in moments her breasts were free of the small scrap of silk and lace.

"Ah, that's better. You have the most spectacular breasts." He gathered them again, cupping the weight of them.

She moaned.

"Your skin is like satin. I love the way you feel. The flesh so heavy. So full." He brushed his fingertips over her nipples, and they grew impossibly hard. Then he twisted them, making her gasp. Somehow, they went even harder.

"Ah, you love this. Your body speaks for you."

Before she had a chance to answer he thrust his hand between her thighs, beneath her silky underwear, into the wet, heated folds of her sex.

"Oh!"

"Beautiful, how wet you are. Look at me, now. Hold on to my shoulders and look into my eyes as I work your sweet pussy a bit."

She did it, hardly believing she was being so compliant, even as she knew she couldn't be anything else with him right now. It was hard to hold still while he did exactly as he said: worked her with his fingers. He had two inside her, his thumb circling her clitoris. Pleasure was a keen buzzing in her body, her head. He was forcing her to keep her eyes on his, his green gaze glittering with desire. For her. It was powerful. Nearly overwhelming.

She was going to come. She dug her fingers into the bulky muscles beneath his black T-shirt.

"Ah, no you don't, my girl."

He slipped his fingers from her and she couldn't help but sigh her disappointment.

He chuckled. "You didn't think it would be so easy, did you?"

She had to smile, a little shakily. "No."

"Up we go, then." He stood, set her on her feet. "Let's off with these pretties," he said, slipping her panties down her legs, helping her to step out of them, leaving her in nothing but her black high heels.

She was so full of pleasure and need and the exquisite wonder of being close to him, having him touch her, that she hadn't really been aware of the transition going on inside her. Perhaps that had been his intention in getting her so worked up before putting her on the cross. But that was exactly what he was doing now: leading her to it, kissing her wrist, then placing it in one high cuff, closing it, adjusting the buckle. Then the same with her other hand, a small kiss on her wrist, closing the leather over it, both wrists bound now so that she was facing the cross. She had some vague sense that she was really going down into subspace. That lovely, ethereal place where her mind swam, emptied out of any unnecessary thought. It was all about Connor. What he was doing to her. What her body was feeling. It was sensation, response. The tangy scent of leather. The air of expectation in the room, coming, she knew, from other people who were experiencing these same things.

But these thoughts went through her mind in a flash of abstract sensation. She didn't linger on them. It was too hard to focus on anything but Connor's wide back as he knelt to buckle her ankles into padded leather cuffs attached to long lengths of chain, which were bolted into the wood floor. She moved one foot a little, simply to hear that primeval clank of the chain. A shiver went up her spine.

He stood, pressing his body close into her side.

"You like being strung up like this."

"Yes," she answered, her voice a whispering breath.

"You look damn beautiful." His accent was thick. "You look like heaven. I'm going to do some very bad things to you. And also some very good things. And soon it won't matter whether it's good or bad. It'll all be good."

He pulled back enough so that she could see the gleam in his eyes, how the lights caught the gold flecks in them, making them shine. She felt beautiful, more than she ever had in her life. She felt proud of her curvy body, her nakedness. The way she must look, bound in chains, her body stretched out with her arms over her head and spread wide.

"Every eye is on you, including mine. I can barely stand to tear my gaze away to dig in my bag, but I'm going to do it. To find my tools, lay them out for use. I want you to hold very still while I do it. To breathe as I showed you before. To close your eyes and get inside your head. Come on now, close them."

He brushed gentle fi ngers over her eyelids, forcing them closed. She did as he'd instructed, taking a deep breath into her lungs, blowing it out, focusing on the way her wrists and ankles felt in the cuffs. How it felt to be bound. She felt calm in some odd way, knowing Connor was right there.

There was a sharp snap, a wisp of wind at her back and startled, she laughed, knowing instantly he meant to get her attention.

He came up behind her, wrapped his hand around the back of her neck. His face was next to hers. "Ah, you like that, do you? You'll like it even better when I use it on you."

She had no idea what he held in his hand—whip or flogger or cat-o-nine tails. But she felt ready for anything. *Wanted* it.

Had she ever wanted anything so badly in her life? She didn't think so. Could hardly think at this moment of anything *but* the moment. Her nakedness, being at the club. Being there with Connor. The lovely and wicked things he would do to her tonight.

She didn't want to question her need, the yearning that was an almost palpable scent in the air. The yearning for Connor. To have him touch her. Bring her pleasure. Bring her pain.

To do as he wished.

She realized in some far-off fashion that this was what turning herself over to him meant. And she was doing it now, no questions asked. There would be plenty of time for questions later. But for now, it was all about her and Connor and what they would create here together.

She couldn't think even for one moment how temporary "together" might be for them.

six

She heard him—sensed him—stepping back, away from her, then there was a pause in which she drew in a long breath and held it. She waited, her skin alive, as though every nerve ending was on high alert. She let out her breath, drew in another. And again, she waited while the music beat a sensual cadence around her. Behind the music were the sounds of other people: voices talking in low tones, sighs, moans of pain or pleasure. The sounds that were particular to this sort of place: the quiet hiss of ropes moving, the clink of metal on metal, the slap of leather on flesh.

Still she waited for something to happen. She let her breath go, stopped thinking so much about it. Made a conscious effort to slow her hammering heartbeat. To calm her nerves. To block out the sounds of the club and look within.

Her body was simmering, a low, steady beat of desire, a thrum of anticipation so strong it felt like electricity in her veins. An acute awareness of Connor standing behind her, as if he were almost a part of her body, so that knowing he was there did nothing to pull her back out of herself, away from this inner exploration.

She felt beautiful. Turned on to an almost ridiculous degree. Lost in need.

She let out her next breath on a long sigh. And before her lungs had emptied there was a sharp snap in the air and an even sharper sting on the left cheek of her ass.

"Oh!"

It was followed immediately by Connor moving in to cup his big palm over the sting.

He didn't say anything, just stepped back after a moment and hit her again.

This time she was less surprised by it. More able to let her body sink into the sensation. A small crop, she thought, from the light weight of it on her flesh. He hit her again, a little harder this time, and for some reason it made her smile.

Oh, this is where we really get into it.

It was what she wanted. *Needed.*

Another stinging rasp, then another. He was picking up speed, working in a crisscross pattern over her buttocks and thighs. With each stroke pleasure rose, as though embedded in the stinging sensation itself. She was squirming just a little, just enough to absorb the impact, to ride out the surges of pleasure.

He began to hit her harder. Harder and harder, until she was breathless with it. Finally, one really hard nick with the leather tip of the crop and she cried out.

His arms were immediately around her waist, his enormous body pressing into her from behind. His hands went to her breasts. He caressed them lightly, his fingertips dragging over her skin, then circling her nipples.

"You're doing very well," he whispered into her hair. "Amazing, to see the way you respond. Just like this . . ."

He pinched both nipples with hard fingers, and she jumped, her eyes flying open.

A low chuckle from him. "Ah, I love to see that. I love to bring you pain, almost as much as I love to bring you pleasure."

His hand smoothed down over her belly, between her thighs, where he found her clit right away. She arched her hips into his hand as he rolled the rigid flesh between his fingers.

"Tell me, darlin', are you wet for me?"

"Yes," she gasped.

"I'll have to see for myself." He slipped his hand into the wet heat between her thighs, his fingers pushing inside her. "Ah, beautiful."

"Connor . . ."

"What is it?"

"I need . . . more . . ."

Another low chuckle from him, then he let her go, moved away from her again, making her groan in disappointment. She could barely stand it, his teasing of her. The way her cuffed ankles forced her thighs apart, the air cool on her soaking pussy.

He began again, a slow volley of smacks with a flogger this time—she knew by the feel of thick suede on her back. He used a crisscross motion again. It didn't really hurt at first. It was simply a means for her to fall into a rhythm as he kept time with the music playing through the speakers. She closed her eyes again. Let herself sink into the fall of leather on her flesh. Although thinking of it as "letting" was silly, she thought from the far-off place in her head. She was helpless against it: the rhythm, the pleasure, the need for exactly what he was doing to her.

It went on for a long time, it seemed, before he began to use a faster pace, to hit harder. The thud of the flogger became sharper, the impact making her body bow. When he moved it lower, smacking her hard across the ass, she yelped. He stopped while she stamped her feet, pain reverberating through her body like an echo: a stinging heat, a strange sort of ecstasy. And after the pain was a rush of endorphins, making her float.

"Oh . . ."

"Good, darlin'?"

"Oh yes."

He let her sail on the chemicals flooding her brain for a few moments before he struck her again. Another hard hit, the flogger biting into her flesh. She handled it better this time, in silence. And again he let her ride out the pain, allowing her time to revel in the chemical rush, the pure pleasure of it. The pride in being able to take it.

He struck again, a powerful blow. Her body moved under the heavy impact, but she remained silent, even as pleasure flooded her body, surged through her.

She felt the small trickle of her own juices slip down the inside of one thigh.

He was behind her again, his hands on her, and she curved her back, pressing into his body. Felt his erection through the denim of his jeans against the crease at the top of her buttocks.

He wrapped one arm around her waist again, his hand splayed across her stomach. The other hand he used to smooth over the sore skin of her back, up and down her spine, soothing her. Then he did something that was entirely new for her. He took the soft skin at her side, just below her underarm, and grabbed it, pinching it hard.

She gasped.

"Does it hurt you, sweetheart?"

"Yes!"

"But is it good?"

Her mind was spinning, her body cycling through pain and

pleasure so quickly she could barely keep track of which sensation was which. "Yes . . . it's good."

He did it again, fast, aggressively, grabbing and pressing handfuls of skin in his big hand, letting go, moving down and doing it again, then up again, until she was squirming hard against his arm, unable to hold still. She was panting as the pain got worse. And just when she was certain she couldn't take any more, he stopped, his hand slipping around her to massage her aching, swollen clitoris, flooding her with pure pleasure. At the same time he placed soft, tender kisses at the back of her neck, the top of her spine, between her shoulder blades, making her body, her heart, melt.

What was happening to her? Not the pain—she understood that on some very primal level. But her heart—how had that become involved?

The idea was so vague in her dazed mind she could barely hang on to it. She was too far gone to be really frightened by it. All she knew was a sense of wonder. A sense of alien unfamiliarity.

Later . . .

Yes, everything else later but what was happening *now*. What she needed. What *he* wanted of her. The driving need to please him that had been growing since the moment they'd walked into the club.

He was really working her clit now, exquisite sensation pouring through her, making her writhe, only the cuffs and Connor's strong arm around her keeping her on her feet.

"Connor . . ."

"What is it, my girl?" he murmured into the back of her neck.

"I need—" She gasped as pleasure arced through her like a thousand-watt jolt. "I need to . . ."

"Come?"

"Yes!"

He worked her swollen clit harder, making it hurt, pinching and tugging. He lowered his other hand and used it to pinch her pussy lips painfully. It was exactly what she needed.

"Oh!"

"Come then, my darlin' girl. Come in pain, come with pleasure. Come into my hands." His voice grew stern with command. "Do it now."

Her body exploded, sensation lightning hot. Electric. She arched hard into his hands, cried out. Came so hard she shook with the force of it, her body shuddering with wave after wave.

Still he worked her clitoris mercilessly, the lips of her sex, then he plunged his fingers inside her, curving them to hit her G-spot. And before she was really done coming another climax ripped through her—or perhaps it was simply more of the first. She didn't know. It didn't matter. Nothing did but his big hands on her. Bringing her pain and pleasure so intertwined there was no way to tell the two apart. It all merged in her system, in her head, shattering her completely.

She was sagging against the cuffs, against his arms around her, the weight of her as sweet to Connor as her scent. Her damp, perfumed flesh. A faint scent of come in the air. He breathed it in, held it in his lungs for a long moment. Then he reached up and uncuffed first one delicate wrist, then the other. He checked them for circulation and was satisfied with their color before bending to release her ankles, then he carried her to the chair behind the cross and laid her on his lap.

She weighed nothing. She was fucking beautiful.

He could feel the heat of the welts across her back, her buttocks, even through his jeans. He'd been careful not to break her skin, to damage her tattoos. All that was left was this lovely heat, the gorgeous flush on her skin. The pink of the welts from where he'd flogged and cropped her. The pretty pink on her cheeks, her breasts. The deeper red of her nipples that were almost as beautifully scarlet as her lush mouth. The indescribably luscious pink of her shaved pussy resting against his thigh.

He tore his gaze from her body to look at her face. Her eyes were a blue glimmer from beneath half-closed lids, her long lashes resting against her high, rounded cheekbones.

Christ, but she was lovely, this girl. In every possible way. His cock was a raging hammer of desire between his legs, the pulse-beat of need driving into his belly. But the need was more than the desire to push inside her body, to fuck her as hard as he could, although that was certainly there. He wouldn't be human not to feel those things right now. But it wasn't just the sex or the power play. It was Mischa.

He gently pushed a stray strand of pale hair from her face. Her expression was dazed, serene. She was full of endorphins. Which was a good thing because he needed a moment to get his racing pulse under control.

Control.

That was the key. He'd come to know it early on, long before his first forays into the BDSM scene. He'd known it even as a boy, when he didn't yet have enough of it to stop his father . . .

Don't think of him now. Don't let him ruin this.

Ah, but ultimately, he'd let his father ruin everything, hadn't he? His childhood, his mother, every relationship he'd ever had. Which was why he no longer had them.

Why, then, was his God damn traitorous heart telling him *this* woman was meant to be his? Not even a full week he'd known her . . .

"Connor?"

He heard the doubt in her voice.

"Yes?"

"Are you . . . Did I do well?"

And damn it, he'd let her see some expression, some scowl, that had let her think he wasn't pleased with her.

"You were amazing. Perfect."

He stroked her cheek again. Not because there was any hair there to push away, but simply to feel the satin of her skin beneath his fingertips. To see the smile it brought to her face.

He kept her there, lounging in his lap. Kept his hands on her: her face, her shoulders, her stomach. He was still hard, so hard it hurt. But the sex didn't seem to matter as much as just doing this did. Watching her come down from her endorphin high. Watching over her.

He always felt protective with any of the girls he played, but with Mischa it went to a whole other level. It was more than him doing his job as a good dominant. It was more than a sense of responsibility. It was, in the simplest terms, what he most wanted to do at that moment.

Insanity.

Yet he was still doing it. Still wanted to.

She was shivering the slightest bit, and he pulled a blanket off the back of the chair and wrapped it around her shoulders, massaging her arms. She sighed, leaned her head against his chest. And soon she was asleep.

He stayed still with Mischa on his lap, watching her sleep as he had when they'd been in bed. When a dom unknown to him approached, whether to ask if they were done with the cross or simply to introduce himself, Connor warned him off with a long, hard glare. They were still in scene, as far as he was concerned, and he wouldn't allow anyone to intrude. No one was going to disturb his girl during aftercare. No one.

He looked down at her face once more, and realized how fiercely he felt the need to care for her.

Hell, he *did* care for her.

There was no way he could bullshit himself out of this one.

Because he *had* to, suddenly, he whispered to her, "You've turned my head but good, my girl. If I'm to be perfectly honest with myself—something I know damn well I don't always do—it happened almost right away.

"You're absolutely the kind of woman a man can have an evening of fun with, whether sex or dungeon play or both. I hardly judge you for that. I've never seen anything wrong in sex for the sake of sex. The pleasures of the flesh are one of the things that makes life worth living. I think you understand that as well as I do. I don't understand all the rules people put on how and when it's acceptable to indulge." He paused, checked her loose features carefully, listened to her even, shallow breathing to make sure she was still asleep before he went on. "My only rule, in the end, is that no one gets hurt. Not in terms of the pain play I prefer—and there's a difference between hurting someone for pleasure and doing damage to them."

Then leave the girl alone.

He took in a long breath, held it in his lungs until it burned.

"I *will* hurt you, damn it. That's certain, if I don't walk away soon enough. Even a girl as tough as you, as strong as you, can be hurt. Damaged. I can't fucking stand the idea of doing that to you. Not you. But I can't tell you all this to your face. Which makes me a fucking coward, doesn't it?"

He breathed out a long sigh. He had to be honest with her. To make sure she understood what he was and was not capable of.

Even if she was just in it for the sex, the BDSM play. He owed it to her to be clear. He owed it to himself to keep her safe.

To keep her safe from *him*.

He ran an agitated hand over his chin, rubbing the stubble there.

They just needed to talk, despite the fact that he really didn't want to. To have it all out on the table. They didn't have to stop what they were doing. As long as he told her . . .

She moaned, her long lashes fluttering open, then her brilliant blue eyes were staring up at him.

"Hey," she said, her voice a little rough.

"Hey yourself." Had she heard his mutterings? He didn't think so. "How do you feel?"

"Sore. But really wonderful."

She smiled, wiggled in his lap, this warm, naked girl under the blanket. Nice. Making him go hard all over again, his mental meanderings taking a backseat.

He grinned down at her. "You're still high on the endorphins."

"Yes. I like it. No crash this time. Or, not so far."

"Are you hungry?"

She shook her head, and he reached up and unpinned her hair, watched it fall down around her shoulders, ran a hand through it. Like fucking silk.

"What do you need?" he asked her.

"Nothing, right now. What do *you* need?"

"Ah, don't tempt me, girl."

"I mean to."

She squirmed some more, her naked sex settling right over his growing erection.

"Did I say you could do that?"

"Not yet."

She was grinning, an impish sort of grin. He knew she wasn't completely out of subspace, but he liked this playfulness. Then her face sobered and she dropped the blanket, baring her gorgeous breasts. She cupped them in her hands, lifting them.

She said, her voice very low, "I'm asking again, Connor. What do you need?"

He groaned. His cock pulsed.

"Come on, then, and suck me. Right here. In front of all these people."

She slid down to her knees before him, unzipped his jeans and pulled out his cock, held it in her hot little hand. She glanced up at him and he nodded.

"Do it, Mischa. Now."

She bent, her hair falling across his thighs, and he had one moment to wish he was feeling it on his naked skin. Then her mouth closed over the head of his cock and his mind emptied.

"Ah . . ."

She let her tongue swirl over the head of his cock, slip into the opening, something he loved and few women ever thought to do. Then she curled her tongue around the tip again, again and again. She was working only the swollen head, her fingers light on the rigid shaft, driving him crazy. Crazier still when she pulled away, blew a soft, hot breath onto the tip, then enveloped him with her mouth once more.

Pleasure surged into him, his balls pulling tight. He wanted to pump up into her hot, wet mouth, to fuck her mouth. But he also wanted to see what she might do. To let her torture him a little.

She kept using her tongue on him, swirling, dipping. When she finally slid her mouth all the way down the length of him, all at once, he groaned aloud.

"Ah, Christ, that's good."

She took him deep into her throat, paused, took him deeper. Then she began to move.

He pushed her hair from her face, held it back so he could watch her pretty mouth sliding up and down on his cock. Desire was like fire in his veins, building, building. Pleasure was even hotter, all driven by her lips and tongue. So damn wet, her mouth.

She began to suck.

"Ah . . ."

He could feel the head of his cock hitting the back of her throat, and she kept stroking the underside with her tongue even as she sucked him hard. So hard he was on that keen edge of pain. Fucking gorgeous, the way this woman gave head. Fucking perfect. The sight of her plush red lips taking him in . . . he could barely stand it. Could barely stand not to thrust right into her, to choke her a little with his cock, something he loved. But he knew if he did it now he'd come too soon.

To calm himself he glanced up, looked around the room, caught sight of the people watching them. A couple at the play station next to them, the dom standing next to his girl, who was on a spanking bench. The dom caught his eye, gave a small approving nod, and Connor's excitement spiraled. He looked further, found a threesome—a man and two women—doing nothing but standing there to watch. The women were smiling.

He couldn't help himself now. He looked back at Mischa's pale blonde head, grasped her hair in his hands, pushed deep into her throat. She took it, swallowing him down.

"Ah, that's perfect, darlin'. Yes . . ."

He was going to come soon. And she damn well *was* perfect: her wet, sucking mouth, her gorgeous hair, the way she worked his cock. The fact that she had no inhibitions about sucking him off in front of the crowd.

He pulled her hair tight enough to hurt and there was a quiet, muffled moan from her. Then he was doing it, fucking her mouth in hard, punishing thrusts. And right as he was about to come, she reached into his jeans and pinched a small bit of skin at the base of his sac between her fingers, sending him hurtling over the edge.

"Christ . . . Fuck, Mischa! Fuck . . ."

He was coming in ripples; it wouldn't stop. And she drank him in, swallowing his come down her lovely throat, sucking him to the end.

When his body calmed he let go of his grip on her hair. She pulled back, his still-hard cock slipping from her red lips. She looked up at him, her eyes the bluest he'd ever seen.

Christ, this woman.

Mine.

For now, maybe. Only for now.

But *now* was fucking perfect. He couldn't think of anything else.

Connor was parking at his place after getting her dressed, bundling her into his Hummer. She didn't remember much about the short drive—nothing more than feeling incredibly relaxed. Sated but still excited, needing more. She hadn't been sure where they were going until she'd asked him, and he'd told her he didn't think she was ready to be back at Dylan's place alone.

She didn't think so, either. She was aware that she was still floating, that she hadn't really come down yet. And that she wasn't ready for him to be done with her. She'd been too pleased at his response to her. Too taken with the sense of power she'd had with his cock in her mouth and him groaning, his fingers buried in her hair.

She was still feeling it now, how pleasure equalized them. She'd had some sense of it before, watching his face as he came inside her. But tonight she felt it so much more. As though he'd let down some walls in letting her take over, set the pace, bring him to climax by *her* actions, by what *she* chose to do to him.

He got out of the car, came around to open her door and helped her out.

"Let's get you upstairs."

He kept an arm at her waist, as he always did. She loved it. And that part of her that hated to admit how much she enjoyed his sense of protectiveness was growing more and more quiet the more she was with him.

He helped her up the stairs. Her legs felt a bit shaky, but in a good way. She couldn't explain to herself what that meant, only that she felt damn good.

He opened the door and they moved inside.

"Are you cold?" he asked. "I'll turn up the heat. You're hardly dressed under that coat."

She started to slip out of it. "I'm warm enough."

"Some tea, then?"

She smiled. "Is it the Irish in you that offers a girl tea?"

"Don't you drink tea?"

"I do."

"Well then, Irish or not . . ." He shrugged as he accepted her coat and hung it in a small hall closet. "The kitchen is this way."

He seemed a little out of sorts, suddenly. She wasn't sure why. Or maybe she really was coming down now and she wasn't seeing things clearly.

"I'd actually love some tea," she said to his retreating back. "Oh, this kitchen is great."

It had obviously been redone recently. The walls were spare white, long rectangles of sleek pale green subway tiles on the counters and on the backsplash behind the stove. The appliances were all black, the curtains at the window white with a wide black border. Very masculine.

"I'm glad you like it. I made Alec help me set tiles over the summer."

He smiled as he spoke, and she relaxed again. Maybe that tense moment had been her imagination after all.

"Here, sit down."

He guided her to a small built-in nook with a white finished table and black padded benches. She watched as he busied himself around the kitchen: turning on an electric teakettle, setting a pair of black-and-white plaid napkins on the table, a white sugar bowl. The kettle whistled when it boiled, and he poured, bringing a pair of black mugs back to the table.

He sat down across from her and she found herself wishing he'd squeezed onto the small bench seat next to her. She glanced at him as he spooned sugar into his cup, then placed her hands around her tea mug. She was being ridiculous. He was right there. He'd invited her into his apartment. Everything was fine. This was just a little bottoming out. She was fine.

"How are you feeling? Come down yet?"

"I think so."

"That's good. Good." He looked down, brought his cup to his mouth and sipped. "Shit! Burned my mouth."

He wiped his lips with one sleeve, grimaced.

"Are you okay?"

"What? Yeah, I'm fine. Fine."

Wasn't that what she'd been telling herself a few moments ago? What was going on here?

"Connor? Is something wrong?"

"No, of course not. We had a great night, didn't we?"

"I thought so."

"I think the same." He paused, and her stomach sank for some reason. "I just think we should talk."

"About what?"

"You know I'm enjoying spending time with you. I don't want you to question that."

"But?"

"There's no 'but' as far as that's concerned. I just want to be honest about my intentions."

She almost laughed. "Your intentions? Connor, no one is standing over you with a shotgun. When did I strike you as the kind of woman who was worried about anyone's intentions? I know we're not heading into a relationship. I wouldn't even call this dating."

"Well, we're seeing each other."

Where was he trying to go with this?

"Yes. So?"

"I believe clarity, transparency, is the best way to go. I don't want you to have any unrealistic expectations."

"Is this the kiss-off talk?"

"The what?"

Her heart was a hammer in her chest, in her ears.

"You know. The talk where you basically tell me that you've had a great time, I'm a good fuck, but it's time to kiss off." She got to her feet, her blood boiling. "Because if it is you can save your breath. I have no desire to be with anyone who isn't into me. In fact, I hardly *need* to do that."

"No, I'm sure you don't. Mischa, that's not what I'm saying."

"Isn't it?"

And why did it matter so damn much? She'd known him less than a week!

It was his turn to get to his feet. He towered over her as he reached to the other side of the table, dragging her closer.

She smacked his hand away. "Don't manhandle me."

"I was under the impression you enjoyed that."

"How dare you." She was fuming now. "How dare you use that against me!"

"Mischa . . . Shit, I don't mean it that way. Fuck."

He let her go and she took a step back. Pushed her hair from her face.

"Maybe you don't. But Connor, what the fuck is going on here? Because I am not one of those girls you need to have a 'talk' with. I'm not going to ask you where we stand or where we're going. I thought that was clear from the beginning. I have a life in San Francisco. I have my business, my friends, my writing. I'm not looking for anything else. I'm happy. With my *life*. And I've been happy to fuck you, to play at your kink."

His tone was low. "I think we've been doing more than playing at it."

"Yes. Okay. Maybe so. But it doesn't mean . . . that I'm going to want more from you."

God, she was a liar. She wanted more from him already. Even if she didn't know what it was, exactly. Hell, she didn't have a clue. She wasn't sure what the tears stinging her eyes were about—that he was angry, that she didn't want to care.

"Fuck. Fuck, I'm sorry, Mischa. This is not the time . . . You're barely down from subspace, if you even truly are yet. I should have kept my mouth shut until tomorrow, at least." He paused, scrubbed a hand over his jaw. "I can't believe . . . I never lose control. I never lose it."

"Is that what this is, Connor? Because I don't like it one bit." A small rage shimmered through her, bit into her stomach. "I don't know why I thought you would behave better than I've come to expect of the average man."

"No, you're right. I expect the same of myself. I expect that I'll . . . behave better than I've a right to expect of myself, maybe."

That made her pause, almost made her want to laugh. She pushed her hair from her face. "God, we're fucked up, aren't we?"

His tight features loosened a little. "Yeah, I've been trying to get over it most of my life. I guess I'd had myself talked into thinking I had."

"Me, too. I'm sorry," she told him, her shoulders relaxing. "I didn't need to get so pissed off."

He cracked a grin. "You did, though, didn't you? I kind of liked seeing you like that. All that fire."

She did laugh then. She couldn't help it.

She really was losing it. Furious one minute, laughing with him the next. The man was driving her crazy. But mostly it was a good crazy.

He reached out and pulled her to him with one big hand wrapped around her waist.

"Come here and let me feel the burn, my girl. Let me see if I can work it out of you."

He kissed her, his lips coming down hard on hers, and she found herself melting into him, her anger, her tension, dissolving. Somehow, with Connor, the world always melted away, allowing her to let go.

Maybe that was why she'd been so mad. Because the notion that anyone could make her let go, make her really lower her boundaries, her walls, was too damn scary to contemplate.

He kissed her harder, started to push her dress up her thighs.

She pulled back. "Connor. You're making it impossible for me to think."

"Then don't. Don't think." He wrapped a hand in her hair and pulled her head back, kissed her throat. "Just hold still while I kiss you, touch you. You can think later. Right now I think I need to fuck you on this table."

"Oh . . ."

And as he pulled his shirt over his head, then her dress, all she could think of was the heated press of skin against skin. The taste of him on her tongue as he started kissing her again. The way her body heated for him. And knew that right now, this was all she wanted.

seven

Mischa yawned, stretched, pointing her toes, her arms overhead. And remembered she was in Connor's bed.

She smiled.

"You're happy this morning," he said, his voice husky with sleep.

She opened her eyes to find him propped up on one elbow, looking at her. In the dim morning light coming through the rice paper shades, his eyes were more a deep gold than green. His jaw was shadowed with beard stubble, which she found incredibly sexy. Almost as sexy as the lines of his bare, muscular shoulder. She reached out to trace her fingers over the black and red Celtic knot work tattooed around his right biceps. "Are you insinuating you're not?"

"Ah, no. Just the opposite."

"You do seem to be happy most of the time," she remarked.

"Do I?"

"Why do you look so surprised?" His features went dark, as though a sudden cloud had settled over him. "Connor? What did I say?"

He scrubbed at his face with one hand. "Nothing. I'm just . . . not always so happy. Or, I haven't been. Christ. Sorry. Not what you want to talk about first thing in the morning."

"No, it's fine." She shrugged. "I don't know anyone who doesn't have some sort of past . . . something they don't like to talk about. There are certainly things I don't like to talk about. Things that have made me less than happy."

"Like your mother?" he asked quietly.

"What makes you say that?"

"That first night we met. You mentioned something about how she'd never really been anyone's mother. I'd imagine that would leave a person with some bitterness."

"Yes, I suppose so," she answered warily.

"And . . . I need to apologize again. It's in my nature to pry. It's part of being a good dominant, getting to know what motivates the person you're playing with. But you don't need to tell me anything you don't want to."

She shrugged again, plucking at the edge of the gray quilt with her fingers, looking down at it. "Oh, you know, absentee parents. Or . . . a flaky mother and a totally absent father. I'm sure you're familiar with that story."

"Not from personal experience. Most of the time I wished my father were *more* absent. He was a right asshole."

When she looked back up at him she could see the pain in his eyes; maybe he wasn't awake enough yet to hide it.

"I'm sorry, Connor."

"Yeah, well. That's my bitterness, I suppose."

"I never knew my father. He left before I was born."

"Some people might say you're better off."

"Maybe. I'll never know, will I?"

"You could find him, meet him, maybe."

"Evie never told me who he was," she said softly, hardly believing she was telling him this, but wanting to for reasons she couldn't explain to herself. "I'm pretty sure she doesn't know. We lived in a series of communes and odd share rentals. Who knows how many men she came into contact with? She's beautiful. There's never been any shortage of men for her. And she was a real free spirit. Still is."

"You said she's an artist."

"Yes. She paints. Works in clay. Makes jewelry. She has real talent, but she's never done much with it. She was always too busy moving us around when I was a kid. Sometimes we'd pick up and go, and she'd leave a dozen canvases behind. Amazing work."

"That must be where you get your artistic abilities."

"Yes. That's the one thing she's given me." She paused, had to swallow the gnawing ache in her throat that came with that admission. "No, that's not entirely true."

"That must be where you got your beauty, from your mother," he said, his green and gold eyes shining. Sincere.

"Well, thank you. But I meant my sister, Raine."

"Are you two close, then?"

"Not so much anymore. We grew in different directions at some point, except that I guess you could say we're both . . ." She trailed off, not sure if she was revealing too much.

"You're both what?"

"We're both sort of . . . hyper-responsible."

"Why was that difficult to admit? I am myself."

"It just sort of slipped out. I've always thought of myself—consciously, anyway—as hardworking. Hyper-responsible sounds a lot more neurotic."

Connor grinned. "If you're neurotic, then so am I. But in my mind hyper-responsible is a hell of a lot better than irresponsible. Tell me more about you and your sister."

"When we were kids it always seemed like just the two of us against the world, Raine and me," Mischa went on. "We were a team. Except that her dad was around and mine wasn't. I mean, I didn't resent her for it. I was glad she had a father in her life. I was just . . . envious."

The truth was she'd always wondered why Raine was good enough for her father to stick around and she . . . obviously wasn't. She could see in her head the movie that had been playing over and over for most of her life: the cards and gifts arriving on Raine's birthday when there were none for her. The front door shutting as Raine went out for a day with her dad, leaving Mischa behind. It still hurt, a small, empty stab to the chest. But she wasn't going to say any of this to Connor. She'd said too much already.

"What about you?" she asked, anxious to change the subject. "Are you close with your sisters?"

"Not so much. They're a bit younger than I am. Clara by eight years, Molly by nine. Hard for a boy to relate to little girls. By the time they were more grown I was gone. Moved to the States."

"That's when you got married?"

"Yeah." He went quiet, and she was about to steer away from the topic, but he took a breath and went on. "I was twenty. It seemed like a good idea at the time, which is a sorry excuse for mucking up someone else's life. I wanted to get away from Ireland. Which is an even worse excuse."

"What did you need to get away from?"

He looked at her, his pupils dark, liquid, as his brows drew together. "My father. He was not a nice man. This tattoo here reminds me how much I don't want to be him," he said, sitting up and stretching out his left forearm.

"What does it say?"

"*Cha tèid nì sam bith san dòrn dùinte*. It's Gaelic for, 'Nothing can get into a closed fist.'"

Connor shook his head, trying to shake away the reason for the tattoo. Memories of his father coming home drunk. It had been nearly every damn night. And when the man was drunk, he was hard on his mother. On him. He'd been a hard man when he was sober. But he'd treasured his girls. Connor would never have left them behind if it had been otherwise. He hadn't been that self-serving, even at twenty.

Not quite. He'd left his mum to deal with the old man, hadn't he? And he'd used Ginny in the process, by marrying a woman he hadn't truly loved, which made it even worse.

Don't think of it.

Not now, with this woman in his bed, so sexy with her mussed hair, her fair skin gleaming in the morning light.

"Does that have anything to do with the scar under your eye?"

"Yeah. Bar brawl at eighteen, like any good Irish lad." He tried to keep the bitterness out of his voice, but her small, brief frown let him know he hadn't entirely succeeded.

"You don't have to say any more," Mischa told him.

He smiled at her. "We've had a baring of souls this morning, haven't we?"

She smiled back. Beautiful, brilliant smile. "We have."

"Perhaps that's enough for one day, then. How do you feel about a long, hot shower?"

"I definitely need one. So do you, frankly."

"Ha! Nice of you to tell me so. Come here, you wicked wench."

He grabbed her and rolled her into his side, then slipping his arm around her waist he lifted her from the bed, carrying her toward the bathroom.

"Connor! Put me down!"

"Not a chance. You're the one who's demanding we shower."

She struggled, but he held her tight. And didn't admit to himself how damn good it felt, his arms around her sweet flesh.

Her naked flesh.

Yes, concentrate on that.

That was easy enough, focusing on the squirming armful of gorgeous girl. He got to the bathroom, reached in without letting her go to turn on the water. He felt her body loosening, accepting his hold on her. Yielding to him. Whether it was his sheer strength that was overpowering her or something else didn't matter. He liked that it was happening.

He was getting hard. Not that it was any surprise. She did that to him, easy as silk. He could get hard just thinking about her. He had the few times they'd been apart, had jerked off to her image in this very shower, coming hard as he remembered the feel of her, the taste of her. How many times in the last week? Less than a week.

Was it only six days ago they'd met? Why, then, did it seem so natural to pull her into the hot shower with him? To start soaping up her body, his hands running over her sleek flesh, as though he'd done it every day of his life?

Don't be stupid.

That was what she did to him. Made him stupid. With lust. With . . . something else. He didn't know what to call it. He'd just met the girl, for Christ's sake. And he wasn't going to go all philosophical now. She was naked in the shower with him, the water running down their bodies. Making her breasts look spectacular. Succulent. He ran his hands over them, pausing to pinch her nipples.

"Hey!"

"Are you protesting because you don't like it?" he asked her.

She laughed. "I think the answer to that is obvious," she said, her fingertips briefly caressing her hardening nipples, making his cock jump with need. "But we're dirty."

"Yes, we are," he said, grinning. "I rather like that about myself. Even more when it comes to you."

"Clean fi rst," she said, her lush mouth setting in mock sternness.

"Ah, she's bossy this morning."

"I promise to be quite submissive again once I'm clean," she answered, grabbing his bottle of shampoo and starting to lather her hair, then spreading the lather over her body.

"I'll see to it you are," he told her, trying to sound grim and failing utterly. He gave up and started to soap himself.

"I'm sure you will. You always do."

"Complaining, are we?"

"I . . . take the Fifth."

"Ha. There's no constitution around here, my girl. Here, time to rinse."

He used the shower wand to spray himself off, then her, doing a thorough job on her silky skin, between her thighs.

"Oh, that's nice," she murmured.

"It looks nice." He moved in closer, swiped at her shaved sex with his free hand. "Feels even nicer."

She sighed, her lashes fluttering. He loved when she did this. When she gave herself over to whatever was happening. Pleasure. Pain. His command. She was submitting to him even now, through the sensation of his hand between her thighs.

He set the shower wand back on its hook.

"Mischa, turn around."

She didn't say anything, just blinked up at him for a moment, then turned around. He ran his hand over her tattoos, taking a moment to admire the delicate lines and shading in the orchids, lotus blossoms and chrysanthemums, the scattered cherry blossoms, all of the work done in classic Japanese style. Beautiful. So much a part of her.

She shivered as he feathered his fingertips over the curve at the small of her back, then he slipped his hand lower, over the perfect heart shape of her ass.

He didn't give her time to consider his actions; he just gave her a good, hard smack.

"Oh! Connor . . ."

But before she could protest her words faded away. Her body went soft. She braced her hands against the white and gray tiles of the shower wall.

"Ah, good girl," he said.

He gave her another smack, the sound of his hand on her wet skin ringing in the shower stall. He'd always loved spanking a woman in the shower. He knew how much sharper the sensation was on wet skin. He did it again, her body moving a little, just a small undulation that signaled the pain as well as the pleasure.

He slapped her harder, and there was a small puff of breath from her.

"God, that really hurts," she said.

"Too much, my girl?"

"No. No, it's really good, too . . ."

He grinned, a little wickedly, if he was being honest with himself, and smacked her again, hard enough to make his palm sting. Her pale flesh was pinking up beautifully. He did it again. And again. First one round buttock, then the other. He was growing harder with every stroke of his hand. Watching the way she was responding: the softening, the sighs. Her welting flesh. Gorgeous.

He kept it up, the spanking growing harder, faster, until she was breathless, squirming. He knew it had to hurt like hell at this point. But she was handling it. He leaned in and ran his mouth over the back of her neck as he smacked her ass, tasting her skin, drawing a long groan from her.

When he paused to slip his hand around the front of her body, between her thighs, he shivered at the heat of her. The slickness of her pussy as he pushed his fingers inside her.

She spread her legs wider immediately. Silently. And as he began to work her with his fingers, pumping in and out, she didn't say a word. Didn't do anything but arch her hips into his hand, keeping up a sensual rhythm.

He wanted to control himself. Wanted to make her come before he took his pleasure with her. But her gorgeous pink ass was so close he couldn't help but press up against it, his cock slipping between the cheeks.

That was it for him. There would be no more self-control. With a groan he reached behind him to shut off the water. He picked her up, kicked open the shower door, and set her on the tiled counter. He fumbled in a drawer, found a condom, sheathed his aching erection. He looked into her eyes, found them wide and blue and wanting. Parted her thighs and plowed right into her.

"Ah . . . yes, Connor . . ."

Her legs wrapped around his waist, her arms around his neck, and he bent his knees so he could thrust deep. She was so damn tight. Tight and wet and fucking beautiful. He drove into her, watching her face. Her plump red mouth. Her glossy blue gaze on his. Intensity. Pure sex. Fucking amazing.

He wanted to kiss her. He wanted to watch her as he fucked her even more.

When she started to come he felt it deep in her pussy before he saw it in her face. Her lips parted, she moaned, panting in fast little breaths.

"Connor, I'm coming . . . oh . . . oh . . ."

Then he was coming, too. Pleasure making him shudder, making his legs shake so damn hard he wasn't sure he could hold himself up. But she held on to him, helping him to ride it out as sensation slammed into him like a wall. Even after the orgasm had faded away he kept pumping into her; he couldn't seem to stop. Not until his cock had gone soft and he had to pull out, to rid himself of the condom.

He realized then that they were both soaking wet from the shower, water dripping all over the counter, on the floor. Mischa was quiet, her blue eyes drowsy. She was fairly deep in subspace, he knew. He grabbed a towel and began to dry her off, holding her steady on the white tiled counter with one hand. She sat perfectly still, letting him do it. When he'd reached everywhere he could he lifted her, stood her on her feet on the bathroom rug and ran the towel over her bottom. She let out a sigh.

"Sore?" he asked her.

"Yes. I love it, though," she answered, leaning into him a little. "I love the soreness. It's my badge of honor. Do you know what I mean?"

"Yeah, I do."

When he ran the towel between her thighs she sighed again, shivered. If he'd been physically able it would have made him hard all over again.

Lord, he couldn't get enough of her. Not for one damn moment. But they couldn't fuck and play all the time, could they? Not that he'd mind trying. But he wanted . . . to *talk* with her, as well.

He didn't want to question it. It wasn't as if he'd never taken a woman to dinner before, but that was usually as a prelude to sex. To dungeon play. This was different.

"Mischa, come to dinner with me tonight."

"Oh, I can't." She pushed her wet hair from her face. "I have a meeting this afternoon with my friend Greyson and I'm not sure how late that'll run."

"Ah, the new tattoo shop?"

"Well, the possibility. Nothing's been decided for sure. I'd really like to open a place here, but we need to talk more, make sure we're on the same page. We have a lot to discuss."

"Tomorrow night, then," he said, toweling himself off.

"Tomorrow's Thursday?"

She was still sleepy. Still under.

"Yeah."

"I have a dinner with Dylan and Kara and their friend Lucie."

"All right, then."

Why did he feel sort of crushed? Desperate to see her?

"Friday?" he pressed.

She smiled. "Friday."

He smiled back, pulled her in to kiss her. He couldn't help himself. Which had been happening a lot with her.

Don't lose it over this woman.

He pulled his mouth from hers with some effort. "Dinner, then the club on Friday," he said, the authority in his own voice making him feel better. "Wear something sexy and red for me."

"You're going to tell me what to wear now?" she asked, looking up at him, one pale brow arched.

"As a matter of fact I am."

Yes, that was better.

She grinned. "Okay."

"Okay? No argument from you?"

"Not this time."

"Don't think for a moment you'll be arguing anything on Friday night," he said, giving her ass a playful pinch.

"Hey!"

"Ah, you are arguing now."

She gave him a grin, turned and bent over a little, making her gorgeous ass a perfect target, looking over her shoulder at him, posing like some pinup girl.

Maybe he *could* get hard again . . .

He gave her a smack and she took it, then straightened up. "I have to go, Connor. You're going to have to wait until Friday for that."

"I'd have never taken you for a tease, sweetheart."

She laughed and grabbed another towel from the rack, drying her hair as she moved back into the bedroom.

He'd never have taken himself for the kind of man who would be unsettled by a woman. Any woman, no matter how gorgeous. How full of fire. But that's exactly what he was. Unsettled.

It didn't have to mean anything more than that. And he would find a way to be sure he was directing the show once more. He'd take her to the Pleasure Dome on Friday. Maybe do a little pre-club mind fuck with her at dinner. Make it clear to her that he was the one in command, which was the only place where he was comfortable.

He knew just how to handle things. He always did, didn't he?

He would ignore the small voice in the back of his head that was whispering, *Maybe not this time.*

Mischa pushed her way through the doors of the Mexican restaurant where she was meeting Greyson Lee, fellow tattoo artist and one of her mentors under whom she'd apprenticed ten years earlier at his shop in Berkeley.

The restaurant reminded her of one of the funky eateries

in Berkeley that surrounded the university campus. It was small, dark, with tables crammed close together, crowded even at lunchtime on a Wednesday afternoon. And it smelled divine.

She spotted him and waved as she crossed the room. When she reached the table he stood and hugged her.

"Mischa, great to see you. You look great. As always."

He stood back and she took in his handsome, familiar face, his dark brown eyes. She liked a shaved head on certain men, and no one wore it better than Greyson. Six foot three, he was all long, lean muscles, with a natural swagger that somehow seemed charming on him. If he hadn't been her mentor something probably would have happened between them, but they'd always been careful not to cross that line. Instead they'd become good friends, and now, perhaps, business partners.

"You look great, too. You have some new ink, I see," she said, glancing at his forearm, where he'd rolled the cuff of his shirt. "You finally finish that sleeve?"

"Yeah, there's a guy here who does beautiful classic Japanese work. In fact, I wanted to talk to you about him, maybe have you meet him. But let's sit down and have a margarita first. I already ordered for you."

"That sounds perfect."

He held her chair for her, something she'd always loved about him. The same old-world manners Connor had. In fact, when she thought about it, they both had that same tendency to take over in any given situation, a mixture of old-fashioned gentleman and that manly commanding thing. Although with Connor there seemed to be more emphasis on the command. She sighed quietly, trying to focus on her meeting with Greyson, to push thoughts of Connor from her mind, which was getting harder and harder to do.

"So, how are the wedding plans going?" Greyson asked as the waitress arrived with their drinks.

"Okay so far. I don't really know what the hell I'm doing, and neither does Dylan, but we'll get through it. I'm meeting with a couple of her other friends tomorrow night; they'll be a big help. How are things with work?"

He grinned. "They'd be a lot better if I was working at my own shop. *Our* own shop. I think we could make a go of it, Mischa. There's no shortage of work here for good artists. And I have two locations for us to look at today, if you have time."

Mischa sipped at her margarita, sweet and cold. "You know I'm seriously considering doing it. If I'm going to have a partner, you're definitely my first pick. And I'd need to have someone here to hold down the fort when I'm in San Francisco, so this is the only way I could even consider expanding."

"How often do you think you'd want to travel back and forth?"

"I'm not sure yet. It'll depend on which shop is busier, I guess."

And how much there was to come back to in Seattle, aside from work.

Was she really thinking Connor would be any sort of permanent fixture in her life? Even if she did work half the time in Seattle, they'd both be moving on sooner or later. Probably sooner.

"Mischa? What's on your mind? Are you having doubts about going into business with me? Because if you are, I have a long list of reasons why this would work."

"What? No. Sorry." She laughed, but it came out a little hollow. "I'm just . . . distracted."

"By?" Greyson asked.

She waved her hand. "A man. I know. Classic."

"Not for you."

"Hmm . . . no, not for me. Grey, can I ask you something?"

"Sure. Anything."

"You've never really been a relationship guy, have you?"

"Not really, no."

"And I've never been in a real relationship in my life. Do you think . . . that can ever change? That people like us can ever change?"

"I don't know. Maybe. If there's something that gives you a good reason to *want* to change. Personally, I'm pretty damn happy with my life the way it is. Seems to me you always have been, too. Do you want to tell me why you're asking?"

She sighed, letting out a long breath. "No. I guess I don't." She lifted her glass, sipped her drink. "Can we talk business instead of me going all girly on you?"

He grinned. "Yeah. Sure."

"Okay. Talk to me about this tattoo artist who finished your sleeve. Because I can tell you're already thinking you want him to come work with us if we make this thing happen."

It was almost ten when Mischa got back to Dylan's apartment. Greyson had taken her to look at both possible locations, and she'd liked them—either one would work beautifully. Plenty of space, good street traffic, both in areas that would attract a good clientele. And he'd come armed with information and statistics that showed her opening in Seattle would be a sound investment. There was a lot to think about. She wished she could call Dylan and talk it out with her, but she knew she and Alec had been meeting friends for dinner, and were probably either still out, or having some alone time at his place.

She kicked off her shoes and carried them into the bedroom, unzipped her dress and hung it up. The apartment was chilly, with her having been gone all day. She wrapped herself in a robe, slid her feet into her favorite fuzzy pink slippers and flipped on the heater as she padded back into the living room. She grabbed her phone out of her purse and sat on the sofa to check her messages. And was surprised to find one from Connor. He didn't say much, just asked her to call him when she got in, no matter how late.

She curled her feet under her, leaning back into the pillows. It wasn't like him to call to chitchat; he must have something specific to talk with her about. Maybe he needed to change their Friday night plans?

Her stomach twisted a little at the thought.

Don't be silly.

She bit her lip and dialed his number. Took in a deep breath when he answered.

"Mischa, hi."

"Hi. I got your message."

She wanted to ask him if everything was all right, but she didn't want to sound . . . needy. Girly. Which was funny, since she was a total girl in every other way—clothes, makeup, perfume, shoes—except when it came to men.

"How was your day?" he asked.

"Good, thanks. The meeting with Greyson went well. I think we may really go ahead with opening a new shop. We still have to hammer out the logistics, but the business plan he drew up is sound. So are the locations we're looking at. We'll meet again next week."

"And this Greyson guy—you've known him awhile?"

"Forever. I apprenticed under him for four years."

Was that a hint of jealousy she heard in his voice? It couldn't be.

"Married? Girlfriend?"

It *couldn't* be.

"No, neither."

"Ah. Well."

She was smiling to herself, glad he couldn't see how pleased she was. Maybe she was more of a girl than she'd thought.

"Anyway, I think we might really make this happen. There are still a ton of details to figure out."

"Like what?" he asked.

"Well, we have to choose the location. Both these places would work—we just have to sit down and weigh the pros and cons."

"What are your options?"

"Are you sure you want to go over this stuff with me?" she asked. She was surprised by his conversational tone. By the phone call altogether.

"Sure. Why not? Sometimes it helps to hammer things out with an objective party."

"It does. I was hoping to talk to Dylan . . ."

"You can talk to me instead, if you like. Although I'm not as pretty as she is."

Mischa laughed. "I might beg to differ."

"Ah, now you insult me. You don't call an Irishman pretty, my girl."

Those words. *My girl*. Why did they go through her like melted butter? That soft and sweet. And she loved this bantering with him. Without his sense of humor he'd be too dark. Lacking balance. Not that she didn't appreciate his dark side . . .

"So, tell me about the buildings you looked at."

She did, describing the neighborhoods, which he was more familiar with than she was.

"It sounds as if the Belltown shop would be best," he told her. "There are a lot of tattoo shops here already, but that's also where the clients will go looking to get tattooed."

"That concept has worked for me in San Francisco. It makes sense."

"We can always use more good artists here. I've been looking for someone myself. Plenty of artists. Not as easy to find one of really good quality."

"I could tattoo you," she said, almost biting her tongue as the words left her mouth.

"Could you, now? Do you have your equipment with you?"

"I'd planned to do some work on Dylan and Alec while I'm here. A sort of early wedding gift."

"If Alec will let you tattoo him then you must be good."

"Oh, I'm good. Very good," she teased, her tone low, flirtatious.

He picked right up on the bait, his tone lowering to match hers. "Yes, you are. *Very* good. At several things. So, do you have time now?"

"Right now? To tattoo you?"

"Yeah. I could be there in ten minutes. Unless you're tired from your day."

"Not at all. I'm sort of wound up, actually."

"Care to take out some of that energy on me?"

A shiver went through her at the thought of tattooing him. The buzz of the needle, the ink pushing into his skin . . .

"Yes. Absolutely. But give me twenty."

"See you then."

They hung up and she went to run a quick shower, her body heating up. She wasn't sure why she was so in love with the notion of working on Connor. Maybe it was the idea of leaving her mark on him, shaking things up between them a little bit. Equalizing them.

Not that she didn't see them as equals, in spite of the fact that he was definitely the one on top when they were in their roles as dominant and . . . submissive. God, she could barely even think of the word in relation to herself. But she knew it was true.

When it came to Connor, she was totally submissive.

As submissive as she was capable of being. Still no slave girl. But it was so much more than she ever could have imagined.

How had he opened her up that much? She must really trust him to let him take her so far.

The idea hit her like a blow.

She'd always thought of her forays into BDSM as her being open to the idea of the extreme experience. A sensation junkie, she knew people in the BDSM arena called it. But she *was* submissive with Connor, even before she was deep down in subspace. Something she'd never achieved with any of the other men she'd done this sort of power play with. Because she'd never met anyone she trusted enough. She'd never given them a chance to show her that she could. But with Connor, things had happened naturally.

She gazed at her reflection in the big mirror through the steam gathering in the room. She didn't look any different. A little more flushed at the moment. A little more dilation to her pupils. Shock? Or just a surge of pure anticipation? Maybe a bit of both.

The trust was beginning to happen on a deeper level, whether she wanted to think about it or not.

Tonight, she'd see if that trust went both ways. Tonight, she would be the one in control. She could hardly wait.

eight

Mischa was just adding a touch of her signature red lipstick when the buzzer rang, and she went to let Connor into the building. Her pulse was racing while she waited for him to make it upstairs. Her temperature went molten hot when she opened the door.

She always forgot how big he was, really hulking. The way his dark sweater stretched across his massive shoulders.

Stop gawking and say hello.

"Hi."

"Hey."

He stepped through the door, took her in his arms and kissed the lipstick off her, leaving her breathless.

"Better stop this if I'm to get a tattoo tonight," he said, wiping at his lips with the back of his hand. He was grinning, but his eyes were dark with desire.

She knew just how he felt. She smiled, took a step back to steady herself.

"I'm getting things set up in the kitchen," she said. "Can I get you anything to drink?"

"No, I'm good, thanks. So are you. I like this look on you. I've never seen you in casual dress before. Other than when you're naked."

She glanced down at her gray yoga pants and her long-sleeved black Ramones T-shirt. "I'll probably work better like this."

"Better than you would in a dress? Or better than you would naked?"

She laughed as she turned to lead him to Dylan's kitchen, everything sleek and modern: white tile halfway up the walls, gray granite counters, polished maple cabinetry and brushed-steel appliances. "Both. I've set up at the bar counter. But we need to talk about what you want."

"I brought some images with me," he said, handing her a sheaf of papers she hadn't noticed he'd been carrying. "I did them myself, so you may want to make them more conducive to the lines you'll need for a tattoo. I don't know if my work will translate directly."

She looked through the pencil sketches of a Celtic dragon, drawn from several different angles. She loved the design immediately.

"This will translate nicely. Just give me a few minutes to draw something up."

"Sure."

"Where are we putting this?"

"I want it to cover the entire upper portion of my back, from the waist up, maybe."

"I don't think we can do that large a piece in one session."

"That's all right. You're in town for another couple of weeks, right?"

"Yes, but you need time to heal in between sessions. Maybe

if I do it in sections, rather than the entire outline, then adding color later . . . Okay, we'll find a way to make it work. Make yourself at home for a little bit."

He nodded, wandered around the open apartment while she began to draw on the transfer paper, following his sketch.

He wouldn't have asked her to start such a large tattoo if he didn't intend to keep seeing her, would he?

Stop questioning everything, being such a girl.

"Dylan has a fine collection of photography," he said from the living area.

"She does. She has amazing taste. I've always thought of her as a frustrated artist, she has such a great eye. Speaking of artists, I'd really love to get a closer look at your work some time."

"Well, I'm not an artist the way you are . . ."

"Are you kidding? I've seen a little of your stuff. It's all over your apartment."

"It's just commissioned work." He came back into the kitchen, and she felt the heat of his presence as he stood looking over her shoulder. She made an effort not to breathe in his scent. "This is beautiful. Much better than my sample sketches."

"Your stuff's not all commissioned work, Connor. What about the erotic pieces?"

"I've just started doing them. I'm not sure they'll turn out to be anything that'll be taken seriously."

"Why not?" She looked up at him. "They're beautiful, from what I've seen."

"Do you think so?"

"Yes. Absolutely. Spare, lovely lines. You have a good eye for the human form."

"Good enough for you to pose for me?"

"Yes."

She'd said it without thinking about it, of what it meant. That he'd have an image of her after she'd returned to San Francisco, to her life. That he wanted to.

Don't make too much of it.

"Maybe this weekend?" he asked.

"Maybe. I have to be available for Dylan. I'm not sure what the weekend plan is yet."

"Of course."

"Here, I think I'm done. Let me know how you feel about it. I can change something, if you want."

"It's perfect."

It *was* perfect, exactly what he'd had in mind. Connor looked at the quick sketch she'd done, marveling at her skill. The dragon was reminiscent of the Celtic tribal work, but with something entirely unique in the graceful lines. The scales were worked into complicated knots. The wings were a pair of long thorned branches, the head regal, fierce, the twisting body powerful.

"I was thinking of doing it in black with a few touches of red, like your warrior armband," she suggested. He was leaning over her shoulder to look at the drawing, and he couldn't help but take one long, lingering breath, drawing in her warm, spicy scent.

"That's exactly what I was thinking," he agreed.

"Great. Let's get started."

She gestured for him to sit on a stool at the high granite counter, which he did after pulling his sweater over his head. He saw that she had a workstation set up, with a piece of plastic wrap stretched tightly over the granite, the thimble-sized plastic cups full of black ink stuck to the wrap with what he assumed was antibiotic ointment, as he'd seen when he'd been tattooed before. Her machine was laid out next to the inkpots and her red boxy power supply unit stood to one side of them. She turned on her iPod, which was sitting in its dock on the counter, and some old punk tune spilled out.

"Is the music okay with you?" she asked.

"Yeah, I love punk. Especially this old-school stuff."

"It's some of my favorite music, although I like a little of everything."

"Me, too. I like the old Irish folk ballads, even. And my mum got me listening to opera when I was a child."

"Opera? Really?"

"You sound surprised."

"I am," she told him. "I go to the opera at least a few times a year."

"Ah, that doesn't surprise me."

She pulled up a stool behind him. "Okay, ready?" she asked him.

"Ready."

She wiped his skin with an antibacterial wipe, shaved off the tiny hairs with a disposable razor, then wiped his skin again before pressing the transfer paper to his back, then pulling it off slowly, all of which he felt with that nice buzzing awareness that it was *her* hands doing these things.

"Do you want to go into the bathroom to check the placement?"

"No. I trust you."

He did. To tattoo him, and in general. Strange. He couldn't remember the last time he'd gotten to know a woman long enough to trust her, other than a small handful of female friends. Not a woman he was sleeping with.

He compartmentalized his relationships with women, he realized. Friends in one spot, lovers in another. But the lines were blurring with Mischa.

"I know you've done this before," she said, "but the back can hurt more than other areas sometimes. The bones are so close to the skin."

"Do I hear a certain degree of glee in your voice?" he teased her.

She laughed. "Maybe you do. Here we go."

The needle buzzed to life, and he felt the first tickling hum of it on his skin.

"Are you doing all right?" she asked.

"Yeah, fine."

They sank into a rhythm, then, neither one talking much. Just listening to the music, the gentle sound of the tattoo needle. He felt himself focusing inward, on the sensation of the needle on his skin, her gloved hand as she wiped the excess ink away. The scent of her perfume was everywhere, and he inhaled, taking it in, making it a part of the experience. The sensation went from the first mild tickle to a low, steady burn, but he didn't mind it.

"How are you doing?" she asked again after a while, checking in with him in much the same way he did when he was playing her.

"I'm feeling it."

"And?"

"It's bearable. But I wouldn't mind if it was worse. For me, the pain is a part of being tattooed, a part of the experience. I like to challenge myself a bit, if that makes sense. It's a sort of trial by fire. Like I've earned my ink."

"I feel the same way. About being tattooed. And about the pain play. I didn't realize it until just recently. But there's that part of me that's getting off on seeing what I can take. And I don't mean I'm one of those people who will hold out on using a safe word when it's needed. But there is a certain pride in it—in taking the pain."

"Exactly. The trial by fire."

He smiled to himself. They were on the same page about a number of things, apparently. He didn't know why that should matter, except that he was finding her to be excellent company, in addition to being an excellent sexual partner.

Great company, amazing sex. Things could be worse.

If only he didn't have to end it.

No.

What was he thinking? Of course it would have to end. They both knew it. They were both the kind of people who went in fully aware of that. Who didn't want more. Wasn't that one of the things they were on the same page about? He wasn't going to turn her into another Ginny. There wasn't going to be another relationship with a woman who deserved more than he could give, and who got too much no woman should have to put up with.

No, there was not going to be another Ginny. He was not going to make another mistake someone else ended up paying for. His mum, Ginny . . . that had been enough.

"Connor, try not to tense up, if you can. It makes it harder for me to get into the skin."

"Ah, sorry."

He forced his shoulders to loosen. Forced his mind away from the old hurt and guilt spinning through his head. And soon the needle was hitting directly on his spine, sending pain lancing through him.

"Oh yeah, there it is," he said, his jaw clenching a bit.

"Hurting?" she asked, pausing in her work.

"Yeah. But keep going. I can handle it."

"I don't want you passing out on me or anything."

"Ha. As if. And you're going to pay for that remark later, sweetheart."

"I hope so," she said, a sensual tease in her voice.

And damn if his cock didn't go hard, hearing that tone.

"Mischa," he said, keeping his voice low.

"Hmm, what?" She had gone back to tattooing him, the needle burning into his skin.

"I'm going to give you a right spanking later. And then I'm going to fuck you until you scream."

The needle stopped.

"If you keep talking like that I'm never going to get this tattoo done. I'll still be trying to finish it a month from now."

That didn't sound like a bad idea to him, for reasons he was not going to think about.

"I'll behave. I promise," he said, then muttered, "only 'til you're done. Then all bets are off."

"I'll count on it. Now shush and let me work."

He chuckled. He couldn't help himself. He was damn delighted with her.

"So, tell me what the dragon means for you," she asked a few minutes later. "I know it's a classic Celtic symbol, but a lot of people put their own spin on things. Symbols are different for each person."

"It's a symbol of power, which is the most obvious meaning, in that I'm a dominant. But they're also guardians."

"What do you need guarding from, Connor?" she asked.

It was a simple question, asked innocently enough. But his gut twisted.

"Myself, maybe." He paused, trying to figure out how much he wanted to say. Mischa remained quiet while she continued to work on the tattoo, giving him time to think. "If you go back to the Greek origins of the word 'dragon' it can also mean 'I see clearly,' something I try to do. Something I *need* to do. I spent the early years of my life clouded. I screwed up a few things royally because I couldn't see past my anger."

"But you got to a point where you decided to change all that."

"I got to a point where I *had* to, or my life wasn't going to change. It needed to."

Mischa was trying to take in what he was saying, letting it mill around in her mind as she worked. He was a complex man. It sounded as if he'd been through a lot. More than he was saying.

"I'm glad this has a symbolic meaning for you," she told him. "I don't like to do meaningless tattoos on people who think something simply looks cool. I think symbols are important." She paused, thinking about symbols in terms of doing this tattoo for him. "It seems symbolic to me somehow that you're enduring the pain—really feeling it, I can tell. Yet you're no less a dom because you're willingly sitting here, because you've volunteered for the pain."

"There's strength in enduring pain, whether dom or sub or neither. But I see what you're getting at. Are you also feeling some sense of role reversal because you're the one delivering the pain?"

"Maybe." She was quiet for several moments. "Except that I'm still doing this at your direction. Just as if you were directing me at any task."

It was his turn to be quiet, thoughtful. There was no sound in the room but the buzz of the needle on his skin. "Do you want me to give you tasks?" he asked, finally.

"Like cleaning the floor with a toothbrush, or reporting everything I eat? Like some slave girl? No—that's not me at all. Despite where you've taken me when we're in role . . . no. I'll never reach that level." She sat back, looking at her work, wiping the excess ink with a paper towel. The tattoo was going to be beautiful, one of her best pieces, probably. On the most spectacularly muscled back she'd seen in her life. Even now, as focused as she was on creating art on his skin, she couldn't help but appreciate the sight of him. It made her sex ache, her mouth practically water. "But if you want to tell me how to suck your cock exactly the way you like it, then we're on."

He sat up straighter, stretched his arms, the muscles rippling. "Are you done for the moment?"

"We can take a break," she answered.

He turned around to face her, his eyes sparking with equal amounts of lust and good humor. He said, "You do seem to enjoy it when I direct you, Mischa. When I take command."

Her body was heating up, going warm and liquid. But she wanted to finish the conversation. "Only when we're in those roles. The total submission thing will never work for me."

"Except that it does." He reached out, laid his hand on the back of her neck, squeezed just a little. He said quietly, "I've seen you go down, Mischa. Deep into subspace."

She swallowed. "Only in response to the pain . . . the sensation."

"Isn't it all the same thing? No matter what gets you there. It's more than the endorphins, the chemical response to stimuli. You start going down when I clasp your neck, as I'm doing now. I see you fighting it, but if I don't stop soon you'll go down, anyway."

Was he right? She didn't want him to be. But she was already feeling that buzz in her body, in her head.

She let out a sigh on a long breath. "Connor . . ."

He pulled his hand back. "We can argue about it later, if you like."

She wanted to be annoyed with him, but he was grinning at her. Pleased with himself, she could see. Charming as hell. And half naked, which was enough to make any woman swoon. Which she was not going to do, despite the incredible breadth of his

shoulders, the hard planes of his chest, his dark nipples as entic-
ing as his defined six-pack abs.

She bit her lip.

Pull yourself together.

Ridiculous that she couldn't decide between being a little mad
and being stupendously—stupidly—turned on. Either way, they
had work to do.

"Am I going to finish this tattoo or are you going to keep
taunting me?" she asked, trying to regain some command of the
situation. Of herself.

"Both, probably."

She laughed. "Probably. See if you can behave yourself for
another hour or two."

"I'll do my best, but no promises," he said, turning his back
to her once more.

Oh, his back was a symphony of muscle. Almost as beautiful
as the front of his big body . . .

She pulled in a deep breath, dipped her needle in the ink,
and forced herself to concentrate.

It was nearly two in the morning when they stopped and she
gently cleaned his skin and rubbed on some ointment. The tattoo was less than halfway done.

"Don't worry," she assured him. "I'm working in sections
so we don't have to wait weeks for you to heal before I can finish.
If we start earlier next time I may be able to get it done in one
more session."

"Either way. Except that I know you have to get back to San
Francisco."

She paused in cleaning up her workstation. Why did he have
to remind her of that? And why did her heart sink a little thinking
of leaving Seattle?

Leaving him.

Stop it.

"It'll be all right if I sleep on my back, won't it?" he asked, rolling his shoulders to stretch them out.

"Sure. Just be prepared to leave some ink on the sheets."

He reached for her, pulling her close. "Tell Dylan I'll replace her sheets."

Her heart was hammering, her body going soft and hot all over. "You're planning on staying?"

"Am I invited to stay?"

"I thought you were the one to make all the decisions," she said a little breathlessly. His mouth was only inches from hers.

Just kiss me . . .

"It's always consensual, darlin'. You know that by now."

She nodded. Her legs were shaky, her breasts full, her nipples stinging with need. Her lips ached for his as he moved close enough that she could feel his warm breath.

"Does that mean yes?" he murmured against her mouth.

All she could do was nod once more.

He kissed her, then. A firm press of his lips, then his tongue sliding in.

She sighed, let herself melt into him as he deepened the kiss. He was taking command with his mouth. And she was giving herself over to it.

He wrapped his arms around her, held her tight enough to nearly bruise her, her breasts crushed to his wide chest. His hands went to her ass, and he pinched her skin hard, over and over, still kissing her. His mouth was demanding. Hungry. His punishing hands telling her that he was, once more, completely in command.

Her sex was going wetter and wetter as the pain built. His silky tongue was driving her crazy. Her clit was pounding with need, a pulse-beat of raging desire. She squeezed her thighs together, but she knew nothing would do but his touch.

Touch me . . .

As if reading her mind—not for the first time—he used his thigh to part hers, pulled her in hard with his hands so that her aching cleft was tight against his muscular thigh. She arched her hips, rubbing against him. It wasn't enough. She knew he meant for it not to be.

She groaned into his mouth. He pulled back.

"Turnabout is fair play," he said, a teasing note in his low tone. But it was just as full of need. "Don't you think, darlin'?"

"Yes . . ."

She was ready. For whatever he wanted of her, frankly. He'd been right earlier. It didn't take much for him to send her hurtling into subspace. Her mind was emptying already. All she knew was how much she wanted him. How willing she was to endure almost anything he asked of her. Not only willing, but eager.

He stripped her down without another word, yanking her yoga pants down, her underwear. He helped her to step out of her slippers before he tore her shirt over her head, then he turned her around. She felt gloriously naked, her breasts heavy.

"Nice that you weren't wearing a bra. Beautiful. Now bend over and brace your hands on the seat of the stool. Yes, just like that."

She did as he asked. She couldn't do anything else.

"Ah, but your ass is superb," he said as he began to stroke the flesh there, long, feathering caresses that tickled and excited her at the same time. "Have I told you how perfect it is? Two handfuls . . ."

He cupped her ass cheeks in his hands, lightly at first, then harder, digging his fingers in, making her gasp with pain and desire. "Spread for me, Mischa. Very good." He slipped one hand between her thighs, swiping at her soaking cleft, spreading the moisture back, between the cheeks of her ass. "Take a breath, darlin'," he said.

She did, and before she had time to think about it, he slipped the tip of his finger into her ass, wet with her juices.

"Oh . . ." Pleasure shimmered over her skin, through her body.

"Breathe, Mischa. I want you to relax."

She nodded, took a deep breath. He pressed his finger in deeper. There was a slight burn as he pushed past the ring of tight muscle, then nothing but pleasure as he inched his way in.

"Christ, but you're tight. Your ass feels like velvet inside. Can you take more?"

"Yes," she gasped. "Yes."

He moved in deeper, slid his finger out a bit, then pressed in again.

"You take it like a champ," he said, pleasure in his tone as he moved his finger in and out of her. "Watching the way you move your body when I fuck your ass with my hand. Moving like a mermaid in the water . . . You make me so damn hard."

He pumped in and out of her ass, and she breathed into it, letting her body open to him.

"But it would be even better to have my cock there. To sink deep inside you."

"Oh yes . . ."

"Do you have any lube?"

"I do. It's . . . oh . . . ," she moaned as he slipped his finger from her body. "It's in the bedroom."

"I'll get it."

"It's in the silver train case next to the bed."

He leaned over her, kissed her between her shoulder blades,

making her shiver. He whispered, "I don't want you to move. Do you understand? I want you to hold absolutely still and wait for me."

"I will."

She felt a loss of heat as he moved away from her, but she didn't so much as turn her head. She closed her eyes, waited, her body loose, her mind blank of everything but her need for him, her need to please him.

He was back quickly. She heard the tearing of a foil packet and shuddered with anticipation. Then his finger was back, rubbing the lube on that tight opening, pushing a little inside.

"Are you ready for me?"

"Always," she said, understanding that it was true.

He moved in behind her, and she realized he was naked as he pressed close to her. His thighs were strong on either side of hers. One arm went around her waist, holding her tightly in the way he often did, making her feel the power of his big body. Making her feel taken over, but in some lovely way. With his other hand he parted the cheeks of her ass, and she felt the tip of his sheathed cock pressing there, then slipping inside.

"Breathe," he told her as he had before.

She took in a deep breath, concentrated on relaxing her body. His big cock surged past the tightest muscles, and she exhaled.

"Take another breath, sweetheart," he said, his teeth clenched in pleasure—she could hear it in his voice.

She inhaled, and he moved deeper. She trembled with need. She wanted to take all of him. Wanted him to fill her completely.

"Connor . . ."

"Shh. Stay quiet, darlin'. Follow my lead. Only tell me if it's truly too much."

She calmed herself. Waited, her body wanting, wanting.

Finally he thrust in slowly. There was the smallest bit of pain, and only because of his size. But the pleasure was an aftershock that rocked her.

"Oh . . ."

He pulled his hips back, his cock slipping almost all the way out, then he arched into her again. She pressed back against him, taking the length of him into her.

"Ah, that's perfect," he murmured. "So damn good. Your ass is unbelievable. The way it feels. The way it looks. Making me damn crazy. I just need to fuck you. To really fuck you. Talk to me now, Mischa. Can you take it?"

"I can take it, yes. Just do it, Connor. Fuck me."

"Ah . . ."

He began a slow thrusting motion. Surging in, pulling out. With each thrust pleasure moved through her, first in liquid, undulating waves, then building into something sharper. She loved the pulling sensation as his cock slid out. The enormous pressure as he filled her in a way she'd never been filled before. She could almost come just from this . . . almost.

And once more he read her mind, read the need in her body. He reached around her and began to roll her tight clit between his fingers.

"Oh God, Connor."

"I want you to come. I want you to come as I do. And it's going to be soon, you feel so good." He gave a sharp jerk of his hips, pleasure and a lovely shard of pain driving into her. But the pain only made the pleasure more keen, lent it a sharper, deeper edge. "I'm just going to . . . fuck you. Until we both come . . ."

He drove into her, his fingers working her clit as mercilessly as his big cock was working her ass. Her body was soaring with sensation, flying higher and higher. She was arching back against his impaling cock, forward into his hand on her needy clitoris. She couldn't get enough. It was too much. Overwhelming.

He angled his hand and pressed two fingers inside her, thrusting deep. His hips ground against her, his cock pushing, pushing, into her ass. She'd never felt so filled in her life, stretched tight. He curved the fingers inside her until they hit her G-spot. And she came hard, her climax like the dazzling light of the sun going off in her head, her body.

"Connor!"

"Ah, I'm coming, darlin' . . . coming so damn hard . . ."

He was driving into her, his hips jerking. And she kept coming, her climax shivering through her body like a small earthquake, shaking her to the core.

Maybe it was being filled, ass and pussy simultaneously. Maybe it was that sense of being so absolutely taken over. Maybe it was the dark, earthy scent that was *Connor*, wild in her lungs as she panted out her pleasure. Panted in time with him. With his plunging cock, his fingers still surging in her clenching pussy. She felt as if she might lose her mind, lose herself and never come back.

Indescribable pleasure, being with this man, the things he did to her.

Too much, maybe.

As the last of her orgasm echoed in her body, faded away, she felt tears sting her eyes.

What the hell was wrong with her?

She sniffed, clenched her teeth. But the tears came, anyway.

Damn it.

"Mischa?"

Connor pulled out of her, which only made it worse, somehow. There was a brief pause, and she was vaguely aware of him grabbing some paper towels from the roll she'd left on the counter. Then he was turning her in his arms. She tried to fight her way out of his embrace, knowing it was futile, but she had to try. To get away from him. Or from herself. Her head was spinning, her body still pulsing with sensation. She couldn't make any sense out of what was happening to her.

"Mischa, talk to me."

"No."

She ground her jaw harder. It didn't help. The fucking tears were falling down her cheeks. She couldn't stop them.

She tried to yank her way out of his hold, but he grabbed her wrists.

"Mischa, look at me."

She'd never heard him so stern. It made her want to melt into him. It made her want to fight him all the more.

He said very quietly, "God damn it, Mischa. Look at me. Do it."

She moved her gaze to his, meaning to argue, but all that came out was a gasping sob.

He lowered his head, evening his gaze with hers.

"This is bottoming out. That's all. You're going to be fine. But you have to stop struggling. With me. With whatever it is you're feeling."

"I don't know what it is. It's . . . fucking alien to me. I don't know . . ." she repeated. "I don't know how to handle this."

"I'll help you."

"I don't want your help. I want you to let me go."

She knew she was being childish. She couldn't help it. She felt totally out of control. Scared as hell.

He said more gently, "Come on, darlin'. You know I'm not going to do that until I know you're feeling better."

"Because it's your duty as a good dominant? I'm not somebody's duty! I never have been." Fury burned in her veins. She knew he didn't deserve all of it, but she couldn't seem to help herself. "I'm not somebody's . . . anything. I don't belong to you, Connor."

"I never said you did." His tone had gone a little flat, a shadow passing over his face.

What did that mean? She couldn't figure it out right now.

"But it is my job to take care of you when we're together," he went on. "And I intend to, whether you want me to or not. That's something I won't compromise on."

He gave her a small shake, and anger surged through her. But she was paying attention to him, which was probably why he'd done it, she realized in some vague way.

"I am not going anywhere while you're like this," he told her. "I won't leave you alone to deal with this. Do you understand me? We're going to draw you a bath and you're going to get in it. You're going to do exactly as I say. I know you don't want to."

Another small sob that she couldn't help before she was able to answer stubbornly. "I don't."

"But you will do it."

He wasn't budging an inch, his hands still hard on her shoulders, his fingers biting into the flesh. But that hard hold, the force of his tone, made her feel better. Safer.

"Connor . . . I'm so . . . I'm just so *mad*. I am not this emotional, childish person, God damn it. This is not who I am."

She wiped at her teary eyes with both fi sts, her fi ngers clenched so tight the nails dug into her palms.

"I think you've never been allowed to be," he said quietly.

"No. Never. Because Evie has always been the child in our family. And Raine, for a while, until she was old enough to feel the same sense of hyper-responsibility I have ever since . . . as long as I can remember. I've had to take care of everything. Making sure everyone ate, and the rent got paid. But it didn't half the time because how the hell was I supposed to make that happen when I was ten years old? God! I've never been able to be a child, and I don't want to be one now. I don't want to do this. But I can't seem to help myself and it's all your fault!"

He didn't even blink as she hurled the accusation at him she knew was ridiculous the moment it left her lips.

Instead, he picked her up, and although she couldn't relax in his arms, she let him do it. Let him carry her to the bathroom, set her on her feet. She'd begun to shiver, and he pulled her robe from the hook on the back of the door and wrapped her up in it before he let her go only long enough to turn on the taps in the tub. He came back to her, rubbing her arms with his big hands.

He was watching her quietly as the water ran, the room filling with steam. He handed her a tissue and she wiped her eyes, her nose. He took it from her and tossed it into the wastebasket. Through it all he was naked, she realized. Totally unself-conscious about it. No less commanding.

She was beginning to calm down. The tears stopped, for which she was grateful.

When the tub was full he slipped the robe from her shoulders and helped her step into the warm, soothing water. She sat down, pulled her knees to her chest. Connor knelt on the bath mat next to the tub. He grabbed a sage-green washcloth from a wicker basket on the floor and dipped it in the water, squeezed it out and began to smooth it over her back.

"Did I hurt you?" he asked, his tone a low rumble. His dark brows were drawn together.

"What? No. Not at all. That's not what this is about." Strange that he seemed to need reassurance from her now. But he obviously did.

"You're sure?"

She understood what he was asking. Understood the difference between the pain play that was all about elevated levels of sensation and really being hurt.

"I'm sure. Absolutely."

He let out a long breath. "Okay. Okay, then."

They were both quiet as he moved the washcloth to the back of her neck, holding her hair up with one hand. It felt lovely. She still felt raw. Wide open. Scared. But she was beginning to relax a little, her shoulders loosening under his tender ministrations, her gaze on the small ripples in the water.

He *was* being tender with her. Unbelievable. Confusing.

"Why are you being so nice to me? After I've been . . . so . . ." She stopped, shook her head.

"You've been fine. This happens sometimes."

"But we weren't even doing any real pain play."

"That's not always what brings it out. Some people reach this space just having a massage."

"The tears?"

"Yes."

"I don't cry. I didn't even as a kid. This is not normal for me."

"Nothing is normal for me right now," he said quietly.

"What?" She turned to look at him. His face was perfectly serious, a study in concentration.

He stroked the wet washcloth over her back a few more times before answering. "Mischa . . . I don't know what's going on here, between us. But it's different. I don't believe I'm imaging it."

She bit her lip. "No. You're not."

"There's a connection . . ."

"Yes."

Her heart did a small flip in her chest as she waited to hear what he would say.

"That might be why you're bottoming out so hard."

"Maybe. Maybe it is. I really don't ever cry, Connor. Even when I broke my arm when I was nine . . . I sat in the emergency room, totally quiet. The nurse told me I was brave but . . . I don't know."

"What don't you know?" he asked.

"I don't think it was bravery. It was because Evie was sitting there with me, wringing her hands, her face looking . . . like she was going to break, just fall apart like she did after one of her men left her. She kept asking me over and over if I was okay. As if I was supposed to just say I was fine and it would all go away. And Raine, she must have been six at the time . . . she was in the chair next to her, looking so small. Crying. And I was . . . the only one there who could handle it."

"Christ, Mischa. That's a lot for a nine-year-old."

She shrugged, but she still felt the pain of it, of the other things about her childhood she usually did her best not to think about.

"I don't know why I'm telling you this," she said finally.

"Because of that connection, maybe. Look, Mischa, you need to know that it's okay to tell me these things. I'm not here to judge. I won't hold it over your head, ever. I can promise you that. And the tears . . . that's not something you have to fight so hard to hold back."

"But I do have to."

"Why?"

Her heart was racing. She had to push to get the words out, and even then it was a small whisper. "Because letting go is too scary."

"Ah, for me, as well."

They remained quiet for a while. He started dipping the washcloth into the water, squeezing it out over her back again, and she watched the small ripples in the water. He was giving her time to calm, to absorb everything that had gone on. Everything they'd said. Maybe to calm himself, as well. And she felt as cocooned by her admissions to him, by his calm voice, as she did by the steam, moist and warm in the air. She felt emptied out, a little raw. But she also understood, at least to some extent, that it had been necessary. For her. For whatever this was between them, maybe.

After some time had passed, long enough that the water in the bath had started to cool a bit, he asked, "Do you need anything? Can I get you a drink of water?"

"No. Just . . . stay with me."

She looked at him, found his steady green gaze on hers as he nodded. He picked up her hand, curling her fingers around his, brushed a kiss there.

"Whatever you want, darlin'."

How strange that he should say those words to her. That he should *mean* it. Even stranger that this was all she wanted. For him to simply be there. With a fierceness she'd never felt before. It was strange. Wonderful. Scary.

She didn't want to be caught up in the fear. She wanted to revel in the wonderful part. Wanted to let herself have this for the first time in her life. To relax a little. Not question any of it: the rawness, the honesty they'd shared.

Right now, she would allow herself this moment.

nine

Connor swung his duffel bag onto his shoulder and walked down the long ramp to his gate at Sea-Tac airport. He pulled his boarding pass from his shirt pocket and checked it one more time. Gate B 11. He could stop by the Starbucks and grab a coffee.

He hadn't eaten yet, but he wasn't hungry. He'd spent the late morning after he'd left Mischa's place—Dylan's apartment—and the early part of the afternoon running on pure adrenaline: making a few business calls to one of the gaming companies he did work for down in the San Francisco Bay Area, booking the flight, the hotel in San Jose. All of it with his heart working like a small jackhammer in his chest, his head spinning.

Whatever you want, darlin'.

He'd said it. What's worse was, he'd meant it.

He couldn't feel this way about a woman. *Couldn't.* He hadn't even really been in love with Ginny and look what he'd done to her! Oh, he'd never hit her, but a few fists through the wall was every bit as unacceptable. His surly attitude. All of it too reminiscent of his father. Emotion brought it out in him. Which was why, after Ginny had left, he'd made the very conscious decision never to put himself in that position again. And now, apparently, here he was. Feeling things he shouldn't be feeling. He had no *right*.

The way he felt about Mischa . . . it had disaster spelled all over it. He couldn't stand the idea of her seeing him for what he was—a man incapable of love. A man incapable of restraining his inner rage without the strength of the walls he'd built so carefully around his emotions.

No, emotion equaled that loss of control he couldn't afford to risk again. He needed some time away to get things back into perspective.

He reached his gate, dropped his bag on the floor, settled his computer case a little more gently and sat in one of the long row of chairs. Outside the wide windows the late-afternoon sun was breaking through the clouds, the rays silhouetting the planes on the runway. He didn't know why it seemed odd to him that the sun would be shining with him feeling so dark inside. It wasn't as if the damn universe had to be in accord with his moods.

He was in one hell of a mood. Which was why he was getting the hell out of town.

His cell phone rang and he pulled it out of his jeans pocket and squinted at the caller ID. Alec. He answered.

"Hey."

"Hey, Connor. You up for dinner with Dante and me? Dylan's meeting with Mischa, Lucie and Kara at his place. More wedding stuff. Mischa may have told you about it."

He didn't like to admit even in his own head that it was like a small stab in his belly to hear her name. "Can't make it. I'm headed down to San Jose for work. I'm at the airport."

"Right now?" Alec asked.

"Yeah. Right now."

"You didn't mention you were going out of town."

"Must have slipped my mind."

"It must have." Alec was quiet for a beat. "You want to tell me what else is going on?"

"What do you mean?" He hadn't meant to be so sharp with him; it had just come out that way.

"Come on, Connor. We've known each other long enough. You're grouchy as hell. There must be a reason why."

He sighed, ran a hand across his chin. He'd forgotten to shave that morning. He'd woken up with Mischa snuggled up naked against him, his heart dissolving in his chest, just melting away. Because of the way her warm body felt in his arms. Because of the driving *need* to protect her. From everything. The world. Him.

Mostly him.

How could he hurt her after all she'd been through as a kid? After the way she'd been let down? He couldn't do that to her. He had to get out before . . . before what?

He *would* hurt her if he stuck around feeling the way he did. Of that he was certain. There was no way he could give her all she deserved to have from a relationship. Letting Mischa think she could have that with him . . . it would be cruel.

"I can hear the gears turning, Connor. They sound rusty."

"Ha. Thanks."

"So?"

Alec waited patiently.

"So . . . The girl is . . . She's under my skin, you know?"

"I'm familiar with the feeling."

"Yeah, well . . ." Christ, why couldn't he finish a sentence? "I don't like it."

"We usually don't, guys like us."

"You mean guys like *me*. *You're* getting fucking married." He paused, blew out a long breath. "Sorry. I don't mean that the way it sounded. I'm happy for you and Dylan."

"I was that guy, too, Connor," Alec said. "Or have you forgotten already?"

"Things changed for you."

"Yes, they have." Alec's tone was low, certain.

He wasn't saying the rest, but Connor got the implication that it was possible he could change, too. He simply didn't agree with it.

"Okay," Alec said after a few silent moments. "Go work, take some time to get your head sorted out. Whatever you need. I won't give you a hard time about it. Did you at least say good-bye to her?"

Anger rose, the skin at the back of his neck prickling with heat. "Of course. Who do you take me for? I'm no oaf, Alec."

"I'm just checking. Mischa's a tough cookie, but she deserves that much."

"You don't have to lecture me about what she deserves, my friend. I know it damn well. Why do you think I'm taking off like this?" He stopped, ran a hand through his hair. "Fuck. I'm sorry. I'm being an ass."

"You are. But I can let it go. Call me when you get back. When you're in a better mood. Or when you're in a worse mood. If you need to talk."

"I will. Thanks, Alec."

"Any time."

They hung up, and Connor stared out the window at the planes gliding down the tarmac, the sun reflecting off the tiny port windows.

This woman had really shaken him up. Shaken him to the core.

He felt like a damn coward, running like this. He *was* a damn coward. But it would be better this way. He needed time, some distance, to get his head together. To forget the sleek, pale polish that was her bare skin. The generous curve of her breast in his hand. The blue of her eyes . . . The way that blue had pierced him right through to the heart when they'd filled with tears.

He shook his head.

Leaving for a while was best. He'd cool off. Regain the control he'd always counted on, and which Mischa had, bit by bit, chipped away at. He couldn't stay in San Jose forever. A few days was all he'd need. He'd be fine. Just fine.

Why, then, had it pained him to leave her? To walk out the door knowing he was going to get on a plane as fast as he could? Why did it hurt to know the only way to continue with her was to shut down the part of himself that felt so fucking amazing because of *her*?

He massaged his chest, as if he could rub away the ache there.

He cared for the girl. That was it. Wasn't it? Caring for her didn't mean . . . anything else. It didn't *have* to. He simply had to get back in control of his ranging emotions.

Control was key, he reminded himself.

He had a feeling that phrase was going to be a necessary mantra in his foreseeable future.

It was Thursday evening and Mischa was in a cab on her way to Kara and Dante's place on the waterfront, just south of where Dylan lived, to go over wedding plans.

It had been a seemingly endless day alone in Dylan's apartment. She and Connor had slept until almost ten, then he'd gotten up and left in a rush, telling her he'd forgotten he was going out of town that afternoon for a few days on business. He'd apologized, asked her over and over if she would be okay. She'd assured him she would be, of course. But she wasn't certain that was true.

She'd holed up in bed, watching movies while she worked on some drawings, her sketchpad in her lap, napping on and off until it was time to get ready to leave. Which was totally unlike her. It was a rare day that went by when she wasn't working. At the shop. Drawing. Writing. Creating new business plans. Hibernating had felt strange, but necessary. She didn't understand it. It surprised her that she'd given herself over to it. And now being out in the world felt a little like some sort of culture shock.

She was still trying to tell herself that everything was fine—that Connor just had to work—when the cab arrived at Kara and Dante's building, a soaring structure seemingly made of glass overlooking Elliott Bay. She paid the driver, got out and took the elevator to the twenty-second floor, found their apartment and knocked. Kara opened the door, a smile on her face. Her long, light brown hair was pulled back into a ponytail, a pair of reading glasses pushed up onto her head.

"Mischa, come on in." Kara stepped back to let her through the door. "Let me get your coat."

Mischa looked around the loft apartment as she slid her trench coat off and handed it to Kara. "Wow. This place is amazing."

"I still can't believe I live here, sometimes." Kara was grinning. "God, sorry. I don't mean to sound snooty."

"You're not, don't be silly," Mischa assured her, giving her arm a squeeze.

"She *is* silly," Dylan called out as she came in from the kitchen area. "Silly in love."

"You're the one getting married, Dylan. You're in no position to tease *me* about being in love," Kara answered.

"Excellent point." Dylan smiled.

Mischa just shook her head, turning to explore the art on the living room walls. To get away from all this . . . happiness, for a moment.

"This is some great photography," she said, gesturing to a grouping of architectural prints on one wall over the sleek cream-colored sofa piled with brocade pillows.

"Thanks," Kara answered. "I've been collecting for a few years. By the way, are you guys okay with eating as soon as Lucie gets here? I'm starving. Mischa, we ordered Chinese. Dylan said you liked curries, so we got some Singapore street noodles for you. And . . . too much of everything. I hope you're hungry."

"A little," Mischa answered, although that wasn't quite true. She'd hardly been able to eat all day, drinking tea and nibbling on toast. Trying not to question why Connor had somehow overlooked the fact that he was going to have to leave town today until they woke up this morning. Until the day after they'd had some of the best sex of her life.

It was more than great sex. It was soul-baring, gut-wrenching conversation about things she'd only ever confided with Dylan.

The door buzzed and Kara let Lucie in. The petite blonde gave everyone a hug, including Mischa. She had a sweetness about her; Mischa had liked her on sight when they'd met at the engagement party.

Where she'd met Connor.

Why did every thought circle back around to Connor?

"The food's already out. Let's eat," Dylan said, leading them all into the dining area at one end of the loft apartment. White take-out boxes were lined up along the center of the enormous table that looked as if it was made of reclaimed wood. Italian dishware in looping patterns of blue, terra cotta and yellow were set at four places.

They all picked a place and sat while Kara poured water into tall glasses from a pitcher.

"I have Tsingtao beer, too, in honor of our Chinese cuisine, or sake, if anyone wants it. Or I can make tea."

"I think I need some alcohol to get through this," Dylan said with a small sigh.

"Don't worry," Lucie assured her, "we'll be fine. All that's left to figure out is the music and the menu. Have you guys decided if you're writing your own vows?"

Dylan groaned, pushing her abundant red curls from her face with both hands. "I'd forgotten about the vows."

"Luckily I have my books with me."

"Books?" Mischa asked.

Lucie twisted to pull several paperbacks from the large tote bag she'd hung on the back of her chair, making a small pile on the table. "I have a few books with wedding ceremonies and readings. I got them when I started making wedding cakes. Weddings can be overwhelming—people are always forgetting some small detail."

"Ah, don't say that," Dylan said. "Kara, I think I need that beer."

"Coming right up. Lucie? Mischa?"

"A beer sounds just about perfect," Mischa answered.

"Beer is good," Lucie said. "Let me help."

Kara went to the kitchen and Lucie followed her to help carry the drinks back.

Dylan leaned over and asked quietly, "You okay?"

Mischa flipped the linen napkin into her lap, fiddled with the edge of it. "Fine."

"Don't make me fight you for it, Misch. They'll only be gone a minute."

Mischa bit her lip. "A minute isn't long enough to talk about it."

"Okay. Why don't we hang out at my place after and we can talk before I head back to Alec's?"

Mischa nodded as Kara and Lucie came back into the room, their hands full of beer bottles.

"That would be great. If you don't mind."

"Of course not." Dylan gave her hand a quick squeeze under the table.

The evening was a long one, with detailed discussion about the pros and cons of hiring a band or a DJ. Kara argued for the DJ, Lucie argued for a live band, and Mischa was somewhere in between. Dylan finally settled on a string quartet for the ceremony and a band who specialized in big band–era swing for the reception. The issue of writing their own vows was left for another day. Still, it was after eleven when they all decided they'd done enough, and Dylan and Mischa said their good-byes.

Dylan was mostly quiet as she drove them back to her apartment. The stereo was playing, and she chatted about wedding details as she navigated the now-rainy streets. She parked and they got out, running through the rain to the building. Inside the apartment they got out of their wet coats and Dylan moved automatically into the kitchen to make tea.

"So, talk to me, Misch," she said, pouring hot water into a pair of mugs and handing one to Mischa, who was sitting at the counter.

She shrugged. Now that it was time to hash it out she didn't know where to begin.

"Connor left town today."

"Did he?"

Dylan was trying to look as if this didn't concern her, but Mischa could see it did.

"Alec didn't know about this, either?"

"I don't think so. He told me he was going to ask him to have dinner with him and Dante while we monopolized the apartment tonight. He didn't tell you in advance that he was leaving town?"

"He said he forgot until this morning. Is that . . . Do you think that's bad? I mean, not bad that he forgot, but . . . yeah, bad that he forgot to say anything about it sooner?"

Dylan blew on her tea for several moments. "You know, Alec did some crazy stuff when we were first together."

"We aren't 'together,' exactly," Mischa protested. "We've been seeing each other for a week. Almost every night, but still . . . We live in different cities. And when was the last time you saw me in anything long term?"

"I never have. But that doesn't mean—"

"Yes, it does." Mischa stood, crossed her arms over her chest, turning away from Dylan to move into the kitchen. She stopped at the sink, leaned against the counter, gazed through the sheer curtains at the night sky. The moon was visible between the clouds, casting a dull silver glow.

"Okay," Dylan said slowly from behind her. "Then why are you so upset?"

Mischa exhaled on a short, sharp breath. "Because I'm an idiot."

"Misch . . ."

She dropped her arms to her sides and turned around. "No, I am. Somewhere—and I have no idea how this got there—I seem to be thinking that Connor owes me something. Some explanation, when in fact, he doesn't. He doesn't owe me a damn thing. He can do whatever he wants, go anywhere he wants. It's not as if he has to ask my permission. He was perfectly capable of making those decisions all on his own before I came along. So was I."

"And?" Dylan prompted, one auburn brow arched.

Mischa's shoulders slumped. "And now I don't like that he didn't give me a heads-up about this trip. It seems . . . rude after we've been sleeping together all week."

Dylan grinned at her. "So, how is it?"

"It's fucking amazing," Mischa answered without much enthusiasm. "That's all it is, though. Incredible sex."

"Are you guys talking at all, in between the amazing sex?"

"Sure we are. About all sorts of things."

"Like what?" Dylan asked.

"Like . . . everything. My business, family stuff."

"Really?"

"Why are you arching your eyebrow at me again?" Mischa asked, crossing her arms over her chest once more.

"Because we knew each other for a good year before you said anything to me about your family."

"Maybe that was . . . good practice for me."

"Maybe."

"Okay. I don't mean to bullshit you, Dylan. This is just hard for me to face, never mind admit to someone else."

"What are you admitting to, exactly?"

She pushed her hair from her face. "I've told him about Evie. About how bad it was living with her as a kid. About how fucked up she was, how it affected me. I still can't believe I told him."

"So, you really went into detail?"

"Well, yes and no. I've told him a bit. I didn't go into all the stuff like . . . Raine and me going hungry before I was old enough to get into her wallet and walk to the store by myself. I didn't tell him how she'd leave us alone for days at a time. Not the really ugly stuff. But enough that he has some idea . . ."

"I'm so sorry, honey."

Mischa shook her head, shook the mist from her eyes. "It's okay. I'm a big girl now. I've learned to deal with it. I learned years ago. Learned how to buy groceries, cook, keep Evie from wasting away during her post-relationship meltdowns. I made my way through school on my own, saw to it that Raine did, too. And we've both done damn well. You'd never even know where I came from, would you?"

"Misch, calm down, sweetie. It's okay."

"God. I'm sorry. I'm . . . a little bit of a mess today, I guess." She paused, rubbed her arms with both hands. "I don't know why being with Connor is bringing up all this old history. Maybe it's the BDSM play."

"It can open you up."

"It sure as hell has done that to me. But I'm trying to just roll with it. And not doing the greatest job with that." Mischa blew out a long breath. Dylan sipped her tea, waiting. Finally Mischa came back to the counter and sat on a stool, lifting her mug to drink some of the warm, soothing tea. "Dylan? Do you honestly think this means anything?"

"Tell me what you're referring to when you say 'this.'"

"I mean that it bothers me that Connor left town so suddenly. Because if it had been any other guy I'd probably be too busy with my own life to notice. I like it that way. And I *don't* like that . . . I suddenly feel I have too much time on my hands, even though I'm here helping with the wedding and putting together a new shop with Greyson. I don't know. Maybe time is an issue. Maybe I'm having too much time with *him*. And do you think there's more to his sudden trip than that he forgot to tell me? We had plans for tomorrow night and now I don't even know if that's happening."

She blew out another breath. She really was losing it.

"I don't know about him, Misch. Men are still largely a mystery to me. I barely have Alec figured out, although a lot more than he'd like to admit. But *you* I know. And I'd say it does mean something that Connor has so much of your attention. It's definitely unusual for you."

"I should stop seeing him." Mischa brooded into her tea.

"Do you think so?"

"What else can I do?"

"Maybe just relax and enjoy him while you're here."

"If he still wants to see me when he gets back."

"He'll want to see you," Dylan said, her tone certain.

"I don't know . . ."

"Come on, what man wouldn't? You can have your pick of men, and you know it."

Mischa tried to smile, but in her head was the disconcerting thought that maybe the guy who might *not* want her was the one she *did* want. Really want. For the first time in her life.

Her cell phone brought her out of sleep three nights later. She glanced at the clock as she grabbed for the phone on the nightstand. One a.m. Who could possibly be calling her? She answered without trying to open her eyes enough to peer at the screen.

"Hello?"

"Mischa, it's me. Connor. I know it's late."

Her heart skipped a beat, her brain shifting into high gear. *Connor.*

"It's okay. I haven't been asleep long." That was a lie. It wasn't okay. Not that he'd woken her. But the whole damn thing wasn't okay at the moment. "Where are you? Are you back in town?"

"I'm still down in San Jose. I'm coming back tomorrow. Look, I'm sorry I took off without some explanation."

"I thought you went there to work."

"I did." He paused, and she could hear him breathing on the other end of the line. "But I also came here to get away."

"Well, that's encouraging."

"I don't blame you for being angry."

"I'm not angry. I'm just . . . annoyed."

How could she admit it pissed her off that he hadn't so much as called? Texted her? She had no claim to him. No right to protest, other than about him flaking out after asking her out for Friday night, which she didn't even want to bring up right now. She didn't want him to know what a *girl* she was being. She didn't want to admit to herself how much it reminded her of how Evie would angst over men, or of how badly that had always ended for her mother.

She *knew* better. Didn't she? Yet here she was mooning over some guy she'd just met.

He's not just some guy. He hasn't been from the first moment.
Stop it.

"All right," he said quietly. "I'll take that."

She sighed, sat up in the bed, turning on the lamp on the nightstand. She was not going to let this guy—any guy—crush her like her mother had allowed too many men to do to her. "So, why are you calling me now?"

"To apologize. To talk."

"Okay. Talk."

There was a long silence on the other end, then she heard the soft exhalation of his breath. "You have every right to be sharp with me."

She shook her head as though he could see her. "No. I don't. I'm sorry, Connor."

"There's no need. I deserve it. I know it. After the other night the least I should have done was . . . Hell, I have no idea what I should have done. Mischa, this is new ground for me."

"What is?"

"Giving a shit about what a woman I'm seeing thinks, to be honest. I know that sounds crass, but that's where I've been in regards to women for a long time. Years."

Her heart beat a small, sharp staccato in her chest. What was he saying, exactly?

"I've been in the same place about men, when it comes to any personal relationship, if you even want to call it that. Probably always."

"So this is equally weird for you, if we're on the same page at all."

It was her turn to pause. She felt as if she were balanced on her toes on the edge of a cliff. Was she ready to dive off? To take that risk? But maybe if they weren't actually asking each other for anything but that acknowledgment, the risk wasn't really that high. Maybe they just had to say it so they could be clear with each other. Get it out of their systems.

The coiled muscles in her neck and shoulders loosened a bit.

"Mischa, did I lose you?"

"I was just thinking. And . . . we are on the same page."

"Good to know."

She could almost hear him smiling on the other end.

"So what now?" she asked.

"Now we either agree to go our separate ways before this gets any more complicated." There was a pause in which she could feel her pulse beating at her temples. "Or we agree to keep seeing each other and not allow it to."

"Okay."

"Okay what? Because, Mischa, I would really prefer the latter. That's what I figured out, being away for a few days." Another pause, longer this time. "I missed you."

Her heart tripped. Had he really said that to her? God, she missed him, too. But she didn't know how to tell him that. Didn't know how to take that high a dive.

"I came to pretty much the same conclusion," she said, side-stepping the issue a bit. "I'd like to see you again, too. Why don't you let me know when you're back in Seattle?"

"I will. What are your plans tomorrow?"

"I'm going to the caterer with Dylan and Lucie to finalize menu options, then Greyson and I are meeting with an attorney."

"When will you be done?"

"Probably by five."

"I'll pick you up at seven."

There it was, that air of absolute authority she loved, responded to. Even now her body was surging with need, simply hearing his voice. His decisiveness.

"Where are we going?" she asked, twisting a lock of hair around her finger.

"Dinner. Then back to my place."

"That sounds good. I'll see you tomorrow night, then."

They hung up, and she found herself smiling.

Don't be an idiot.

Not the first time she'd told herself that since meeting Connor Galloway. It probably wouldn't be the last. But she liked where they were, where this conversation had led them.

She slid back down under the covers, burrowing beneath the blankets, then reached to turn out the light. But she couldn't get sleepy again. She was too worked up after Connor's call. Which was not good, considering the long day she had planned tomorrow. But the truth was, her body was as active as her mind. Hearing his voice, thinking about seeing him, had kicked the low simmer that had been burning in her since the moment they'd met into a sizzling fire. The heat flowed through her veins, her sex, making her ache.

Need him.

She groaned. Tomorrow night would not be soon enough.

And she would never get to sleep with desire coursing through her as if he'd kissed her, touched her, rather than simply talked to her on the phone. It was that voice. So damn sexy, with that soft Irish brogue, deep and rumbling. There was something sexy in the way he'd sounded a little uncertain at the beginning of the conversation. Even more at the end, when he'd slipped so seamlessly back to that natural tone of authority. It immediately reminded her of the way he held her down when they were having sex. The rough way he handled her . . .

She ran her hands over her stomach, cupped her breasts, brushed her nipples with her thumbs. They were hard. She pinched them and a lovely jolt of need arched through her. She did it again, harder this time, really making it hurt, and her pussy went wet all at once, just from the pain. That, and the image in her head of Connor doing this very thing to her with his big, clever hands.

She sighed, let one hand wander lower, slip between her thighs. She was soaked already. Wanting like crazy. Wanting more than her mere hand could do.

She rolled onto her side and flipped open her train case, pulled out her largest vibrator, a flesh-colored phallus made of pseudo-skin. It was huge, lifelike, except that it carried a powerful vibration. And it was exactly what she needed.

It took her a few moments to find an outlet behind the nightstand to plug it in—vibrators this powerful were never cordless—but finally she had it. She stripped her nightgown over her head before she lay back on the bed, the big vibe between her spread thighs.

She closed her eyes, teased herself with images of Connor: his big hands, his bare body rippling with muscle, his lush mouth. She could remember exactly the way he tasted. The touch of his hands on her flesh. The lovely sting of his palm as he spanked her.

Her body was heating as she played the images like a movie in her mind. Her pussy was pulsing with need, yet she didn't touch herself yet. She wanted to draw it out, the way Connor did, making her wait.

She spread her thighs wider, pictured his big, beautiful cock, the skin a golden brown, the head slightly darker, swollen, glistening with a pearly drop of pre-come.

"Fuck me, Connor," she whispered into the dark as she finally let herself switch the vibrator on.

She touched the lips of her aching sex lightly, shivered in response. She did it again, still teasing herself. She thought of the bottle of lube in her train case, but she didn't need it tonight. She was plenty wet. She pulled her knees up to her chest, spreading herself open, and slipped the tip of the big vibe inside.

"Ah . . ."

Connor's cock was every bit as big as her favorite toy. Bigger, maybe. She pushed it in deeper, her hungry sex taking it easily. She was shaking all over, pleasure trembling through her in long waves. And Connor's face in her mind, held over her as he slipped his cock inside her.

"Oh yes."

She pulled the vibe out a little, drove it hard inside her, imagined Connor doing the same as pleasure made her body clench with the first edge of orgasm already.

"Come on, Connor," she murmured. "Fuck me hard."

She pumped her hips, taking the vibrator deep, her pussy clenching around it. She was fucking the toy in sharp thrusts of her hips, grinding on it. Beginning to come.

"Connor . . . fuck me . . . just fuck me . . . yes!"

Her climax hit her hard enough to blind her, to make her yell his name.

"Connor!"

Still she pumped the huge vibe into her pussy, needing more. *Not enough . . .*

It wouldn't be. Only Connor himself would be enough.

Finally she stopped. Pleasure still shimmered deep in her body. Need was just as deep, just as powerful a force. Need for *him*.

Connor.

She was trying to catch her breath as she pulled the big phallus from her body, switched it off. Her body was still burning, still hungry for satisfaction. But she knew she could fuck herself with her vibrator all night long and never feel the satisfaction she craved. That was something only Connor could supply. His touch. His command. His presence.

She had to wonder if she would ever be truly satisfied, or if he'd ruined her forever, somehow.

Either way, she would see him tomorrow night. And that was really all that mattered right now.

At five minutes to seven Connor pulled up across from Dylan's building. He looked up, found the lights on in the apartment, knew Mischa waited for him up there. He could get hard just thinking about her. Seeing her, imagining all the dirty things he would do to her back at his place after dinner.

"Down boy," he muttered to his rising cock, pressing a hand over the crotch of his jeans. It didn't help much.

He swore under his breath as he got out of the car, crossed the street, rang the buzzer. She didn't say anything over the intercom, just buzzed him into the building.

He leaned against the wall of the elevator as it carried him to her floor.

Have to see the girl. Have to get my hands on her.

It had been too damn long.

Four days?

But he didn't have time to question himself. The elevator opened and he was in front of her door. He knocked. She opened it looking like every fantasy he'd had of her since he'd left town. Except that she had too much clothing on.

But he liked it. A wrap dress in a black and red print that skimmed her curves, showing plenty of cleavage. The high black heels he loved seeing on her, like a little touch of fetish. And fucking fishnet stockings.

She was smiling at him with that lush red mouth of hers.

"Aren't you going to say hi?" she asked, laughing a little.

He stepped in, kicking the door shut behind him.

"No."

He made a grab for her, yanked her in close, turning her so her back was to the door as he pushed her up against it. Then his mouth was on hers and he was kissing her, his tongue driving inside. She tasted of toothpaste and flowers. Which didn't make sense. He didn't care. He breathed her in, drank in her hot, wet tongue. Crushed her breasts beneath his palms, feeling the hard swell of her nipples through her dress, her bra.

He stopped kissing her only so he could rake his tongue along the slender column of her throat, needing to taste her.

"This is a hell of a hello," she gasped as he pushed her dress aside, reached into her bra and pulled her flesh free.

He bent to take her dark red nipple in between his lips, licking, then sucking, then biting hard.

"Ah, that's good, Connor . . ."

Her hands were on either side of his face, holding his head to her. His were snaking up under her dress, lifting the hem as he slipped up her thighs, found that the stockings were held in place by a garter belt. There was nothing else under there. He would have smiled if his mouth hadn't been filled with her sweet, fragrant flesh, the swollen tip of her nipple. He kept sucking on it as he cupped her ass with one hand, kneading, pinching. The other he slipped right into the wet folds of her pussy.

He began to work her right away, thrusting two fingers inside her, pressing on her clit with the heel of his hand.

"Fuck, Connor."

Yes, fuck her . . .

His cock was hard as steel. He let her ass go long enough to unzip his jeans. To pull his cock out and sheath it with a condom from his coat pocket, then he impatiently fought his way out of his coat and dropped it to the floor. Then he was on her. He picked her up and she wrapped her legs around his waist even as he plowed into her body. Her pussy enveloped him, hot, wet flesh tight around his cock.

"Ah, Christ, Mischa. This is what I needed. To fuck you. Just. Like. This."

Each word was punctuated with a sharp thrust of his hips as he drove into her, pressing her back hard against the door. Pleasure was the only thing counteracting the hammering in his chest. The only thing to feed the pulsing beat in his cock. The only way he could be a part of her.

She was moaning, her hands clasped behind his neck. He held on to her ass and plunged, again and again, while she arched her hips into him. While she came, her pussy squeezing him like some hot, silken fist around his cock. Then he was coming, shouting, fucking her as hard as he ever had. Needing it to be this hard, this primal.

His legs were shaking, and he had to pull out, to ease her onto her feet. Her cheeks were flushed, her gorgeous tit still out of her dress, the nipple enticingly red. He ran a fingertip over it, felt her answering shiver. When he looked back to her face, her eyes were a brilliant blue, glossy with her recent orgasm.

She was breathing hard. So was he.

"Well," she said after a minute. "Welcome home."

It did feel like being home, he realized. Being there with her. Being inside her body.

Can't think like that.

He couldn't seem to stop.

I am in big trouble.

He wasn't going to think about that, either. Instead, he smiled at her. "Ready to go to dinner?"

She laughed. "I might need a quick whore's bath. And to change my panties. If I were wearing any."

"Bathe away. No panties," he told her. Commanded her.

She gave him a mock salute before she went off to the bathroom. But he didn't mind her being a little sassy. He was back in the driver's seat, which was exactly where he needed to be. And where he intended to stay.

ten

Mischa loved the little downtown Italian place on sight—one of those old-school restaurants with big red vinyl booths and checkered tablecloths. The kind of small restaurant only the locals would know about. She was sure the food would be wonderful.

"They make one hell of a *puttanesca* here," he told her as they slid into the booth.

"The whore's spaghetti?" she asked, grinning.

"Well, you did take a *courtesan's* bath before leaving the apartment." He gave her a wink, his brogue heavy. "I thought it only fit."

She laughed, not for the first time that evening. "*Puttanesca* it is, then."

He ordered the wine without consulting her, which she had to admit she rather liked, and the waiter brought it quickly.

She'd noticed before how almost everyone sort of jumped for him. She didn't think it was his size, although that could be in-

timidating. She figured it was his natural air of authority, something people probably responded to without knowing they were
doing it. She sure as hell did. Even when she was fighting it.
Which she wasn't doing tonight. It felt good.

She felt good. Still buzzing from the fast, hard fuck they'd had
up against the door the moment he'd arrived. And maybe simply
because he was *there*.

The wine arrived, a California Zinfandel, and Connor had the
waiter pour for them. He handed her a glass and raised his.

"Cheers," he said, clinking his glass with hers.

"What are we toasting to?"

"I'm Irish. We're good toasting to the drink."

"Come on, Connor. Surely you can be more creative than
that," she teased.

"Well then, you mouthy little minx, how about we toast to
the absolutely spectacular fuck we just had, and to more later on.
With some spanking thrown in for good measure. My hands are
itching to feel your fine, sweet ass."

It wasn't what she'd been expecting him to say. She didn't
know what she *had* expected. But it delighted her, making her
grin widen.

"You are a vulgar man, Connor Galloway."

He raised a brow. "But you like that about me."

"I do."

They clinked glasses, drank.

"How was the caterer?" he asked.

"It was good. We managed to pick a menu. Everything seems
to be on track. Although Dylan and I are both grateful as hell for
Lucie. She's the only one of us who seems to know anything about
this wedding stuff."

"And your other meeting?" He sipped his wine, the glass looking ridiculously small in his big hand.

"That was good, too. Productive. Greyson and I met with an attorney and went over the paperwork to set up the partnership, and had him look over the lease before we sign it. I'm getting excited about opening another shop, although it's going to be a huge headache to get it started. There's all the hiring, the build-out, ordering chairs and supplies. Thank God I have a partner this time; that's going to make it only half my own headache, anyway. We stopped and had some lunch and brainstormed shop names, but haven't come up with anything solid yet."

"Lunch, eh?" He sat back in the booth, crossing his arms. "Then what?"

"Then we opened a bank account for the new shop."

"A joint account?"

"Well, we both have to be able to sign on it, of course. Greyson will be the one who's here the most to oversee construction and . . . Why are you looking at me like that?"

"Like what?"

"As if you're pissed off about something."

"Do I?"

She leaned in closer, examining his darkening features. Oh yeah, he looked annoyed as hell. Trying to cover it up and not doing a very good job of it.

"You want to know if we've slept together, don't you?" Why was a part of her pleased about it?

He paused, unfolded his arms, as if he'd just become aware of his defensive posture. "I've no right to ask."

"No. But I'll tell you, anyway. Nothing has ever happened between us. If it had I wouldn't be going into business with him. I don't think business and pleasure mix well. Once you sleep with someone the dynamic between you changes."

"In what way? I'm not questioning the concept; I'm wondering what your thoughts on it are."

"You can have a one-nighter with someone and if you're never going to see that person again, then that night is what it is—good, bad, whatever. But if you're going to see each other again, well, it had at least better be good."

"Excellent point, that."

"If that person is a friend," she went on, "then you *will* see them again, and the friendship will forever have that extra weight of the sex. Which can be really awful if the sex didn't go so well."

"Are you insinuating that sex with Greyson wouldn't go well?" he asked, a grin on his face, one dark brow quirked over his green eyes.

She laughed. "No, not at all. Although I can see you'd *love* for me to say so. What I'm saying is, if you're friends, then you're taking a risk with that friendship. And if it does go well, and you continue to see someone, friend or someone you've just met . . ." She paused, pushed her hair from her face. "Okay, look at us, for example. We've been seeing each other, sleeping together, for almost two weeks. But it's been a very condensed less than two weeks. Maybe because we both know my time here is limited."

"And also because of the intensity of the power play dynamic."

"Yes," she agreed with a nod, "everything is more intense because of that. And now we've ended up . . . here. Having to wade through this connection thing. If we had met at Dylan and Alec's engagement party, flirted a little, but never taken it that one step further, things would be completely different between us at, say, their wedding, than it will be now."

He moved in closer, lowered his voice. "Yeah, because if we hadn't already slept together I'd probably have to take you into some back room during the wedding and fuck your brains out."

She laughed. "Well, there is that."

He gave a small nod of his chin, his eyes sparkling. "I may still have to."

"That's . . . a possibility. But does what I'm saying make sense to you?"

"It does. I agree with all of it. But let me ask you what conclusion you've come to?"

She took a few moments to collect her thoughts, her fingers toying with her wineglass. "The fact that you felt you had to go away for a while, the fact that we've had to have a sort of revealing conversation, come to some agreement about how we do things from here, proves my point. If this were Greyson and I having this conversation, it could make being in business together a little . . . loaded, as I said earlier. Definitely more complicated."

"Are you saying you can't have sex with someone without becoming attached?"

"I'm saying that sometimes we do, despite ourselves. Even if it's in some small way that we ultimately have a handle on. Even then, at that point we have to be careful . . ."

She stopped, bit her lip. She'd said too much. She was either talking in circles now, or she was about to take the discussion one step too far in a direction she didn't want to go in.

Except that some small part of her did.

"You're not saying much," she said more defensively than she'd meant to.

"Yeah. Well. I'm thinking about everything you've said."

She wanted to prompt him to tell her what he was thinking. Instead she said, "Anyway . . . I hope this is the last of the Greyson inquisition?"

"Ha. Hardly an inquisition, my girl. I'd do that with the aid of about thirty feet of chain and some hot wax, at the very least."

Her pulse heated and she leaned further into him, batted her lashes for good measure. "I might like that," she said, glad for the shift in conversation.

"You would, I promise you. I'll have to get you back to the club sometime soon."

"I'd like that, too."

Their food arrived, a fragrant pasta with chunky tomatoes and capers tossed in olive oil. She caught the slight scent of anchovies as she brought the fork to her mouth and tasted.

"Well?" he asked.

She chewed for a moment, savoring the flavors. "Light and fresh and perfect."

He nodded, self-satisfaction in his expression. Which was one he wore often. It was cocky, no denying it. But something about him . . . even when he was being cocky, it was as though he *deserved* to be, and she never found it obnoxious. Only a man like Connor—that truly self-assured, that naturally powerful—could get away with it.

They finished dinner, relaxed, talking about movies and art, the places they'd each traveled to, the places they'd still like to go. Japan was at the top of the list for them both. Mischa had always wanted to go to watch the Japanese masters tattoo.

"Which reminds me," she said, "we have to finish your tattoo. How is it healing?"

"Doing fine, I think. Itches like mad, of course."

"When do you want me to work on it?"

He shrugged. "Whenever you're ready."

"Tomorrow? No, tomorrow I have a dress fitting. And on Wednesday Dylan and I are going to a day spa, then having dinner with the girls. What about Thursday? Greyson and I are meeting with a contractor he knows about the build-out on the new shop, but I'm free later on. Or do you have work to do?"

"My work is by contract. I'm not currently on a big project. Thursday it is."

She liked that they were making plans, even if it was to finish his tattoo. Even if it was only three days ahead. There was something nice about it—not leaving things totally open-ended, which was how she usually operated. She was normally too busy to tie herself down to plans with a man. And frankly, she hadn't met anyone she wanted to spend this much time with.

She picked up her glass, swallowed against the strange lump forming in her throat.

It doesn't mean anything.

So they liked each other? So what?

So, the point at which they decided to cut this thing off, whenever it was, was going to be hard. Which was exactly the sort of thing staying busy, working so hard, had always kept her safe from.

She took a good, long gulp of her wine, nodded when Connor offered to refill her glass.

She was liking him more and more. Enjoying their conversation, their easy banter, as much as she did the sex. Well, almost as much. Because the sex was frankly off-the-charts mind-blowing.

If she could just stay focused on that, everything would be okay.

After dinner they got into Connor's Hummer and he drove back to his place. They chatted during the drive, while they made their way up the stairs. The evening had seemed to be going at a more relaxed pace, maybe because they'd sort of rubbed one off before dinner. But now that they were about to be alone she couldn't get to him soon enough, her body burning with need the moment he shut the door behind him.

He took her coat from her just inside the door, held it in his hand as he took off his own.

He gave a small nod.

"Strip."

"What?" She laughed a little, totally taken by surprise after their casual evening together.

He remained silent, watching her, his green and gold eyes gleaming in the dim light of the one lamp burning in the living room. She could tell by his expression that casual time was over. That the mood had shifted and they were suddenly in the roles of dominant and submissive. And something in her responded to it as easily as if he'd placed his hand behind her neck, exerting that gentle pressure, as he so often did.

She licked her lips, kept her gaze on his and untied her wrap dress, let it fall to the floor. She paused, waiting for some cue. All she got was another brief nod of his sculpted chin. She wanted to make some little joke. She wanted to make him fight her for it. But she knew damn well she wasn't going to do either of those things. She was soaking, aching, already.

She brought her hands to her breasts, smoothing her fingertips over the red lace of her bra before undoing the clasp in the front. She pulled off the bra, reveling in the weight of her freed breasts, the way the cool air touched her nipples, making them go hard instantly. She held the bra out, let it dangle from her fingers before dropping it next to her dress on the floor.

She was about to remove the red lace garter belt that held up her black fishnets, but Connor put a hand on hers, stilling her.

"Leave those. And the shoes. Come with me."

He turned, and she followed him, her heels clicking on the wood floor. He paused to drop their coats on the sofa, then he continued toward the bedroom. He didn't turn around for one moment, simply assuming she would follow. She did, of course. There was no question about it, even though she had yet to conquer that small part of her that still thought she *should* question it:

his absolute command of her once they were in role. But most of her was ready to simply turn herself over to him. Eager to.

Once there he gestured to her to stand at the foot of his bed, facing him. He hadn't touched her yet, which was making her shiver with need. The need to feel his hands on her skin. For him to come closer.

He was watching her in that way he had. His eyes were burning with gold and heat and something else she didn't understand. Intriguing. Yet she couldn't get her mind to work enough to figure it out.

"Mischa," he said, his tone low, "tonight is going to be about pinching. The sensation is different from any other, yes?"

"Yes."

Her breath was catching in her throat already, heat melting between her thighs.

"Have you ever played with clothespins?" he asked, stepping back to the tall dresser behind him. Without taking his eyes from her, he reached for a bag made of red velvet sitting on top of the dresser. Her glance flicked to it, then quickly back to him. She knew he didn't want her to look away, to stay focused on him.

There was something insanely sexual about the fact that a man of his sheer size and strength, a man with his thoroughly dominant attitude, would possess an item like a red velvet bag. Not that he wasn't a sensualist. But it seemed in direct opposition to who he was sexually. Raw. Primal.

She licked her lips. "I've seen it done. I haven't done it myself," she answered.

"And what about these?" he asked, pulling a pair of nipple clamps from the bag, a long chain dangling between them. They were tipped in black rubber, she could see, although beneath that soft rubber was, she knew, a row of evil little teeth.

She swallowed. "I've only used them on others. When I was topping."

"Why?"

"I don't like . . . the idea of them. They seem like such a submissive thing to me."

"And what are you doing, standing here mostly naked at my command, if not submitting to me?"

Her fingers curled into fists at her sides. She felt her eyes blazing. "I am submitting to you. But I don't like the idea of the damn clamps."

He grinned at her, which surprised her. "We'll have to use them tonight, then, won't we?"

"Connor . . ."

But she didn't know what she wanted to say. She wanted to argue. Yet she didn't want to, at the same time.

"Tell me, Mischa. Are these a no for you? Or a maybe?"

"They're . . . a maybe," she said, keeping her gaze on his, feeling the fire in it. She would give in to him. But she could still let him know she wasn't happy about it.

He stepped closer, until she swore she could feel the heat emanating from his body, even though he was still a good foot away. He reached out, stroked his fingertip over her cheek, trailed it down the side of her neck.

He said, his voice soft, "Do you remember when I talked about pushing you on some of those maybes?"

She nodded.

"Say it, Mischa."

"I remember."

"This is one of those things. Particularly because you seem so pissed about it. We'll find a way to work through that. To work it out of you."

God, why was her body heating at that thought? Betray-
ing her. Her sex was going wet. And she realized only then that
she *wanted* to be pushed. That no one had ever done that with
her before. No one had dared. And certainly no one she'd ever
trusted.

Had she ever really trusted anyone?

No one but Connor. Not like this.

His finger had paused at her collarbone, but he moved in now,
using his whole hand to cup her breast, making her draw in a
breath as pleasure hit her, simmered in her blood.

"You have the most beautiful breasts I've ever seen," he murmured. "I can't wait to torture them. But we'll start with the pins."

He gave one nipple a tweak, resulting in the tiniest bit of
pain. But it was enough to excite her. To make her want to clench
her thighs to ease the ache between them. She clenched her jaw
instead.

"Don't move," he told her.

He opened the bag and she heard the sound of him spilling
the clothespins out on the bed. She was starting to shiver all over,
just a small trembling that was adrenaline, maybe. But also partly
the desire coursing through her at a dizzying pace.

He was standing behind her now, pressing his body against
hers, and it was all she could do not to press back against him, into
the firm, muscular planes against her back. The hard ridge of
his erection beneath his jeans that was at the small of her back.

One hand came around her waist, held her tight enough to
give her that sense of his absolute authority. His breath was warm
in her hair.

"I need to prepare you," he said quietly. "To make your body
ready to handle the pain. I would do it, regardless. But all through
dinner I was thinking of the feel of your wet slit. How the soft
lips of your cunt swell when you're excited. How they swell even

more when I touch them. When I put my hands on you. My mouth."

She flexed her fingers, her knees, wanting—needing—him to touch her.

"And when I was drinking my wine, I was remembering the way you taste, your sweet pussy. How fucking wet you get. It makes me a little crazy, I'm not ashamed to tell you—that you get so soaking wet for me."

She bit her lip, her entire body throbbing with need as he spoke.

He splayed his hand on her stomach, sliding it lower, inch by inch.

"Tell me, darlin'. Are you wet yet?"

"Yes," she whispered, her eyes closing.

"Shall I feel it for myself?"

"Yes," she said more loudly, spreading her legs wider for him.

"Ah, I love that you're so eager for me. Perfect, that you spread without me even having to ask."

She waited while he kept his hand poised at the edge of her lacy garter belt. Her clitoris pulsed.

Touch me . . .

"You want my hand on you," he said. "Don't you, sweetheart?"

"Yes . . ."

"You want me to fuck you with my fingers. Tell me."

She swallowed. "Yes. I want you to fuck me. With your hand. Any way you want to."

It was all she could do not to arch her hips as he slid his palm lower.

He waited. She drew in a breath.

"Say please, Mischa."

"Please," she breathed.

He brushed just the tip of her needy clit and she gasped.

He stopped.

Her pussy, her entire body, clenched. She shook her head, her hair sweeping her shoulders.

"What is it, Mischa?"

"Nothing." She bit her lip, squeezed her eyes tighter.

He feathered his fingertips over her tight clitoris again, and she moaned.

He stopped again.

"This is making you wetter, isn't it?"

"Yes, damn it," she muttered.

There was a low chuckle from him. "I know it is. Which is exactly why I'm doing it. When will you learn to trust me? To turn yourself over to me entirely? I'll take care of everything. I do everything with intention. Surely you've come to see that by now. You don't need to make any decisions here. This is the key in what we do together. It's all about trust. Now. Tell me please like you mean it."

Why were tears stinging behind her eyelids? But she did as he wanted. As *she* wanted. Strange that it was the same thing. "Connor, *please.*"

"Ah, that was nice, darlin' girl."

He slipped his fingers inside her, and she was panting immediately. He began to pump.

"You feel so damn good," he murmured against her ear. "Like silk. So fucking hot. I could throw you on the bed and fuck you until you scream."

"Yes . . ."

"But we have other games to play first."

He pulled his hand away and she stumbled. He caught her, his arm around her. She leaned against him, trying to catch her breath.

"I'm going to have you sit on the end of the bed," he said after a few moments.

She nodded.

He helped her sit down and stood in front of her.

"Open your eyes, Mischa."

She did. It was almost a shock to see him. His beautiful, rugged face. His lush mouth. Those penetrating eyes. She noticed the small, ragged scar beneath his eye, felt the pure masculinity of it.

"This is what I'm going to use on you," he said, holding up a handful of colored plastic clothespins. "They're going to hurt going on. They're going to hurt much worse coming off as the blood rushes back into the areas that have been deprived of circulation while the pins are on. Which will entertain me greatly. But you should also get an enormous rush of endorphins. Here we go."

He knelt in front of her and took one of her breasts in his big hand, kneading the flesh. It felt lovely, her nipple hardening. Then he used his fingers to pinch a bit of skin together at the underside of her breast and placed a pin there. The moment his fingers let go pain rushed through her.

"Oh!"

He smiled. "Yes, it's a surprise, isn't it? Breathe through it. You can do it. Inhale."

She did as he said, following his instructions as he took her through some breathing. The pain was intense. So was the pleasure as endorphins flooded her brain, her body.

When he put a second clothespin on her she remembered to breathe. It still hurt. And brought an even heavier surge of desire. She knew she was absolutely soaking wet. She was hyperaware of it. Of the feel of the fishnets pressed into her skin beneath her thighs. The garter belt tight around her hips. The high heels on her feet. Hyperaware of everything, including—or maybe most especially—Connor. His dark earth and rain scent. The rhythm of his breathing that caught a little at the same time hers did when he placed a pin on her. The heat of his hands as he pinched another fold of skin and put another clothespin on her.

When there were four or five—she'd lost count—he moved to the other breast. Pinched the underside of her breast in his fingers, clamped a pin on.

"Good?" he asked after she'd gasped, caught her breath.

"Yes. It's good."

He smiled once more. Then he leaned in and kissed her. His mouth was an unexpected shock of sweetness, then his tongue as he slipped inside. His hunger was another surprise as he absolutely devoured her mouth. And once more she felt a knot in her throat, tears that wanted to come. And unbelievable desire arcing between her thighs like electricity.

Need him . . .

He seemed to read her mind—not for the first time—as he slid a hand between her thighs and over her tight clit.

She moaned into his mouth. He kept kissing her, rubbing at her clit. Her hips arched into his touch. She thought she would come, kissed him harder, her breath coming in ragged pants.

He pulled away.

Desire was etched on his face, his mouth soft and loose. His eyes burned with golden fire in the green depths.

"What you do to me, girl," he said quietly. He pulled in a deep breath. She did the same. If her mind wasn't so muddled with desire and pain there would have been a dozen questions to ask him. She didn't know where to begin. Couldn't think now.

He blinked, ran a hand over his jaw. Reached behind her for another clothespin.

He put two more on her in quick succession, then touched the first one he'd attached to her aching flesh, pulled on it gently. Pain shivered through her. She breathed into it, her body bowing a little. Pleasure was quick to follow.

"Ah, I love the way you respond. But I'm going to have you take in a deep breath for me. And as I pull the first pin off, breathe it out. And keep your eyes on mine, darlin'."

She nodded, just a small tilt of her chin to let him know she understood. She took in a breath, held it in her lungs as he released the first pin.

Pain was a sharp lance, deep into her body.

"God!"

"Yes, breathe into it, Mischa. You can do it."

He wrapped his palm around the back of her neck, massaged it as she tried to inhale, tried to do as he said. But the pain was a terrible thing. Until the endorphins kicked in again and her head swam with pure pleasure. It leached into her system, fueling her body. Her sex gushed with it.

"Oh . . ." she moaned.

"Yes, it's good, isn't it? Ride it out."

She was dazed. Need and pain made her mind soar.

"I'm taking another one off," he told her.

She inhaled deeply, let it out as the pain broke over her like a crumbling wall, shards biting into her: skin and body and mind. And panted until she melted once more in a pool of unbelievable desire.

He did it again and again, and each time was a new rush of pain, blade sharp, seeming to go deeper than her skin. Each surge of pain was followed by a lovely release of the brain chemicals that made her feel nothing but pleasure, her body burning with it. She thought wildly that she might be able to come, simply from this heady mixture of extreme pain and extreme pleasure, and all of it having to do with Connor.

When the final pin came off, her body arched into his, and she didn't know whether she slipped off the bed or he pulled her off. But suddenly she was in his lap on the floor, and he was kissing her again, even as she rode out the last waves of pain. Her skin was on fire. Her pussy aching, soaking wet. Needing him.

He gathered her breasts into his hands, kneading the sore flesh, bringing a new rush of sensations. She pressed into him, drinking in his flavor, sucking his tongue into her mouth. Her hands were tearing blindly at his clothes. He pulled off his shirt, and her palms found the dense muscle of his chest, found his nipples and tugged on them, hard. He groaned. She did it again. One of his hands went to her hair, burrowed in, pulled her head back until she slipped from his lap and she was laid out on the floor.

He was on top of her, his thighs kicking hers apart, his jeans somehow gone. Then his cock, swollen, enormous, was at the entrance to her body, slipping in the wet folds. Her arms went around his wide back, trying to bring him closer.

"Come on, Connor," she begged.

"I can't . . . wait, damn it. Condom."

He reached to one side; she turned her head and saw him pull a condom from his jeans pocket. Was grateful that he was prepared; she couldn't have waited another second for him. She didn't have to. He sheathed himself, held her thighs with hard hands and slid into her.

"Ah, God, Connor."

His cock was huge, filling her, fucking her in deep, punishing strokes.

"Mischa . . ."

She looked up at his face, torn with pleasure. And once more she felt the tears brimming in her eyes. She didn't know why. Her body was loving this, the good, hard fucking. His command of her as his fingers dug into her inner thighs, holding her open and wanton for him. He was looking right at her. Seeing her tears, she knew. She was helpless to stop them. Even as his expression changed, his brows drawing together.

He stopped. Pulled her up into his arms.

"God damn it, girl," he muttered.

He gave her one final squeeze before turning her in his arms until she was on her hands and knees on the soft Persian rug, and he was poised over her, spreading the cheeks of her ass apart so he could take her from behind.

She wanted it, that little bit of anonymity that came with him fucking her from behind. She closed her eyes as he slid his cock into her waiting pussy once more.

Yes, just sink into the sensation. Into his command. Don't think of anything else.

Not even why the damn tears were coming, just from having sex with this man.

Soon enough it was easy to do that, to feel his big cock driving into her, bringing pleasure with it. He had one arm around her waist, his fingers twisting her nipple, drawing it out, making it long and hard as he thrust into her. His breath was at the back of her neck, then his mouth as he latched on to her flesh, sucking and biting.

"Come on, girl. Come again for me."

She knew she would. Pleasure was spiraling inside her, a tight knot that was unraveling, blossoming in her body, spreading outward as his cock hit her G-spot over and over.

"Do it for me now," he told her, his harsh tone leaving no room for argument. "Come, Mischa."

She did, crying out, shivering in his tight grasp, her hips arching back, into his body, taking him deep.

"Damn, girl. So fucking tight." He plowed into her, hard

enough to hurt. But she was still coming, sensation shimmering in her system. She didn't mind it, yearned for the pain. For the sense of being taken over.

"Fuck me harder," she ground out between ragged, panting breaths.

"Ah, Mischa, my girl . . ."

His hips slammed into her, his arm tightening around her waist.

Still she needed more. It wasn't enough.

"Come on, Connor."

"You want more?" he demanded.

"Yes. I need it. I need you to . . . *own* me."

She couldn't believe she'd said it. But it was true. She felt strange. As if she was poised on the edge of a great chasm, and only his roughness could hold her safe.

"Take in a breath," he growled in her ear, his breath hot.

She did as he told her.

His hand came up around her shoulder, closed around her throat. He held her there firmly. It was a moment or two before she realized she could barely breathe.

He thrust hard into her a few times, let her throat go, and she pulled in a gasping breath.

"Again," he told her.

She inhaled, his fingers tightened on her throat, and he fucked her hard as she exhaled, her breath a small trickle, before she inhaled, no more than a small, shallow breath.

She understood right away that she was in no danger. That he had it all under control.

Trust him.

Yes, completely. That was what this was about. She was in no real danger, even though the way he was temporarily cutting off her air felt a little scary. But after he did it once more, the fear dissolved in the absolute certainty of her trust in him, and in his absolute command.

"No more," he said, his hands going back to her waist as he rose up behind her. "Keep your head down, my girl."

He held on to her as he drove into her in sharp thrusts, harder and harder, hammering blows that made her surge back into him, wanting every inch of him.

In moments she was coming again, unexpectedly.

"Connor!"

"Yes . . . Mischa!"

He came with a roar, his fingers digging into her flesh. And she loved it all—his throaty voice, his cock pulsing in her body with his pleasure.

He lowered his body over hers once more, and she felt him shiver. Just a small shudder that let her know his climax had been as powerful as her own. That he was affected by what had just happened between them.

What had just happened?

It had seemed to make sense in the moment. Now her mind was spinning out a dozen possibilities.

He'd been too rough with her.

She could trust him utterly.

No man should have that much control over her.

She was completely safe in his hands.

It had always been about being in his hands. Never another's.

Dangerous. Not the sex. The feelings.

But it was Connor. Connor.

She loved him.

Jesus.

She pushed forward, disengaging from his body, his cock slipping from her.

"Mischa?"

She shook her head, unable to speak.

"Did I hurt you?"

She shook her head again, crawling away from him, onto the bed. Crawling until she reached the pillows. She curled into them, letting her hair obscure her face.

"Hey," he said, his tone more gentle than she'd ever heard it as he knelt at the foot of the bed, knowing not to get too close. "I didn't mean to scare you, darlin' girl."

"No. It's not that."

"What is it, then?"

"I . . ."

But she couldn't tell him. Not Connor. Not *her*, for God's sake. She would not turn into her mother. She would *not*.

She took a long breath, tried to force her voice to sound normal despite the hammering inside her brain. "It was just a little . . . much for me, maybe. I just need a minute."

"Okay. Okay." He got up and sat on the foot of the bed, waited a few moments, moved closer, slowly, until he was right next to her. He stroked her hair from her eyes, his fingers so gentle she wanted to cry. "You're sure you're all right? I've done a lot of the breath control before. I would never have hurt you."

"No. I know that."

"Do you?"

His gaze was dark, searching hers. She turned away. She didn't dare look at him. She was afraid he might see the truth in her eyes.

"May I have some water?"

"Of course."

She felt the mattress shift as he got up, heard the padding of his bare feet as he left the room.

What the hell was she going to do now?

She pushed her hair from her face, looking around the room.

It had become so familiar so quickly. Too familiar, maybe—the modern black furniture, all sleek lines, that nevertheless felt like warmth to her. The streetlights gleaming through the rice paper shades, how the light diffused, made everything in the room appear softer. Even the scent of Connor's bedroom made it feel like home. More home than even Dylan's place.

Maybe more than her own home in San Francisco, which seemed so distant right now.

Stop being an idiot. This is just another kind of bottoming out.

But was it?

She pulled in a breath, blew it out slowly, willed herself to calm down.

She would keep this to herself. Maybe take some time tomorrow, maybe over the next few days, to dissect it, see if it was simply a natural reaction to the extremity of their power play. Just because she'd thought the words didn't make them true. Did it?

eleven

Connor pushed away from his drawing table and stood. He'd been up since seven, had been trying to work all day, but his concentration was shit. It was nearly three and he'd gotten almost nothing done. He rubbed a hand over his head, his gaze going to the row of windows. He'd hung the same shades in here as he had in the rest of the apartment when he'd turned this second bedroom into his office, but in here he kept them raised, leaving the windows open to the Seattle sky. He liked to see the shifting shades of gray in fog and clouds, those rare moments when the sun peered through. He liked to feel the pace of the city. It inspired him. Usually. Not today.

As he'd told Mischa, his work was by contract, and he was between deadlines. But he had a few ideas he was knocking around for a new video game for a company out of L.A., and he needed to put some drawings together sometime in the next few weeks. The last two days had been a wash and he'd ended up going to the gym both days, working out like a fiend. Working off . . . what?

Whatever it was that had blown his focus.

You know damn well what it is.

Mischa.

He couldn't fucking believe it. And how many times had he said that to himself since they'd met? It was getting old.

It was the truth.

He blew out a breath, sat down at his drawing table.

"Just do it," he said aloud.

He picked up his pencil, bent his head to work.

But all he could see in his mind's eye was the creamy skin of her shoulders, the rich red of her mouth. And instead of the interior of the interstellar ship he was supposed to be working on, it was her face that began to appear on the page.

"Fuck it," he muttered.

He gave up and let his hand show him the way. The curve of her cheekbones, her jaw, her long, thick lashes. Then her eyes . . . except that there was something in them he couldn't get quite right. He needed to have her in front of him, needed her to pose for him.

They'd talked about it. Had talked about her tattooing him later today. And he was as eager as a puppy, waiting to hear from her. Which made him feel like an ass.

He got to his feet once more and began to pace. Back and forth over the wood floor, passing the bookcase filled with art books he'd collected over the years: comic illustrations, classical art, photography. In front of the books were a few framed photographs: his sisters, Clara and Molly, his mum in her garden. They had been the only women in his life—*really* in his life— since Ginny.

He shook his head. He'd never quite let Ginny in, either.

And why was that? What was he so damn afraid of? Because—
and he was seeing it for the first time—it was fear that was holding him back. He knew it because Mischa Kennon scared the shit
out of him.

He jumped when his cell phone went off. Muttered a curse
as he picked it up.

"Alec."

"Someone's in a bad mood."

"Yeah. Sort of. Brooding, maybe. Sorry."

"Do you want to tell me what's up?" Alec asked.

"Yeah, not really."

"Okay."

"You're too fucking agreeable sometimes, you know."

Alec laughed. "Funny, no one's ever told me that before."

"Well, I will tell you. Because I'm crawling out of my skin
over here, to be honest." He paused, and Alec waited for him to
go on. "You remember we talked before about Mischa."

"Sure."

He started to pace again, putting the phone on speaker, gripping it in his hand. "It's gotten worse. I'm waiting to hear from
her today. *Waiting*, Alec. I've never waited on any woman. Not
my ex-wife. Not anyone. So what the hell does this mean? No.
Don't answer that. I don't want to hear it."

There was a long pause on the other end of the line, just
enough time to make him feel even more foolish.

"I don't know what you want me to tell you, Connor. That you
shouldn't see her again? That you'll grow bored and stop feeling
like this eventually? I can't tell you that. I don't know what will
happen. Everyone is different. You need to calm down and see
where this goes."

"The whole 'seeing where it goes' thing sounds an awful lot
like going in blind. No control over the situation."

"Sometimes that's all we can do. Even guys like us. One thing I've figured out is that we're still human. You, me, Dylan. Mischa. And that makes us unpredictable."

"I don't like unpredictable."

"You like to *be* unpredictable," Alec said. "You just don't like it when someone else is."

He let out a short laugh. "You're right there. But part of the problem is that right now I don't even know what *I'm* going to do."

"You'll figure it out. I say let it ride for a while. She's in town for another two weeks."

"What? I thought it was one more week."

"She told Dylan last night she needs to extend her trip to finalize some things with the new shop."

"Ah. So." He stopped pacing, ran his hand over his head again. He wasn't sure what he was supposed to think about this new piece of information "So why'd you call?"

"There's a dom support group at the Pleasure Dome tomorrow night. Maybe you'd like to come along and talk about your feelings?"

"What?"

"Just kidding."

"Ass."

Alec chuckled. "I called to see if you and Mischa want to have dinner with us tonight. Or is that too weird?"

"It's too . . . couple-like."

"All right. We'll table it."

"Anyway, she's doing some more work on my tattoo later," he said, picking up his pencil and tapping it on the edge of his drawing table.

"I didn't know she was tattooing you."

"Yeah. Her work is amazing."

"It is. She did a small piece for Dylan and me both last night."

"Ah, she mentioned she was going to do some work on you two."

"You seem to know an awful lot about what she's doing for someone who's not into the 'couple-like' thing."

"Fuck off, Alec."

Alec laughed. "Hang in there. I'll talk to you soon."

They hung up, leaving Connor feeling a bit more centered. Alec was right. He could let this thing play out. Just let it be whatever it was. Great sex with a gorgeous woman who would, in two weeks, take off for California, go back to her life. He didn't have to remind himself that once this new tattoo shop was set up, some of her life would be here in Seattle.

But two more weeks, rather than one . . . that was good, wasn't it? He shook his head, gripping the pencil in his hand. He wished to God he knew.

Mischa raised her hand to knock on Connor's blue door. Her heart was tripping in her chest. She pulled her hand back, biting her lip.

She was being ridiculous again. Just because she'd realized how she felt about him . . . God, she couldn't even think the word in her own head. But that didn't have to change anything. That's what she was trying to tell herself, anyway.

She shifted the big, boxy red leather case that held her tattoo equipment to her other hand and knocked firmly.

There, that was better.

Until Connor opened the door.

The breath just went right out of her as she stared at his massive chest, a black sweater stretched tight across it. It was even worse when she raised her gaze to his green eyes, felt as if she was falling into their gold-sprinkled depths. There was so much in this man's eyes . . .

"Hey," he said, his voice that low throaty tone that turned her knees to mush.

"Hey."

She smiled, tried to get her composure back as he took the case from her, took her hand and led her inside. He set the case carefully down on the floor, slipped her coat from her shoulders, then pulled her in close and even more carefully kissed her.

His mouth was hard and soft all at once, his tongue sweet as it slipped into her mouth. Then he was really kissing her, and her whole body was lighting up with need as he crushed her to his chest. She sank into his kiss, into *him*. Her brain was starting to shut down already.

He let her go, held her at arm's length.

"Jesus, Connor."

"Yeah. I know. That's why I stopped. We have work to do."

She swallowed hard. "Yes."

He stared at her for several long moments, yanked her in again, his mouth coming down so hard she thought her lips might be bruised. She didn't care. He opened her mouth with his tongue, all sleek velvet as he pushed inside. One arm went around her waist, held her tight. The other went around the back of her head, under her hair, so that she could feel the heat of his big hand.

Lovely.

She went loose all over, her body yielding even before her mind had time to consider it. All she could do was grip his arms, use them to hold herself upright as her sex pulsed with need. As her heart beat with it even harder. A different need . . .

Need him.

He pulled back with a snarl. "Mischa."

"Connor?"

"We need to . . . talk."

Her head was spinning now. "About what?"

He drew in a deep breath; she could see the way he filled up his lungs, his chest expanding even more. He held her shoulders with both hands, watching her face as he spoke, his dark brows drawn.

"Look. This is . . . Things are getting intense here. Do you agree?"

"Yes."

"Does it freak you out at all?"

She couldn't help the small, nervous laugh. "It does."

"Yeah, well, it does me, too. And I am not the kind of guy who has conversations about where we're going, or any of that."

"I wouldn't expect it of you. And I'm not the girl who does that, either."

"Right. But here's the thing. I think it's necessary to say something now. About what's happening between us. Because we're spending a hell of a lot of time together; the time has been condensed."

"Yes," she agreed. "But I'll be going home soon, so there's really nothing to talk about."

Why were her own words making her heart sink? Maybe because she knew damn well she wasn't being honest.

"Yeah, two more weeks."

"How did you know I was staying longer?"

"Alec told me. But look, can we spend these next couple of weeks together? I mean, whatever time we have here. Can we agree not to question it, just be in the moment? Do you understand what I'm saying?"

She nodded. "I get it. And I don't see why not."

When had she turned into such a good liar? She had nothing *but* questions. For him. For herself. Questions she probably didn't want to know the answers to.

God, she was a mess.

"Good. That's good," he said, dropping his hands from her shoulders.

She bit her lip, waited for him to say more. When he didn't she asked, "Why don't I start work on your tattoo? There's a lot to be done, still."

"Sure. You can set up in the dining room, if that works."

"That should be fine as long as there's good light."

"There is."

He picked up her leather case and she followed him, watched him put it down on the floor, then concentrated on setting up her workstation at the big glass dining table while Connor moved into the kitchen to get them both some bottled water.

She needed to calm herself. To stop trying to dissect what this odd little discussion had meant, if anything. She really couldn't make heads or tails out of it. Obviously he still wanted to see her. The way he kissed her would have told her that, if he hadn't indicated it himself. But he didn't want anything more from her. He'd made it clear that once she returned to San Francisco, they would be done. Hadn't he?

Which would be for the best. She couldn't afford to let a man throw her like this—she had too much at stake. Her focus had to be on opening the new shop. Her business, her success at it, was who she was, every bit as much as the art itself. She wasn't about to throw it all away because of a man, the way Evie had. If she compromised even a little on the promise she'd made to herself long ago—so long ago she couldn't even remember when her mind-set had been any different—it would ruin everything she'd worked so hard to build for herself.

Just stay on course.

When Connor returned, handing her a bottle of water, she accepted it with barely even a small patter in her chest. She'd always known what she wanted. And even Connor Galloway, even the way she felt about him, was not going to steer her down another path.

"Okay," she told him. "Let's get to work."

They spent the next five hours with the tattoo needle whirring against a backdrop of music playing on Connor's iPod. Neither one spoke much other than to comment on a song, or when Mischa checked in to make sure he wasn't getting too sore or tired. She liked these long tattoo sessions. A lot of other artists would limit their sessions to two or three hours, but she enjoyed having the opportunity to really concentrate on a piece, to let herself fall into the work. It was meditative for her, made her feel more connected to her art.

She was making excellent progress, the lower half of the dragon taking shape, the detail in the wings. Finally, she got to the point where she'd worked on every bit of skin available that wasn't still healing from the previous session, and stopped. She sat back to look at the overall piece, pleased with what she saw. This was going to be really beautiful when it was done.

"Do you want to take a look in the mirror, Connor?"

"Sure. Yeah."

She followed him into the bathroom, remembered in a shivery flash the times they'd had sex in the shower, the water spilling all over their naked skin. She pulled in a breath.

Calm down.

Connor was standing with his back to the big vanity mirror. Mischa handed him the hand mirror she always kept with her tattoo equipment.

"What do you think?" she asked him.

"It's incredible. Looks even better on my skin than it did in your sketch. I can't believe how much work you did today."

"Well, I work fast. And you took it like a champ. Not everyone can sit for so long."

"That's my Irish peasant blood. I come from sturdy stock." He winked at her, grinning.

All tension seemed to be gone. On his end, anyway. She was still feeling a little uncertain, especially now that she'd stopped working on his tattoo. She wanted—needed—to regain some sense of control. Not that she was ever the one holding the reins with Connor . . .

"Oy, I'm stiff from sitting still so long."

He set the hand mirror down on the counter before raising his arms over his head to stretch. Mischa eyed the ripple of his abs, the narrow line of dark hair leading into the low-riding waist of his jeans, her body going warm in a flash.

Without saying a word she pulled her knit dress over her head. Connor's eyes widened but he didn't move to stop her as she unhooked her bra and let it fall to the floor, leaving her in nothing but her thigh-high sweater tights. As she sank down to her knees on the bathroom rug and unzipped his faded jeans, the last thing she saw of his face was his wide grin.

Then it was his cock taking all her attention. The shaft was thick, the flesh a pale gold, the head swelling already, growing darker as she moved in, letting the warmth of her breath bathe his flesh.

His hand slid behind her head, but he didn't hold her firmly, as he might have before. He seemed to sense already that something would be different this time. He twined his fingers in her hair, but his touch was light. So was the first flick of her tongue on the tip of his rising cock. He groaned softly.

She smiled, did it again. Waited with a sense of glee as he

pulled in a hissing breath. She moved in and let the flat of her tongue rest against the head and held it still there, simply letting him feel it while she felt the beating pulse of his desire against her tongue.

"Ah, come on, sweetheart," he said finally.

She didn't move, heard him take in a long, slow breath, then pause before he blew it out.

"So that's how you're going to play it, is it, darlin'? You know I could pick you up and turn you over my knee right here, don't you?" When she didn't react, he went on, "You are a little minx, aren't you? But that's one of the things I love about you, Mischa. That you'll only take so much shit from me."

She would not focus on the fact that the word "love" had just come out of his mouth. No she wouldn't. But she would certainly make him pay.

She opened her lips and slid her mouth down the length of his cock, swallowing him deep all at once.

"Ah, Lord, girl!"

His fingers flexed in her hair, but still he didn't do anything to try to control her. She moved back, sliding her lips up the heavy shaft until she'd reached the tip, let her tongue swirl there, dipping into the hole. Loved it when he shivered. She did it again, really pushing inside, and his hips arched. She drew back.

"Payback is a bitch, is that it?" he murmured, but his voice was heavy with pleasure.

She felt it—that she had the power right now. That he was entirely at her mercy. It was what she needed at that moment. And she loved what she was doing to him. Loved the flavor of his big cock, the weight of it in her mouth. The moans of desire, the way he shuddered with each touch, each stroke of her tongue. She smiled to herself again before she yanked his jeans down a little, giving her better access. She grasped the base of his cock with one hand, her fingers barely managing to wrap around it, and gave it a squeeze. He groaned. She felt the tension in his thighs as he tried not to move.

Very good.

Then she reached between his muscular thighs and cupped his balls in the other hand.

"Oh, that's good . . ."

She glanced up. Connor's eyes were closed, his head tilted back, one hand behind him on the bathroom counter, steadying him.

She licked her lips, gazed once more at his beautiful cock. It was all hers tonight. *He* was all hers.

She grazed the engorged tip with her lips, just a soft brushing, back and forth. Let her tongue dart out to taste him, teasing him. She took the head into her mouth, sucked hard enough to hurt, she knew. Connor was beginning a shallow panting, which pleased her enormously—that he was so lost in desire, and that she was the cause. Her own sex was damp, aching with need. But she wasn't inclined to stop. She kept up the teasing: a flicker of tongue, a brush of lips, a small nip with her teeth at the underside of the shaft, just letting his balls rest in her hand. Then, finally, she swallowed his cock, letting her throat open up as it hit the back of it.

"Ah, you're killing me, Mischa."

She began to stroke him with her mouth, sliding up, pressing down, while her tongue danced along the rigid shaft. And she began a gentle massage of his balls, moving them in her hand, while with the other she used her grasping fingers to follow the stroking rhythm of her mouth.

When he began to rock his hips, arching into her mouth, her hand, she knew she had him. Knew he'd lost control—or at least given it up. Given it over to her.

She paused to suck one finger into her mouth, along with his cock, then she slipped it out, moving it back, behind his balls and slowly slid it into his ass.

"Christ, woman!"

But he didn't move. Just held still, his breath even more ragged than before. She felt a small clenching in his ass, slipped her finger in deeper as she sucked his cock hard.

"Ah . . ."

When he tried to press on the top of her head, to guide the motion, she put one hand up to still him. And he cooperated, taking his hand from her hair.

She really went to work, then: sucking his cock until her cheeks hurt, until she was hurting him a little, she knew. And knew he loved it. Sliding her finger in and out of his ass, massaging his prostate. Using her other hand to make a tight ring around the base of his big cock. Faster and faster. Harder and harder. And all the while she was growing absolutely soaking wet, as if his mouth was on her, his hands on her body. She felt the power of what she was doing to him. Felt his pleasure as if it were her own.

"Mischa!"

He came, shaking all over, groaning, calling her name again and again.

"Mischa! Christ, girl! Mischa . . . ah . . ."

She felt him shoot down her throat, the salty-sweet heat of his come. She kept working him until she was sure she had every last drop. By the time he was done she was trembling as hard as he was. He slid down onto the bathroom rug, pushing her down on the floor. The soft rug was beneath her, but her shoulders were lying against the cool tiles, making a lovely, sensual contrast to the molten heat of her body.

He was kneeling over her, his cock still out of his jeans, glistening with her saliva and a little of his come. Her pussy was pulsing with desire, her breasts aching to be touched.

"You know what I want, Connor," she told him, power still heady, making her dizzy. "Come on. Give it to me."

He smiled, that quirky grin of his. Then he got on all fours over her, bending to lay a quick kiss on her mouth before moving down.

He began to lick her breasts, first one, then the other. Long, sinuous strokes of his tongue. The mounded flesh, the undersides, around the nipples, then finally pulling her stiffening nipples into his mouth. First one, then the other, back and forth, his mouth on her driving her crazy. She wrapped her legs around his back, trying to pull him closer, but he was too strong; she couldn't budge him.

"Connor."

He laughed then, a muffled sound, as he had one nipple in his mouth.

"Connor, come on. Suck me."

He did, hard, sending a small, lancing pain through her. But pleasure ran just as deep.

"Oh, that's good," she murmured.

He moved to the other side, did it again, that rough sucking into his hot mouth, and she had a moment to wonder how his mouth could be so silky and so hard all at the same time. But in moments he was sucking, sucking, and she was losing herself in pleasure. Her hands went into his hair, but he reached up and held them firmly out to the sides, pinning her down.

She didn't care any longer. Didn't need to be in control. It felt too good to just let him go, let him do what he wanted. Once he realized she'd stopped struggling he let her go, and she left her arms where he'd placed them, feeling open, a little wanton.

She let her thighs fall open and he instantly pulled away from her breasts and slid down her body. Her pussy squeezed in anticipation.

She didn't have long to wait. In moments he was tonguing her slit—long, lovely strokes, up and down. She was soaked, her hips rocking, needing to come almost instantly. When he sucked her clit into his mouth it started—spirals of pleasure moving through her system like some lovely, high-pitched keening at the edge of her hearing. He pushed his fingers inside her, and her pussy tightened, pleasure spreading, into her belly, her breasts. Her nipples went tight. Her climax spread like lightning heat, that fast, that hot, scorching her in its wake.

"Connor, I'm coming . . . oh . . . oh . . ."

He let her ride it out, just as he did when it was pain he was giving her, rather than pleasure. Or maybe it was all the same. Her mind was swimming.

Connor raised his head, his eyes twinkling. Devilish. "Did you like that?"

"Loved it," she breathed.

Love you.

Don't.

Don't love him. Don't think it.

"I'll love it even more when you can fuck me properly," she said instead. It was just as true.

"Ah, give the girl a little power and she runs with it." He reached down and squeezed one of her breasts in his hand, and she surged into his touch, her body still buzzing with her climax. "Don't think I won't fuck you good and hard shortly, darlin'. I'll fuck you and spank you until you're coming and screaming and crying all at the same time." He gave her nipple a good, hard pinch, making her breath hiss through her teeth. "You know I will." His eyes were dark, glittering.

"Yes." She smiled.

"That's better."

He sat back on his heels, looking down at her, a small smile on his handsome face. She felt dwarfed by his size. But she felt no inclination to get up off the floor. She loved the way he made her feel. So female. No, it was more than that. He made her feel utterly *feminine*. She didn't want to stop to consider why she reveled in it.

"Time to feed me, woman. Have to replenish my strength."

"Good, I'm starved. What are you making for me?"

Before she even had time to flash him a grin, he'd pulled her into his lap and turned her over. His hand came down on her ass in a solid smack.

She gasped. "I know you think you're punishing me," she said from between gritted teeth as pleasure poured through her system.

"On the contrary. I'm giving you a little gift of endorphins to carry you through what I plan to do with you later, once I've eaten."

"Mmm . . ."

She was trying to think of a witty reply when the spanking began in earnest. There was a volley of quick, sharp slaps, then the angle changed and it was the whole hand hitting her, his hand cupped so that his fingers and palm made contact, making for a heavy, thudding sensation, rather than just the sting. She knew he would bruise her. She didn't care.

No, that wasn't quite true. She wanted it. Wanted him to mark her.

The pressure built inside her quickly, so quickly she wondered if she could come simply from him spanking her. That and the feel of his muscular thighs under her belly. She arched her hips, found that she could press her mound into his thigh, pressing her needy clit against him.

Oh yes, that was enough. Pleasure spiraled along with the pain. Her ass was a mass of sensation: his hard hand coming down on her aching flesh over and over, the sting turning into a lovely burn. The desire blossoming between her thighs. She parted them a little, really grinding down on him. And he was letting her do it, she knew from some vague, endorphin-filled place. Letting her get off on his thigh while he spanked the hell out of her.

She was hovering on that edge, her orgasm just out of reach. She angled her hips and he shifted a bit beneath her, the ridge of his big thigh muscle hitting just the right spot. And as he smacked her ass she swore she could feel the reverberation echo through her body, setting her off. She came in a torrent of pain and pleasure, grinding her mound against him, her clit swollen and pulsing.

She was left gasping, her climax still sending small ripples through her body when she realized the spanking had stopped. Connor lifted her until she was cradled in his lap. He was grinning down at her.

"That'll teach me," she murmured, her eyes half-closed as she rode out the last lovely brain chemicals surging through her.

Connor chuckled, a deep, infectious belly laugh, and she found herself laughing with him.

"You are the strangest woman," he told her.

"But you like it."

"I do."

"You must be starving by now."

"About to faint away," he agreed.

"We can't have that, can we?"

"I'd lose all my dignity."

"Well, if you'll let go of my left nipple, maybe we can get up and find some food."

He looked down to where he'd been squeezing her beautifully sore flesh between his fingers, grinned.

"Ah. Right. Up we go, then."

He lifted her to her feet as he stood. She was a little dizzy. With her stunning climax. The aftereffects of the hard spanking. With the dynamic between them.

Something had shifted the moment she'd gone down on her knees and taken control. And even though the control had very clearly shifted back to him, something had remained changed.

She would still submit to him. There was no question about that any longer. But something in the way they related to each other, both in and out of those roles, had shifted. They were more just people together, who they each were. It was less about those roles, suddenly.

More dangerous.

Yes, but more enjoyable, too.

She was going to miss him.

Stay in the moment.

The moment was awfully damn good. She didn't want to miss a second of it dwelling on things she'd rather not think about.

He pressed a finger to the spot between her drawn brows.

"What's going on in there?"

"Um . . . just thinking about food. I really am starving."

"It's too late to order out. I'm afraid you'll have to put up with my cooking."

"I'm sure I've had worse."

He yanked her in close, gave her sore bottom another smack. "Think I'll poison you, do you?"

"Let's hope not. We still have one more session to go on your tattoo."

"Smart little minx," he muttered as he handed her dress to her, then zipped up his jeans. "Come on."

He brushed a kiss over her cheek, then turned to leave the bathroom.

"I'll be right there. Give me a second."

She closed the door behind him, taking a minute to wash her hands, to splash some water on her face and give herself a quick whore's bath with a washcloth she found rolled up on a shelf. She used her fingers to smooth her hair into place, looking at her flushed face, her blue eyes sparkling.

No one had ever made her feel alive the way Connor did. No man had ever brought out her humor—not one she'd slept with, anyway. She was more often funny with her friends. That was who she felt relaxed enough with to be herself. So what did it mean that her personality was coming out with him?

And when was she going to stop questioning every single thing when it came to Connor?

They'd just agreed to let things be, hadn't they? She needed to stick to her end of the bargain. No matter how hard it was going to be later on.

Stay in the moment.

That was the key. To simply be in the *now*. Tomorrow—figuratively speaking, since the tomorrow she was dreading was still two weeks away—would be here soon enough.

"Mischa? You staying in there all night? Food's nearly ready," Connor called through the door.

"I'll be right out."

She took a deep breath and opened the door.

The apartment smelled wonderful, and when she went into the kitchen she found Connor standing over the stove, a spatula in one hand, which made her smile.

"Do you need some help?" she asked him.

"Nah, I'm good. Just an omelet. I hope you like mushrooms and tomatoes. You're not one of those health nuts who won't eat cheese, are you?"

"I love cheese. I love almost everything."

He glanced up at her, flashed her a quick grin before returning his gaze to the pan.

"Have a seat, then."

She did, sliding onto the bench in the breakfast nook, where a pair of napkins and forks were neatly placed. She watched him expertly flip the omelet, then a few moments later he slid it onto a plate. He set it down in front of her.

"Scoot over—we're sharing," he ordered.

She scooted, loving it when he moved in close beside her, his big arm brushing hers.

"This looks great. I didn't know you cooked."

"Nothing gourmet, but enough to keep myself fed. I stay up late working a lot, so I often find myself eating late at night. Here, how is it?"

He picked up a fork, cut a piece and fed it to her. The cheese melted on her tongue.

"Mmm, very good. Do you like to cook?"

"I don't mind it. But I'd prefer someone else cook for me, which has never really happened. And which is why I also eat out a lot." He paused to take a bite himself.

"No one's ever cooked regularly for you?" she asked as he prepared to feed her another bite.

"Sure, my mum, growing up. Then Ginny, for a while. Ah, sorry. Shouldn't have brought her up."

"No, it's fine."

He chewed another forkful of omelet. "What about you? Do you cook?"

"I don't have much time to cook these days, with running the shop, doing tattoos, writing a few novellas a year just to keep my hand in it."

"That's right—you're a published erotica author, like Dylan."

"Yes, just a few stories out there. It's not my main career focus, obviously, but I love it. It exercises a different part of my creative mind. And that's how I met Dylan."

"That's good, then."

"It is. But I end up eating out with friends or ordering in a lot, too. I can cook, though. I had plenty of practice as a kid. I cooked for Evie and Raine all the time."

"As a kid? Your mother didn't cook for you?"

"Sometimes, but to be honest it was mostly tofu and whole grains and green stuff I could barely recognize. Raine and I liked it better when Evie would forget to stop painting, or working on whatever art project she had going. I'd grab some cash out of her wallet and we'd go to the nearest grocery store. When I was nine I bought myself a copy of *The Joy of Cooking* and taught myself a few things. Raine became my sous chef as we got older. She's a really great cook, now. I don't know how she does it, with her job and everything. But Raine is a bit of a powerhouse. She always told me she'd rise above the hippie name Evie gave her, and she has. In spades."

"What about you? Have you risen above your name? Which I don't think is exactly a hippie name, by the way."

"Not like Raine is. But yes, I've absolutely risen above it. Above everything."

Connor set his fork down, and she realized they'd polished off the omelet.

"What do you mean by 'everything'?"

A small knot was forming in her chest as she realized what had somehow leaked from her mouth while they were eating. Why had she babbled on about her family to him?

She shook her head. "You don't want to hear all this stuff, Connor."

"Sure I do. Why not?"

"Because it's . . . not the happiest story."

He shrugged, the muscles in his bare shoulders rippling. "It doesn't have to be."

"Well . . . I guess 'everything' is just . . . growing up with Evie. Are you sure you want to hear this?"

She looked at him, found his expression softer than she'd ever seen it.

"Yeah, I do."

She bit her lip. "Everything" with Evie was a hell of a lot. "She'd forget about us fairly often, you know? She'd get caught up in a painting or a sculpture or sitting at her potter's wheel, and Raine and I would just disappear for her. And if there was a man around . . ." A short laugh slipped from her. "Well, she was just gone. Sometimes literally for days at a time. Until she got tired of him, or he got tired of her. You'd think she'd have learned, after my father disappearing, then Raine's father breaking things off with her after she told him she was pregnant with Raine. Evie would always swear she wasn't going to fall for that again, but she did, every time.

"It was a little easier when we lived at the communes. There were other adults around to sort of take up the slack. We'd get a hot meal. Other kids to play with, whose mothers would sometimes make us clothes or read to us when they did that stuff for their own kids. But still . . . we knew something was off in our lives. That this was not how people lived. Without televisions and a mother who would make it to parent-teacher night at school." She paused, sighed as she pushed her hair from her face, her gaze going to the empty plate. "Kids need that stuff."

Connor laid a hand on the back of her head, stroked her hair. "I'm sorry you didn't have it."

She looked up at him. There was still a softness in his features. Not pity. Just sympathy.

"It sounds as if you missed a lot from your childhood, Connor."

"I did. Which is why I know how it hurts. But we'll save that tale for another day."

"All right."

She didn't mind. She didn't take it as a bad sign that he wasn't ready to share the details of what had happened with his father. It was enough that she'd felt so able to talk to him about her past, ugliness and all. It was enough to sit in his warm kitchen, the rain starting to come down outside, making her feel safe and cozy with Connor sitting next to her.

It had been a long time since she'd felt this safe with anyone. And never with a man. She'd never felt about anyone else the way she did about Connor.

But it was enough to revel in the comfort, right now, rather than question it. She'd save that tale for another day.

twelve

Connor kept his hand at the small of Mischa's back as they moved through Koi, the Japanese restaurant where they were to meet Alec and Dylan for dinner. It felt somewhat strange going there together, almost as a couple, but Alec had asked him again, told him he was overthinking it and to just come. It was something he hadn't experienced for a long time, not like this. It was different from taking a woman to a party, or to the Pleasure Dome. But there was also something that felt natural about it, because it was Mischa.

Everything felt natural with her. Things had been easy between them this past week, since the night she'd worked on his tattoo. Even the revealing talk they'd had at his kitchen table. Well, revealing for her, at any rate. But he was glad they'd talked. She'd been more open since then, on every level. It had made the sex, the power play, thrilling as hell.

And he'd be lying to himself if he thought that was the only thrill.

Not now.

No, now he spotted Alec's hulking figure at a table near the rain-spattered window, Dylan looking tiny beside him. Their heads were together, her dark auburn hair shining in the dim light of the restaurant. Pretty hair, Dylan had. But not the pale spun gold like his Mischa.

His.

Lord.

He let his fingers tighten possessively at her waist—*needed* to for a moment—and she turned to him, her blue gaze questioning. He smiled, and she shrugged, letting it go.

"Hey." Alec stood to greet them, giving Connor a good pounding on the back, leaning over to kiss Mischa's cheek before Dylan got up to hug them both.

He helped Mischa into her chair, then sat beside her at the table.

"Hope you haven't been waiting long. Traffic was hell," Connor said, flipping his napkin into his lap.

"Just a few minutes," Dylan answered. "We hit traffic, too. But we've already ordered some calamari and a round of beers. Hope that's okay."

"Oh, you are the little subbie girl," Mischa teased her.

"Ha! You're one to talk, these days, hon." Dylan beamed even as she protested, and Alec grinned down at her.

"You two," Connor said. "Grinning like fools."

"Like happy fools," Alec said, lifting Dylan's hand to his lips to drop a quick kiss there. "You should try it sometime."

"Nah, happy isn't for me."

He realized only as he said it that a good part of him truly believed it. He glanced at Mischa, shook the thought away. He was happy enough at the moment, wasn't he?

The waiter came with their beer and he poured his into a tall glass, then poured Mischa's, too. He took a swallow. "So, where are you in wedding details? Just about finished up by now, I'd imagine?"

"God, no." Dylan shook her head. "There are still a thousand things to do. I had no idea weddings were so much work."

"Good thing this is the only wedding either of us will have to have," Alec said, looping an arm across her shoulders.

"And good thing Mischa is here to help."

"I wish I was of more help. Honestly, if it wasn't for Kara and Lucie I'd be totally lost. And I'm sorry I have to get back to San Francisco, Dylan. I wish I could stay right up to the wedding."

So do I.

Connor took another long draught from his beer glass. He had to stop thinking that way. There was no point.

A small twist in his gut, but he wasn't having it. He took another swallow, saw that he'd nearly drained the glass already, realized what he was doing and set his glass down. He wasn't going down that road, drowning the thoughts roaring in his head with alcohol.

"Don't worry, Misch," Dylan said. "I understand. You have a business to run. Speaking of business, how are things going with Greyson?"

Another odd twist in his gut that he chose to ignore. He didn't like hearing that man's name. Didn't like to be reminded of how close Mischa was to him.

Fuck. He was being a right idiot.

"Everything's going really smoothly. Opening a new shop with a partner to do half the work is a lot easier than it was doing it myself with Thirteen Roses. We've already had a preview peek at the architectural plans for the build-out, and it's looking great. And we finally chose a name—1st Avenue Ink."

"That's exciting," Alec said. "When do you think you'll open?"

"Oh, it'll still be a good four months or more. That's if the build-out goes well. But I'm counting on a few hitches. Contractors aren't always the most reliable bunch. And even if Greyson's guy is as good as he says he is, I know things happen he can't foresee." Mischa shrugged.

"But you'll be back to check on things before then?" Dylan asked.

Connor clenched his jaw, trying to ignore the way his chest tightened. He glanced up and found Alec watching him.

"Definitely," Mischa answered. "We still have to hire artists and a shop manager, and we've agreed we won't take anyone on until we've both met them. We don't plan to hire any artists just from seeing their portfolios. We want to be sure they're a good fit in every way. Personality clashes can ruin a tattoo shop—the clients always feel the tension, so we're being careful."

Alec raised an eyebrow at him. Connor pretended he had no idea what the question was.

"How often do you think you'll make it?" Dylan asked her.

Connor's fingers flexed on his glass. He hadn't let it go, apparently. Alec noticed it, too. He was still watching him, and he knew damn well his friend was taking in every response, the same way he would a sub he was playing. The man was too damn well trained in the art of observation.

"Probably at least once a month, for a few days or a week at a time. It depends on how busy the shop in San Francisco is. But it'll be good practice for Billy for when I'm splitting time between the two shops."

"You'll need a place to stay when you come," Dylan suggested.

Mischa waved a hand. "I can camp at a hotel until I find a place of my own."

"Don't be silly, Misch. I was going to rent my apartment out after the wedding, but that can wait. Why don't you stay there?"

Or at my place.

What was he thinking?

"I don't want to put you out. You'll have to at least let me pay you some rent."

"That's not necessary."

"Of course it is, Dylan. I won't even consider it otherwise. But if you're really okay with it I'd love to stay at your place; I'm always so comfortable there. And it'll be nice to have a home base with all the stress of opening a new shop."

"Consider it done."

Mischa smiled at Dylan. "You're a doll. Oh, calamari! I'm starved."

Connor let out a long breath when food was laid on the table and they were all distracted. He didn't want to think too much about Mischa returning to San Francisco. Or what would happen—or what wouldn't happen—when she came back to Seattle regularly.

No expectations. Wasn't that what they'd agreed on? Why the hell couldn't he stop wondering? And wasn't wondering a mere step away from *expecting*?

Mischa felt Connor tense beside her, wondering what was wrong with him. She was having a good time, and he knew Alec and Dylan—he should be as much at ease with them as she was. The Japanese beer was good, the tempura-fried calamari even better. And better still, the promise of some amazing sex later, as always. What was going on with him?

She turned her head, trying to read his expression as he stared at Alec, who was staring back at him. Men! Impossible to decipher. She decided to give up and return her attention to the meal.

During dinner Connor finally seemed to relax a bit as talk turned to the upcoming wedding, mutual friends due to arrive for the event, and why Dylan and Alec wanted to skip the traditional wedding shower and bachelor party.

"Mischa, come with me to the ladies' room?" Dylan asked once the plates had been cleared.

"Sure, hon."

"Why can't women go to the bathroom by themselves?" Alec asked, standing as Dylan got out of her chair.

Connor did the same when Mischa stood, and she had to admit to herself once again how much she loved these old-world manners she saw in the truly dominant men.

"We have to disappear once in a while so you guys will remember to appreciate us," Dylan said.

"I always appreciate you, baby," Alec told her, adoration for his future bride clear on his face.

Dylan grinned at him, leaned in to give him a kiss while Mischa's stomach began to churn. Would Connor appreciate her more once she'd returned to San Francisco? How screwed up was that? That she'd have to leave the damn state before he'd miss her.

And why did she have to care so much?

"Come on, Misch."

She shook her head, trying to calm her wandering thoughts as she followed Dylan toward the back of the restaurant. The restroom was as sleek as the rest of the place, with bamboo-covered walls and an elegant lounge area. Dylan grabbed her hand and pulled her to sit down on a black leather love seat.

"Mischa, what is going on with you two?"

"What do you mean?"

"Oh, come on. Don't tell me you failed to notice Connor glowering all through dinner."

"He did seem a little wound up tonight, but I don't know what it was. Things have been good with us. Really great, actually. Maybe he's just having a rough night, or there are some issues with his work. Honestly, I'm trying not to trip on it too much. I make myself crazy enough over him as it is."

"Why are you getting crazy if things have been good between you?" Dylan asked.

"I don't know . . . maybe because things *have* been so good." She stopped, biting her lip for a moment. "Sorry. I know that doesn't make much sense. I just . . . I don't like to think about me going home and both of us just moving on as if nothing has happened. I can't wrap my head around that."

"Because?"

"Because . . ." She had to stop again, blow out a long breath. "Because something *has* happened. *Is* happening. This was supposed to be fun. And it has been, in spades. But it wasn't supposed to be anything else. Anything *more*."

"Misch, what are you trying to say?"

"That I'm . . . having feelings for Connor. And I don't know how to deal with this. I don't really want to. This is *so* not what I need right now."

"Maybe it is," Dylan said quietly.

Mischa shook her head. "No, it's not. How can it be? I'm opening a new business, and that is no small feat. There will be months of planning and interviews and building permits, then trying to promote the new shop, attract a clientele. Not to mention preparing my San Francisco shop for me to start splitting my time between cities. I'll have to look for an apartment eventually. There are a thousand things to do, things I *must* focus on. God, the other day I was late to a meeting with Greyson because

I was lounging around in bed with Connor. Grey made some snide remark about how apparently I'll forget all about the business now that I have a boyfriend and even though he was joking, that really hit me where it hurts. And Connor is not *even* my boyfriend. Not by a long shot."

"Misch, no one doubts your devotion to your work."

"Well, it made me doubt it myself. For a minute, anyway." She shook her head, frustrated that she was having so much trouble expressing herself. "I mean that it made me recognize that I *am* distracted. And I can't afford to be. I don't have time for this!"

Dylan put a hand on her arm, gave it a small squeeze. "Okay, hon. Calm down."

"Don't you see, Dylan? I can't fucking calm down. That's the problem."

She wiped a stray tear from her cheek with an impatient hand, watching confusion pass over Dylan's face. They were both quiet for several moments.

"Wow," Dylan said finally.

Mischa sniffed. "Wow what?"

"You love him."

Mischa covered her eyes with her hands. "Please don't say it," she whispered.

Dylan's hands covered hers as she pulled them from her face. "Mischa, it's okay."

"It's not. It is absolutely not okay. I have a career to think of. I have a life."

"And you can't have those things and love, too?"

Mischa just shook her head helplessly.

"I have all of those things."

"That's you," she protested.

"Why do you have to be any different? Misch, I understand

how you feel. I was in the same place not all that long ago—you know that. Until I found Alec. Until loving him made me realize that *he* was what I'd been missing. That loving him was what I'd been missing."

"I don't think that's who I am, Dylan, and it's certainly not who Connor is. We've been clear with each other from the start. I can't expect him to change. That's not fair. It's not realistic."

"The way he looked when you mentioned Greyson's name tonight tells me something different."

"What look?"

"Like he was ready to tear Greyson's head off and eat it with his sushi."

That made her smile a little. "He did not."

"Okay—maybe it wasn't that bad. Still, the man was jealous."

"Jealousy doesn't equal love."

Dylan shrugged. "Maybe not. But it also doesn't equal a guy who doesn't care."

"It's just a sense of possession. Isn't that a part of the dominant and submissive thing?"

"Yes, to some extent. But when a man feels that you're *his*, well, that's a whole different story."

"He's never said I was *his*."

"He's thinking it."

"How can you be so sure about that?"

"I've seen that look before. On Alec. On a dozen other men, within the BDSM scene and out of it. I was writing about it even before I experienced it for myself."

"I don't know, Dylan. I don't know what he's feeling. It's confusing. Because even if I did know, I sure as hell don't know what to do about it. I don't know if I can have this, do you understand what I mean? And wanting it if Connor doesn't is foolish. Dangerous."

"Don't you think it's worth it, Misch? I won't say it's easy, but I'm telling you it is absolutely worth it."

"I don't know. Despite your surety about love I just can't grasp it. All I feel is the danger, and none of the joy that's so apparent with you and Alec."

All she knew was that loving Connor meant her whole life, everything she'd worked so hard for, could crumble beneath the crushing blow of him turning away from her.

But she couldn't turn away from Connor. Not yet. She had to find some way to handle her feelings, to stay with him as long as she could. To ignore the fact that there was a finite ending to what they had.

She swallowed hard, trying to get her throat to work past the tight lump in it.

"I just need to gather my strength," she told Dylan. "To continue on as I always have. That's the only option for me."

Dylan frowned. "Okay, hon. If that's how you want to handle things, I'm behind you, no matter what. But I do wish you'd think about it."

"I appreciate it, Dylan—everything you're saying. But I'll do better if I stop thinking so much. I really will. Okay?"

"Yes, of course. Okay."

Dylan gave her arm another squeeze. It was meant to reassure her, Mischa knew. But it felt too much like the dull squeezing of her heart as she swallowed down the rising pain, the emotion that threatened to choke her if she dared to really let it out, even for a moment.

She had to stop thinking about any possibility of a future with Connor. She had to focus on her work, the one thing that had always saved her. She was used to it, focusing on work. Getting all of her self-worth through her career as an artist, her other career as a writer. Being a successful business owner. That was what made sense to her. What she wasn't used to, what didn't make sense to her, was being in love.

After dinner they stayed and drank tea and talked for another hour, giving Mischa time to calm down. She was glad she had a better handle on herself by the time they'd said good night to Alec and Dylan and were riding back to Dylan's place in his big black Hummer. They were both quiet on the short drive—the muffled splashing of rain on the tires, the gentle surge of the windshield wipers, soothing her.

Once inside the apartment Connor helped her out of her damp coat and took off his own, and she hung them up before they moved into the living room. There was a distant rumble of thunder as they sat on the green suede sofa.

"Do you need anything to drink?" he asked her, ever the gentleman, even in her own temporary home.

"No thanks, I'm good. What about you?"

"I don't need anything more to drink; I must have had an entire pot of tea."

"I meant, are you good, Connor?" she asked quietly, not wanting to startle him, but needing to know. *Needing*, which she didn't like at all, but the feeling that something was wrong was too strong to ignore.

"What? Sure, I am. Fine."

"It's just that you seemed pretty wound up at dinner."

"Did I, now? Well, work has been a bit rough. Nothing I can't handle. I'm a little behind on my next project, is all."

"Do you need to go? I don't mean to keep you from working. I know it's important. You don't need to stay."

She started to get to her feet, but he stopped her with a hand on her wrist.

"I don't need to leave, Mischa. I'll stop brooding over my work; you don't need to worry about it. I have everything under control."

She settled back into her seat. "You always do."

He cocked an eyebrow.

She shrugged. "I wasn't being facetious, Connor. It's true, you are always in control."

"Are you saying you don't like it?"

"No. You know I do. And I don't mean just the sex, the power play. I like that you're someone who's in command of his life. It's the way I like to run my life, too. Organized. Career-driven."

"Yeah. So, what are you leaving out?"

"Why do you think I'm leaving something out?"

"I'm trained to read the subtext, aren't I? And there's more beneath the surface with you."

His eyes were gleaming in the lamplight. Watchful, as always, but she could still swear there was something else going on in there.

"Isn't there with everyone?" she asked.

"Yeah, sure. But something specific is going on with you right now."

"And there isn't with you?"

He was quiet a moment, a frown passing over his lush mouth. "Touché," he said softly.

Despite their uneasy banter she was acutely aware of the heat of his body next to hers. No matter what she was angsting over—and she had to admit she was, too often these days—that part never went away. And now, when he was a little uptight, maybe even a little angry—even though *she* was a little angry—she felt the fire of his presence down to her bones.

"Connor, I don't mean to . . . Hell, I don't know what I'm doing. Annoying you. Making you mad."

"I'm not mad."

He reached out, tucked her hair behind her ear. A small shiver went through her. His gaze met hers, a smoky green in the soft light coming from the floor lamp, the reflection of streetlights gleaming through the bank of tall windows. There was a tenderness there, a bit of rawness. Maybe a little of the anger—or whatever it was—glittering in his steady gaze. And so it surprised her when he pulled her in hard, crushing her breasts against the solid planes of his chest, and kissed her. Surprised her again when his kiss was fierce enough to take her breath away.

The man was all contradictions, which confused and enticed her at the same time. But in moments, she was unable to think about it. To think about anything. He undressed her quickly, with rough hands, never taking his mouth from hers. Her dress slipped from her shoulders, then her bra. He slid the fabric from beneath her body, taking her panties along, too. And still kissing her, he unzipped her boots, pulled them off, leaving her in nothing but her thigh-high knit tights.

He was still kissing her as he undressed himself, pausing to pinch her nipples, to reach under her and squeeze her bottom just a little too hard as his clothes came off. When they were both naked he pressed her down into the cushions and immediately lowered his head as he held her down, one hand on her belly, one on her thigh, spreading her open for him.

He dipped his head and went right to work, taking her clit into his mouth, sucking hard.

"Jesus, Connor. Give me a second to . . . oh . . ."

His tongue was swirling on the tip of her clitoris. She felt that small nub of flesh going hard, growing longer as he sucked her into his hot mouth.

He was still holding her down, and when she tried to shift position he held her harder, not allowing her to move. And there was not one part of her that wanted to rebel against his hold on her. She was loving every moment of it, needing to be taken over by him, to lose herself in it.

Pleasure poured through her, wave after sinuous wave, curling deep into her belly, spreading to her already clenching pussy, her hardening nipples.

He pushed his fingers inside her, and her body arched off the sofa.

"Oh!"

He began to fuck her with his hand, hard and deep and fast. His mouth on her was just as demanding. Demanding of her pleasure. Demanding that she come. She felt desire rising to a dizzying peak so fast she couldn't even question it. His hand on her thigh gripped harder, digging into her flesh, and she knew that he was *owning* her in exactly the way she craved. Needed.

Connor. Make me come.

She was unable to speak the words aloud. Yet he got the message, loud and clear. He pumped into her, curving his fingers to hit her G-spot as he sucked on her clit, over and over, his tongue slipping into her opening along with his thrusting fingers. Sensation was an ocean, drowning her as she fell, into the depths, her body shaking as she came.

"Oh . . ."

He paused to murmur, "That was beautiful, Mischa. Again."

"Connor, I don't know—"

"Come again for me."

He bent to her soaking cleft once more, taking her sore clitoris into his heated mouth. This time he ran his tongue over the swollen tip, gently, gently, making desire course through her, liquid and hot. He understood she was sore, sensitive, but he knew exactly what to do. His fingers pressed into her, more gently this time, barely moving, then he added two more, filling her.

"Ah, God, Connor, that's so good."

He twisted his hand as he pressed into her, twisted again on the way out, creating a spiral of sensation that took her right back to that keen edge. And as he gently sucked her needy clitoris into his mouth, his tongue dancing on the tip, she came again, trembling, crying out.

"Connor!"

He shifted, withdrew his fingers, his mouth leaving her, and she was dimly aware of him pulling a condom from the pile of clothes on the floor, the crinkling sound of foil tearing. She forced herself from her post-climax stupor to watch him roll the condom over his big, beautiful cock, watched as he squeezed the base of his thick shaft, heard the small gasping intake of his breath.

She waited, but he held himself over her for a few moments, looking at her.

"You have the most perfect breasts I've ever seen, have I told you that, darlin'?" he asked, stroking the curve of them with gentle fingers.

She smiled. "You have."

"Well, 'tis true." His accent was heavy, his voice low and rough. "And your eyes are the most startling blue. Like the sky. I feel like . . ." He paused, one finger reaching out to stroke her cheek. " . . . Like I can fall into them. I do, every time I'm with you, Mischa, my girl."

What was he saying? Tears stung at the back of her eyes. Her heart was hammering in her chest.

"And when I'm inside you, in your fine, tight body, nothing else matters." His dark brows drew together. His face was full of need, and something else she couldn't identify. He slipped his hand between her thighs, into her wet heat, and she moaned. "This is heaven, my girl. But it's not all of it. Not just the way you look, the way you feel. It's your God damn skin. It's the scent of you making me crazy every minute of the day. It's . . ."

He stopped, and she felt as if her heart stopped beating for a moment, waiting for him to finish the sentence.

He shook his head, his gaze going even darker with desire. "I have to just fuck you now. Do you understand?"

She nodded, even though she didn't, really. She didn't know what he meant, what he'd been about to say, but hadn't. All she knew was that if he wasn't going to tell her, having him fill her was the next best thing.

"Open for me," he said, his tone quieter, yet as commanding as ever.

She spread her legs, wrapping them over his wide back, and he slid home.

His rigid flesh filled her, a little bigger than she could take, but still never enough.

Never enough of Connor.

Don't think about it.

No, she thought only of the immense pleasure, the shimmering desire flowing through her. The lovely feel of his hard-packed, muscular body crushing her into the sofa cushions. The weight of him holding her down. His heart beating against hers.

Connor closed his eyes, arched his hips, pushing into her slowly, slowly. Pleasure was thick in his veins, in his cock. In his chest, somehow. He didn't dare open his eyes, to look at her face at this moment. He knew he'd lose it if he did. But when she sighed, he couldn't help himself.

It was as bad as he'd thought it might be. Or as good. Better. Her cheeks were flushed, her pupils dilated, her blue eyes glossy. Her mouth cherry red, even with all her lipstick kissed from her lips.

She was the most beautiful woman he'd ever seen.

She was the only woman he wanted.

No.

Just fuck her, now.

He arched into her, felt the tight, velvet sheath of her pussy clasp his cock. Her hands were on his shoulders, then slipping down over his back, making his skin tingle with heat. Making it fucking sing beneath her touch.

Focus.

He slipped out of her, almost to the tip, then plunged deep.

"Ah, Connor."

Yes, say my name. Need to hear it.

No.

He pulled out, thrust again, harder this time, their pelvic bones crashing. He did it again and again. Her arms went around him, held him tight. Fucking *held* him.

His heart twisted in his chest even as pleasure swarmed him, making his entire body go hot and loose. He was melting. Melting into her.

He kept fucking her, driving deep, his hands in her hair, hanging on to the silken strands as if they were some sort of lifeline. He knew he was pulling too hard, hurting her with his pummeling cock, his hips. Loved that she didn't do anything but pant, moan. Hold him tighter.

His vision blurred, and she was a watercolor wash of blue eyes, red lips, that perfect porcelain skin. And as his climax roared through him his vision went black and he fell into her. Into her arms. Into her body.

Mischa.

He was in love with her.

No.

He was shaking with an indescribable pleasure. With the pure thrill of coming into this woman. And with a bone-shattering fear.

I cannot love her.

But I do.

God fucking damn it.

He wanted to pull away from her, but he was too weak from coming. Too weak with the emotion surging through him, like some physical sensation weighing him down. All he could do was collapse onto her, her body soft and still beneath his.

He couldn't think about this now. Couldn't figure it out. But there was nothing to figure out. It simply *was*. Not a damn thing he could do about it.

It wasn't about the sex, no matter how mind-blowing, how fucking divine it was with her, even though that's when it had hit him. Like a God damn brick wall. But no, it was her. Who she was. The way she thought about things. Her creativity. Her drive.

Had he ever even been capable of this much lucid thought so soon after coming?

He pulled in a breath. Pulled in the scent of her—some exotic spice he could identify only as *Mischa*.

He needed . . . what? To feel that connection with her in some way other than the sex. Fucking crazy. But it was what it was.

"Mischa."

"Hmm? What is it?"

Her hands made a languorous exploration of his back, soft fingertips stroking his skin, and he had to pause for several moments simply to feel it.

"Can you work on my tattoo?"

"Of course. When do you want me to do it?"

"Now."

"Right now?"

"Do you feel able?"

"I can always tattoo," she answered, a cocky tone in her voice—that fire in her he loved.

"I know it's late. Can you finish it tonight?" he asked her.

"I don't mind it being late, and one more long session is really all it'll take. But you'll have to let me up."

He moved off her with some effort. So tempting to stay right where he was, his weight crushing her pliant body into the pillows. But he *needed* her to tattoo him. To work the ink into his skin. To have that moment where it was just the two of them and the sound of the needle buzzing, the endorphins flowing through his system. Her doing what she loved. Doing it with *him*.

She disappeared into the bedroom while he slipped back into his jeans. She came back in black yoga pants and a hot pink thermal shirt that clung to her curves. Her pale hair was the slightest bit tousled, her cheeks still a lovely, blushing pink from the sex. She smiled at him as she passed him to get her red leather equipment case by the front door, and he grabbed her and kissed her briefly but hard on her way back. When he let her go she stepped back, pressed her lips together as she looked up at him, quiet for several seconds. He knew she was wondering what was up with him. He couldn't explain it to her in any way that would make sense.

Finally she took another step back and turned away. "It'll take me a few minutes to set up," she called over her shoulder, moving into the kitchen. "Do you want tea?"

"I'll make it."

"The tea is in the cupboard by the sink."

"Sure, I've got it."

He found the tea, two big white ceramic mugs, and filled the kettle, set it on the stove to heat while she covered the granite bar counter in plastic wrap, squeezed some antibiotic ointment onto the plastic as he'd seen her do before to hold the tiny plastic inkwells in place. She filled them with black and red ink. He couldn't tell exactly what it was she did with her machine—something involving some rubber bands and making small adjustments. He'd ask her about it sometime. But not now. Now he just wanted to get started.

The kettle sang and he made their tea, being sure to place her mug a careful distance from her setup on the counter.

"Are you ready?" she asked him.

He nodded, sat on the high stool, leaning his elbows on the sleek, cool granite.

She smoothed an antibacterial wipe over his skin, then went to work right away.

The moment the needle touched his skin was almost like some sense of relief. He breathed into it: the sound, the small sting. The idea of Mischa quietly concentrating behind him. He sank into it, in much the same way a submissive sank into the rhythm of a flogging, or being bound for hours. It was just the two of them, shrouded by the night sky outside the vaulted loft windows. Nothing between them but the humming tattoo needle, her art, his flesh. He let his body relax, his mind as well. He didn't want to think too much about what was happening to him. About what he felt for her. Some distant part of him could almost accept it. For now, he would let it be—and ignore that "letting it be" had become his new mantra when it came to Mischa, as well as the question of how long he could continue to do that.

Mischa bent over Connor's enormously wide back, her machine familiar and warm in her hand. So strange that he had asked—demanded, almost—that she tattoo him tonight. Right that minute. Not strange that he was demanding. That was pure Connor. But that he would come out of sex asking for it. What was that about?

Of course she had said she would do it. She found it hard to refuse this man anything. Which wasn't entirely about his air of authority. But why now?

The sex tonight had been different. No real kink at all, other than that subtle undertone of Connor being in command. But she didn't think he could be any other way, with her or anyone else, in any aspect of his life. She'd felt so much . . . had had several moments in which she was almost certain he was feeling it, too. And now he wanted her to tattoo him. Not just tattoo him, but finish the job.

Finished.

Was that what was going on? This instant demand to complete the tattoo. Had he decided he was done with her and he didn't want the job to remain unfinished?

Don't get distracted.

But she was good enough at what she did that she could allow a small part of her mind to run independently of the needle. And she knew exactly the detail she wanted to add to this design, had been thinking about it for the last few weeks.

He didn't act as if he was done with her. But then, she'd always been the one to finish with a man. She had no idea what it was like to be on the receiving end. Maybe this was some sort of divine retribution.

She was waxing too philosophical. Too much while she was working. Too much, period.

She was probably just being paranoid. But she couldn't help that small, nagging voice in the back of her mind that kept telling her it was over. That they'd had their run and it had been lovely, but Connor had had his fill. Too bad she hadn't. Too bad she didn't think she ever would have her fill of Connor Galloway.

thirteen

It was after five in the morning when she was done. She wiped his skin one more time, admiring her own work. The dragon was massive, covering his entire upper back. It was some of her best work to date, the details perfect: the shaded scales, the red lashing tongue, the wicked points of claw and wing. The attitude of the dragon was perfect for Connor—a beast of elegance and power.

"All done," she told him.

Can't even think those words.

"Ah, good. Let's go look in the mirror."

She followed him into the bathroom and handed him the hand mirror she kept in her kit, which he held up so he could see the reflection of his back in the enormous pewter-framed mirror over the sink. She looked with him, over his shoulder—or rather, around it. Enjoyed the heavy muscles there, the way they flexed as he shifted position, as much as the tattoo she'd done.

"This is amazing." There was real awe in his tone. "Better

than I could have imagined. Odd how it all seems to come together in a new way, now that it's completed. Except that I see the same thing in my own work, at times. No matter how you imagine it, how the lines flow together while you're working on it, the final product has some magic all its own."

"I feel that way about my work a lot. It's never really complete until it's finished. Not even the image in my head."

"Yes, exactly." He put the mirror down on the edge of the sink, leaned in and pressed a kiss on her forehead, which was achingly sweet to her. "Thank you. It's beyond beautiful."

"You're welcome."

He leaned back against the counter, staring down at her. His expression was dark. Unreadable. "I like that we understand each other. That we're both artists, of a sort. Not that what I do equals your work in any way."

"Of course it does. I don't understand when you say that."

"Contracted work is not art."

"But it is. And that's what I do most of the time, anyway. My clients give me specifics that I have to follow. It's still art because it's our interpretation of the image. It's our artistic voice that goes into it every time."

"Hmm, I suppose you're right. I don't usually think of it that way. I guess . . . that I feel there's some value taken away because I get paid to do it."

"Sounds like some latent guilt to me," she teased, their easy banter helping her to relax.

"Well, I was raised in the Catholic church, so the guilt goes without saying, doesn't it?"

"So I've heard."

His expression had shifted as they talked, and now his eyes were sparkling a lovely deep green, the golden highlights gleaming.

"Mischa. Let me draw you," he asked suddenly.

"Okay."

"Now."

She laughed. "Now?"

He pulled her into him, kissed her hard, his mouth sweet and firm. He pulled back. "Come on. The light is perfect at sunrise. And there are all these windows . . ."

She laughed again. "Okay. Let's do it."

It made her heart soar a little that he'd asked to draw her. She remembered the first time he'd brought it up. She'd been excited about the prospect then, too. And now her body was heating up at the idea of stripping down for him, sitting perfectly still in exactly the way he wanted her to. There was something submissive in the act, she thought. But it was also just very simply sexy as hell.

They went back into the living room and she lent him one of her drawing pads, some charcoal pencils.

"Take off your clothes," he said with a small nod of his chin. "I turned up the heat; I don't want you to chill."

She stripped down, tilting her head as he stared at her. She loved the way he was looking at her, his gaze appraising, but in a way it never had been before. She imagined he was taking in the lines of her body, her face, his eyes catching where the light and shadow hit. And was acutely aware when his gaze lingered on her bare breasts, the naked vee between her thighs. She grew wet again just having him look at her this way. Being naked. Feeling more naked than she did when they were about to have sex. When he was going to spank her. This was more like it had been when she was naked at the Pleasure Dome, that same sort of thrill of exhibitionism, even though he had, of course, looked at her naked before. It didn't quite make sense, even in her own head. All she knew was that this felt different. That it felt amazing.

"Beautiful," he said. "We'll do one of you standing first, just like that, by the windows. That's perfect, with the morning light coming in from behind you. A quick sketch. I won't leave you on your feet for too long. I want you to take a deep breath, relax. Yes, with one knee bent, so that your weight is resting on the other leg. Let your arms hang at your sides and tilt your chin a bit. Perfect. Hold it right there."

The pencil was already moving as he spoke. He drew in quick bursts, looking at her carefully then glancing down at the pad of paper. And she stood there, motionless as a statue, something surging in her at the effort it took to hold still. At the yielding in her body, her mind. In doing what he wanted of her.

He was true to his word; he sketched for maybe fifteen or twenty minutes before he told her to sit down on the sofa.

He came to stand over her, and she noticed the smear of the charcoal on the fingertips of his right hand.

"Let's lay you back a bit. Yes, lean on your elbows. And one knee up." He used his hands to position her leg exactly where he wanted it, and his touch was like a small frisson of flame on her skin. "How long can you hold your head back? I want you in a pose of ecstasy, your head thrown back, if you can. I want your hair sweeping the surface of the sofa."

"I can hold it," she told him, feeling a sense of pride. She *would* do it.

"Excellent."

He was drawing again, crouching on the floor, then standing, looking at her from different positions. And to her amazement he paused now and then to touch her, running his hand down her calf, or over the shape of her foot, her hip, her belly. And finally he touched his fingertips to her jaw, her lips.

She was shaking. Not with fatigue, although she felt that, too. But with a simmering need for him. She was a little out of her head from not sleeping. But it was also that this time together was dreamlike, with the misty morning light casting a pale white and golden glow everywhere in the room. Over her body, tipping the rise of her breasts and belly. She thought of the way the ocean around San Francisco looked in the morning, at times, the crest of the waves tipped in fog-shrouded light. How soft this sort of light was. And she felt soft all over—her body. Her *self*.

She wasn't even quite sure what she meant. Maybe that the hard shell she'd created for herself as protection was . . . melting away. And because she knew that even now, while Connor was drawing her rather than spanking her, being in those active roles, she was just as much *in his hands*. And it was where she wanted to be.

"Mischa, let's have your head back up, now."

He placed one hand on the back of her neck, smoothed it upward, beneath her hair, making her shiver, helping her to raise her head. "Are you cold, darlin'?"

She shook her head. "No."

"You're sure?"

She nodded. It was all she could do.

"All right, then." He took a step back, then another. "Look at me. Tilt your chin down, but let's have your gaze on me. Ah, so sleepy," he murmured. "Sexy as hell, the look in your eyes."

He moved back in, swept her hair away from her face, paused with his hand on her cheek. She closed her eyes, absorbing the heat of his hand. His hand was replaced with his lips, and he trailed small, fiery kisses over her jaw, down the side of her neck. Her nipples came up hard, her clit pulsing.

"Oh, you are too tempting," he said, his voice husky, his accent a heavy rolling on his tongue.

He brushed his fingers over her breasts, circling the nipples for a moment, making them ache. Then he lowered his hand between her thighs and pressed on her clitoris. Her eyes flew open and she caught his gaze on her face as he stroked her wet cleft.

"Love that you're always so ready. So wet." Keeping his gaze on hers, he drew his fingers to his lips, slipped them briefly into his mouth. "Love the taste of you. Pure honey, it is."

She moaned, her lashes fluttering. He was killing her.

"Connor . . ."

"Shh. You're going to lie perfectly still and let me draw you before I fuck you again. Oh yes. Don't question it, my girl. If you had a free hand I'd have you feel how rock hard I am for you. But I will wait until I'm done with this. Until I've captured you on paper. Tell me, do you want me to fuck you, Mischa?"

"Yes," she breathed.

"Say it."

"I want you, Connor," she said quietly. "I want you to fuck me. Hard, the way you do."

He laughed, a raw, sensual sound. "I will. Don't doubt it, darlin'."

When he got up and moved back she watched him, his big body graceful, the hard ridge of his erection straining against his jeans.

She was soaking wet. Her body, her mind, buzzing.

Love you.

She couldn't say it aloud. But she could think it. And at this moment, there was nothing in her that was able to fight it.

He kept moving around the room, turning over pages on the tablet, starting a new sketch, then very quickly going to another page once more. After a while she came to see there was a rhythm to his movements, to the way he changed positions, drew from different angles. And she sank into that rhythm, very much in the same way she did when he was spanking or flogging her.

Eventually he said to her, "Turn over, Mischa."

"What?"

"A little spaced, are you? It happens. And I like to see you this way. In fact, it's perfect for what I have in mind."

"What's that?" she asked.

But before she got an answer he'd flipped her over onto her stomach as if she weighed nothing in his big hands, and started to spank her.

"Oh!"

He didn't say a word, just kept up a hard, punishing pace, his palms coming down on her hot flesh until her buttocks were on fire. And need burned just as brightly between her thighs.

He stopped and she swore she heard his panting breath as he slipped a hand between her thighs, swiped at her juices, making her pussy clench.

"Must draw you now, with your ass this beautiful shade of pink."

She stayed where she was on her stomach on the sofa, holding her upper body up, braced on her elbows. Her breasts brushed the suede surface, the upholstery soft on her engorged nipples. If only he would take a moment to touch them, pinch them . . .

But soon enough she was falling into that easy pattern of breath and stillness, giving herself over. Her head hummed, her eyes half-lidded in the fog-clouded light coming through the windows, invading her mind like a veil. Time passed, but she'd lost track. It didn't seem to matter.

"Mischa," he said finally.

"Hmm?"

"It's time."

Suddenly he was behind her, his naked hips pressing against her still-sore buttocks, his arm wrapping around her waist, pulling her to her knees. Then he was parting her thighs with his knees, sliding the tip of his sheathed cock between her swollen pussy lips. She loved how he did this, took her by surprise. Started right in on her with no warning. It was too good.

"Connor . . ."

"Going to fuck you, my girl. Going to drive in hard. Take a breath."

She obeyed, trembling all over, going wetter, impossibly. He ground home with one thrust.

"Ah, God, Connor."

He pulled back, slung his hips and arched into her, his heavy cock filling her, hot and pulsing. Pleasure was like an arc of lightning, searing her. Shocking her.

She pushed back against him, taking him deep. His hands came up to cup her breasts, his fingers tugging on her nipples as he fucked her. His cock was a solid shaft of velvety flesh. Desire was like some radiant light, insinuating itself in every fiber. Pleasure came from every direction at once: her pussy, her nipples, even from his hips grinding against her body. It was his scent, his skin.

It built, potent, undeniable. And finally, irresistible as her climax came crashing down on her. The light filled her mind, dazzling her as she came.

"Connor! Oh . . ."

"Darlin', yes . . . yes . . . come for me. Christ, I'm coming, my girl. Ah . . ."

He arched into her, driving her orgasm on. And even through the condom she felt the heat, the power, of his climax. Then his big body shaking, the panting heat of his breath in her hair.

"Ah!"

It was a primal sound, an animal sound of exquisite pleasure. She knew it, felt it reverberate deep in her body.

He slipped out of her, dragging her with him until they were lying together on the sofa, Connor behind her, spooning her.

She felt loose all over, relaxed. Trusting that they were on the same page. That she didn't need to question what was happening between them.

They'd had a strange and amazing night, unlike any experience she'd had with a man. She was exhausted, limp. Too tired to question any of it, as she normally would. And maybe, just once, that was a good thing. For now she would simply enjoy Connor's big body solid behind hers. The way he'd looped one arm around her waist, his hand splayed across her stomach, his hold possessive.

Yes, for once in her life, she was ready to let go the rein she always held so tightly. On her life. On herself. On her heart. She was ready.

With that thought, that trust, in her mind, she closed her eyes against the pale light of morning, and slept.

Connor opened his eyes, guessed from the angle of the sun coming through the windows that they'd slept no more than an hour or two. Mischa's breath was a quiet rhythm. She was still asleep. So soft beside him. So perfect in his arms he could barely breathe.

His pulse ratcheted up, his heart beating out a frantic cadence against the cage of his ribs.

He had to get up.

He shook his head, rubbed a hand over his eyes. He couldn't calm himself.

He moved carefully, not wanting to disturb her. But he was desperate to get up, to get some distance between them. Some space to think. To breathe. When he managed to get up from the sofa, she sighed, her eyes still closed, and rolled onto her back. He stood and stared at her. She was that fucking beautiful. She was that good.

Too good for the likes of him.

He shook his head. Ran a hand over the short stubble of his hair.

Fucking idiot, to fall for this girl. To let things go this far.

His heart was a small hammer in his chest, growing larger by the moment.

Have to leave.

He shook his head again. He couldn't just leave her. It was wrong, to leave after the night they'd had. Without seeing to her, making sure she was down from subspace. To make sure she was okay.

He wasn't okay.

Fuck.

He stepped backward, his bare foot coming into contact with his jeans on the floor, and beside them the sketchpad. He bent down and took the pad in his hands, glancing at the sketches there. He'd almost captured her.

Almost.

He looked once more at where she lay quietly on the green sofa. She was naked, and so damn gorgeous it made his chest ache. How could any woman look like this? Flesh over bone in perfect, rounded proportion. And her face . . . His fingers ached to reach out and touch her cheekbone, her closed eyelids. Her red lips. But he wouldn't do it. Couldn't do it.

And Christ, her scent was all over him.

He gently pulled a throw blanket over her still form before he picked up his jeans, took them along with the sketchpad into the bathroom. Stared at himself in the mirror.

He was a fraud. Posing as some responsible dom when he was about to leave this woman after he'd played her only a few hours ago. Without checking to see how she was doing. Oh yes, he was leaving.

Love her.

No.

Impossible. It was *him*, for God's sake! He could not do this. To himself, maybe. But certainly not to her. He would fuck it up royally, just like he had with Ginny. Just like his father had with his mum. It was in the genes. It was in the lousy fucking example he'd been given of what a man was. He may have spent the last number of years trying to learn to be a better man than he used to be. A damn sight better than his father, sure. But it was the bounds within the roles of BDSM, those rules involved in being a responsible dominant, that kept it all in check. Those were the boundaries in which he could function as someone in command of himself. If he were to have more with Mischa those roles wouldn't always be present and he . . . he wasn't certain what might happen. He couldn't risk it. That in itself would be a loss of control to some degree he hadn't ever experienced. And letting go control . . . Well, that would be a disaster for him. And more importantly, for Mischa.

He would not do it. He'd come too close already. Taken things with her too far. His own damn fault. Unforgivable.

His chest felt like a raw, open wound as he slid his way into his jeans, ripped the sketches from the pad and held them carefully as he made his way back into the living room to find his shirt, his shoes, his coat. He took one last look at her, so damn lovely it tore at him.

His hands were fisted at his sides, the one hand crushing the edges of the sketches as he watched her sleep for as long as he dared. When he knew he couldn't possibly take it any longer, he turned away, opened the door and walked out.

Mischa woke knowing something was wrong. It wasn't simply the absence of Connor's big body next to hers. He could have been in the kitchen, the bathroom. But somehow, even before she opened her eyes, she knew he wasn't.

The pain began instantly. Why would he have left, if it wasn't what she'd been dreading nearly the entire time they'd been together?

She made herself get up, pulling the throw blanket around her bare shoulders. She didn't remember how it had gotten there—they'd gone to sleep naked. Pressed together.

She bit her lip against the tiny sob that wanted to escape.

She moved into the kitchen, rubbing her eyes, trying to clear the grainy blur from lack of sleep. If he'd left a note for her the most obvious place would be on the high bar counter. There was nothing there. Somehow, she'd known there wouldn't be. And yet, she made herself check the coffee table, the bathroom mirror, the front door.

Nothing.

The emptiness threatened to open its yawning mouth, to suck her in. She steeled herself against it.

Don't be dramatic. It could be anything.

She knew it wasn't true even as she dialed his cell phone, which went right to voice mail.

"Connor, it's me. Mischa. I just . . . was wondering where you wandered off to this morning. Okay. Call me when you get a chance."

She sounded so casual. What a good little actress she was. What a good little liar. Because beneath the words, the tone, she was a fucking mess. Barely fending off collapsing into tears.

No.

This was exactly what she'd never wanted to do. To turn into Evie. She was not that person. She was a hell of a lot stronger than that.

She could almost smell the stench of stale pot smoke in the air.

Could almost feel the birdlike bones of her mother's arm as she helped her into the bathtub after too many days of lying on the couch. Evie had always looked so utterly blank during one of her dark times. No expression as the silent tears would wash down her cheeks.

Sometimes that was the scariest part of it all—that her mother had been so rendered numb it was as if she wasn't *in* there anywhere. Just . . . gone. Leaving a nine-year-old Mischa—or eight- or seven- or even six-year-old—to try and handle everything.

She shivered, the cold biting deep.

It was damn hard at the moment to remember her strength. Maybe she couldn't do this alone.

She picked up her phone again and dialed Dylan's number.

"Hello?"

"Dylan, it's me."

"Hi, Misch. What's up?"

"Do you know, by any chance, if Alec has talked to Connor this morning?"

"I don't know. Alec left early, and I haven't talked to him other than a brief text a few hours ago. Why? What's up?"

"He was . . . He was here last night." She had to pause, her throat going tight.

"Misch?"

She drew in a long breath. "This is probably just me being paranoid."

"Okay," Dylan said slowly. "I might believe that if I'd ever witnessed you being paranoid. *Ever.* Just tell me what's going on."

"Nothing." She took a breath, tried to keep her voice from shaking. "It's nothing. We were together last night and we . . . I finished his tattoo. And then . . ." She stopped, biting her lip. "Dylan, I feel like an idiot. Because I know better, you know? I do. And this is just . . . stupid beyond belief. He's probably at home working. He probably forgot to tell me he had to get an early start."

"He didn't say good-bye? Leave you a note?"

"No. Nothing."

Nothing. That's what I have.

That chasm threatened to open up and swallow her again.

"I don't like this," Dylan said. "Let me call Alec and—"

"No, please, don't do that. It's bad enough that I'm being foolish in front of you."

"Oh, honey, you're not being foolish. Alec won't think so, either, I promise."

"Just . . . let's give it a little more time. I'm sure he'll get my phone message and call me back later. I'm being stupid."

"Did he play you last night?" She heard the sharp edge in Dylan's voice.

"Well, it was more early this morning. Just some spanking. Nothing too heavy."

"Misch, these guys—Alec's particular circle of friends—are *always* playing heavy, no matter the pain level, or even the absence of pain. They are very serious players. The dynamic is always there."

"Yes," she said, more meekly than she'd wanted to.

"Then he's an irresponsible asshole to take off without doing proper aftercare. This is not okay. And I'm sorry to be ranting. Are you all right? Do you need me to come over?"

"No, don't disrupt your schedule. Like I said, he'll show up sooner or later. I just need to chill."

"Are you sure? It's not a problem. I can be there in twenty minutes. If you're bottoming out I should come—you shouldn't be alone."

Mischa ran a hand through her tangled hair. "Please don't worry about me, Dylan. I can handle this. I'm a little raw, but I'll be fine. Maybe I just need to wake up, have some tea."

"Well, call me later. Let me know what happens. Let me know if you need anything."

"I will. Promise."

They hung up, and she felt like more of a liar than ever. She'd lied to her best friend. She was absolutely not okay. And she knew already that Connor was not returning her call. Not now. Not ever.

She spent the day wrapped in the same small blanket, staring at the television. She rarely watched TV, but the only other option was reading, and she knew she didn't have enough concentration to take in anything she might read. She could have drawn. But drawing, even looking at her sketchpad, after what had gone on that morning, was out of the question. She may as well just pierce her heart with a kitchen knife and be done with it.

Instead, she drowsed her way through several old black-and-white movies, an animal documentary, spent twenty minutes at a time flipping through channels, barely aware of what she was looking at.

By the time the sun was going down, the evening sky paling, the television making a blue-washed flicker against the tall windows, she still hadn't heard from him. And as ridiculous as she knew it was, she called him once more.

"Connor, it's me again. Mischa, in case you've forgotten who I am. Which you have, apparently." She sucked in a breath. "Shit. I'm sorry. I don't mean to sound so . . . Anyway. Call me, okay?"

She slammed her cell phone a little too hard on the coffee table.

God damn him!

She tried to shake it off—she hated being angry. It wasn't a constructive emotion. But she was pissed.

Her phone buzzed and she grabbed for it, her heart thrumming like a small caged hummingbird in her chest.

Dylan.

She couldn't talk to her. Couldn't face her sympathy, or even her being enraged on her behalf. She let the call go to voice mail.

She got up, then, went into the kitchen and found a bottle of wine. A good California Cabernet, probably much too good for what she had planned for it, but she'd repay Dylan later. She opened it, took it back to the sofa and curled up with it in her lap. She stared at the TV as she drank, one swallow, then another, straight from the bottle.

It was an ugly thing to do; she knew that. But this was what she needed right now. To stop thinking, dissecting. To make herself numb. Not like Evie. *Never* like Evie. Just for a little while. Just for the night. She would allow herself this one thing. Tomorrow she would get back to her life. Business as usual, with her in control.

She tilted the bottle, took another long pull on it. She was right; the wine was excellent. Even drinking as fast as she was, she could taste it. But she got no pleasure from it. Not even from the small buzz that was loosening her muscles already.

She had a feeling it would be a very long time before anything felt good to her again.

When she woke up with the new day's sun shining too brightly into her bone-dry eyes, she knew she'd been right. She felt like absolute crap. She was hungover, stiff from spending an entire day and night on the sofa—and hell, much of the night before, too. And that deep, aching dread of Connor's absence was like a weight on her chest, threatening to crush her.

I won't have it.

No, today she would pull herself together. She'd start with a shower.

She got up, dropping the blanket, and moved into the bathroom. She turned on the taps, avoiding her reflection in the big pewter-framed mirror while she waited for the water to heat. When the room began to steam up, she stepped in.

The water felt surprisingly nice, the warmth seeping into her skin, easing her aching head as she let it run over her hair.

It was then the tears started.

She moved her face under the warm spray of water, let it wash away the tears. She didn't want to acknowledge them. She was not that girl—the girl who cried over a man. Who fell in love and had him fucking leave her.

She was not her mother.

Her hands flew to her stomach, an unreasonable fear rising like bile in her throat, but she knew she couldn't be pregnant. They'd practiced safe sex, and she'd been on the pill since she was seventeen. She let her hands drop, feeling foolish. But Evie had had her heart broken even after Mischa and Raine had been born. She'd been broken over and over, every time she opened her heart to another man who eventually stomped on it.

Just like her father had. Like Raine's father had. And now, despite her best efforts, it was happening to her.

The tears grew hot, scalding her eyelids. Hot with anger. Hot with fear—the fear of what this made her. The scorned woman.

Connor.

She could see his face behind her tightly shut eyelids. Almost too handsome if it didn't have that rugged edge: the square chin, the strong jawline, and the scar beneath his eye to set off the lush mouth, the dark lashes, the gleaming green and gold eyes.

She'd sworn she'd seen emotion in those eyes. But then how could he just take off without another word to her? Without even telling her it was over?

"God damn it, Connor," she muttered.

She pulled back, shook her head, steeled herself as she swept her wet hair from her face.

She was not having this. She would not be so damn weak. She would not waste her life, not one more breath, on tears over this man.

He was dangerous. She'd known it right away. And hadn't heeded her own instincts. She'd told herself she could handle it. It had been a lie all along.

He was far too dangerous for her to stay in Seattle. She couldn't see him, not before she'd really had a chance to pull herself back together. Even though right now it felt like that might never happen.

She booked her flight using her laptop. Amazing how quickly one could buy a plane ticket, make a quick escape. A few minutes later she was tossing her clothes into her suitcase, carefully cleaning and packing up the tattoo gear she'd let sit out all night. Irresponsible of her. But that's what he did to her. He turned her head, made it impossible to think. And that was exactly why he was such a danger to her. She could lose everything, being distracted by him. Her business, her success, everything she'd spent her life working so hard to build. Everything that made her feel she had some value. The things in her life that kept her safe.

She waited until she'd called a cab before she sent Dylan a text explaining that she was leaving immediately for the airport, promising to be back in time for the wedding. She felt terrible leaving Dylan with only a few weeks to go and still so much to be done. She felt selfish. But she also felt it was a matter of survival, at this point. She knew Dylan would be understanding, but she couldn't bring herself to talk to her. Couldn't bring herself to say out loud what she was going through.

She had to get out of Seattle. Had to get as far away from Connor as she could.

Connor.

Her chest surged with emotions, everything tangled up into one razor-sharp ball of pain: love and rage, fear and a terrible, tearing sadness. Love.

Love . . .

Fuck.

She cursed the damn tears that squeezed from her eyes as the cab made its way to the airport. The sun was setting, the gray sky lighting for a while with a wash of pale silver, and as they left the city proper, left Connor Galloway behind, it began to rain.

But the truth was, *he* had left *her.* Left her alone without so much as a note, a call, a good-bye. Left her with nothing.

She had to clench her fists until her short, red-lacquered nails bit into her palms, had to grind her jaw against the pain that slammed into her like a wall. She bit back the tears, her throat aching, burning.

She had no idea how she was going to endure this. She almost wanted to call Evie and ask her how she'd survived this. But she knew from a lifetime of experience that Evie had no coping tools other than checking out. She'd put on a pretty dress, search out some drum circle or art festival where she could meet the flaky artist and musician types she was always drawn to—the supposedly spiritual types, which was a joke—and she'd forget herself in a new man's arms.

Mischa didn't want anyone else. And she knew damn well that wasn't a fix for this.

She'd simply have to find a way to get through this. To survive her first heartbreak.

She swore it would be her last.

fourteen

Sweat rolled down Connor's forehead as he pressed the barbell up, his jaw ground tight. He tried one more rep, barely made it, and with a groan he jerked the weight back onto the bar. Four hundred pounds on the bench press was his normal weight, but he'd been spending most of his time at the gym the last four days, working out until his muscles screamed. Until he was so exhausted he'd go home and fall into bed after a brief hot shower. Now he was drained, plain and simple. He knew he'd pushed his body too far.

He sat up, wiped his face with a towel, breathing hard, nausea roiling in his gut.

He couldn't stand to stay in the shower long enough to soak out the pain in his muscles. It made him think too much of *her*. Hell, everything did. Which was why he was practically living at the gym. It was the only place he could go where there were no reminders of her.

Except that he was there, and he was still thinking of her, wasn't he?

He couldn't take any more working out tonight. His body was done. He had to go home.

He grabbed his water bottle and sipped slowly, waiting for the nausea to calm before he stood and headed out to the parking garage. After the heat of the gym the Seattle cold hit his sweat-soaked skin like a small shock, making him shiver.

He was turning into one hell of a pansy. But it was more than the fact that he'd maxed out at the gym. That he was feeling the cold down to his bones. It was that he'd never felt like such a coward, so damn weak, in his life. Not since the last foolish wall-punching episode. And he'd been young enough then to have some sliver of an excuse.

He got into his Hummer and turned the engine over, his gaze on the stark gray concrete wall in front of him. But it was no help. He saw her in his mind's eye every time he got into his car. The way she'd go so still and quiet in the plush seat, as if the size of the vehicle itself sent her down into subspace. Maybe it did. He'd seen it happen with other women.

He didn't want to think about other women. He hadn't wanted to since the minute he'd laid eyes on Mischa.

Don't think her name, damn it. Don't do it.

His cell phone buzzed and he cursed as he hit the answer button, forgetting for a moment that he wasn't talking to anyone, that he hadn't since he'd crept out of Dylan's apartment like some thief, leaving Mischa behind, four days earlier. Fucking four and a half, if anyone was counting, which he was, apparently.

"Who's calling?" he growled.

"Jesus, Connor. Someone piss on your parade?"

"Alec."

"Yeah. Should I even ask how you're doing?"

Connor rubbed at the back of his neck. He hadn't intended to talk to anyone, but Alec was on the phone and he had to say something, didn't he? "Not so good, to be honest. Which is something I haven't done much of lately."

"What's going on? I've been calling you since Monday. Not to go grandma on you, but you sound like shit, brother."

"Feel like shit."

"Want to tell me about it?" Alec asked.

"No, not really."

"Let me guess that it has something to do with Mischa taking off back to San Francisco Sunday night?"

"What? She left?"

"She hasn't talked to Dylan about it. I assume that means you two haven't talked, either."

"You'd assume right." Connor couldn't keep another growl out of his tone.

"And," Alec continued, "I assume that's why you're in such a shitty mood."

"Shitty mood doesn't begin to describe it."

Alec was quiet a moment. "I know we're not all about sharing our feelings, Connor, but tell me what the hell happened. And before you tell me you'd rather not, that's already obvious. Do it, anyway."

Alec was right. He didn't want to talk about it. He didn't want to talk about anything. How he'd been ignoring work. How he'd been brooding like a kicked puppy. He didn't want to talk about the fucking *weather*. But he couldn't stand feeling like he was about to explode every single waking moment of the day.

"I left her." His stomach tightened into a hard knot, his free hand gripping the steering wheel. "And I didn't do it right. I didn't check in with her. I didn't make sure she was okay. I didn't do any of the things we've been trained to do. That *I've* been trained to do. Totally fucking gutless and irresponsible, I know it."

"You left after you played her," Alec said. It was a statement, not a question.

"I did." He could rake himself over the coals again for it, but he was too damn tired.

Another long pause on the other end of the phone. "We'll talk about that part later. What else? And don't make me pull it out of you. Spill."

"She called me a few times. I didn't pick up. Never called her back."

"Because?"

"Because I fucking can't, Alec! I can't do it. Can't talk to her. Can't see her again."

"You're making a hell of a big deal out of this, Connor. In the past you would have just sent the girl home, whoever she was. End of story. You told me before that things were different with Mischa. So what happened with her that made you act like such a God damn jerk?"

"I know it. So . . ." He paused, ran a hand over his head. "I can't believe I'm saying it, but I love the girl. I think she loves me back."

"Are you fucking crazy, Connor?"

"Probably. Yeah, I'm thinking I am."

"Why the hell would you leave like that if you love her? Did you two have a fight?"

"No, no fight. I don't know. No. I do know. She's better off. I have my reasons, Alec."

"Did you ever consider that maybe your reasons are bullshit? Mine were, back when I didn't think I could be with Dylan."

"I don't know . . ." But his mind was churning. What if Alec was right?

"Something to think about. That's all I'm saying."

"So I'm thinking."

"Okay. Let me know how things work out."

"Yeah. Will do."

They hung up quickly. He liked that about Alec—that he knew when a conversation was done. And he had other things to do. Right now.

He dialed Mischa's number, his head reeling as he waited for her to pick up. What the hell would he even say to her? But after a few rings it went to voice mail.

"Hey, Mischa, it's me, Connor. Look, I know I owe you a damn big apology. Let me make it. Call me."

He hung up, feeling like a fool. That hadn't been what he'd meant to say. What needed to be said. Not by a long shot. But he couldn't say it to her voice mail. He had to talk to her.

Fuck.

He gunned the engine, drove out of the garage and headed toward home. If she wouldn't answer his call, he'd have to find another way.

Mischa glanced at her cell phone's caller ID.

She picked it up. "Hi, Greyson."

"Mischa, what's up? I thought we had a phone conference set up at four with the attorney."

"Oh no! I'm sorry, Grey. I forgot. I was at the shop today and I . . . I'm sorry," she said again. "I just forgot."

"Everything okay with you?"

"Yeah, sure." She sat down in the overstuffed red velvet

chair in the living room of her Victorian apartment. "No. Not really."

"Tell me you're not having second thoughts about going into business this late in the game, Mischa."

"What? Of course not. Do you really believe I'd do that?"

"Nope. So, you want to tell me what's really up? Does this have something to do with why you left Seattle early and canceled this meeting with the lawyer in person with no explanation? Because I know you. If it was a family emergency or something with Thirteen Roses you would have told me instead of sending me that vague text telling me you needed to reschedule the talk with the lawyer by phone from San Francisco."

"Grey, I'm just . . . I needed to leave. I needed to get my head together."

"It's that guy Connor, isn't it?"

She sighed, pushed her hair from her face. "Yes."

"Do I need to hire a hit man?"

She laughed a little, the first time she'd even cracked a smile in the five days since she'd been back in San Francisco. "No, that won't be necessary."

"All right. But tell me if you change your mind. I can always use the cash I have stashed away for 1st Avenue Ink."

Smiling hurt a little, but she couldn't help it. "Thanks, Grey. You're a real friend."

His tone sobered. "I am, you know."

"I know."

"So . . . this talking about feelings stuff is new territory for us, other than bitching about our families or work, but if you need me, I'm here."

"I appreciate it. I really do."

"But you're not going to tell me about what happened with you and Connor."

She shook her head, even though she knew he couldn't see her. "I can't right now. I'm mad. And I'm . . . *hurt*. And I just can't talk about it yet."

Even admitting that much out loud was like having a hot poker driven into her chest, and she had to take a slow, steadying breath.

"Well, I'm here," Greyson said again.

"Thank you. And thanks for not drilling me about it."

"Any time."

After they'd rescheduled the phone conference with their attorney and hung up she stood and went to the window. Her apartment was on a quiet street in North Beach, one of a long row of gorgeously detailed Victorians. The sun was just setting, the last rays of the day touching the scrolling gingerbread work of the homes across the street with a pale winter light.

She hated this time of day lately. Ever since she'd returned from Seattle. The nights were endless, and as pretty as she'd always found the setting sun, now it was nothing more than the harbinger of the long, dark night ahead.

She'd tried to stay busy, to stay as late as possible at the shop, but today she'd had nothing booked later than three. She'd attempted to hang out, finding busywork, but eventually she'd had to leave—it wasn't enough to distract her, and she knew she was driving her employees crazy. Working on a tattoo was the only time she was really able to lose herself enough that the constant, drumming pain faded away.

Some ridiculous part of her, she now realized, had thought that if she just came home everything would be okay. But it wasn't. This had been the longest five days of her life.

Damn it, Connor.

Her body was going hot all over. Not with lust, but with a simmering rage. How could he do this to her? How could she have let it happen?

Need to slow down.

She pulled in a long breath, then another. Flattened her palm against the cool window. But once the anger had dissipated all that was left was the part that hurt so badly she could barely breathe.

A short sob escaped her and she clamped a hand over her mouth, trying to hold it in. Trying to get the pain under control. But that was the problem. Connor had opened her up, and her emotions were something over which she no longer *had* control. Her safety net was gone, the one thing that had held her together most of her life. All those years when she'd had to be the adult instead of a child. Control was what had carried her through life, had helped her *make* a life.

She shook her head, willing the fear and confusion and grief away. It didn't work, of course. She had to do *something*. Maybe a long hot shower would help. It would ease some of the tension from her tight shoulders, anyway. They felt like they were made of solid granite, hardened from all these days of holding back the tears with a steel-hard grip.

She turned from the window and made her way down the narrow hall to her bedroom. It was normally her haven, with its white iron bed piled high with pillows and its fluffy lavender down comforter, the highboy dresser she'd found in an antiques shop across the Golden Gate Bridge in Sausalito, the black-and-white fleur-de-lis print curtains she'd had custom made from her own design. But now what was once her favorite room seemed nothing more than an empty space. She'd spent every night since her return on the velvet sofa in the living room. Which didn't make sense. He'd never been with her in her own bed, yet she couldn't stand to sleep in it alone.

With a small sigh she kicked her way out of her Ugg slippers, stripped off her yoga pants and her hooded sweatshirt and took her pink satin robe into the bathroom. There, she turned on the taps, letting the water run to heat up, which took forever in these older buildings.

She caught her reflection in the oval mirror above the pedestal sink. She was pale. Not that she wasn't always pale, but her fair skin had a distinctly gray cast to it. Her eyes were huge. Haunted. Which was exactly how she felt, so she shouldn't have been surprised. But she was. Seeing the pain so stark on her face came as a shock to her. It was why she'd put on her makeup the last few days using her tiny compact to see just one eye at a time, just her lips, her brows. Luckily she was able to do her hair with little effort and without really looking. Because seeing her face like this was too damn awful.

She turned away. She'd have to continue avoiding mirrors for a while. But what really concerned her was that she'd have to return to Seattle soon for Dylan and Alec's wedding; it was only two weeks away. The idea seemed impossible at the moment. It made her stomach churn, her pulse hammer in her veins.

She reached in to the old black-and-white-tiled shower stall to check the water temperature, adjusted it before stepping in, getting under the warm spray.

Yes, this was what she needed. A hot shower to relax. Maybe a few glasses of wine after. She just had to wind down. Because there would be no avoiding Seattle. No avoiding Connor. She would simply have to find a way to do it.

Damn it.

Connor got out of the cab at the address Alec and Dylan had given him after a little strong-arming, some begging, and making them promise not to tell Mischa he was coming, to let him work this through with her on his own. It seemed strange now that

Mischa had never given it to him herself. Or maybe not. Things hadn't been like that between them. No talk of a future beyond what they might want for dinner, what the coming weekend might bring. Certainly nothing beyond Alec and Dylan's wedding.

He stood in front of a row of older homes, Victorians and Tudors that had probably been split up into apartments in this part of town—North Beach, the old Italian section of the city. There were a lot of good restaurants in the area, he knew. It was also home to a number of tattoo shops. He wasn't surprised that this was where Mischa lived.

Her address was a pale pink Victorian with gray and white trim. Pretty place, he could see, even though the sun was mostly set. There were three heavy oak doors at the top of the stairs, with planter boxes on either side of the narrow porch. He checked the address one more time and saw that her door was the one on the left.

He made himself drop his shoulders before ringing the bell, heard it echo somewhere inside, and waited for her to answer. And waited. He listened carefully to see if he could tell if she was in there, but he had no idea which floor she was on, if he'd even be able to make out where any sound might be coming from. And there were the noises of the city all around, as there were at his place in Seattle: cars going by, the voices of people walking down the street, the noisier chugging of a bus somewhere.

Impatient, he rang again, but still, there was no answer.

He took a breath, pulled in the damp San Francisco air that so reminded him of Seattle. It calmed him a little, for some reason, that tiny bit of familiarity. He'd better calm, he guessed. There was nothing for it but to wait until she got home from work, or wherever she was. He set his overnight bag down on the porch and settled on the top step, watching the traffic go by, letting the hum of cars and people and city life lull him.

"Excuse me, young man, but you'll have to let me pass. And tell me who you are. I don't know you."

He looked down at a woman who had to be at least ninety, with a frail, tiny frame and a wrinkled face with dark, wizened eyes framed by thin wisps of white hair. He didn't know her, either, but his manners were good enough that he knew to introduce himself in the presence of a lady. He got to his feet and said with a slight bow he couldn't quite help, but which made him feel a bit foolish under her discerning glare, "I'm Connor Galloway, ma'am."

She continued to stare up at him from the bottom of the stairs. "Hmm. What are you doing loitering on the steps to my building?"

"I'm waiting for Mischa to get home."

"She is home."

"I don't mean to argue, ma'am, but I've tried the bell."

"Then maybe she didn't feel like answering."

"That had occurred to me," he admitted.

"Anyway, her lights are on. She's not one to waste, so my guess is she's in there. Stand aside."

The tiny, commanding woman took the stairs more quickly than he would have given her credit for, passing him and raising her gnarled fist to knock on the door. He stood behind her, his heart hammering.

To his surprise the door opened. Mischa stood in the doorway in a pink silk bathrobe. Even with her damp hair flowing around her shoulders she looked like some glamorous 1940s film star.

"Mrs. Tucci, I . . ." She caught sight of Connor, then, and her mouth made a small *o*.

"I came for the rent. Your check is late."

"I'm sorry, Mrs. Tucci. You know I'm never late, but I've been traveling. I'll bring it over as soon as I'm dressed."

"I was just checking. I know you'd never skimp on the rent. Oh, you have a gentleman caller."

Mischa's gaze flicked back to Connor, her tone going a little dead. "Yes, I see that. Thank you."

The woman—Mischa's landlady apparently—turned with a sniff and batted Connor's hand away when he tried to help her down the stairs.

Once she was gone he stayed where he was. He could tell from Mischa's expression she wasn't happy to see him. Not that he'd expected her to be. Not entirely, at any rate. Why couldn't he find his voice, damn it?

He tried clearing his throat. "Mischa—"

She cut him off, saying flatly, "I'd have argued the point about you being a gentleman but I hate to upset Mrs. Tucci."

"You're right."

She pulled the tie around her waist tighter, and he couldn't help but notice how the pale shade of the silk made her skin look even more like milk. "And yet knowing that doesn't help."

He moved up the stairs, then, until he was on the small front porch. Until he could see the shadows under her blue eyes, the wary, haunted expression on her face. Beautiful as ever, but she looked wrung out. It made him feel like shit. "Let me in, Mischa. We should talk."

"Should we? We really should have talked days ago. Like the day you left me asleep on the sofa. Or even the day after. We should have talked when I called you. Or at the very least, when you called me back. Except that you never did."

"I did call," he protested. "You wouldn't pick up."

"Too little, too late, Connor."

"I know. But I'm here now."

"And I'm supposed to be impressed and go all girly on you?

Melt at your feet, as I've done all too often? As dozens of women have before me, I'm sure."

There was a hardness, a flintiness, to her blue eyes he'd never seen before.

"Mischa, I get you being mad."

"You're not the only one with a temper, Connor, Irish or not."

He was momentarily stunned. He rocked back on his heels, felt his nostrils flaring. His voice was a low growl. "I never once showed temper to you. Not once."

"Oh, get over your sore spot, Connor. I'm just being pissy."

"Fuck. I know that. I . . ." He paused, scrubbed a hand over his head. "I don't blame you. I was an ass of a million kinds. My actions were unconscionable. And I came all this way to apologize. Please let me in. Let's talk this through."

"Why, Connor? Because you can't stand losing?"

"This was never a competition. I don't even understand that. Who would I have been competing against?"

"Yourself, maybe. I don't know, Connor. All I know is that I'm over this."

"Over this?" he repeated.

"Over the dancing around it all as though we're not supposed to have any feelings—you and I, who are far too cool for all that. Right? The badass dom. The badass tattoo artist. Well, we *are* tough. Or, we were, in the beginning. And personally, I plan to get back to that place. Where I don't have to worry about all this . . . bullshit. Where I don't get led on, then fucked over."

"Mischa, please . . . Look, everything you're saying is fair, I won't deny it. I'm not here to argue."

"Why are you here, Connor?"

She sounded tired now. But not defeated.

He was tired, too. Exhausted. And although he'd expected her to be angry, he hadn't expected her to be so strong in her convictions. So steadfast in turning him away.

"I didn't think you'd have a good answer for me," she said quietly, beginning to shut the door.

"Mischa, wait!"

He lunged, but stopped himself just as the door clicked shut. What the hell was he going to do? Jam his foot in the doorway? What kind of jerk would he be?

But he hadn't had the chance to tell her why he'd come. That he was there because he loved her.

Even if he had, he wasn't sure she'd believe it. Or, at this point, if she'd even care.

Mischa took a step away from the door, then another. It was almost as if she could feel the heat of his big body on the other side. She clenched her hands into fists, her nails biting into her palms until it hurt. But she needed it to ground her.

Her pulse was thundering in her ears, her head spinning.

What the hell had just happened?

Connor, here on her front step. What was he trying to prove? Was it some Dudley Do-Right thing that he felt he had to redeem himself for his crappy behavior? Well, she wasn't having it.

She took a tentative step toward the door, peered through the peephole. He was standing at the foot of the short flight of stairs, his back to her, staring out at the street. If he'd been any less hulking in stature she wouldn't even be able to see him down there. But he was so huge.

There was a time when she'd found the sheer size of him comforting.

She watched through the tiny hole as he stepped into the street and flagged down a cab.

It was then that she cried.

The tears were no small thing this time, but enormous, wracking sobs that instantly made her ribs ache. She wrapped her arms around her body as if that alone could hold them in. Hold her together.

Why had he had to come to San Francisco before she'd had time to gather her strength? It was too much, seeing him. Wanting nothing more than to be in his arms, no matter how angry she was.

But what he'd done was unforgivable. And even if it wasn't . . . well, she wasn't going to take that chance. She couldn't do it. No man was worth losing everything for, feeling this terrible emptiness, this pain for.

Except that some small part of her was telling her he was.

She realized she had pulled the belt to her robe so tight it was cutting off her circulation. She let it go, flexing her fingers, taking in deep breath after deep breath, pacing her living room.

How had she let this happen? How had she let herself care so damn much?

She knew she'd been horribly rude in not at least letting him come in and have his say. Knew she'd been impatient, that if she'd given him a few moments to speak he might have said . . . something she wanted to hear. Wanted too damn desperately. Which was why she'd had to turn him away.

She shoved both hands into her damp hair, let herself fall into her big velvet chair. God, she could barely stand the idea that he'd been right there at her door and she'd let him go. But even more, she couldn't stand what might happen if she'd let him in, let him talk, let things go any further with a man she cared about. *Loved*, for God's sake! It was too damn risky. And she was still just mad enough to feel some sense of self-righteousness. The fact was, he had left her, snuck out while she was sleeping. She didn't care what the state of their relationship was, she didn't need to be treated like some cheap one-night stand. She deserved better than that. Yes she did, damn it!

Feeling a little stronger, she stood and went back to the bathroom and began to brush out her hair.

He'd done wrong by her. Even worse than if he were just some guy she'd been sleeping with. But after all that talk about what being a good dom meant, all that crap about what a responsibility it was . . . He'd used that line as he pleased to keep some control over her, but when it was time to carry through on his end, look what happened.

The brush caught in a tangle and she ripped through it with a savage yank.

"Ouch!"

She shook her head at her reflection in the mirror.

She was not going to ruin her hair over this man. She was not going to ruin anything: her hair, her business, her *life*.

So she was in love with Connor Galloway. So what? She'd get over it, in time. She had plenty to keep her busy. Her shop to run. The new shop opening. Dylan's wedding.

Fuck.

Dylan's wedding. Connor would be there.

Well, she'd simply have to find some way to deal with it. And the wedding was two weeks away. Plenty of time for her to get a handle on her ranging emotions. She would make sure that whatever was happening—or wasn't—between her and Connor didn't get in the way of her best friend's wedding day. No matter how it broke her heart to think of seeing him again. No matter how it had broken her to see him today, her heart like a thousand fucking pieces on the floor.

The damn tears started again, and she gave up, dropped the brush and braced both hands on the counter, let the tears fall.

She was never doing this again. Never risking this kind of pain. She would never love another man again.

No. Because the only man she would ever love was Connor.

The phone woke her, not for the first time that morning, but she decided she'd better find out who it was.

She saw Dylan's name on the caller ID.

Mischa rubbed her aching eyes. Too much crying had made them feel like they'd been sandpapered. Or tattooed. It was that same kind of sharp, insistent irritation, a stinging, raw ache.

The ringing stopped and she put the phone back down on her nightstand, turned her face back into the pillows. The ringing started again.

With a small sigh, she answered, "Hello?"

"Mischa, are you okay?"

"What? Sure. Fine."

"I don't think so."

"What are you, a mind reader now, Dylan? Just because I haven't felt like answering my phone." She stopped, jamming a hand into her hair. It was a tangled mess again, something she never let happen, but which had been happening all too often lately. "God, I'm sorry. I'm . . . sorry. I don't mean to be such a bitch."

"It's okay. Just tell me what's going on."

"You know Connor came here?"

"Yes, but Alec hasn't been able to reach him, and I haven't been able to reach you. I tried the shop and Billy said he hasn't heard from you since Friday—he sounded concerned, although he was trying to hide it. And for you to miss work . . . Either things are very good or very bad."

"They're not good," she admitted. There was no point in

trying to get around it. Dylan would see right through any excuses she tried to make.

"I had a feeling. What can I do?"

"Nothing." She paused, sighed. Tried not to let the sigh turn into a sob. "I just . . . have to get over this."

"Oh, honey."

"No. It's okay. I'll be fine. I can do this."

"Where have you been for the last two days?" Dylan asked softly.

"I've been here. In bed."

"For two days?"

"Um . . ." She looked at her clock. Nine p.m. She'd somehow missed all of Saturday and most of Sunday. All she'd done was lie in bed and cry, get disgusted with herself, stomp around the apartment, go back to bed and cry some more. Somewhere in there she'd slept. A lot. Yay for escapism.

"Mischa?"

"Sorry. I'm here. I've been sleeping. And feeling sorry for myself, to be perfectly honest. But I'm done with that, I swear. I'm done and I'm going to pull myself back together, get everything under control. I'll be up there to help with the wedding, I promise. I won't let you down."

"I'm more worried about you. Are you going to be okay seeing him? Because if not, you don't have to come. Kara and Lucie will help me and, well, it would never be the same without you, hon, but if it's going to be too hard . . . I would never do that to you."

"Dylan, I wouldn't miss your wedding. Never! Please, don't even worry about that. Don't worry about me. I can handle this. I swore I would not let him change the way I do my life, and this is part of it. An important part."

"I've just never seen you like this."

"Neither have I. And now we know why I didn't want this to

ever happen to me. But Dylan, I won't let it get the best of me. I won't. I'm going to be fine. I'm coming back to Seattle a few days before the wedding and we'll pull this thing together. You're going to have the best wedding ever. And you're going to be so happy . . ."

The God damn tears burned behind her eyes, clogging her throat.

"Oh, Misch."

"No. No. It's okay. I'm just so happy for you."

She was a lousy liar. She knew it, Dylan knew it. But Dylan was kind enough to let it go.

"All right, hon. But you know I'm here if you need me, wedding or not. Just because I'm getting married doesn't mean I'm some delicate flower. If you want to talk this through—and I can see you don't want to right now—I'm here for you. Okay?"

She sniffed. "Okay. Thanks. And thanks for understanding."

"You're not a spiller. I know that about you. I can't wait to see you, hon."

"I can't wait to see you, too. Everything's going to be beautiful. Everything's going to be perfect."

She would make sure Dylan's wedding was perfect. None of her aching grief over a man—a man!—was going to ruin it. No one had died, after all. So why was she acting as if someone had?

She threw back the covers and got out of bed, pausing to let her head stop reeling. If she was going to pull herself back together the first thing she needed to do was eat something before she passed out.

Yes, it was time to get on with her life. The pain was going to be like a heavy weight she carried in her chest, but she could do it. Man or no man. Love or no love.

No love.

No Connor.

Fuck.

fifteen

Mischa stood in front of the wide windows in Dylan's Belltown apartment. It was a scene that had become familiar: the gray skies overhead, the colorful cafes, shops and galleries below, the funky urban architecture she loved as much as her Victorian in San Francisco. It was the middle of November in Seattle and it was raining, of course, but she didn't mind. She'd always loved the wistfulness of the rain, and now it suited her mood to a tee. She knew she was being dramatic, but that was how she felt inside. As much as she'd wanted to have a handle on her emotions by Dylan's wedding date she was still as raw as she'd been the day she'd gone home to San Francisco. Maybe more so now that she was there, in the same city as *him*.

She laid her fingertips on the windowsill, absorbing some of the cold seeping in. She often went to a window when she was upset, she realized. She'd done it ever since she was a kid. Whenever she felt . . . trapped. But all she was trapped in now was misery of her own creation.

I miss him.

But she was still mad, too. And the mad was a lot easier to deal with. She'd hold the mad close in order to get through seeing him tonight at the wedding.

"Misch, will you come help me decide on this jewelry?" Dylan called from the bedroom. "I haven't been able to make up my mind."

"Sure."

She joined Dylan, who had a rather large selection of accessories laid out on her bed.

Mischa laughed. "You haven't been able to narrow it down at all?"

"Every time I think I have I end up pulling out every piece I own. Do you think this means I'm turning into a bridezilla?"

"Sweetie, if that was going to happen you would have had all our heads months ago. Certainly mine, when I abandoned you."

"You did not abandon me. I thought we talked about that already. Don't make me have to argue with you on my wedding day." Dylan raised her gaze to Mischa's, her gray eyes pooling with tears. "Oh my God. I'm getting married."

Mischa was by her friend's side in an instant.

"Don't tell me you're getting cold feet?"

"No. No, of course not. I'm just so damn happy. I can hardly believe it's real."

Mischa smiled at her, reached out to squeeze her hand.

Dylan sniffed. "Do you want to know a secret?"

"Always."

"Every time I even think the words 'my husband' it makes me giggle like a fool."

Mischa had to laugh. "I'm sure you'll get used to it. Just don't do it during the ceremony."

Dylan groaned.

Mischa took her by the shoulders and turned her toward the bed. "Time to pick something."

"Okay."

"I think you should keep it simple. The dress is so streamlined and glamorous; you should let it take center stage. What about these diamond studs and this bracelet? I'd skip a necklace."

"Of course you're right, as usual. If you ever give up tattooing—not that you would—you'd make a great stylist. Or a lady's maid."

The buzzer rang and Mischa moved back into the living room to answer it. It was Kara and Lucie, along with a tall, striking woman with high cheekbones and long, shining jet-black hair.

"Mischa, this is Veronica," Kara introduced her friend, who Mischa had heard would be doing Dylan's makeup.

Veronica smiled, setting down her makeup case, which was a large silver train case, very much like the one Mischa always transported her sex toys in. She hadn't brought it this time. Hadn't opened it in weeks.

"It's good to meet you." Veronica smiled, a gorgeous flash of white teeth. The woman was model-perfect.

"You, too. And I'm sure Dylan will be glad to see you—she's starting to really chomp at the bit. I think she'll feel better once we get things rolling."

"My cue to set up. How about over here on the bar?" Veronica suggested.

Mischa had to swallow the memory of tattooing Connor at that bar. This wasn't the time. It was Dylan's wedding day and she'd vowed not to let Connor—or her powerlessness over how she felt about him—ruin it.

Veronica went to work on Dylan's makeup while Lucie made a cup of tea for the bride and Kara went over a list of vendors and contacts at the wedding site, making a few last-minute phone calls to confirm that everyone was where they were supposed to be. Mischa was glad it was her job to do Dylan's hair. She needed all the distraction she could get.

Two hours later Dylan was ready, stunning in her glamorous 1940s-style sheath of ivory silk that shone like liquid champagne against her fair skin, the small train a graceful sweep behind her. Mischa, Kara and Lucie were in their attendants dresses, all of them in various vintage styles of calf-length rose silk.

"Are you nervous?" Lucie asked.

"I'm just ready," Dylan answered, happiness shining through in her smile, in the sparkle of her gray eyes.

Mischa, on the other hand, was wishing she had a Xanax handy. But she bit back her nerves and helped Dylan into the creamy faux fur wrap for the limo ride to the Asian Art Museum.

The women chatted in the limo as it splashed through the streets, and Mischa did her best to be present in the moment that was so important to her best friend. But she couldn't help that undeniable part of herself that was filled with dread at the idea of seeing Connor. And the small pit of excitement in her stomach. By the time they reached the museum, the sun setting behind the silvery clouds, her pulse was jangling in her veins and she felt as if she'd downed more than the single glass of champagne they'd all toasted the bride with on their ride over.

The car pulled up in front of the museum where Dylan and Alec had first met. Luckily, the rain had stopped, and they all got out, making their way carefully in their heels across the paving stones of the walkway that led to the grand entrance of the art deco structure.

There was barely time to marvel at the architecture inside, or to peek into the Garden Court, where the ceremony and reception were to be held. The site's wedding coordinator, Betsy, a cheerful brunette as petite as Lucie, whisked Dylan and Mischa into an elevator to take them downstairs while Kara and Lucie went into the Garden Court to see how many of the guests had arrived and to make sure everything else was ready.

"How are you doing?" Mischa asked Dylan as they were ushered into what looked to be a boardroom.

Dylan squeezed her hand. "Just excited. I just want to do it, to be married to Alec. And . . . a little shocked at how 'bridal' I'm being."

Mischa set her tote bag holding flats for Dylan, touch-up makeup, hairspray, bottled water and other wedding day emergency items on the big table. "You are getting married today, sweetie. I think you're allowed. Do you want to sit down?"

"No, I don't want to wrinkle the dress. And I'm too jumpy to sit. How are you doing, Misch?" Dylan's auburn brows drew together.

"I'm fine."

Dylan drew closer. "Are you, hon?"

Mischa blinked, forced herself to smile naturally. "I'm good. Really. I'm thrilled for you, Dylan. For you and Alec both. You're going to be so happy together."

She would never worry Dylan today, of all days. Would never tell her she felt as if her heart was about to burst out of her chest. Was ashamed to admit even to herself how distracted she was simply knowing he was there, in the building.

Stop it. Calm down.

Kara came into the room. "I think everyone's here. Lucie is just checking in with the caterers. It's time, Dylan."

"God, maybe we should have had a real rehearsal last night," Dylan fretted, pulling a small mirror from the tote bag to check her lipstick.

"We're not doing a traditional procession," Kara assured her.

"The guys are already waiting up front. All we have to do is move down the aisle when Betsy tells us to. Easy. Anyway, it was important that you saw your family last night. Oh no, honey, don't cry. You'll ruin your makeup."

"Dylan, what is it?" Mischa quickly found a Kleenex and carefully dabbed at her friend's eyes.

"I wish Quinn was here," Dylan said softly, referring to her younger brother, who had passed in an accident years earlier.

Mischa took her hand and held on tight, finding some comfort even as she was giving it. "He'd be so happy for you. Just focus on the happy part, okay?"

Dylan sniffed. "I can do that." She smiled. "I guess a little bridal meltdown is requisite."

"So I've heard," Kara agreed. "Something for me to look forward to."

"Kara?" Dylan turned to her, eyes wide, and immediately grabbed her left hand. "Oh my God! You haven't said anything and we've all been too distracted to notice. It's gorgeous!"

Kara beamed, letting Dylan and Mischa examine the emerald-cut diamond. "I didn't want to steal your thunder."

"When did this happen?" Dylan demanded.

"Last night. I guess the wedding fever is contagious."

Dylan pulled her in for a hug, then Mischa did the same.

"Congratulations," she told Kara, letting her go. "You've found a wonderful guy. I'm so happy for you."

She was. Thrilled for Dylan, and for Kara. Wondering if she'd ever find real happiness again herself. She'd thought she was happy on her own. Running her life the way she chose to. Hell, she *had* been happy. But now, everything had changed . . . or maybe this wedding fever stuff really was contagious. She was being overly sentimental.

"Okay," Betsy announced, "it's time, ladies."

Dylan found Mischa's hand and held it as they rode the elevator back upstairs.

"It's really happening."

"Yep," Mischa told her, smiling. "Everything's going to be great."

Lucie was waiting when the elevator doors opened, and there was a small flurry as Lucie, Kara and Mischa fluttered around Dylan, straightening her dress, patting her hair, making sure the orchids pinned there were secure.

The music started, the lovely first notes of the opera *Lakme*'s Flower Duet.

"You're first, Mischa," Betsy whispered, "then Kara, then Lucie. You'll all line up to the right of the officiant, with Mischa standing closest to Dylan. Dylan, you'll go as soon as they take their places up front."

Mischa nodded, stood at the foot of the small flight of stairs leading to the Garden Court.

"And . . . go," Betsy told her.

She started up the stairs, almost wishing she had a bouquet to hold just so she'd have something to do with her shaking hands. She saw first the small pieces of Southeast Asian art mounted on some of the higher shelves on the walls of the court, intricately carved pieces in wood and sandstone. As she mounted the stairs she saw the rows of seated guests, their backs to her. And when she reached the top she saw Alec and his best man, Dante, standing at the other end of the lovely slate-tiled room with its vaulted, greenhouse-like glass-paned ceiling.

Next to Dante was Connor.

It took her breath away to see him. He was so damn handsome in his dark suit, his ivory shirt and tie. So sophisticated. And he was watching her from the moment her foot found the top step, even before anyone else had noticed her. Watching her in the way he always did. Carefully. Thoughtfully.

She thought her heart was going to pound its way right out of her chest. And she wanted more than anything to turn and run. Well, more than anything except make Dylan's day what it was supposed to be: perfect. So instead she took that first step and began to move down the aisle, inexorably toward him.

Just keep breathing.

She was vaguely aware of the guest's eyes on her as she found her place at the front of the room, remembered to send Alec a small, encouraging smile. She watched as Kara, then Lucie, made their way down the aisle and took their places next to her. Then finally all heads turned as Dylan moved down the aisle, and Mischa was distracted from the grief inside her as she saw the expression of pure joy on her best friend's face, her flawless skin glowing. She was absolutely overwhelmed by Dylan's beauty at that moment, and her friend's happiness, the excitement she saw on Alec's face, settled over her like a lovely warmth.

The ceremony began with the officiant, an old friend of Alec's, reading pieces from Rumi, talking about the enduring bonds of love. Mischa glanced at Connor, found his gaze held steadily on her. She tried to look away, but his eyes were blazing, electric. She swore she saw pain there. Confusion. Anger. The same things she was feeling herself.

She shifted her balance from one foot to the other as the ceremony continued, and when the officiant talked about the imperfection that was real love, she finally had to tear her gaze away. She looked instead at the guests, focusing on Dylan's grandmother in the front row, who was happily leaking tears into an embroidered handkerchief.

Dylan and Alec exchanged rings and said their vows. And beyond them, Connor's steady green gaze bore into her.

Why wouldn't he look away? Leave her alone during the ceremony, at least, when they were supposed to be focused on their friends' wedding? Instead he was making her damn uncomfortable. Making her tremble with yearning to be with him, damn it. And with that small rage she hadn't been able to leave behind.

Don't think about it. Don't look at him. Be here for Dylan.

With some effort she drew her gaze back to the happy couple as they finished their vows, then kissed as they were pronounced husband and wife. A small cheer went up from the guests and the wedding party, and she joined in as Alec dipped Dylan, their kiss long and passionate.

Alec straightened, his grin full of mischief as he muttered, "What the hell," and lifted Dylan into his arms, carrying her back down the aisle. Everyone laughed, and Mischa followed, only to be joined by Connor. He took her arm as they made their way between the rows of chairs. There was nothing she could do about it.

"Nice to see you," he said quietly.

She turned to look at him, found a smile on his face as he nodded to the guests. She tried to do the same.

"Is it?" she asked.

"I'm the one who came to you, Mischa, remember?"

She didn't know what to say.

"We need to talk," he said out of the corner of his mouth as they reached the doorway at the back of the room.

He led her down the stairs, where she broke free of his arm. She turned to face him, doing her best to remain calm despite the racing of her pulse, the heat in her body from being so close to him, her throat so tight she felt she could hardly speak, all of which she wanted to deny, and couldn't.

"This is their wedding!" she hissed under her breath, her gaze darting to where Dante was coming down the aisle, Kara on one arm and Lucie on the other, then back to Connor. She moved toward the front doors and he followed. "This is hardly the time or the place."

"No, the time and the place were when I came to see you in San Francisco," he said calmly, but there was banked emotion beneath the quiet tone of his voice. "And I know damn well if I let you walk out of here tonight you won't let there be another chance. I have no intention of allowing that to happen."

The command that had always melted her was there, and it had the same effect on her now. She silently cursed herself.

"What if I promise you we can talk tomorrow?"

A small shake of his head. "Not good enough. I don't want to make a scene here, but we can find a quiet corner before the night is over."

"You're not going to take no for an answer, are you?"

He shook his head, his gaze hard on hers. God, she'd nearly forgotten how green his eyes were, how the gold flecks made them look as if they were lit up from within.

Stop it.

"Okay," she finally relented. "We'll find some way to talk before the end of the night."

"Yes, we will."

She huffed, indignant at his insistence, his relentless bossiness, but also at her body's undeniably electric response to him.

Kara, Dante and Lucie joined them, followed by the guests. Waitstaff were roaming around with trays of champagne to keep everyone busy while tables were being moved into the Garden Court and set for dinner and dancing.

"They should have the room set up in about twenty minutes," Lucie told them. "Alec and Dylan are having a few private moments in one of the side alcoves."

"I'm sure they'll need more than a few moments," Dante said, grinning.

Kara rolled her eyes. "You have a dirty mind," she told her fiancé.

"You like that about me," he said, his eyes twinkling.

Kara grinned. "Lucky for you, I do."

"Definitely lucky," he said, taking her hand and brushing a kiss across the back of it.

Mischa's stomach twisted as she remembered the touch of Connor's lips on her hand. And it made her damn uncomfortable to think about it while he was standing right next to her, making her miss the way he kissed her. Making her miss *him*.

Inexplicably, her eyes misted, and she excused herself to make her way to the ladies' room.

She dabbed at her eyes, checking her reflection in the mirror to make sure she hadn't mussed her makeup—and couldn't resist taking a moment to shake her head at herself. She must be crazy to even allow herself to think for one moment that anything could come of this conversation with Connor tonight. He was not the kind of guy to really want anything from her. And she didn't want anything from him. At least, she didn't *want* to want anything. But the horrible truth was, she did. She'd known it for a long time. Had known it when she'd left Seattle—and him—behind. Had known it deep in her soul the moment she'd seen him tonight. But how could she possibly get past the fact that the very wanting scared her just as deeply? How could she get past the certainty that loving him meant the end of everything she'd worked so hard to build for herself? Her business, her independence. Her sense of safety.

She knew on some level that she felt safe only because she'd built a defensive wall around herself, one no one could break through. Except that Connor had found the chink in her armor. And she wasn't sure she'd ever be able to repair it.

The fact also remained that she wasn't even certain he wanted to do anything more than get an apology from her for being so rough on him. Maybe he'd had enough. Maybe he simply felt a need to tell her that.

Tears stung her eyes once more, but she was *not* going to cry.

She laid a hand over her pounding heart. She had to calm down, to be there for Dylan. She was strong enough to hold it together for one night, damn it, Connor or not.

She pulled in a deep breath, straightened her dress, and made her way back to where the guests were mingling while they drank their champagne. Dylan found her and introduced her to her grandmother, who Mischa could see now looked a lot like an older version of Dylan. Dylan passed her then to some friends, including Veronica, the gorgeous makeup artist she'd met earlier at Dylan's place, then Kara introduced her to two women she remembered seeing from a distance at the Pleasure Dome. Which brought her thoughts back to Connor.

Glancing around, she saw him talking with a group of men. He looked up, caught her gaze, and for a moment that lasted a little too long, their eyes locked. Her body went hot all over in a flash. She was the first to look away, sipping the glass of champagne she'd grabbed from a passing waiter's tray.

Finally it was time for everyone to file back into the Garden Court, where round tables were gorgeously set with ivory linens. In the center of each was a glass globe vase, smooth stones lining the bottom, miniature pale green and creamy white calla lilies mixed with trailing stems of tiny white and green orchids. The dishes were a simple rippled and frosted glass, leaving the beautiful, ancient artwork lining the walls as the main focus of the room.

The DJ, who was mostly hidden from view in one of the side alcoves, was playing some light jazz, soothing, elegant dinner music, as everyone found their seats. Mischa went to the table set aside for the wedding party and was glad to find she was seated next to Dylan, and relieved to see Connor sitting between Lucie and Kara.

She focused on Dylan, chatting about what a beautiful bride she made, how perfect the ceremony had been, all the time watching Connor from the corner of her eye, acutely, disturbingly aware of him. She found his gaze on her several times, but he was too hard to read. There was a fire burning in his green eyes, but what did it mean? Anger? Passion? Which one frightened her more?

Dinner was served, but she could barely taste her miso-glazed salmon. She washed down the few bites she had with a few sips of champagne. If she was going to have to have a talk with Connor later she'd need to keep a clear head; she was being very careful about how much she drank.

Dante stood and rang his glass with a spoon, announcing it was time to make the toasts. His was partly funny, partly sentimental. Mischa tried to focus on the words, but the entire event, much to her dismay, was going by in a blur.

Dinner ended and Dylan and Alec moved to the small dance floor at one end of the court for their first dance. She couldn't help a small sigh of envy at how utterly romantic it was as Alec swept his bride over the floor, at the way they looked at each other. She didn't think she'd ever seen such love in two people's eyes, and her own threatened to fill with tears once more.

Kara and Dante joined them on the dance floor, and Lucie's roommate Tyler took the petite blonde by the hand and led her to dance. She didn't have time to consider what might come next before Connor was at her elbow.

"Mischa."

She hated that her entire body responded to the sound of her name on his lips with a long, lovely shudder.

She started to shake her head. "Connor . . ."

"It's expected," he said. "We're part of the wedding party."

She sighed, but stood and let him lead her to the floor, let him put an arm around her waist and pull her in close.

"Try to relax and look natural, will you?" he prompted.

He was right. She let her body go loose, melt a little against his.

"There, that's better," he said, his tone softer than it had been with her all evening. "Not so bad, is it?"

"Maybe not," she said, not willing to give in. They moved over the floor, his grace surprising her. "I didn't know you could dance."

"There's a lot you don't know about me, apparently," he said, his accent as thick as it had ever been. "Like the fact I can be quite stubborn."

"I think I've seen that."

"You haven't seen the half of it, sweetheart."

She pulled back a bit, looked up into his too-handsome face. His expression was perfectly serious, a little hard and sharp around the edges.

She kept her tone low, her expression as neutral as possible, aware that they were surrounded by wedding guests. "Connor, I don't know what all of this macho bravado stuff is supposed to mean. It's different from your usual domly air of authority, which I get. But I'm not getting what's going on right now at all. You've been awfully casual about what was happening between us until now. Or until you showed up at my place in San Francisco, anyway."

"Maybe I was," he said gruffly.

"I'm going to be living part of the time in Seattle," she went on, unable to stop herself now. "In your town, socializing with your friends who happen to be *our* friends. Yet you've never mentioned anything past Dylan and Alec's wedding. As if the future didn't even exist."

"Neither did you."

"God, men can be so dense!" she exploded, then glanced around to see if anyone had noticed.

"Don't toss me in with the rest of them, Mischa. I'm not your father or Raine's father or any of the men who treated you carelessly."

"I've never *allowed* a man to treat me carelessly."

"Maybe because you never let anyone matter. You never let anyone close enough. You never open yourself to the possibilities, good or bad."

"You're one to talk!"

She couldn't believe they were having this conversation while dancing. She could barely believe they were having this conversation at all.

"That's true enough. True even about Ginny." He paused, and they stopped dancing. He looked down at her, his expression softer than she'd ever seen it. She thought her heart would break. He went on, his voice low, husky. "I want to change that. Hell, Mischa, you *have* changed that. That's what I'm trying to tell you. Look, can we go find someplace quiet?"

She nodded, too stunned by the sudden change in his attitude, by what he'd just said, to argue. To think straight.

Half-numb, she let him lead her from the dance floor, through the Garden Court and back down the stairs to the entryway, which was empty now. He took her up another short flight of stairs to the left and into a gallery that was dimly lit, filled with Meiji woodblock prints behind glass. In the center of the room was a long, narrow bench, and they sat down.

"So?" he asked, one dark brow raised. He was close enough that she could inhale his scent: the dark earth and the rain that was his skin. She closed her eyes, letting it mix with the pain for a moment before opening them to look at him once more.

"You never let anyone in, either, Connor. You said it yourself. Not even the woman you were married to. How could I have possibly changed anything for you?"

"Ah, but there's the catch. You got in, anyway. I'll admit I fought it. Almost as hard as you're fighting it. But you got in, Mischa." He took her hand, and when she would have pulled away he only gripped it tighter. "Right under my skin. Into my heart."

She shook her head, tears burning again, so fiercely this time she didn't know if she could hold them back. "Stop it, Connor." She pulled her hand away then. It hurt too much to feel his fingers wrapped around hers.

"Why? Because it's uncomfortable to hear? Believe me, this is way out of my comfort zone, too. But I have to say it."

She shook her head again. "Not because it's so hard to hear, but because it's difficult to believe."

"I'm no liar." His tone was low, dangerous.

"It's not that I think you're lying. It's the . . . believing part that's hard for me."

"Oh, ye of little faith," he said softly.

A small smile crept through the pain and tension that had drawn her lips into a hard line. "Yes."

"What if we just threw caution to the wind and risked it, Mischa? What if we tried it? Because I don't know about you, but I'm going fucking mad without you. I don't think things could be much worse for me."

Her heart wanted to soar. She couldn't let it. What if she soared, only to come crashing back to earth?

"And if we try it and it doesn't work?" she asked, her throat thick with emotion as she voiced one of her worst fears.

"Then at least we'll have tried. What do you think will happen if it doesn't work?"

"I don't know. Something . . . awful. All I know is what I've seen."

"Are you referring to your mother? Because it seems from all you've told me that you're a hell of a lot stronger than she is. You've already done so much with your life. I don't see me—or anyone—causing you to give all that up."

"It feels that way. I *know* I'm stronger than Evie ever was. But I'm just as certain there's some fatal hidden flaw. That there's some inevitable disaster underneath. And frankly, Connor, making myself vulnerable enough to be in a relationship with someone who's . . . Well, you're every bit as tightly controlled as I am. As closed off. I'm sure you have your reasons, and you've shared some of them with me. But you haven't shared enough. And in my world, men always leave. My father, Raine's father, every man my mother's ever fallen for—and there have been more than a handful. The only reason I haven't been left is because I've protected myself from it. I've never gotten involved enough that it ever came up. How do I know you'll stick around?"

"How do you know I won't?"

He reached for her, but she shook her head, warning him off.

"How do *you* know, Connor?"

He blinked, as though it took him a moment to understand what she was asking. She held her breath as she waited for his answer.

He lowered his long, dark lashes for a moment, let out a sighing breath before he looked up, focused on her again. "I'll admit, this is something I've struggled with. But let me tell you some things. It'll take a few minutes. Will you listen?"

She nodded, her insides still coiled up tight.

"I never told you why I got divorced, did I? It's not something I tell people often. Alec knows. Maybe no one else. And maybe me telling you now will only make things worse, but I have to say it to get to the next point. So . . . It was Ginny's choice, the divorce." He stopped, pulled in a deep, sighing breath, scrubbed at his jaw. "I don't blame her for it. She left in large part because of my temper. The one I inherited from my asshole of a father. Not that I blame him entirely. Because once we're adults, we have a choice, don't we? And I chose to indulge in my temper until after Ginny left. I never hit her. But I hit the wall a few times."

He stopped, watching for her reaction.

"I've never seen you lose control, Connor. Not like that. You obviously have a handle on it."

Why was he telling her this? This wasn't what they needed to talk about.

"It was a long road to get here," he admitted. "I've always thought the temper was a part of me, just as my father's genes are: his dark hair. His height. I've been damn careful, always mindful of it. I'm telling you this now so you understand what the need for control is about for me. And that need extends beyond the BDSM dynamic."

"You think I don't know that?" she demanded, getting up to pace the polished floors. "You think that's what holds you together, but it also holds you back. And even though I see the same control issues in myself, it still pisses me off that you *never* let it go. That you can't open up. It makes it pretty damn scary to even consider getting into some sort of relationship with you when we're both so . . . damaged."

He said quietly, "I know. I do. Please sit down, Mischa."

She looked at him, wanting to rebel, but she went back to the bench and sat down, her arms crossed over her chest.

"What I'm trying to tell you is that things have changed for me. At some point there was a shift between you and I. Or maybe how I felt about you caused me to see things differently. But one day it just fucking hit me like a blow to the gut. I'd always felt that way. Damaged. And I designed my life around fighting against what I thought was inevitable. But it hasn't come to pass.

Oh, I have some temper still, it's true. But it hasn't gotten the best of me the way it did my old man. And what I finally realized was, I may have some of my father in me, but I'm not *him*. And what made me realize it was you."

"Me? I don't understand."

"Everything you told me about your mother. You're so afraid you'll end up like her—that inevitable disaster—but that's not even a remote possibility. I think everyone but you can see it. It made me think. Because it's not remotely possible I'll end up like my father. The drinking, the violence—it's something I've always rejected. That stupid punching the wall crap was just me being young. Being an idiot. I've known it for a while. But the need for control, that wasn't so easy to get rid of. It's habit, maybe. Programmed in by now." He ran a hand over his hair, mussing it a little, making her want to reach out and smooth it down. "Lord, I haven't talked this much my whole life."

"Maybe it's time you started," she said quietly.

"Yeah. It is. I'm trying here, Mischa." There was so much in his green eyes. Emotion. Fear, maybe. Hope.

"I'm sorry. I know you are." She took a breath, giving herself a moment to take it all in. And she still had questions.

"Connor, tell me about Ginny. You were married, went through a divorce. But you've never said anything about how you felt about it, about what happened other than you being grumpy, having those wall-punching asshole moments a lot of young guys have."

"No . . ." He gave a small shake of his head. "Look, this is something I'm frankly a bit ashamed of. But I'll tell you now. I was never in love with her. Which is a pretty rotten thing to say of a girl I married."

"Why did you marry her, then?"

"She was a good girl—a nice girl. She'd come to Dublin to

study for a semester. That's how we met. She loved me, though God knows why. And you have to understand, in Ireland people get married young, so it seemed the thing to do, especially when she pushed for it. I thought I'd come to love her. But soon after the wedding reality set in, and it was just two people who weren't really suited trying to live together. So even though she was the one who chose to leave, it would have come to that one way or another. We stayed together for nearly two years, and by the end all I felt was relief. Which only makes me feel like more of an asshole. But I'm trying to get over kicking myself for it, to recognize that at twenty we all make stupid mistakes. I only wish she hadn't had to pay for it. I swore I'd never do that to another woman. So there hasn't been anyone else, not beyond a temporary play partner."

"But now . . . ?" She couldn't help it; she had to ask.

"Now there's you. And I can't turn away from you. From what you make me feel for the first time in my sordid life."

The ice in her veins was beginning to melt as she began to understand what Connor was telling her. He was saying he'd made some discoveries about himself. So had she. She was starting to truly believe in herself. Maybe, if she could do that, she could believe in him, too.

"Connor, I want to be with you. I want to try . . . "

"But?"

"But . . ." Her head was spinning with a million thoughts. "If we're going to do this . . . relationship thing . . . You're not going to boss me around all the time. Just to be clear."

"I wouldn't think of it." He paused, caught her gaze with his. His green and gold eyes were twinkling. "All right, I *will* think of it. But you won't let me do it. Because you're your own person, Mischa. That's one of the things I love about you."

She was desperate suddenly to hear it—that he wanted her.

That his need for her was anything close to the yearning she'd felt for him almost from the start. The need that had made her run from him. But she couldn't run anymore. She wasn't sure any longer that she had to.

"Tell me more, Connor."

He moved in closer, touched his fingers to her hair, making her body go warm and liquid. "I love your blond hair, the silk of it. How you keep it so perfectly. And your lips. The wicked scarlet of your lipstick, how red they are even bare of it." He traced his fingertips over her lower lip, making her shiver. "I love the art you created on my skin, that your creativity is so much a part of you, that you're able to understand that in me—how important it is. I love your motivation and drive. I love that you have this need to conquer the whole damn world. Your passion. Your fire."

He paused, and she couldn't stop the tears pooling in her eyes. That any man—but especially *this* man—would say such things to her!

"I need that," he went on. "I need a woman who's strong enough to stand up to me when necessary. Someone who isn't afraid to do that. Because even though all of my partners have been submissive women—and I won't pretend I don't want that, too—what I've really needed is a woman who can submit to me in the bedroom or at the club, and who, when all the role play is over and done, is as strong as I am. An equal. Because you can't have a partnership if it's not between equals. That's the mistake I've been making over and over for years. But you are my equal, in every way. I've never doubted that for a moment."

He was so damn beautiful, this man. She could see him so clearly in the dim lighting of the closed gallery. Every perfect line and plane of his features. The scar below his eye. The raw emotion on his face. It scared her. *He* scared her. She was trying hard to fight it, but the fear still lingered "This is crazy, Connor."

"Yeah. Probably. We have some shit to work out, the both of us. But I don't see why we can't do it together. Are you willing, Mischa? Tell me you are before I lose my mind for good."

"Connor, I want to. I do. I'm still trying to understand it all and it's . . . overwhelming, trying so hard to trust that this could work. There's the distance issue—"

"You'll be here half the time. You've said so yourself. We can handle it."

"And there's the issue of your stubbornness." She went on when his brow furrowed, "And mine, I know."

"Stubbornness can get you through the hard times, too. You know it as well as I do."

"But Connor . . ." She had to stop, her heart a small, fluttering hammer, her pulse hot and thready. But she had to ask. "What else is there to hold things together? To hold *us* together?"

He took her face in his hands, forcing her to meet his gaze. "There's love, my darlin' girl. That's what I've been trying to tell you. And would have if you'd stopped trying to argue your way out of it. There's love."

sixteen

"Connor? What are you saying?"

He looked down at her blue eyes pooled with tears. Had he scared her? He hadn't meant to. He'd only meant to assure her that he was *in* this. He'd only meant to tell her what he had to before he fucking exploded.

He smoothed a tear from her cheek with his thumb, leaned in to lay a gentle kiss on her ruby-red lips, pulled back. He caught her gaze with his, needing her to see his face, needing her to believe him. "I'm saying I love you." She stared at him, her blue eyes unblinking, so he went on, "*This* is where I've lost all control. Saying this to you, feeling it, is one of the damn scariest things I've ever done. But I have to tell you. I love you."

A small sob escaped her, and she buried her face in her hands. "Mischa?"

What did this mean? He'd opened his heart to her. He'd thought she felt the same. Was he wrong?

He took her face in his hands once more, forcing her to face him.

"Mischa, what is it?"

"Just that . . . I love you, too."

She was laughing then, and he thought he'd have a heart attack simply from being so damn happy and relieved.

He pulled her in for a kiss, tasting her tears as he pressed his lips to hers. Nothing had ever tasted so sweet as his Mischa.

His.

Finally.

He pulled back. "God damn it, woman. Do you know what you did to me just then? Nearly gave me a stroke."

She smiled through her tears. "I'm sure you'll let me make it up to you."

"Damn right."

"Still the boss, Connor? Even now?"

"Always, love."

"We may have to work on that."

"We'll be a work in progress."

"Meanwhile, why don't you work on kissing me again?" she demanded.

He wrapped his arms around her, holding her close, loving the scent of the flowers in her hair, the delicate silk of her dress, and even more, the woman beneath it. He kissed her hard, opening her lips, diving into her sweet mouth. He was going hard; he couldn't help it. He wanted her. More than he ever had. Part of it was her lush breasts crushed up against him, the feel of her softly curved body in his arms, the eagerness of her mouth. But a big part of it was that he needed to be closer to her than being in public, than wearing clothes, would allow.

He pulled away again, growled in her ear, "I can't wait to get you someplace where I can get my hands on you."

She kissed his neck, a trail of fiery kisses that had him groaning.

"I can't wait, either," she whispered against his skin. "But we're at our friends' wedding. I think we'd better get back in there before we do something inexcusable."

He groaned. "I hate it when you're right."

"I'll do my best to make that up to you later, too."

She was grinning, her gorgeous mouth looking well kissed, which pleased him. Hell, *she* pleased him, in every way.

He swept a hand over her cheek. He couldn't help it; he had to touch her.

"I love you, Mischa."

"And I love you."

She felt as if her heart was bursting at the seams, but in the best possible way. It was an amazing thing, how wonderful it felt to tell him. To hear it from him. To believe it, and to believe *in* it. How knowing he loved her and voicing her own feelings drained so much of the fear and doubt away.

He helped her to her feet, kissed her again, lightly this time, before pulling back and smiling at her.

"This is the best wedding I've ever been to," he told her.

"Wait until you taste the cake," she teased.

"Ah, what I've already had is far sweeter."

She stood on her tiptoes and kissed his mouth. "I love it when you're corny."

He reached behind her and smacked her bottom. "Better get used to it."

"It may take some effort, but I'll try."

He held her, both hands on her shoulders, bending a little to look into her face. "I mean that. You had better get used to it. And I can't believe this is me saying it. But that's how it's going to be."

"Well, then. Yes, sir."

His face broke into a grin. "Sassy wench."

She nodded. "That's how it's going to be, too."

He shook his head at her. "Back to the wedding with you."

She laughed, took his hand and together they moved back toward the light and the music and the sound of laughter.

How was it possible that this pair of optimists was *them*? But love was a strange thing, she realized. A force more powerful than their fears, the skewed images they each had of themselves. Love had changed them both. Transformed them into something better than they'd been before. She felt the strength of it flow through her, simply from having her hand in Connor's. From knowing he loved her. From the strange certainty that somehow, it was going to be okay.

As he spun her back onto the dance floor she laughed, joy like some tangible element in the air. As they danced she watched Dylan and Alec, their heads together, intimate even in this crowd of people. She saw Kara and Dante holding each other close, their eyes closed, as if the world around them had ceased to exist. Maybe it had, for them. And for the first time, she understood what it meant. What it felt like.

"Connor."

"What is it, darlin' girl?"

"I'm still scared."

"Sure, so am I. I'm man enough to admit it."

"But that doesn't mean I have to run away anymore."

His hands grasped her waist so tight she gasped. "I won't let you."

She leaned her head against his broad chest, breathed in the scent of him. "Don't ever let me, Connor."

He didn't say another word, just held her close, swaying with her to the music. And it was exactly what she needed. *He* was all she needed. She was so glad she'd finally figured it out.

*   *   *

They left the wedding together after seeing the bride and groom off on their honeymoon, which was just as well. Mischa wasn't ready to explain things to Dylan. She just wanted to enjoy Connor for a while, to have him to herself.

It was raining as they rode in the taxi back to his place, the droplets turning the city into a watercolor of silvery moonlight, golden streetlights, everything in metallic tones. They were quiet, holding hands, glancing at each other, neither daring to do or say more until they could be alone at last.

When they reached his apartment it was dark other than the streetlights shining through the rice paper shades as he closed the door behind them. He hadn't let go of her waist since the moment he'd helped her from the cab.

"Connor? When are you going to kiss me?" she asked.

"In about two seconds, darlin' girl. I wanted to wait until I truly had you alone."

"Why is that?"

"Because as soon as I kiss you, things are going to get very naked very fast."

"Oh, I like the sound of that."

She sighed as he undressed her, more carefully than he usually did, yet she felt the carefully restrained passion in every movement of his hands, in the panting of his breath even before he'd really touched her. It excited her, to think of him being so turned on just ridding her of her clothes, even after all the things they'd already done together. And she was just as excited by it, his careful stripping of her body. From simply knowing how he held himself back. That he had to.

"Come on, Connor," she begged, needing to feel his bare flesh under her hands.

He took a small step back, and in the moonlight and the filtered light from the street below, she watched him. Watched as he took off his jacket, his tie, then his shirt, as the massive muscles of his shoulders and chest came into view. She wanted, as she had before, to trace her fingertips over the outline of his tattoos, to feel the ink in his skin, especially the ink she'd put there herself.

Marking him . . .

Yes.

Rather than waiting for him to set the pace, to make the first moves, as she normally did in deference to their roles as dominant and submissive, she reached out, stroked her fingertips over his biceps. Took his hand with hers, turning it over so she could trace the words in Gaelic on his inner forearm: "Nothing can get into a closed fist." She knew it was his pledge to himself to be a better man than he thought he could be. He already was.

She moved her fingertips to his chest, drew a long, slow line downward, over his tightly muscled abs. Delighted in the shiver that went through him. She looked up at his face as she unbuttoned his slacks, reached in and took his hardening cock in her hand. Loved the quiet moan that slipped from him as she wrapped her hand around the heavy shaft.

"Ah, you're killing me, my girl."

"Not quite yet . . ."

She smiled at him as she sank to her knees. Grinned when he groaned aloud. Then she slipped his slacks down and took him into her mouth. Just the tip at first, swirling her tongue around the head of his cock. She wrapped her hands around the back of his thighs, felt him tense when she slid her mouth down the length of him. She sucked him hard, taking him deep into her throat, and he buried his hands in her hair. She could no longer argue the part of her that loved serving him in this way. Loved the wood floor hard under her knees. The knowledge that even as she served him, the power was *hers*. It was a heady idea, that and the sweet taste of his flesh in her mouth.

"I'll come if we don't stop, love," Connor warned through gritted teeth.

She took him deeper, pulling him in with both hands on his buttocks.

He laughed, told her in a throaty tone, "Oh no you don't."

Before she had a moment to think about it he knelt on the floor, lifting her, spreading her thighs and wrapping her legs around his body. She knew he could feel how wet she was for him, her sex open against his stomach.

He shifted her, and his cock impaled her in one sharp thrust.

"Ah, Connor!"

They began to move together, his lips feathering kisses over her neck, her collarbone, her shoulder. Their arching hips were like liquid at first, a slow, undulating motion. Pleasure seared her, burning in her veins like wildfire—as wild as the emotion she could no longer control, and no longer wanted to.

"Connor . . . I love you," she panted.

"Love you, darlin' girl."

He stopped for a moment, took her face in his hands, looked into her eyes. "I do. I never thought I'd mean it this much."

She smiled at him, happiness suffusing her, a lovely, seeping warmth unlike anything she'd ever felt before. She leaned into him, wrapped her arms around his neck, and they held still for a while, silent, their bodies joined, simply *feeling* each other while thunder rumbled outside, while sensation thrummed through their bodies.

After a while he pulled her hand to his lips and kissed it, tiny, fleeting kisses that set her on fire all over again. She kissed his muscled shoulder, the side of his neck, and they began to move once more, his cock pressing into her, gently at first, then a harder, driving rhythm. The soft, tender need grew, spiraled, until they'd reached that primal place that had first brought them together. That primal rhythm their bodies knew, and needed from each other.

Thrusting hips to thrusting hips, their bodies grew slick with sweat as they held on tight. They were both panting, grinding into each other, the need as much about emotion as it was physical desire.

The pleasure built inside her, coiling tight. Her nails raked the back of his neck, his fingers dug deep into the flesh of her hips, his teeth sank into her throat. But it was *them*, and the pain only carried them higher, faster.

He drove into her, over and over and over again. It seemed as if she was poised on that keen edge forever, wanting to draw it out before she came. She bit her lip as the first wave edged closer, fought it as hard as she could. But it was too much: his beautiful cock surging deep, her mound grinding against him, the scent of him, his flesh under her hands. Her climax poured through her like the rain coming down outside. Like thunder, rumbling through her, making her shiver all over. She felt how her sex grasped him, drew him deeper. She trembled in his arms, coming and coming, her head spinning. Out of control. But it no longer mattered . . .

"Mischa, I'm going to come."

"Yes," she murmured.

"No condom. Hang on."

He pulled out of her, but still held her as tight, his cock pressed against her cleft. He pumped his hips, and understanding, she arched into him.

"Mischa . . . ah . . ."

His hips jerked as he came, hot against her skin. And as he came he kissed her, hard, his hands holding her face, his tongue surging into her mouth.

When he stilled against her he kept kissing her, and it was so lovely and sweet, keeping desire flowing between them. Keeping them connected.

They were soaked in sweat, in his come, in hers. Nothing mattered except that they were together. That he was kissing her and kissing her.

Finally he pulled back.

"Shall we clean up and get into bed?" he asked, his voice low as he nuzzled her ear.

"Mmm . . . only if you'll kiss me some more once we get there."

"That I can do. Come on, then."

He stood, taking her with him, carrying her through the apartment and into the bathroom.

"You can put me down now," she told him, laughing as he reached with one hand to turn the hot water on in the shower.

"Eventually," he told her.

He kissed her again as they waited for the water to heat, a slow twining of tongues, a sweet press of lips. He stopped only long enough to step into the shower, where he finally set her on her feet beneath the spray of warm water. He bent to kiss her once more, his arms wrapping around her waist, hers going around his neck.

He stopped to tell her once more, "Love you, my girl."

"Love you, Connor."

"Come on, let me wash you."

He soaped her, rinsed her with the shower wand, then washed himself. And even though they'd spent plenty of time in the shower together, this felt more intimate to her than it ever had before.

"Connor . . . there's something about having admitted this

to you—that I love you—knowing that you love me back, that makes this different."

He nodded. "*We're* different. We let it happen. That *makes* us different."

"Yes, that's it exactly."

They got out and he dried her carefully, then dried himself, and they went to bed, hand in hand. He held her in his arms as they drifted off. Mischa slept, dreamless, the most peaceful sleep of her life.

It was morning, the winter sun slanting through the paper shades like a white mist. Mischa's body was warm beside him, his arm half-numb from her weight resting there, but he didn't want to move.

Connor thought for a moment about the night before, about all that had happened. He felt as if his chest were bursting. It was several minutes before he realized this was what happy felt like.

As he rubbed his free hand over his jaw his stomach rumbled.

He was also starving.

He turned and kissed her awake, grinning when her blue eyes fluttered open.

"Time to wake up, darlin'," he told her.

"Mmm . . . okay, I'm up."

He kissed her again, then dipped under the covers to tug one nipple between his teeth.

"Hey!" She was laughing even as she held his head to her breast.

He came up from under the gray comforter. "I'm making us breakfast."

"Ooh, I get service. Nice."

"Sassy wench."

He turned her over and smacked her lush bottom, making her laugh again before he got up, slipped into a pair of navy cotton pajama bottoms and headed into the kitchen.

As he scrambled some eggs and made toast and tea he found himself whistling, something he hadn't done for years, maybe. He stopped himself, shook his head, then said, "Fuck it," to the empty kitchen and whistled some more.

He brought a plate and two mugs of tea back into the bedroom, pleased as hell that Mischa was sitting in his bed, her blue eyes shining, the swell of her gorgeous breasts peeking above the covers. He sat down next to her, fed them both bites from his fork, and they sipped tea in between.

"So, what are your plans, Mischa? For Seattle, I mean."

He hadn't meant to be so insistent, but he had to know.

"Well, I've talked to Billy at Thirteen Roses, and he's fine handling things there, for the most part. I still have to be there to tattoo once in a while, but he and Greyson and I agree I have to make 1st Avenue Ink my priority until the shop is established."

"And that means . . . ?"

"That means I'll be here most of the time for the first six months, at least. Dylan will let me stay in her apartment until I can find a place of my own."

"Stay with me."

The words came out before he could think about what he was saying. But as soon as he said it he knew it was the right thing.

"Connor, are you sure?" She set her mug down on the nightstand. "This is still so new."

"Yeah, I'm sure. Are you having doubts?"

She smiled at him. "Not about us, no. A little about myself, maybe. I'm not going to be great at this relationship thing, you know. I have no experience. And I don't like doing anything without doing it perfectly, so it's going to make me a little crazy. I might get cranky."

He let the plate rest on the bed, took her face in both hands, gazed into her eyes. Eyes as blue as the sky in Dun Laoghaire. "I don't need you to be perfect. I just need you to be yourself. We've always lived a little like outsiders, you and me. We've embraced it. That's part of the connection, don't you think?"

"Yes."

"I'm going to blow it fairly regularly, I'm certain. Which might make you cranky. Can you live with that?"

"It'll make me feel better about not getting it all right myself."

"So, then." He cocked an eyebrow at her. "Will you at least think about it?"

She threw her arms around his neck, holding on to him tight.

"Do I take that as a yes?"

"Yes, I'll definitely think about it."

"Stubborn girl. I may have to spank you until you see the error of your ways."

She pulled back to look at him, and her eyes were sparkling. Beautiful. "I may have to stay stubborn, then, until you do."

His cell phone rang from the other room, and he muttered, "Crap. I need to get that. I'm expecting a business call." He got up, called over his shoulder, "But then we'll see about that spanking—and how long you think you can hang on to your stubborn streak. I'll make you mine yet, darlin'."

Mischa grinned to herself as she watched him walk out of the room, the flex and shift of muscle in his back. She nearly had to sigh at the sheer beauty of the man. And he was all hers.

Wasn't he?

They'd talked about love. About him wanting her to live with him. But they hadn't talked about commitment. Was that part of the package? Or maybe it wasn't until they'd declared it. He said he'd make her his. She wanted to be. Wanted to *show* him.

Throwing back the covers, she walked naked across the room to his dresser—and saw for the first time that he'd replaced the drawing on the wall above it with a new one. One of *her*.

Her jaw dropped. When had he hung it there? How had she not noticed it earlier?

It was beautifully done in charcoal on thick paper, framed in black against a classic creamy matting—her laid back on the sofa, naked, one knee bent, her head raised, her gaze focused, full of sensual promise. Even though she was alone in the room, even though she'd certainly never been self-conscious about her body, she found herself blushing. It was the sheer compliment of it— that he'd drawn her, had bothered to have it framed, hung it in his bedroom rather than the gallery of his work in the hallway.

There was a surge of warmth in her chest. She'd have to ask him about it later. But right now she had something important to do first.

She opened the top drawer of his dresser, where she knew he kept a number of his toys, including a black leather collar, the one thing she'd always shied away from. It was too much a symbol of ownership, and those who wore them too utterly submissive. But she knew at that moment she *wanted* to wear it for him, wanted him to place it around her neck. Wanted that sensation of being *his*, to feel it deep in her bones. And she understood this was the only way to get there.

She pushed her hair from her face, got down on her knees on the rug at the end of the bed, facing the door, stilled herself while she listened to the soft murmur of his voice in the other room. She didn't mean to listen in, but she liked hearing him talk about his work, his tone all business. Confidant. Utterly capable.

Sexy.

Her body was loose with desire—the physical desire that was purely about wanting his touch, the more powerful desire to belong to him. There still lingered some small shock that she knew so thoroughly she wanted this strange thing she had never wanted with any other man.

She was trembling by the time he came back into the room and found her, arms outstretched, holding the leather collar in her hands. On the floor before her she'd placed a leather blindfold, another previously taboo item, and a pair of leather cuffs.

His brows furrowed. "Mischa?"

"Connor . . ." She had to stop, to draw in a breath. It felt so damn *crucial*. She went on quietly, "I need to tell you . . . I get it now. I understand what it means to give myself to you. I couldn't have done it with a man I didn't feel something for. And I felt something for you right from the start, even though I didn't recognize it then; only in hindsight. But even then, I couldn't surrender to you completely until I trusted you all the way, until I trusted myself. But it goes deeper than that. Because I couldn't find the trust until I found the love."

He moved closer, bent over her. "Mischa . . ." He stroked her face, then touched the collar laid out across her palm. "Is this what you really want?"

She nodded. "Absolutely. This is my gift. Not only the surrender, but the love, Connor. I'm giving you everything."

"And giving up nothing, I promise you that."

"I know."

He stroked her cheek, her hair. "Ah, I love you, my darlin' girl."

"Show me, Connor."

It might not have been the way other people expressed how they felt, but they weren't like everyone else. For the two of them this was exactly right. He took the collar from her hands.

"Stay right there on your knees, darlin', and bend your head for me," he told her. His tone was quiet, but the command she loved so much was there, threaded with emotion.

She did as he asked, a thrill of anticipation running through her. Then she felt him draw the band of leather around her neck, fasten the buckle. He left his hands there for a while as she shivered, as she absorbed the sensation of belonging. It was like nothing she'd ever experienced before. She never wanted to stop feeling this way.

"Connor," she whispered, lifting her gaze from the floor to meet his. His eyes were dark with desire, lit up with love. "I'm yours now. Finally."

"Yes. Mine, Mischa. But you know what a collar between us means—that I belong to you just as much. It's the only thing it *can* mean."

Her heart surged, and she smiled up at him. "That's exactly what I need. That, and to *feel* you. Please, Connor."

He leaned over her and gently laid her down on the rug, the wool pleasantly scratchy against her bare back. Her body was alight with need, desire and love blending in her system like liquid heat.

He drew her arms over her head and used the cuffs to bind her wrists together. She luxuriated in the sensation of Connor overpowering her, in her own yielding. In the way her body was stretched out, elongated. The sense of safety she felt in his hands, under his command, his collar around her neck. She felt treasured, precious, as he gazed at her with raw, naked emotion in his eyes, which had gone a dark mossy green with banked desire.

"Now," he said.

She closed her eyes as he slipped the blindfold over her head. She inhaled the spicy scent of the leather, exhaled. There was one small quiver of fear, but the moment he laid his big hand over her heart, pressing down the tiniest bit, she was reminded of how safe she was with him.

"You all right, love?"

"Yes."

It was true. The last shred of fear faded away and she gave herself over, truly, completely, for the first time.

He kissed her, a light brushing of his lips, and she smiled. What followed was a long, sensual exploration of her body, his hands, his mouth everywhere, it seemed. Kissing her shoulders, her breasts, her belly. Stroking her thighs, her jawline, her lips with his fingertips, until she was shivering with need, desire a languid yet electric current running through her.

It went on forever, or seemed to. And even as the need turned to an ache that nearly screamed to be quenched, there was nothing in her that wanted anything but for him to set the pace.

She knew in some far-off way that she was flying on endorphins. That her mind was a lovely blur of sensation, her body all panting breath and acutely sensitized flesh. Wanting so strong she could barely stand it, yet giving that wanting over to *him*.

Finally his fingers slipped into her aching cleft and she sighed as pleasure swarmed her, hot and liquid.

"Ah, I love to see you like this. Lost in pleasure. And never like this before, darlin'. You've no idea what it does to me. I had no idea what it might do . . ."

She heard him draw in a long breath, knew he was trying to calm himself. Felt pleased that he had to do it. And jumped when he pinched the inside of her thigh.

"Oh!"

"Good, yes?"

"Oh yes . . ."

He knew just how to do it; how to take her to the height of pleasure, then ramp it up by delivering just the right amount of pain.

He pinched her again and she squirmed, moaning, pain and pleasure mixing exquisitely in her system.

"Come on, now, Mischa," he said, using one hand on her hip to still her. "Hold still for me. Just breathe through it." She inhaled, forced her body to lie quietly as he pinched her inner thigh, while his other hand slid into her sex, his fingers pushing inside.

Her heart hammered, her sex tightening.

"Not yet. Don't come yet."

So much authority in his voice, if he hadn't been specifically telling her not to come, she might have, simply from the sound of it.

He kept his fingers inside her, pumping gently, driving pleasure deep. At the same time he slipped a hand under her and pinched the tender skin of her bottom, harder and harder, over and over in the same spot. She got sore so fast it made her head spin. She had to bite her lip to keep from crying out. In sublime pain. In unendurable pleasure.

"You can do it, love. Take a breath."

She did as he said, holding her orgasm back. For him.

"Ah, you're good. So good, my beautiful girl." He stopped pinching her, and she felt his palm resting on her thigh. "Now I want you to relax. I know it seems impossible, but it's not. Do it, Mischa."

She tried, but desire was thick in her veins, flowing through her.

"I don't know how," she whispered. "I need to come. It's too strong."

"Ah, but this is all about you controlling it, darlin'. Controlling it by letting it go. Do you understand what I'm saying? You can do it."

It made a strange kind of sense to her. She took in another long breath, talked her body into loosening, bit by bit, even as his fingers surged inside her, tiny movements that nevertheless brought pleasure to new, stinging heights.

"Ah, there you go. Perfect."

She felt impossibly warm all over, her body lax. She lay back and let him work her, need cresting, making her fly, letting it flood through her body like water.

Finally he said, "It's time, love. Come."

She did, pleasure bursting inside her, flowing to her limbs, the water turning to a deep, thundering roar that filled her head.

"Ohhhh . . . Ohhhh . . ."

She couldn't stop moaning, couldn't stop shivering in long, undulating waves. Sensation was infinite, her body curling into it. And Connor went with her, his fingers inside her, the other hand pulling her into his lap. And still she came, her sex quivering, pleasure seemingly endless.

Eventually his hand slipped from her and he swept the blindfold from her face, covering her with the end of the comforter from the bed. She pressed her face to his chest, reassured by the steady beating of his heart. They sat together on the floor for a long time, and after a while she heard the rain coming down outside again, making her feel safe and warm in his lap.

"Connor . . . make love to me."

She had never said those words to any other man.

So many firsts with him.

They slipped together onto the floor and he covered her body with his. He held himself over her, his green eyes dark with desire. Wide with the wonder of love. She felt it in every look, every touch. And as he entered her she felt it deep inside her body. In her heart.

She hadn't been looking for this. And yet she'd found him, somehow. And now, knowing Connor, knowing love, she couldn't imagine how she'd accepted all her life that she would never have this.

She wrapped her arms around him, then her legs, pulling him closer as desire rose once more.

"Don't ever let me go, Connor," she whispered against his neck.

"Why would I do such a foolish thing? You're everything to me, my love. You're mine. *Mine.*"

His.

It was all she'd ever wanted. More than she'd known was possible.

She knew, for the first time, the beauty in belonging.

Acknowledgments

I must thank my friend and author K. B. Alan for her thoughtful critique; my assistant, the infamous Kitty Kelly, for beta reading this manuscript; and especially the fabulous R. G. Alexander for doing a rush look at the final chapter in the revision phase of this book when I was wracked with the usual neurotic writerly insecurities. You know I love you girls!

I also have to thank my editor, Kate Seaver, for not only allowing me but encouraging me to write these characters who are somewhat outside the mainstream "romance box." Tattooed women can find love, too!

Also available from Black Lace:

Alec Walker should come with a warning.

A man who lives on the edge, he is famous for his love of dangerous sports, kinky sex and independent women.

Dylan Ivory has come to interview him for her latest book but instead he issues her with a challenge – and the perfect way to do her research.

Part 1 of *The Edge Trilogy,* a dark sensual romantic series, perfect for fans of E.L. James and Sylvia Day, from the acclaimed author of *Exotica*

Also available from Black Lace:

Give in to desire . . .

Kara Crawford doesn't expect to find anyone
who can fulfil her dark fantasies until she experiences
one of the most incredible nights of her life with a
man she's always admired from afar.

Dante De Matteo may be a master of control now,
but his troubled past means he won't let anyone
ever get too close . . .

**A dark sensual romantic novel perfect for fans of
E.L. James, from the acclaimed author of *Exotica***